EROS RISING

RICHARD E. WILLIAMS

Contents

To Michelle, may you always find peace and comfort.

Chapter One

Alex had experienced panic attacks before, but this wasn't normal. This shook him to his core, like a harbinger of disaster. As he lay naked in bed next to his boyfriend, Danyal, he struggled to control his breathing. He'd never experienced such security and warmth as when he was in the arms of the man he loved. So why did he feel more scared and alone at this moment than ever?

It wasn't on his agenda to have a near-death experience crossing the street on the way to work. The adage about your life flashing before your eyes wasn't true. Alex recalled blinding lights followed by darkness. The deafening sound as his flesh and bones crashed against metal. The weightless feeling of his body being thrown fifteen feet off the ice-covered ground. The soul-piercing cold on his skin as he landed face down in the fresh snow. The detail that Alex vividly remembered was the look on the face of the driver milliseconds before the collision. It wasn't surprise or panic, but a sinister smile. Just thinking about the look gave Alex chills. He swore that the driver had corrected course to ensure the violent collision.

Debris from the older model deep blue F-150 pickup truck covered the intersection as the driver had wrapped the vehicle around a telephone pole and fled on foot. The EMTs had no clue how Alex had survived unscathed, with only his bruised pride and soiled clothing. Alex could hear their muffled voices. He should be severely injured or dead, they said. How did he survive? Luck or fate?

Maybe it was just the adrenaline coursing through his veins, but he had never felt physically better in his life except for this damned anxiety. Alex focused on his senses to ground himself as he tried to chase it away. He could feel the scratchy flannel sheets on his skin. Alex placed his head on Danyal's soft, bare and draped his arm across his muscular torso. The intoxicating scent of his boyfriend's cologne tickled his nose. Danyal's heartbeat was a mesmerizing lullaby soothing Alex's spirit. He wondered how he deserved a boyfriend like Danyal. He was intelligent, funny, thoughtful, and had a body that would inspire Michelangelo to sculpt a new masterpiece. Everything in his life should feel perfect, but it didn't.

Despite his best efforts, distraction was no match for his worries tonight. Why was Alex's anxiety still growing? It had to be more than adrenaline or a stress reaction from the accident. Was anticipation of meeting Ditta for dinner on his birthday feeding his sense of dread? It was their tradition, but he'd never brought a man to meet her before. How would she respond? Would she like Danyal? Was his decision going to ruin the moment? With each racing thought, Alex spiraled further down the rabbit hole. Fuck it; he couldn't take the chance. There's no way this dinner can happen. He had to stop it at all costs.

"OK, sleepyhead, you better not drift off. We've dinner plans at 8:30 p.m., which gives you about ninety mins to get ready," said Danyal as he passed his fingers through Alex's coiffed hair.

Alex didn't reply and held Danyal's naked body tighter.

"Can we stay in bed forever?" Since the snow was so awful tonight, ordering takeout and staying in bed would help quell his anxiety. Alex hoped Danyal would take the hint and nip the evening in the bud.

"No," said Danyal, "You've been nagging me for weeks to go and meet Ditta on your birthday. You've been raving about your birthday chocolates since we met."

Alex's frustration continued to grow. "Let's wrestle for it. I'm a decorated champion, so you'll lose."

"That was years ago, mister," said Danyal mockingly. "You've gotten old and soft."

"If I win, we skip dinner and stay in tonight," said Alex.

"You've signed your death warrant," said Danyal as he tried to make a stern face.

Alex quickly rolled from the side where he was embracing Danyal to be on top, holding Danyal's arms over his head and pinning him to the bed. The match had already finished, and Alex was ready to claim canceling dinner as his prize.

"What'll it be tonight, Chinese takeout or Mexican?" said Alex.

Danyal took his right hand and grasped Alex from the back of his neck, pulling him forward for a passionate kiss. Alex never wanted this kiss to be over. Danyal paused and looked into Alex's eyes.

"We'll never leave this room if you're going to lie on top of me naked," said Danyal.

Alex chuckled inside that diabolical scheme had been revealed. Operation Cancel Dinner was a success!

Danyal abruptly shifted his body weight, gently throwing Alex to his side before rolling to the side of the bed to stand up.

"We're not staying in tonight; I'll shower first if you don't want to join me," said Danyal as he walked naked across the room to the bathroom.

"I'll be there in a second; I'm appreciating the view." Think, Alex. Time to find a plan "B." Alex carefully watched Danyal, trying to preserve every detail as he crossed the bedroom to the bathroom door.

How could he get out of this dinner? He could admit to the accident, but that would surely start an argument with Danyal for not telling him sooner, and he would drag him kicking and screaming to the hospital. There was too much risk in that strategy. Alex needed something more subtle to sidetrack their dinner plans. Once Danyal had turned on the shower, Alex walked to the dresser, where he picked up Danyal's phone and placed it in the inside pocket of the sports coat he intended to wear. Alex grinned with satisfaction. If Danyal can't find his phone, we'll be late and have to cancel—a quick and easy distraction with a low risk of discovery.

"Hurry up, Alex, we'll be late for your dinner. Are you going to join me?"

Alex responded by pulling back the curtain and stepping into the warm shower.

Dressing slowly, the dread in Alex's chest continued to grow.

"Dr. Lieth, you have your infamous million-mile stare on your face. Be careful. It'll give you frown lines."

Alex smiled at Danyal. He'd been thinking about his relationship with Ditta and how amazed he was she was still in his life. As far back as he could remember, he'd spent his birthdays with her, ever since the death of his parents in a small plane crash when he was eight. He was unendingly grateful for her and her generosity. More importantly, she wholeheartedly supported him at age sixteen when he came out as gay. Until he met Danyal, Ditta had always been the rock that anchored him. Alex especially fondly remembered his birthdays because she pampered him with his favorite artisan Italian dark chocolates. It was their tradition, and in spite of his nerves, he was excited about the chocolates and telling her about the wonderful man in his life.

"Are you anxious about meeting Ditta?" said Alex.

"A little; meeting your surrogate family is a huge step. Not every day you meet a Fortune 500 businesswoman who can make grown men cry with only her stare."

"She's not that bad," said Alex. "She's just shrewd, is all. I guess I get my tenacity from her. She does have a soft side the world doesn't get to see. It's what I love about her the most."

Danyal smiled. "Since I'm an orphan and my adopted family disowned me for being gay, there's little chance of you meeting them. But right now, I'm more anxious about finding my phone than our dinner plans. Have you seen it?"

Alex shook his head no. *Liar.*

"Fuck," Danyal said as he ran his fingers through his hair and let out a guttural growl. "That phone cost me a month's salary! We're not leaving until I find it. It's a small apartment; help me look."

Alex internally breathed a sigh of relief as he rummaged through the blankets on the bed. He knelt and looked under the bed, saying, "It's not here. Did you bring it home from work?"

"I think I did."

"I'll text Ditta. We can cancel, and head back to the café to find your phone."

"No, you've been anxiously anticipating this dinner. You go ahead, and I'll go to the café on my way to the tavern."

"I'm not going without you, Danyal; I'll cancel," said Alex, quickly pulling his phone from his pants pocket to seize the moment.

"Give me your phone, Alex. I'll call my number. I leave the phone on vibrate when I'm at work, so we might hear it."

"Let's head to the café; before they close," said Alex, as his heart jumped into his throat. *Shit! Did he put the phone on silent?*

"No, it might be a wasted trip. Give me your phone."

Alex reluctantly handed it over. He held his breath as Danyal dialed the number and recoiled at the vibration in his breast pocket, which could be heard anywhere in the tiny studio apartment.

"Alex, come here."

"Why?"

Danyal hung up the call and stepped closer to Alex. He pulled Alex closer by the lapel of his sports coat. Danyal methodically patted Alex's pants pockets as he searched for his prize. He stopped searching after putting his hand on Alex's chest.

"What's this, Alex?"

"That's my right pec. You've touched it before."

Danyal opened Alex's sports coat and removed his phone from the inside pocket. "Why did you pull this stunt, Alex?"

Alex looked down at Danyal's chest, avoiding eye contact, feeling his shame rise to the surface.

"My eyes are up here, Alex," said Danyal as he used his left hand to gently move Alex's chin up to meet his gaze. "You know I love you, but sometimes I feel like I live with a twelve-year-old kid. Why would you hide my phone and then pretend to help me look for it? If you don't answer me, I'll get the answer the old-fashioned way by tickling it out of you." Danyal playfully pushed Alex back onto the bed and ticked Alex's stomach and chest. He stopped after feeling Alex's heart racing in his chest and recognizing the tears in Alex's eyes.

"Hey, what's wrong? Tickling has never made you cry before."

Alex looked away from Danyal's gaze, tears rolling down his face.

"Alex, you're scaring me. Your heart is beating faster than a race car engine," Danyal said as he kept his hand gently placed on Alex's chest. "Did you take your anxiety medication?"

Alex turned to his side, facing away from Danyal, and didn't respond. How could he explain his fear when he struggled to put his finger on it?

"Something is bothering you, Alex. Please, answer my question," Danyal said as he gently stroked Alex's face, wiping away his tears.

Should Alex tell Danyal about the accident? No, it would open Pandora's box. He needed a more straightforward answer and decided to go with the truth.

"I'm...I'm afraid," Alex said in a shaky voice, looking Danyal in the eyes. "I can't shake the feeling something bad is going to happen. I'm also afraid when we start bringing other people into our perfect world, it will somehow change what we have. I don't think I could bear it if that happened," Alex said, burying his face in Danyal's chest.

Danyal took his hands and tenderly pulled up Alex's face. "I'm not worried about other people causing problems in our relationship; that can only happen if we let them. I'm worried your first reaction was to hide my phone rather than talk to me," said Danyal softly.

"I tried," said Alex. "I told you I didn't want to go to dinner."

"Try harder, Alex. I love you, but I never know what to expect when I return home each day. Will I get to spend the evening with the sexy college professor, or will you drive me mad watching videos on TikTok?"

Danyal silently stood up and pulled Alex to his feet, before kissing him softly on his forehead.

"Lucky for you, I'm in a forgiving mood since it's your birthday. Just don't pull that stunt again; be honest and talk to me when you're struggling. Now, you're going to wipe away your tears and get yourself ready so we can face your fears together. I'm ordering an Uber."

Alex nodded.

Danyal returned, standing at the bathroom door as Alex splashed water on his face. "The Uber is almost here. You never answered my question."

"Which question?"

"Did you take your anxiety medication?"

"No," said Alex, shaking his head. He had planned to have a beer with dinner and was concerned about mixing Klonopin with alcohol. Dr. Sonja was always warning him about the risks of mixing two sedatives.

"OK, but it makes your anxiety worse. You should take a pill in case you skip the beer."

Alex nodded in agreement.

Danyal paused briefly before proceeding, "How will we handle introductions? Will we start at the table together or make the introduction after you've had time to prepare her?"

"I'm leaning towards having you sit at the bar while I prepare her to meet you. I'll wave you over when the time is right."

"Sounds like a plan, but I do have another question. If Ditta is as refined as you describe her, why did you pick Dante's Inferno Tavern for your birthday dinner? I love it there, but it's not exactly a Bostonian fine dining establishment."

"I guess I wanted you guys to meet on my turf."

"Good enough for me. You've done as much as possible with those puffy eyes; your handsome face looks fine."

"Danyal..."

"What, Alex?" said Danyal as he turned to look at Alex's reflection in the bathroom mirror.

"I'm sorry."

"Alex, I love you, but when you play games, it puts me in the position of being a parental figure. I'm your boyfriend, not your father.

We can face any problem together, capiche?" said Danyal as he blew Alex a kiss and winked.

"Understood," said Alex. He could never resist Danyal when he turned on his charm.

"One last thing," said Danyal as he pulled a small velvet jewelry box from his coat pocket. "It's not a birthday without a present."

Alex smiled and walked over to Danyal, standing next to the bed where he placed the box in Alex's hands. He opened the box and lifted out a necklace with a crescent moon and star encased within an enormous golden heart. "It's beautiful, Danyal."

"I'm glad you like it. It's Turkey's flag, a symbol of love in my culture. It matches the necklace I wear. Now you can say you always have my heart with you, and I'll have your heart with me."

Alex leaned forward and gently kissed Danyal. "I'll treasure it and always keep it close to my heart," he said as he put the necklace around his neck, where it rested on his sweater. Danyal was a romantic, and Alex sometimes wasn't sure what he'd done to deserve him. It was Danyal's Turkish charm that he loved the most.

"Thank you for the gift," said Alex as he hugged Danyal, hesitating to release his embrace.

"There'll be more time for hugging later," said Danyal. "Get your coat, Dr. Lieth. The Uber is here, and we'll face this storm and any obstacles that get in our way together. We can still arrive on time; it'd be rude to be late for your birthday dinner."

Alex held Danyal's hand as they left the apartment. Little did Alex know that his anxious feelings were warranted, and that his perfect world was about to implode.

Chapter Two

Galen

Galen took a deep breath as his stomach turned like a Ferris wheel, and his heart lurched into his throat. Keep it together, mate, don't embarrass yurself. She's the wealthiest and most powerful woman on the planet. Keep yur head on. Straighten yur tie. Everything is good as gold. Any other night, Galen would advise his employer to stay inside with an enjoyable book in front of the fire, or watch a match on the telly, but tonight, she was determined to brave the inclement weather. Remember the rules of engagement. Don't speak unless spoken to. Don't make direct eye contact with her. What wus the cardinal rule? Aye, never touch her if ya value yur life.

Galen stepped out of the elevator into the penthouse. He quickly assessed Ms. Dea, standing at two o'clock at the floor-to-ceiling windows, admiring the driving snow. Nature was indeed pissed tonight. The wall of falling snow completely obscured the lights of the surrounding buildings. The primo view of Boston and the harbor were mere figments of imagination. Galen could tell she was on a mission from the stern look on her face. Galen had only seen Ms. Dea from a distance before tonight. The other security guys' reports of her being a knockout hadn't done her justice. He tried not to gawk. She was tall, striking, and mesmerizing. Being around her made him feel small and sad. He dared not speak and held his breath as he waited to be acknowledged.

"Good evening, Mr. Tucker. A pleasure to finally make your acquaintance," she said without turning toward him.

"Pleasure is all mine, ma'am. Dodgy conditions outside," said Galen in his New Zealand accent.

"The conditions are harsh indeed, a fitting metaphor for life. But nature has never stopped me before, and it won't tonight. I'm on a quest I must see through. May I ask you a question, Mr. Tucker?"

"Yes, ma'am," said Galen, still holding his breath.

"Is this outfit right? Does it make enough of a statement?"

Galen tried to think of the most flattering comment he could pay because he was the last person to advise on fashion, and complimenting a woman had never been his strong suit. He'd never been in the presence of such a posh lady and knew he'd likely never be again. "Yu're a stunner, ma'am."

Ms. Dea laughed softly. "A delightful response, Mr. Tucker. I hope my fashion choices will be moot if the evening plays out as I intended."

"Major plans tonight, ma'am?" Galen winced the moment the words tumbled out, knowing he was being intrusive.

"The biggest ever. Alex's twenty-fifth birthday, and so much more. Tonight, everything changes."

"Let's get ya on yur way, ma'am. Yur chariot awaits."

"Oh, I hope not, Mr. Tucker. Chariots were a dreadful way to travel. Way too bumpy."

Stepping into the elevator, Galen watched the floor numbers as they descended. From the corner of his eye, he noted Ms. Dea carefully patting her coat pocket to ensure the contents were secure. Stepping out of the elevator at the security exit to the building, her driver greeted them.

"Good evening, Ms. Dea. The roads are frightful with a nor'easter tonight; we'll take the Hummer rather than the limo. Boston in the winter is a cruel mistress."

"Thank you, Malcomb, you think of everything," she said, smiling. "How many years have you been my driver?"

"Two decades, madam," Malcomb said as he opened the door for Ditta and closed it before climbing into the driver's seat.

"It feels like only yesterday. I want you to know I trust you completely with my safety and that you'll never steer me wrong."

"Excellent pun, madam. New security tonight?"

"Yes, Mr. Tucker will be accompanying me tonight. Once you drop me off for dinner, you and Mr. Tucker can take the rest of the evening off so you can get home safely."

"How will you return home, madam?" asked Malcomb, his injured pride visible in his darkened eyes.

"I've made other arrangements," said Ditta as she turned to Galen and glimpsed the disapproving look on his face.

"Speak your mind, Mr. Tucker. You obviously disagree."

Galen chose his words carefully before responding. "Apologies, highly recommend against that course of action. There's no way to protect ya if ya send me away."

"I've made other arrangements," she said forcefully.

"That's not necessary, madam. I'm prepared to wait for you all evening to ensure you return home safely," said Malcomb.

"I insist, gentlemen, it's not open for debate. Please follow my orders."

Galen swore her eyes flashed as he nodded silently before gazing at Malcomb. He noted the driver's furrowed brow as they made eye contact in the rear-view mirror. They agreed, but Malcomb shook his head, overruling any further objections from Galen.

"Malcomb, you've been a faithful employee. I deeply appreciate you," said Ditta.

"Thank you, madam; you're going to make me blush. What's your destination tonight?"

"Dante's Inferno Tavern."

"Oh my; that's the last place I expected."

"Why?"

"The tavern is mostly for townies but has become a popular drinking establishment for Harvard students. My son William likes to go there with his friends. It's not seedy, but it's a dive bar by Boston standards."

"Well, if William has the same sensibilities as his father, I'll surely enjoy the establishment. How is he doing?"

"He's due to graduate in May with his degree in engineering."

"Excellent. I'll make sure he receives a wonderful gift."

"You're too kind, madam. Let's get you on your way so you arrive on time."

Galen sat quietly, with his bruised ego barely contained, trying to understand the rules of engagement. Malcomb was breaking every rule, but Ms. Dea obviously didn't care. Had to be his years of service, allowing him to respond so relaxed and informal. Galen carefully sized up Ms. Dea as she stared at the winter wonderland outside the Hummer window. She looked lost in thought until she turned towards Galen with tears building in her eyes. She was packing a sad tonight. She looked so deep into Galen's eyes before speaking that he questioned if she'd read his thoughts. Did she see his every secret?

"Listen carefully, Mr. Tucker. As of tomorrow morning, I'm assigning you as the leader of Alexander Lieth's security detail. Your job is to protect him with your life if needed. I fear that there has already been an attempt on his life. Although this won't make sense now, you must share two gifts to assist him with his journey. The first gift is the knowledge that he can bypass the protections of board members by physical touch, with their consent. The second gift he'll need is this dagger." Ditta picked up her purse and pulled out an elongated box holding a dark brown dagger with a five-inch blade and ivory handle resting on a white silk cloth. She handed the box containing the dagger to Galen. "The dagger is a priceless family heirloom. You must keep it safe until Alex needs it."

Galen sat dumbfounded, staring at the weapon in his hands. He'd held many weapons in his life, but the aura of this dagger was intense. He wanted to drop it on the floor to escape the energy it held.

"How'll I know the right time, ma'am?"

"I trust you'll know the appropriate moment to give him both gifts. You must wait until all appears hopeless to give him the dagger. You must hide it and keep it safe. It will give him courage and connect him with his birthright." Ms. Dea momentarily clasped her hands around Galen's hand. The intense warmth from her skin burned his hand as intense energy waves pulsed through his body. Every hair on his arms stood on end. Galen wanted to recoil from her touch and cower in the corner, but dared not break her embrace or offend her. Galen had heard rumors about what she could do, and he was terrified. He was totally at her mercy.

"I mean you no harm. You must guide Alex with these gifts," she said as she gently released Galen's hands and reclined back in her seat.

Galen could see the tears escaping her eyes. However, he was paralyzed to respond to this woman he'd barely met, but already feared. "Will do mah best, ma'am. Not mah place, but ya, right? Ya seem sad."

"I guess the moment hit me thinking about past accomplishments, failures, and being sentimental. I orchestrated this plan years ago, and now it must happen tonight."

Ditta's musings were interrupted by Malcomb's gentle voice. "We're almost there, madam. Two more lights to go. I can drop you off close to the door."

"Thank you, Malcomb. You're a gentleman, and I hope life continues to bless you."

Stepping out of the vehicle to open the door, Malcomb offered his arm to guide Ditta onto the slippery sidewalk. Galen looked at Malcomb, and the driver was as confused by Ms. Dea's melancholy behavior as he was. Neither man was comfortable with the unusual request to dismiss her driver and security detail in a raging blizzard. She turned, blew a kiss in Malcomb's direction, and made her way toward the entrance of the building.

Galen turned to Malcomb and asked, "What now, mate?"

"In all my years working for Ms. Dea, I've learned it's best to honor her wishes. Step back inside the vehicle, Mr. Tucker, and I'll take you back to headquarters."

Galen stepped back inside the warmth of the Hummer. This situation felt wrong. Something earth-shattering was about to happen. Galen pulled out his phone as it vibrated. The text on his phone read, *Do you want Amara to recover?*

Who the fuck? Stop pissing with me, he texted back to the unknown sender.

You'll be able to save her with our help. All you must do is obtain a sample of chocolate Ditta Dea gives to Alex Lieth, was the reply he received.

Could it be true? Can they save Amara? Galen recognized something in his heart he hadn't experienced in years: hope.

Instinctively, he responded, *I'll do it.*

Chapter Three

Having a panic attack in public was Alex's worst fear, and with his unrelenting anxiety tonight, each moment brought his nightmare closer to reality.

He reached into his pocket and took the Klonopin he'd brought while rationalizing it would be OK since he was limiting himself to one beer. *Focus on the goal of getting through the dinner. At the end of the evening, you can be back in bed in Danyal's arms and properly thank him for his birthday gift.*

Alex tried to distract himself as he looked fondly around Dante's Inferno. The tavern had become his bastion away from the stress of the world. Alex always knew he could come here for a cold drink that would melt away his anxiety. However, his sense of dread remained out of control tonight, even in his happy place and with his favorite beer. He tried to distract himself by thinking about the history of the tavern. Almost every action of defiance or sedition kicking off the Revolutionary War started within these four walls. He always thought he'd found his place here in Boston because he was a rebel at heart.

Although Alex imagined himself a revolutionary who could save the world, college was one realm where he really excelled. Literature and history spoke to him. Books were his domain and his escape from the struggles of the world. Alex wished other areas in his life, such as social interactions, were as enticing and relaxing as an enjoyable book. Only those close to him knew about his struggles with anxiety as he overcompensated by putting up a strong front. Beneath the façade and bravado was his continual pursuit of perfection. But he had learned perfection was where happiness went to die.

Alex raised his head at the perfect moment to observe Ditta cross the tavern's threshold as she gracefully glided across the room. She always looked like she'd stepped off a Milan runway wearing, a long black leather jacket belted at the waist, immaculately tailored black pants, and a blue blouse that perfectly highlighted her figure. Besides her trademark bright red lipstick, he could never tell if Ditta was wearing makeup as her olive complexion was always flawless, with her long dark hair pulled back into a tight ponytail.

She smiled at Alex as they locked eyes. Her classic beauty was striking. Alex wondered if she'd ever share her beauty regime. Danyal was right; she was definitely out of place in this dive bar. Alex was envious of the primal attraction she possessed. He chuckled at the thought, as he knew he was desirable and never lacked companionship in bed. He'd had dalliances with many men, usually ending in an intense blaze of glory. Hookup culture supplied instant pleasure, but Alex knew nothing about love until Danyal. Speaking of Danyal, he was seated at the bar across the room, smiling at Alex with his devilish grin, ready to make his grand entrance after Alex and Ditta had caught up. Danyal's was the drug Alex craved. He could see he was fidgeting, and was already on his second beer.

When Ditta reached the table, Alex stood up and kissed her on each cheek. He pulled out her chair, just like a gentleman. Her sending him to the finest boarding schools had bought him some manners.

"Happy birthday, Alex. Seeing you become such an extraordinary man has been my greatest pleasure. I hope the world is ready for you," she said.

Alex said he had ordered her favorite wine, Cabernet Sauvignon, which paired well with dark chocolate. He laughed softly, opening the small ornately decorated box of Gianduiotto chocolates Ditta had placed on the table before him. Taking the first bite and letting it melt softly onto his tongue was almost orgasmic, and he felt his anxiety ebb away. How could the simple combination of sugar and cocoa be so heavenly?

"Careful," Ditta said, "savor the moment. Viva la vida."

Alex appreciated the chocolates as they sipped their drinks. The moment was almost perfect. Feeling unworthy of Ditta's care and support, Alex said, "I'm so grateful to have you in my life and for everything you've done to support me financially, personally, and academically. I didn't know who I'd be if I didn't have you."

Ditta sat at the table, watching Alex with tears in her eyes. Such a display of emotion surprised Alex. He'd never seen any sadness from Ditta before, and was embarrassed by his confession.

"I'm sorry," he said. He didn't intend to ruin the moment by upsetting her. "Please forgive me."

Still holding back tears, Ditta looked away and took a deep breath before returning to meet his gaze. "Alex, you might not feel this way at the end of this night. You might hate me for what I've done."

"Not possible," he said, as he recognized the depth of the pain in her eyes. He knew instantly something was seriously wrong.

Ditta paused to reflect before speaking. "This birthday will be your most significant yet, and this night will determine the future of your entire life."

Alex, half laughing, said, "It's pretty dramatic as birthday speeches go, but as a literature major, he gave her credit for the vivid imagery."

Ditta's eyes narrowed, and the sadness on her face was replaced with anger. "I'm not joking, Alex. I'm deadly serious. Your life won't be the same if you survive the night."

"Woah, back up. *If* I survive the night?" Had she been hitting the vino on the drive to dinner? Maybe Ditta was having fun at his expense.

"It's my fault, Alex, for keeping you in the dark, but I wanted you to enjoy as much life as possible before this day. Everything changes tonight. So, Alex, impress me with your knowledge. From your studies, what do you know about the ancient gods?" she asked.

This was the most random question Alex had ever been asked. "Are you serious? Are we having an oral exam now?"

"Answer the question!" she snapped.

Alex rolled his eyes and took a sip of beer, before responding that the ancient pantheon of gods was a family unit created by humans to establish societal norms and standards of behavior. Every culture has its own spin on the gods to control the masses. Despite all the art and literature on the subject, no undeniable evidence of their existence exists.

"Your answer is naïve. What evidence would you believe? Would you even know if a god was sitting in front of you? Let's ask this question in Socratic terms. What's my name?"

"Ditta Dea?" said Alex hesitantly.

"What does Ditta mean?"

"I'm not sure," said Alex. Ditta had never discussed much of her history with him, aside from her business accomplishments.

"Think, Alex. You're a smart boy. Go back to ancient literature."

Alex sat quietly for a moment and responded in a questioning voice, "Aphrodite." He was growing tired of the game.

"So, what's the meaning of my name?" Ditta asked again.

"Your name means goddess Aphrodite." Alex felt a little dense for not putting two and two together. He wondered how bullied she must have been at school, being called Aphrodite. But who cares if her parents gave her an antiquated name? No wonder she shortened it.

"Are you angry with your parents for giving you that name?" he said, trying to make light of the strangely intense conversation.

Ditta responded that if she had parents, she'd ask them. She said she'd had many names across history: Venus, Freda, Branwe, Ziva, and Hathor. For Alex's information, she continued, the gods were indeed an elite group or pantheon, as he'd labeled them, but they were never human—in fact they were more like the universal forces of nature. Ditta paused, recognizing Alex's confusion before she continued. She told Alex that Einstein was wrong, that gravity isn't the most powerful force in the universe; rather the gods are the elemental forces of the universe. However, only two universal forces remained throughout the development of human civilizations—survival of the fittest at a cosmic level. Only Eros and Thanatos remained. Creation and destruction. Life and death. Love and hatred. Sex and aggression.

Alex sat in disbelief, wondering what had happened in the past fifteen minutes. All he wanted to do tonight was to have a drink with Ditta, have her meet his boyfriend, savor his favorite chocolates, and fuck Danyal to end his evening. How did he get here? Ditta laughed as Alex looked dumbfounded.

"Mind letting me in on the joke?" Alex said.

Ditta responded she had enlightened him about the true nature of the universe, and there he was thinking about fucking the handsome man at the bar.

How the hell did she know what I was thinking?

Ditta smiled at Alex and told him that he was sitting in front of the goddess of Eros, thinking about sex. There was no way for her to avoid hearing his desires. She told Alex she could hear the carnal thoughts and desires of every person on the planet. For example, she explained, the couple to his right looked to be in love, but he was "fucking" his secretary. The couple to the left of them haven't fucked in years. The two men playing pool were fucking each other, but only when drunk enough to act on Eros. Meanwhile, the woman at the bar in the burgundy blouse was asexual.

The conversation no longer amused Alex. "If...*if* I believed you, Ditta, why are you telling me these universal truths?"

"Because...I'm dying," said Ditta as she looked away from Alex.

"Excuse me?" said Alex. He couldn't believe what he had heard.

Ditta raised her head and met Alex's gaze. "I'm dying, Alex. I thought we'd have more time to prepare you to be the champion of Eros, but it has taken too much of my life force to conduct the experiments to create a new vessel for Eros and to hold back Thanatos to keep the world in balance."

Regardless of her far-fetched stories, Alex could see from the sincerity in Ditta's eyes that she wasn't lying. He leaned forward, placing his hands on hers, and asked, "How much time do you have?"

"I barely have enough energy to prepare you tonight. I won't make another sunrise."

Alex sat back in his chair, placing his right hand over his mouth as he realized his feelings of dread had been warranted. He started to cry and asked, "Is there anything modern medicine can do for you?"

Ditta shook her head. She explained modern science couldn't heal her body. She was losing her connection to the Eros force. Her remaining Eros force must be transferred to him tonight, or they risked the world falling into deep chaos. She couldn't abandon humanity or the universe to their demise with Thanatos. Eros and Thanatos must remain balanced, or the universe will devolve into darkness. Ditta told Alex to look at the course of American history to see the imbalance of forces. When she loved and Eros was abundant, there was peace, prosperity, harmony, civil rights, equality, and spiritual growth. However, when Thanatos was the stronger force, the results were catastrophic: slavery, the Great Depression, two world wars, Vietnam, climate destruction, natural disasters, poverty, famine, MAGA, and Fox News. She said anyone with eyes would know Eros was losing the battle and that is why the universe needed Alex to survive.

Alex sat shaking his head. How could he be the universe's savior? This must all be some sick joke.

Ditta stated the plan was for Alex to replace her as the Eros force. She'd known her time was limited for the past thirty years and had tried so many times to create—through cosmic and supernatural means—the perfect vessel that could become Eros. But after thousands of failed attempts, her energy had been drained and, as a result, the universe suffered. She'd given up and was resigned to her fate until humanity developed scientific and technological advancements in genetics and cloning. She said Alex was the only test subject to survive the genetic cloning procedures and mature into adulthood. She and Alex were the same. "You are Eros, the fusion of science and the supernatural."

Alex ran his fingers through his hair as he tried to process what Ditta had said.

"I'm a clone of a god and the result of a supernatural experiment?" Alex said.

Ditta nodded. Genetic manipulation alone was insufficient in the trials, and other methods needed to be employed to ensure survival.

She said the secret ingredient to the process was ichor which enhanced his chances of survival and immortality. The ichor now in Alex's blood was the supernatural agent that fueled his abilities and immortality. Ditta said mortals couldn't consume ichor without turning their blood to fire and bones to sand.

Alex nervously laughed. Where had he received ichor? With his diet, it must be pizza and beer! Ditta clarified Alex had been ingesting increasing doses of ambrosia every year since birth. Had Alex never wondered why the chocolates she gave him were so especially divine? Turns out, they were Divine.

Alex looked puzzled, realizing Ditta was being totally sincere. He acknowledged he'd never been sick or had a fever. He'd never been to a doctor except for a school-related physical. Alex didn't know if it was the conversation or mixing beer with Klonopin, but his face was burning hot, and his head was starting to throb like a bass drum at Mardi Gras. He sat back in his chair, beginning to sweat as the room spun. His heart raced, and his breathing grew faster and shallow.

Fuck, another panic attack.

Chapter Four

"**A**lex," pleaded Ditta, "focus on my voice. This isn't a mere panic attack. You're starting to feel cosmic energy flowing through your body. You can learn to control it." Ditta reached across the table and placed her hand on Alex's. "Focus on my voice. Let the energy flow through you rather than letting it build up in your body. As you breathe out, let the energy flow back into the cosmos."

He breathed slowly with his eyes closed, before meeting Ditta's gaze. How did she do that? He'd never had a panic attack pass so quickly. Alex could see Danyal rising from his barstool, but raised his hand to signal him not to approach.

"Have you been having more anxiety attacks lately?" she asked.

Alex nodded yes.

Ditta told Alex what he was experiencing was a fraction of cosmic energy flowing through his body. Given his history, his mind had no references to define the experience, so it interpreted the experience as a panic attack. She stated the good news was, he'd learn to control the cosmic energy in time. At this point, Ditta questioned if he still refused to believe her. She continued, saying it was a rare soul indeed that could contain both forces. Ditta asked Alex to look around the room. Each person has a spark in their core that burns bright pink for Eros, or else there's the blackness of Thanatos. She added Alex could see this spark or the void, whether he knew it or not.

Just then, Ditta turned to face the elderly couple in the corner and asked Alex to concentrate and investigate the core being of the woman.

"I'm not playing your parlor game," Alex said, still catching his breath.

"What are you afraid of, Alex? Prove me wrong," said Ditta.

Alex sat quietly and stared at the woman. As his gaze lingered, his face went pale, and his eyes widened like a child's on Christmas morning.

"What did you see, Alex? Something shocked you?"

"The woman has a dim pink spark in her chest. It's faint, but it's there. The husband has a more vibrant pink spark in his chest. Does he love her more?"

Ditta clarified that the man does not "love her more." It's a tragedy, she said. They've been married for fifty-five years, and she's developed dementia and is slowly forgetting him and their love. Ditta said she was pleased Alex noticed the differing intensity of their sparks, and wanted him to try another person. She pointed to the businessman at the bar in the blue suit.

This one posed no challenge, Alex said; his core is solid black.

Ditta agreed, saying the bearded man was a sadist who worked for a banking conglomerate, his driving force being power and greed. His only relationships revolved around power and control, which were aspects of Thanatos. Ditta said she was pleased Alex was getting the hang of it. She added that each human being has a dominant driving force, that doesn't change. For example, Mother Teresa, Jesus, Mohammad, Roosevelt, and Carter were pure Eros. Humans consumed by Thanatos—such as Hitler, Dahmer, Bundy, and Trump were easy to name. Their only goal was bringing about death, destruction, and chaos.

Ditta noted she could see the fear in Alex's eyes; he was afraid to look at Danyal. She gently said to him, "Danyal loves you and has Eros in his core. However, darkness surrounds his heart."

"Stop!" Alex exclaimed. Why was she doing this to him?

"Alex, control your emotions; you're making a scene."

He was making a scene? She was the one putting on her one-woman show about battling eternal forces.

Ditta told Alex that she wasn't trying to hurt him or toy with his emotions. She was trying to prepare him for the next step in his evolution. She recommended they move forward and wouldn't focus on Danyal if Alex was uncomfortable. Ditta added that Danyal had been a much-needed step in Alex's development. "How can you become Eros if you haven't experienced passionate love and desire? You needed to feel the depths of love and intimacy, so I sent him your way to further your development."

Alex interrupted, raising his voice even louder, "What the fuck are you talking about? You sent him my way?"

Ditta asked whether Alex thought it was a coincidence that, the day he and Danyal met, he'd gotten on the wrong bus, that his phone died, and that he had to get off and find a café to charge it, even though he despised café culture. That there was an unexpectedly hot guy serving him at the café, who was into history and struck up a conversation with him. She said it was a small feat to make their paths cross. Did he think it was a coincidence he got on the wrong bus and was lost due to mass transit? Did he think it was odd that his phone was dead, and he sat at a cafe charging it when he despises cafe culture? Unexpectedly, the hot guy deep into history waiting on other guests smiled and started making small talk.

"Within three days, you were in bed together and have never parted because your attraction was explosive. It's been eleven months, six days, two hours, ten minutes, and five seconds since that fateful moment. Eros knows all when it comes to affairs of the heart."

She continued saying that, for the record, the love and lust was all real, but going beyond the passion phase was never intended. Danyal had enough of an Eros spark that could be manipulated in order for him to cross Alex's path. But the Eros Danyal now possessed was an enigma that shouldn't exist. Ditta said Eros can only limit or suppress a being's Thanatos for a brief period. As a result, Eros can't change a human at their core. She'd tried and failed many times to limit the impact of Thanatos. But watching Alex's relationship blossom with Danyal, going against the laws of the universe, Ditta said she realized the only reason Danyal had the growing ability to love Alex, was because Alex was lightening Danyal's darkness. Ditta confirmed she didn't have this ability, and it was the moment she knew Alex's abilities were finally developing, and it was time to accelerate his transformation.

Alex stared at Ditta in disbelief. He grasped the edge of the table so hard his knuckles turned white. What were his options to end this conversation? Should he walk away? Grab Danyal and just leave?

Ditta confronted Alex, saying that leaving would be a mistake and that the next step in his development was to guide or direct the Eros spark in others. She pointed to the young woman at the bar, sitting beside the man with the beard. Her spark was dim, being asexual, but it was still there. Ditta instructed Alex in his mind's eye to imagine her kissing the bearded man and to make it happen.

"So much for the #metoo movement," Alex said sarcastically.

"Funny, Alex. It's Thanatos that's to blame for sexually exploitative behavior. Concentrate, build the spark, then turn the spark into action."

Alex closed his eyes and was silent. He opened his eyes, and to Alex's shock and amazement, the young woman leaned over to the bearded man and kissed him on the cheek before slapping him across the face and walking out the door. Ditta giggled with glee and added that he had wimped out on the kiss, but the slap was appropriate and amusing. Looking around the room, Ditta pointed to the next lesson and said she wouldn't make him do anything more tonight if he completed this task. She told Alex about the intense shame felt by the two guys playing pool who were secretly hooking up. She demanded Alex ignite their spark of attraction and make them kiss publicly.

"No," Alex said sternly. He wouldn't do it. Alex refused to out them for Ditta's amusement.

"Alex, our time is short, and you have two choices. Either you can make them kiss, or I can make them start fucking on the pool table. Your choice."

Alex sat defiantly with his arms crossed, refusing to do as she commanded. Ditta smiled and nodded to the pool table, as both men began to unbuckle their belts.

"Stop this bullshit!" Alex exclaimed as he slammed his fist on the table, knocking over his beer.

"You know how to stop it, Alex. Just one kiss."

Alex turned towards the men and imagined the most passionate kiss possible, and the men willingly played along, entering into an intense embrace that shook them to their core. They couldn't hide their desires any more or their erections. He watched as their sparks burst into a blaze.

"Bravo!" Ditta said and applauded. "You impressed me, but you did one thing wrong."

Alex responded, angry and confused, "I did exactly what you asked?"

"Yes, you did. But look around the room, Alex. Every person in this room is engaged in a kiss."

To Alex's astonishment, the entire bar was kissing except for Danyal. *Stop kissing,* he thought and the room returned to normal as if the kissing outbreak had never happened.

Ditta smiled across the table and congratulated Alex on a remarkable show of Eros. She added the ability to control the entire room except for Danyal, showed considerable control and determination. She smiled and wondered aloud if people were kissing for miles outside the bar. Ditta stated this exercise illustrated his final lesson. She warned Alex he must keep his desires and emotions in check. If he loves too much and loses, the universe will suffer his depression and grief. If his love turns to resentment and hate, Thanatos will take control, and the universe will risk destruction.

Ditta looked at her watch, saying the time was almost nigh, but that she had one last revelation for Alex. She warned him that his transformation into becoming the Eros force wasn't assured. At dawn, he'd either become an immortal force of creation and rebirth, or his body would explode at the cellular level, unable to harness Eros. As his abilities grew, her life force was waning.

With tears in her eyes, Ditta stated the last gift she could give Alex was the time to spend his final fleeting moments of human existence in Danyal's arms. "Eternity is a long time, Alex, and agents of destruction will threaten you. I'd hoped Thanatos had been too distracted by causing death and destruction in Ukraine to notice my plans—but there was no way that a cosmic force would take kindly to a substantial change in the laws of the universe."

She further cautioned Alex that Thanatos rarely gets his hands dirty. "Beware the Sons of Enyaluis, for they are his right hand and do his bidding." She warned Alex to question every decision and think very carefully where he placed his trust. Ditta said she hoped he'd love, and allow his Eros to transform the universe and humanity. She added she wanted him to take this opportunity to enjoy one last night of pleasure, regardless of the outcome. Ditta thanked Alex for giving the universe new hope. "Godspeed," Ditta said as she stood and kissed Alex on the forehead.

"Where are you going?" asked Alex.

"I don't know, Alex. I hope to walk out the door into the unknown peace of oblivion. Freedom is a feeling I have long forgotten, but I embrace whatever comes next without fear."

With that, Ditta turned and walked out into the driving snow. Alex lost sight of her as she disappeared into the snow and darkness of the night.

Danyal quickly approached the table and hugged Alex tenderly. "That looked intense. Are you OK?" Danyal whispered into Alex's ear.

"No," said Alex as he grasped Danyal tightly. He knew his life would never be the same again. He wanted to live this night as if it were his last, in case he didn't survive in the morning.

"Please take me home and never let me go," said Alex. Tomorrow and the universe be damned.

"Bring the chocolates with you; I'm dying for a taste," said Danyal, flashing his devilish grin that stoked the spark in Alex's core to an inferno—one that threatened to consume them both.

Chapter Five

The light streamed through the blinds like a million suns rising on the horizon. Alex covered his head with his pillow, trying to escape the radiant onslaught. His head beat like a Mannheim Steamroller performance, building to a climatic crescendo. The siren outside the window felt like an ice pick to his brain, stabbing with an almost homicidal fury. Waves of nausea flooded his intestines as his bowels churned relentlessly. Each breath seared his lungs. His tears were lava scorching his skin.

A paralyzing thought gripped him. Could the pain assaulting his body be an aneurysm or stroke? How many Klonopin and beers did he consume? Had he been in a freak accident? The mere act of thinking deepened his suffering and confusion by sending a cascading wave of electricity that bounced back and forth in his skull. As he tried to get off the bed, he crashed to the floor with his legs too weak to bear his weight. Alex lay naked in the fetal position, suffering and paralyzed on the cold concrete floor. He prayed for the strength to move, but his prayers went unanswered. His body had become a prison.

Alex didn't know how long he lay on the floor; time had lost all meaning. There was only the pain. Ditta's words began to echo sharply in his mind: "Don't hold the energy. Let the cosmic energy pass through you." Alex took a deep breath and released a wave of energy that violently flung the furniture across the room, crashing against the wall. After expelling several waves of energy, a tingling in his chest slowly spread through his body. This sensation was foreign to him, and he basked in the euphoria of this new feeling of relief.

Inch by inch, he steadied himself to his knees as he crawled towards the fiercely blazing window. Closing the blinds took every ounce of his determination. However, achieving his goal produced a substantial wave of ecstasy throughout his body. His entire being vibrated as every nerve and synapse in his brain fired with elation. Slowly breaking free from his delirium, he attempted to piece together the events leading to this moment. But only fragments of the puzzle appeared. He recalled passionate sex with Danyal, birthday chocolates, and Ditta with her deranged story of gods, Eros, and transcendence.

Wait, did Ditta die? No, that's ludicrous. It had to be a dream.

He'd have to share with Danyal his crazy dream about Ditta and her tale of gods. He would undoubtedly laugh his ass off at that one. Dr. Sonja would also have a field day interpreting this nightmare. Alex's mouth tasted like a dirty penny and was drier than the Sahara. Stumbling towards the kitchen for water proved easier than closing the blinds. With each step, his vision began to focus. Following the trail of clothes and empty chocolate wrappers on the floor, he stopped on his path to the bathroom to pick up the box of birthday chocolates that held only two remaining pieces. The thought of eating even the heavenly chocolates turned his stomach, but he didn't want to waste them. He placed the box on the dresser with one piece inside and slid the other chocolate into the pocket of his sports coat, hanging it on the bathroom door since he intended to wear it to work.

Reaching to turn on the bathroom light, Alex noticed the power was out. He turned to look out the window where the long line of snarled traffic indicated the power was off for at least several blocks. *Shit, what time is it?* He looked at his cell phone and saw it was 11:35 a.m. Alex panicked as he scrambled to turn on the shower. His anxiety quickly dissipated as he deduced it was Sunday, since his birthday dinner with Ditta had been on Saturday night. Danyal had his pickup basketball league at the community rec center on Sunday mornings and would be home by noon. Alex was happy Danyal wasn't in the front row to see the train wreck he was today. He stepped into the shower to wash away his hangover.

Wiping the condensation off the mirror, Alex admired his reflection. His dirty blond hair, square jaw, chiseled facial features, and tightly groomed beard were what drew admirers to him. Ditta always said, "The pretty flower attracts the bees." His lean, muscled body in gay culture would be labeled a "twunk"––a young, muscular gay man. However, Danyal referred to him as his "otter" due to his beard, the light body hair on his chest, and the happy trail leading down his sculpted abs. Alex smirked at his reflection; not bad for a day over twenty-five.

A fast-paced knocking at the front door abruptly disturbed his moment of solitude. Opening the door in a wet towel loosely wrapped around his waist, Alex proclaimed, "Danyal, you know every time you lock yourself out, you owe me a sexual favor of my choice. Quid pro quo."

But to Alex's chagrin, Danyal was not alone and stood beside him was a lean, balding African-American man in a three-piece suit, clutching a briefcase. Alex had never made this guy's acquaintance, and wasn't in the mood to now. He closed the door slightly to cover his nakedness, looking puzzled as he glared at Danyal for bringing a stranger to their door.

"Sorry," said Danyal, "I forgot my keys again. Something weird is happening today. The whole city is in a blackout. All the power seems to be out."

Alex widened his eyes and frowned. "I thought you'd be alone, Danyal."

"It's my fault, Professor Lieth," said the stranger, "please pardon my intrusion. My name is Thomas Brynmor, Esquire. I'm the personal and lead corporate attorney for Ms. Ditta Dea. Since her passing, I need to meet with you to discuss her will."

Alex's heart jumped so fast it nearly burst out of his chest, as he realized the previous night's events had been real. What they say about attorneys and vultures swarming while the body is still warm must be true. It had barely been twelve hours since Ditta made her dramatic exit from the stage.

"Are you going to let us in, Alex?" said Danyal.

Alex didn't respond as he struggled to piece together the events of the past twenty-four hours.

Danyal stepped inside the apartment and nudged Alex with his elbow for his rudeness. Danyal whispered maybe Alex should get dressed before they talked with Mr. Brynmor. He gestured with his left arm to the small table with two chairs in the kitchen, inviting Mr. Brynmor to enter as he apologized for Alex's behavior.

Alex walked into the bathroom and slammed the door behind him. The notifications on his phone showed ten missed messages from Thomas Brynmor. *Fuck, this shit's getting real.* At least Danyal was home to support him through this drama.

Returning to the kitchen in a t-shirt and jeans, Alex sat at the table while Danyal stood leaning up against the counter. Mr. Brynmor fumbled to pull a laptop out of his briefcase. After turning it towards Alex to view, he realized the computer was not working.

"No worries, son," said Mr. Brynmor. "I have a transcript you can review." Thomas fumbled with the file before handing it to Alex.

This can't be happening. Danyal can't find out what Ditta told me this way.

"I'm sorry you wasted your time. I've no desire to be involved in Ditta's affairs under any circumstances."

"I can understand your hesitation, Dr. Lieth. This is a highly unusual situation."

"You think?" said Alex sarcastically.

"If you won't read it, Alex, I will," said Danyal as he scooped up the file off the table before Alex could stop him.

"Danyal, please, don't open that file."

Once he'd opened the gates of Hades, the havoc released couldn't be contained.

Danyal opened the file without hesitation and began reading aloud.

If you're seeing this recording, Alex, I've moved on from this plane of existence, and you've survived your transformation into the Eros force. Although you may have mixed feelings about my passing, I can only imagine your confusion and questions about the changes happening in your body and life. I sincerely apologize for keeping you in the dark and for the abruptness of my revelations. I know my actions were selfish, and I should've prepared you better for the changes you will encounter. However, I assembled help for you in your transition and planned to provide support to help you learn and grow into your abilities. Mr. Brynmor will provide you with the details, as I've gathered a team of experts to guide and advise you on your journey. In addition, I've left you the financial resources needed to change your life. Mr. Brynmor will explain, and supply the details.

I wholeheartedly hope you love, learn, and lead humanity to a new phase of prosperity.

Danyal closed the file and looked at Alex as he raised one eyebrow. "What's she talking about, Alex? What is the Eros force?"

Alex sat in silence, ignoring Danyal's question. The words had been spoken, and the gates of hell were flung wide open, releasing demons into Alex's perfect little world.

"Are you OK, Dr. Lieth?" asked Mr. Brynmor.

That might be the most loaded question ever uttered. "Am I supposed to be, OK? When did the fate of humanity and the universe last drop into your lap?"

"I can't say I've had that experience, sir."

After pausing briefly, Mr. Brynmor added that he must inform Alex of Ms. Dea's steps to assist him. Alex was now the sole benefactor of all her assets, which included all her bank accounts, her personal antiquities collection, and business endeavors. The portfolio was far-reaching. Most businesses came under the umbrella of Palingenesis, LLC. PGC, as the board referred to the company, was a multi-billion-dollar corporation with offices and ventures across the globe. The corporation had opened its headquarters here in Boston. Mr. Brynmor noted PGC had a high rise as the regional headquarters for their business ventures, and that it housed many of their employees. Alex now had access to the fully furnished penthouse there as part of this property. A team of legal experts and financial advisers would be on hand to manage the day-to-day operations. In addition, Alex's safety was paramount, and as of this moment, he would have a twenty-four-hour security team and guarded transportation at his disposal.

Alex sat motionless, staring at the file on the table. *FUCK, FUCK, FUCK!* What had happened to his life in the last twenty-four hours? How could things go to shit so fast? This must be a nightmare! *WAKE UP!*

Danyal walked over to Alex and stood behind him. He placed his hands on Alex's shoulders, offering emotional support. "Do you need a break, Alex?"

Alex shook his head no. "Are you through, Mr. Brynmor?"

"Almost," said Mr. Brynmor, as he added Ms. Dea had established teams of experts to assist him in areas she valued from her experiences. Thomas said he'd coordinated the legal team and had scheduled a meeting tomorrow to introduce Alex to the other team leaders, including spiritual development, emotional health, research/biotech development, and security.

Alex stared at the man across the table with a furrowed brow. "So you're telling me I'm Bruce Wayne or Tony Stark?"

Mr. Brynmor laughed. "No, son, they're fictional and mortal. You're a god with more wealth than Bruce Wayne and Tony Stark combined."

Hearing the "g" word out loud sent cold shivers down Alex's spine. Alex appreciated Mr. Brynmor's humor, but needed to figure out his next step––not to mention working on damage control with Danyal, whose silence scared Alex.

"I can see this is all overwhelming for you," said Mr. Brynmor.

"Mr. Brynmor, you appear trustworthy, but I can't wrap my mind around this. Where are the TV crew and cameras telling me this is all a prank?"

"This isn't a prank, Dr. Lieth. Everything Ms. Dea and I told you is true."

Alex replied there had been a mistake. He was an adjunct professor of twentieth-century literature who might be the most unqualified person to hold the universe together. He was the man for the job if you needed a lecture delivered or a paper graded. His priority was Danyal, and it was none of his business what happened to the rest of the world if his little corner was protected. Ditta should've made a better backup plan, because he had no intention of playing her game.

"Mr. Brynmor, if you would kindly gather your files and leave, I'd greatly appreciate it," Alex said.

"I think that would be a mistake, Dr. Lieth. We ask that you give us one hour tomorrow to introduce you to the board and tour PGC headquarters. What harm could one hour of your day do?"

"I can't blow off teaching my classes tomorrow to attend this meeting."

Mr. Brynmor told Alex he had nothing to worry about, and apologized for not mentioning it, but PGC had obtained Starling University as one of their company holdings. Since Alex was now the boss, any changes he wanted to make at the university were within his power, so they would understand if he missed one lecture.

Alex felt like he was being bribed. The carrots being dangled in front of his face kept getting bigger and bigger. He felt like the devil was trying to buy his soul piece by piece.

"The answer is no; I'm not for sale," said Alex.

Mr. Brynmor added that, with full disclosure, whether Alex came to this meeting or not, there would be a security officer in the hall around the clock, and plainclothes security following him whenever he ventured into public view.

"That information does not help me feel more secure, Mr. Brynmor." Alex was starting to feel like a bird in a gilded cage.

To Alex's surprise, Danyal spoke up. "If there's one trait Alex has in abundance, he's stubborn and won't be pressured by a hard sales pitch. His answer is no, and we won't attend your meeting. Please leave, Mr. Brynmor, and don't return to our home again uninvited."

"Yes, sir. I'll respect Dr. Lieth's wishes. May I at least leave you information about PGC's resources and files on the staff for your review?"

Danyal sighed before responding, "Good day, Mr. Brynmor."

Mr. Brynmor set his business card on the table before quietly leaving through the door Danyal held open. As soon as they were alone, Danyal closed the door and locked it before turning to see Alex lying on the bed sobbing and clutching Danyal's pillow. Danyal said nothing but curled up next to Alex from behind, spooning and gently wrapping his arms around him. Although a gesture of love, Danyal's embrace offered limited protection from the inferno of emotions growing in Alex.

Danyal and Alex lay intertwined on the bed until night had blanketed Boston. Alex hesitated to break the physical peacefulness of the moment. If he let go of his emotions, all hell would break loose. He could barely grasp the magnitude of his situation, and holding Danyal in a continued state of ignorance was cruel.

Alex spoke softly, "If there was ever a time to run for the hills and never return, I think it would be now."

"How would we live?" asked Danyal, gently tightening his embrace.

"By our wits and off the land. You could open a little café, and I could teach English at the local school. It would be picturesque."

Danyal gently kissed Alex's neck.

Alex could only imagine what questions were going through his lover's brain. His mind had been racing for hours, and he was no closer to having any answers.

Danyal quietly whispered in Alex's ear, "This sounds like a fairytale. Who hasn't wanted to be a superhero at some point? All I need to know is how I can be there for you after Ditta's passing, and all the burdens that come with it."

Alex paused. "You're taking this well. I'm scared shitless."

"If you're scared, I'll hold you till you feel less afraid. You're still my Alex, above all else." Danyal hesitated briefly before asking, "What scares you the most?"

"Everything. I like my world, my job, and us. It's enough for me."

"Then it's enough for me, too," said Danyal.

Alex rolled over on his side and made eye contact with Danyal. "So, you don't have other questions? That would be a first, my handsome man."

"Of course I have questions...such as, how you became a...god. And what'll the future look like for us, and is this a blessing?"

"Blessing? It's a curse."

"Is it? We have goals and dreams that can now become reality. The resources you inherited could change our lives forever, and we could follow our passions. Not many people have the chance to do that in their lifetimes."

Alex smiled. "So we'll be Jimmy Carter and travel the world building houses and cafés?"

"If that's what you want, I'd follow you anywhere, Alex Lieth. You could change the world."

"*We* could change the world," said Alex.

"Yes, we. You don't have to decide right now. But, what would immediately make you feel better?" Danyal laughed as Alex's stomach growled before he could even finish his question.

"I think I might need to eat."

"Chinese?" asked Danyal.

"Yes, please."

"I'll place the order," said Danyal as he began to stand from the bed, but was stopped by Alex, who pulled him back for one more embrace. "Don't start anything you're not ready to finish," said Danyal.

Alex smiled and said, "Thank you."

"For what?"

"For being my rock in this crazy world."

"I'll put it on your tab," said Danyal as he kissed Alex on the top of his head, before picking up his phone to order takeout.

Chapter Six

Galen

Not every day ya get to meet a god. Bring him a cuppa, Joe. Maybe he won't smite me on mah first day.

Galen hoped Professor Lieth was a down-to-earth bloke, unlike some of the wankers on the board. He chuckled to himself as he stood in the queue at the coffee shop. Usually, he'd wait until later in the morning for his first cuppa, but today, he wanted to make a good impression. Galen had been secretly following Professor Lieth for weeks, and today would be first contact.

Galen had only worked with the company for a year. Hell, he had only provided security for Ms. Dea on one occasion, and it was the night she vanished. He was usually security for the other board members, and nothing much happened. The security crew had their favorites and would assign each "asset" a codename. Ms. Dea was "Venus," which Galen thought was lazy and shite, but it had been in place for decades. Among the bodyguards, they had a lottery to name Professor Lieth. After suggesting "the Unicorn," Galen had won the pool. He was being cheeky, but the codename stuck, so now Galen was assigned to Operation Unicorn.

Climbing into the limo, Galen secured the coffee in the cup holder before reviewing Professor Lieth's file again. Crikey––twenty-five and already holds two doctorates from Yale in twentieth-century literature and anthropology. Galen had always struggled in school. He only made it through with the help of his twin sister Amara, who was the brains in the family. He'd dreamed of attending university alongside Amara, but rugby was his way out of their wop-wops hometown, achieving stardom on the New Zealand All Blacks national rugby team. At age eighteen, he was on his way to becoming a national hero. He missed playing, and it was his first love. Once a rugger, always a rugger! He'd tried to watch American football but found it grotty. He could do without the dancing and celebrations after making minor plays.

He'd hoped to make rugby his career, but life had other plans for him––including the military at age twenty-three in the 1st New Zealand Special Air Service Regiment. Special Forces training and four tours in Afghanistan didn't prepare him for many jobs except to be a mercenary or private security for posh clientele. The exceptional pay PGC offered was mint, which helped him pay for Amara's care. Galen understood his job was to be a blunt instrument that protected the Unicorn at all costs. Lethal force was always an option. Contrary to the recruiting slogans, the military didn't train its recruits to be peacekeepers. His training had given him the skills to identify, target, and eliminate threats. He was an excellent marksman, proficient in hand-to-hand combat, and skilled with various weapons.

Looking at Professor Lieth's picture stirred jealousy and pity in Galen. The Unicorn was skux—a handsome, stylish, determined, and goal-oriented bloke who made his dreams a reality. The bloke wakes up one day and is a god. Who has such luck? Unlike the uber-wealthy Ms. Dea, whom everyone feared, the Unicorn had lived a life built on hard work. Galen respected this, but the Unicorn was as innocent as a lamb in the lion's den. Ignorance may be bliss, but it could get the Unicorn killed––and Galen had to ensure he survived.

He envied Professor Lieth for having a partner to share his life. A fit bloke, if truth be told. Galen had observed Danyal and the Unicorn together. A blind man could see they loved each other, but relationships complicated Galen's job. If his high-profile clients weren't divas, their partners undoubtedly could be. Galen had no illusions; keeping Danyal safe was only secondary.

Relationships while in the military and private security were rare. All the moving around, odd shifts, secrets, and last-minute trips would take their toll on any couple. Galen had no time for relationships as he was to shadow the Unicorn during all waking hours, usually sixteen-hour days. Another security crew member, Templeton, covered the night shift. Galen liked the day shift because it allowed him to see unfamiliar places, and the premium pay certainly didn't hurt.

Galen had mapped out the Unicorn's daily routine, looking for potential vulnerabilities. His job as Adjunct Professor at Starling University provided his biggest concern. The punters were out in full force on campus; crowds of hundreds of students made it more challenging to observe and intervene. Galen snickered at the thought of getting the Unicorn his own Popemobile to shuttle him around campus, waving to the masses. Galen would have to negotiate with Professor Lieth about how close he wanted him to be during lectures, office hours, and staff meetings. Keeping the Unicorn safe in the university environment was going to be a monumental feat.

Galen's planning was interrupted by the limo stopping at their destination. Taking a deep breath, he exited the limo and entered the three-story, baby blue-colored apartment building. Stopping at the lift to check the security code, Galen shook his head as the lift keypad was broken. That meant the place was wide open to hostiles to enter with no resistance, and would have to be fixed. Otherwise, he might as well hang a sign on the door with his schedule and the best times to be assaulted.

Galen sprinted up the stairs, checking for blind spots and security risks. Fifteen seconds was all it took to storm the third floor; fifteen seconds too quick for Galen. The stair doors at least needed to be locked to delay access. He walked out of the entrance to the third floor and looked at his watch. Cripes, he'd arrived early. *Don't be the prat that disturbs a god. Walk it off. Don't get smited on yur first day!* Galen stepped past the door to 3A to ensure the hallway was secure, and to survey the surroundings. Turning back towards the elevator, the Unicorn and Danyal exited the apartment hurriedly.

"Gidday, Professor Lieth and Mr. Sarif. It's a cracker of a day outside," said Galen. He immediately recognized his greeting had startled the unsuspecting pair. "Sorry, mates, didn't mean to startle ya. Mah name is Galen Tucker. Leader of yur security detail."

"Good day indeed, Mr. Tucker," said the Unicorn hesitantly. "I wasn't expecting anyone to be waiting for us."

"Mah bad, sir."

"I told Mr. Brynmor I wanted nothing to do with PGC. That also includes not wanting any security skulking around after me," said the Unicorn.

Galen was instantly annoyed. He was merely the messenger. If the Unicorn had his knickers in a bind, he should call customer service and complain. He was starting to feel more like a babysitter to the Unicorn, rather than security for a god.

Galen took a deep breath before responding, "Only the messenger, sir. Gotta job to do. Will be following for yur safety with or without yur consent."

The Unicorn was built, but he didn't pose a physical threat to Galen. He could see that behind the Unicorn's eyes lurked a brain that was locked and loaded with intelligence. Galen was ill-equipped for a battle of wits today. From the scowl on Danyal's face, Galen could tell he was being sized up. He knew he needed to be careful around Danyal--an alpha never likes a new threat in their territory.

Danyal responded, "I'll protect Alex. I suggest you find somewhere else to be, Mr. Tucker. I'll call the authorities if you don't back off."

Galen laughed internally, not acknowledging Danyal's remarks. The Unicorn was his client. Galen quickly weighed his options in order to defuse the situation.

"Yur transportation service has arrived, mates." Maybe being useful was a more tactical approach than getting into an argument.

"Transportation service?" asked the Unicorn.

"Yah. My job is always to shadow ya when yu're out in public. Sorting a ride for ya is included."

"We're running behind today, but the bus will be fine," said the Unicorn.

Galen rolled with the resistance; he knew he needed to make it seem like the Unicorn's idea.

"10/4, sir. I'll ride the bus with ya."

The Unicorn looked at Danyal and said, "Can you get us both to work on time, Mr. Tucker?"

"Route is already mapped out. Driver ready to go."

"I wish there was time to get coffee on the way. I rarely drink it, but I must admit I need some liquid inspiration today," said the Unicorn.

"Coffee is waiting for ya. Mocha latte, grande, extra hot, and extra whipped cream. Mr. Sarif, there's a traditional Turkish brew for ya."

"Mr. Tucker, I'm not sure if I should be impressed or concerned," said the Unicorn.

"No need, sir. Social media keeps no secrets."

Danyal continued to glare intensely at Galen without speaking. Galen chuckled inside again as he watched Danyal mark his territory. *Down, boy, no one here is interested in your property.*

"Please ignore him, Mr. Tucker. He's a little grumpy this morning. He tells me often that in Turkey, they have a saying––a cup of coffee commits one to forty years of friendship."

Score!

"Looking forward to our professional relationship, sir," said Galen as he motioned towards the stairs. He was amused. Danyal placed himself between the Unicorn and Galen as they descended the stairs.

Walking out the front door to the apartment building, Galen could see by the look of surprise on the Unicorn's and Danyal's faces that the shiny black stretch limo was a new experience for them. The limo hadn't been Galen's choice. Too flashy and painted a target for inquiring eyes in this neighborhood. But PGC had demanded it, trying to lure the Unicorn in with honey. After Galen opened the door for them, the three men stepped inside and sipped their coffees.

Galen turned to the driver and said they were all secured and ready to leave for the university and Excalibur Café.

"Excellent coffee," said Danyal reluctantly. "It's hard to find good Turkish coffee in Boston."

"Cheers!" said Galen as he raised his coffee. "First time in a limo?" Small talk was hard for Galen, but he wanted to make a good impression.

"Yes, I've only seen them up close at charity functions at Starling University," said the Unicorn.

"Is it everything ya imagined?" asked Galen.

The Unicorn chuckled and placed his hand on Danyal's knee before leaning over and giving him a peck on the cheek, and then asked if Galen could give them some privacy on their way home.

Galen's face flushed at the suggestion, but the Unicorn had potentially committed to another ride––a minor victory. He turned to look out the window to prevent his fellow passengers from seeing his embarrassment. Public displays of affection had always made him uncomfortable. It was best to keep private lives behind closed doors. But apparently the Unicorn was comfortable with PDAs. *Gummon! Get a room, mates.*

Galen was relieved it was a short drive to their first destination: Starling University. Exiting the limo, Galen observed the Unicorn kiss Danyal. He could feel Danyal's eyes burning a hole through him as he closed the limo door. Galen and the Unicorn walked in silence across the Starling University campus. The number of people around concerned Galen; combatants could launch an attack from any angle in the crowd.

Trying to establish the rules of engagement, Galen asked, "There a problem with me sitting in the back of yur class?"

The Unicorn took a lengthy pause before responding.

"I'm not agreeing to anything permanent, Mr. Tucker. But I'll get you the syllabus and reading list if you want to follow along for the lecture today."

"That'd be choice, sir," responded Galen, even though he doubted the Unicorn's conviction.

"I'll lend you the books––but promise me you won't call me 'sir' in front of a room full of hormonal nineteen-year-old students."

"Noted, sir. Don't embarrass the professor on mah first day at university. That's mah promise, scout's honor."

"Your accent and dialect are fascinating. Is it Australian?" asked the Unicorn.

"No, New Zealand." *Fuckin' idiot*. Americans were always clueless about Kiwis being different from Aussies.

"New Zealand was my second guess. I bet you're a hit with the ladies."

"No time for relationships, sir. Job keeps me busy."

"I apologize, Mr. Tucker, for being too personal so soon after meeting. Please feel free to tell me when I'm being intrusive."

Galen nodded curtly. "All good, sir."

Mind yur own frigging business, mate. Not everyone wants to put their business out on display like ya. Stop being a dickhead.

Chapter Seven

Alex

Although Alex had said he had no issue with Galen sitting in the back of his classes, he was concerned about the perception of having a hulking rugby player as his tentative new shadow. If he agreed to this arrangement, ironing out the kinks would be a work in progress.

Fortunately for Galen, Alex didn't have time to waste arguing about the situation this morning. Galen might stick out less if he wore street clothes rather than a black suit and tie. However, Alex decided there was no hiding a tall, dark, and handsome man like Galen, regardless of his wardrobe. Alex was sure the rumor mill on campus would quickly start churning, and hoped none of the nonsense would make its way back to Danyal. Alex loved Danyal for all his strengths, but his major flaw was a jealous streak many Turkish men possessed. Danyal was so insecure about Alex being around other men, that he'd limited his interactions with male students or colleagues at work. He even withdrew from hanging out with his best friend, Shae. Effectively cutting Shae out of his life to appease Danyal's feelings pained Alex, but he had no time or energy to deal with Danyal's jealousy. He knew he was running from the situation to avoid it, and was ashamed for walking away from such a close friendship. He'd been thinking of Shae of late and wanted to reach out, but lacked the courage to face his poor decision on top of addressing Danyal's insecurities.

Arriving at the literature building, Alex was somewhat mortified to show Galen his humorously small office, which barely held his desk, a small bookshelf, and two small chairs. In all honesty, he knew it was nothing more than a converted broom closet, but it was his realm in the hallowed halls of academia. Alex stepped inside his office while Galen stood outside the door several feet away, so as not to draw undue attention.

While he prepared for his lecture, Alex heard a whisper.

"Dammit, I wish he'd be on time for once."

"Did you say something, Mr. Tucker?" said Alex.

Galen stepped to the door and shook his head no.

Alex returned to his work, but was disturbed by another whisper.

"Shit, she said she was late. There's no way she can be pregnant. I'm not ready to be a father."

Alex looked around the hall quickly, only seeing students hurriedly passing by, with Galen leaning up against the wall with a confused look. He stepped back into his office, but the whispers became louder, now verging on screaming.

"Where's my class at?"

"Damn, the tall, bearded guy leaning on the wall is fucking hot! I'd like to get him into bed!"

"Where's Dr. Lieth? I hope he goes easy on the papers! I need to pass his class!"

"I hope Sarah sits beside me today. If she does, I'll make my move!"

"Please don't have a quiz today. I didn't do the reading!"

Alex placed his fingers between his eyes, trying to focus and drown out the disembodied voices. With each passing second, the voices grew louder until they merged into a single booming static that couldn't be deciphered. Alex fell back and sat in his desk chair while his head ached like an axe pounding his skull.

NO! Was it happening again? Please don't let it happen again.

Alex was startled by Galen, who'd entered the office and closed the door. He knelt beside him and leaned over, placing his hands on Alex's shoulders and shaking him.

"Professor Lieth, ya right?"

Alex couldn't respond except to shake his head no. He could feel the pain in his skull reaching the levels he'd only experienced the morning he transcended. Without warning, Alex released all the energy building in his head, sending out a shock wave that threw Galen up against the wall and bursting all the light bulbs in the office and down the hall in a cascading wave of explosions, triggering the fire alarm and sprinklers. Alex helplessly gasped for breath.

Galen pulled himself up from the floor and knelt in front of Alex. "Breathe, mate. Take long, deep breaths. Yu're hyperventilating. Focus on mah voice. Take a deep breath in and slowly let it out. Yu're in control."

Alex followed Galen's commands, and the two men sat quietly, taking deep breaths until his breathing was nearly normal.

"Can ya speak, mate?" asked Galen.

"Yes," said Alex in a weak, hoarse voice.

"Ya right?"

"I don't know," said Alex, breathing deeply. "I suffer from anxiety attacks, but this wasn't anxiety."

Galen squinted, looking concerned. "Ya know what triggered it, mate?"

"I kept hearing voices until I was overwhelmed..." Alex paused. "The noise was so loud I couldn't think. There was this buildup of energy until it was released." Alex looked up at Galen, noticing some blood above his right eye. "Are you hurt?"

Galen reached up to wipe the blood off his eyebrow.

"It's a scratch, mate."

Alex closed his eyes, and his breathing began to increase again. "I hurt you, Mr. Tucker. I'm so sorry," said Alex, now holding his face in his hands.

"Not even hurt, sir. Mah job to make sure yu're safe. Have ya experienced this before?"

"Not with voices, but I've experienced the explosive release of energy."

"Eh, when?"

"Yesterday, right before Mr. Brynmor came to my apartment."

Galen grew silent and sat back against the wall.

Alex removed his face from his hands and looked up to meet Galen's gaze. "What are you not telling me, Mr. Tucker?"

"Don't mean to alarm ya, sir. An EMP anomaly on Sunday crashed the electrical systems on the entire Eastern Seaboard."

Alex raised his hand over his mouth to hide his gasp. "So, you're saying *I* caused the blackouts?"

Galen nodded yes. "PGC scientists believe it's true."

Alex sat forward in his chair. "What do we do now, Mr. Tucker?"

"Need to get ya out of here and checked out by the doctors at PGC."

"No," said Alex, "I won't go there." He refused to make a deal with the devil.

"Come on, sir. Need to know yu're OK."

"No, I'm not ready. Please take me home."

"Too risky, sir," said Galen, shaking his head.

"Please, take me home."

Galen relented and helped Alex stand. "Ya fit to walk?"

Alex, still dazed, didn't respond.

"Can go down two ways, mate. Ya can stand and walk out, or I can pick ya up and carry ya out. Ya choose, or I'll choose for ya."

Alex nodded yes. "I'll walk with your help. But I have a request, Mr. Tucker. Please don't tell PGC or Danyal about what happened today."

"Can only agree not to tell Mr. Sarif if ya order me. Can't keep what happened from PGC. Immediately sacked if I didn't file a report. Understand yur hesitation, mate. Ya consider the risk you pose to Mr. Sarif? What happens if the next time ya've an attack, ya hurt him or even worse?"

Galen stopped walking and looked Alex directly in his eyes, as the water from the sprinklers drenched them from above. Alex lowered his face to avoid Galen's gaze before nodding. He couldn't forgive himself if he hurt Danyal. He'd have to swallow his pride and ask for help.

"Make the call and set up a meeting with PGC tomorrow, Mr. Tucker."

Chapter Eight

Alex

Alex prayed that going to PGC wouldn't be a life-altering mistake as he rode in the back of the limo alone with Danyal.

Danyal leaned over and put his arm around Alex. "Are you nervous?" he asked.

"Immensely."

"Did you take your Klonopin?" asked Danyal.

"Yes, but it's not working anymore. I don't know why," said Alex.

"You were in bed when I got home last night. Why did you change your mind?"

Alex needed to fabricate a plausible answer without admitting the events at the university yesterday. "I decided to gather all the facts to make an informed decision."

Danyal raised one eyebrow as he looked at Alex.

"What?" asked Alex. Was his response not good enough?

"You're acting weird. Sometimes, I wish I could read your thoughts."

Alex turned to look at Danyal and gave him a gentle kiss. It turned out that hearing the thoughts of others was terrifying, and Alex hoped Danyal would never have to experience it.

Upon arriving at the Palingenesis headquarters, Galen opened the door to reveal the entrance to the building. Dorothy and her crew had finally arrived at the Emerald City. Whoever designed the building wanted to make an impression, and Alex could see from the wide-eyed look on Danyal's face that he was also in awe of the towering façade and impressive architecture. Galen gestured for them to follow and said that since it was their first time, they would go through the front lobby for the grand tour. For all other trips, they would use the security entrance. Alex and Danyal followed along, taking in every detail of the building.

Galen explained that the building was completed in late 2019 before COVID exploded—thirty floors with the boardroom on the 28th floor. The 29th floor was the penthouse, and the 30th floor housed the gym, spa, and swimming pool—also, there was a helicopter pad on the roof. Galen added many companies resided in the building, while two floors served as staff housing for vital employees. Rumor had it that Ms. Dea purchased the plot because it falls on an energetic ley line.

"Is that true?" asked Alex.

"Our shaman says it's true," said Galen.

"Careful, Mr. Tucker––don't believe every rumor you hear," said Danyal sarcastically. "It's a sign of a weak mind."

"Ignore him, Mr. Tucker," said Alex, and he jabbed Danyal with his elbow. "It takes a while for Danyal to warm up to strangers and new situations."

Galen proceeded, saying PGC was a more secure fortress than Fort Knox. All eyes were on Alex as they approached the lobby's front desk.

"Good morning, Professor Lieth and Mr. Sarif. Welcome to Palingenesis. Galen, Security delivered a package for you," the guy sitting beside the desk said, handing over two small boxes.

"Cheers, Adam. Ya still getting owned at darts?" said Galen.

"Only because you abandoned the team, you bum," said Adam. "Zoe is still pissed at you for abandoning us, so you might want to stay clear."

"Sorry, mate——'preciate the warning. Duty calls. This way, please," said Galen. He motioned Alex and Danyal to the elevator.

As the door to the elevator closed, Galen opened one of the two boxes and asked Alex to remove his watch. He complied reluctantly, while Danyal watched his every move like a hawk. Galen removed a jeweled watch from the box and placed it on Alex's wrist. Alex asked if the watch was a Rolex, and Galen shrugged. Galen explained the watch was Alex's security clearance to operate the elevator and activate the security features of the building. Alex was advised to keep it on at all times. Galen went on to say that the watch had a panic function, offered biometric monitoring, and had a state-of-the-art GPS system that was accurate to six inches—a smartwatch on steroids.

Galen then handed Alex a new phone and explained it was a significant upgrade on his current model. *Bugger 5G and basic wireless systems; this was a military-grade satellite phone so fast it'll blow their minds.* Galen said PGC satellites have insane encryption, so company communications were secure and private. The phone was hack-proof, virus-proof, and waterproof. All data was securely scanned upon transmitting and receiving with no delay in quality or speed. Galen added the company would also provide Danyal with a watch and phone.

"Pardon me, Mr. Tucker, but this is all getting a bit James Bond. Of the two of us, Danyal is the tech aficionado," said Alex.

"Does the watch have a flamethrower?" said Danyal, smirking.

"That'd be bang-up. Sure, they can make it work," said Galen, smiling as the elevator stopped.

Before leaving the elevator, Alex asked Galen to forgive their moods that morning. He explained they were severely sleep-deprived, and that the past few days had been among the worst of their lives. Alex added he knew Galen was trying to help and didn't deserve their ire that morning. As Alex finished speaking, Danyal rolled his eyes and exited the elevator. Galen smiled and replied things were all good. He added he hoped things would break their way, and that the board could help them.

Alex and Danyal followed Galen down the hall to a massive conference room with seven individuals sitting around the rectangular table, with three empty chairs. The view from the conference room was breathtaking, with a full view of downtown Boston and the harbor. Alex was awe-struck and stared out the window as if looking down on the Earth from Olympus.

Alex took a seat, trying to hide his anxiety in front of a group of total strangers—though, thinking about it, he noticed a few familiar faces among them. Could he keep it together? He was only there to find out what resources the company had to keep Danyal safe.

"Welcome, Dr. Lieth and Mr. Sarif. I'm glad you fine young men came to visit us today. After our meeting on Sunday, I was a little concerned you might be too overwhelmed."

"Good morning, Mr. Brynmor. I'll be upfront that my only reason for attending this meeting is to learn more about PGC's resources." Alex knew the only thing he cared about was ensuring Danyal's safety, and that Galen had conveyed this to the board under the agreement they'd not discuss his recent "episodes" in front of Danyal.

Mr. Brynmor nodded, stated he understood, and thanked Alex for his honesty. He started the meeting and turned the floor over to Yuzuru Ryo.

"Good morning, Professor Lieth. I'm head of security for PGC."

Ryo went on to say he was the rookie of the bunch, since he'd only been with the corporation for eight years. Ryo outlined that he ran the day-to-day tactical security operations of the business, while Mr. Tucker would be in charge of Alex's protection going forward. He stated that Alex's safety was paramount to all of them, and that Mr. Tucker and each team member had been hand-picked for their expertise and unique skills. Ryo added he wouldn't lie to Alex, but that many domestic and international threats would take every opportunity to gain influence or control his abilities to affect global political systems, economic systems, and military engagements. When Alex was in public or at work, Ryo confirmed Mr. Tucker or a plainclothes team member would always be with Alex. When at home, security would be posted outside the apartment. Ryo finished by saying they respected Alex's privacy, but that he should understand there would be a vetting process for all persons close to Alex, to rule out potential threats to his safety.

"You know how to make a guy feel unsettled, Mr. Ryo," said Alex.

Mr. Brynmor passed the floor to the Chief Financial Officer, Kylie Peters. She explained that, as CFO, she ran the day-to-day financial operations of the team. Ms. Peters asked Alex to open the box in front of him, whereupon he found a black credit card. She stated Ms. Dea had left instructions for him to have a monthly stipend of $30,000, with all bills being paid directly by PGC.

Alex thanked Ms. Peters. Thirty grand a month was about half of his yearly salary without tenure. After so many years of living beyond his means, Alex stated he was sure he could make it work, *if* he decided to work with PGC.

Damn, this will blow Danyal's mind. Maybe now we can go on a much-needed vacation!

Ms. Peters said, in addition to the stipend, Ms. Dea converted the 29th floor of the building into a penthouse that was immediately available for Alex's use. She explained he didn't have to decide today if he wanted to use it, but that she'd like to give them a tour after the meeting.

Alex thanked Ms. Peters and assured her they would take the tour when they had time, since their schedule was hectic today. He had no intention of taking the tour, or moving into the penthouse, and only wanted to speed things along.

"May I offer another opinion?" interjected Ryo. "As Ms. Peters mentioned, the penthouse apartment on the 29th floor is available for your use. Ms. Dea had the apartment designed with ultra-modern security features––it was her haven from the world. I'd be negligent if I didn't ask you to consider changing your living arrangements for safety reasons."

Alex stated he'd take their recommendation under advisement. However, he and Danyal needed to discuss the situation. A rags-to-riches story might be appealing in fiction, but it was daunting and overwhelming when it came about in real life.

Ryo stated he understood. He joked he might be the commander at work, but if he decided to move his children and his wife without consulting her, he'd be the one needing round-the-clock security.

Alex chuckled.

"Going around the table next is..." Before Mr. Brynmor could finish his sentence, a short bald man with silver-rimmed glasses and a thick German accent interrupted him.

"I can introduce myself, since I've been working for this company for forty-eight years as the senior member of this board. Hallo, Alex, I am Dr. Walhbert Bruno. The lead scientist and head of the biotech division that developed the cloning and genetic engineering program responsible for your existence. My main responsibility is to keep you healthy. My department will be scheduling several exams and advanced diagnostic testing to determine if there were any detrimental effects following your transition. Being a hybrid being, you're the equivalent of a cosmic anomaly. We must establish your physical limits to determine a baseline functioning for your body."

"Dr. Bruno, I've been called way worse than being a 'cosmic anomaly.' Are we going to address the elephant in the room? You know I've never been a fan of needles because you came to my boarding school and did my physical once a year for about seven or eight years. I think we know each other. You've seen me naked. I'll always remember you brought my favorite cherry lollipops and Scooby-Doo Band-Aids."

"That was many years ago, Mr. Lieth. Age has been kind to only one of us. If you share any similarities with Ms. Dea, your skin may be impervious to the effects of age, and physical injury will be a thing of the past. Don't be expecting any lollipops. I take my work seriously."

Alex had made the naked joke to make light of the situation, but he was surprised to see Dr. Bruno. They shared a past, one he'd not soon forget. In place of the caring doctor he once knew sat a hardened stranger he barely recognized. Alex's gut told him something other than age had changed this man. Sitting across the table from his "maker" made him deeply apprehensive. Alex had many questions, such as how Dr. Bruno had managed to elude the prohibition in the medical field on human cloning. Maybe Ditta had evoked supernatural means. However, the breach of basic medical ethics loomed large in Alex's mind.

"Moving on around the table," said Mr. Brynmor, "it's my pleasure to introduce you to Hokolesqua Mahomet. Hoko, can you tell Dr. Lieth about your role on the board?"

"Yes, it would be my pleasure. Allianchu, Dr. Lieth––that's the traditional Peruvian greeting for 'hello, how are you?'" He added it was a great honor to be at Alex's service, and that his role on the board was to serve as Alex's spiritual guide and to help him strengthen his connection with nature. Ms. Dea valued spiritual practices and ceremonies such as meditation, fasting, feasting, chanting, dancing, altered states of consciousness, cleansing immersion in water, and purification through rites and rituals. He stated he would work in these areas to connect Alex's universal spirit and mystical abilities. He ended by saying Ms. Dea, before her passing, shared that she thought Alex could develop abilities that could surpass her own, and that she entrusted him to help Alex on his journey of self-discovery.

"Mr. Mahomet, in reviewing your file, I was intrigued by your research on Ayahuasca and altered states of consciousness. As a trained anthropologist, I find this fascinating and am keen to learn about sacred and ancient beliefs. I'm honored by your offer of assistance."

"Please, call me Hoko," said Hoko before explaining formal titles can prevent people from connecting with others by causing interpersonal distance. He added that his spiritual advisor told him connection is a true path to growth and prosperity. The heart matters, and it's the right way.

"Thank you, Hoko. I'm grateful for the opportunity to learn." Hoko intrigued Alex more than any of the other board members. Still, there were more introductions to be made.

"Hello, Alex. As you know, my name is Dr. Diana C. Sonja, and I serve as the mental health expert on the board."

Facing Dr. Sonja was the moment Alex had been dreading.

"I'm sorry for any subterfuge in our past relationship," she said.

"What might you be referring to, Dr. Sonja? Maybe the fact you have been my therapist for the past several years and worked for the company owned by Ditta responsible for my creation?" said Alex. He'd shared his innermost thoughts, feelings, and fears with this woman; her betrayal cut him deeply. The idea of being vulnerable in weekly psychotherapy with her alarmed him. Could he ever truly trust her again, given her deception?

"I can only imagine the questions you may have and how you're feeling," said Dr. Sonja.

"You don't want to know what I think and feel, Dr. Sonja. It would be best to finish this conversation behind closed doors where I can be 'authentic' with you."

"As you wish, Alex. Ms. Dea valued psychotherapy as it helped her through many of the trials and tribulations she experienced. There will be weekly and emergency sessions as needed, going forward. Failure to attend sessions isn't an option, I'm afraid, so I'll work around your teaching schedule as needed."

Danyal placed his hand on his thigh under the table. Alex turned to look at him, who shook his head. Alex knew it was not the time or place to air his grievances with Dr. Sonja and nodded back to Danyal, agreeing it was time to move on. Alex took a deep breath and turned to face the rest of the board.

"Excellent. Now that you've met the members, do you have any questions, Dr. Lieth?" said Mr. Brynmor.

Alex responded that he did have one request. While the ride in the limo was very luxurious, it was a little extra for their lower-middle-class neighborhood. He felt like everyone was looking at them, like they were either a celebrity or the mafia. If they decided to work with PGC--a colossal *if*--could another vehicle be arranged for transportation?

Ryo responded that he would investigate the issue and wanted to know if Alex and Danyal intended to drive. Alex answered that they had their licenses but, living in a city with good mass transit and a limited income, having a car was not a priority. Biking in pleasant weather had also been a good source of exercise for them.

Ryo agreed to investigate their vehicle inventory and get back to Alex ASAP. Any vehicle used must meet stringent safety and security requirements, and PGC may have to procure a car with custom specifications. Alex thanked Ryo for his understanding.

Mr. Brynmor stated that, before adjourning, there was another delicate matter he would like to discuss with Alex. He said Ditta, in her will, didn't want a funeral upon her passing, but the PGC staff that worked with her closely would like to have a celebration of life, and would appreciate him and Danyal attending.

Alex's mouth turned dry and tasted metallic as he considered how to respond. On the one hand, Ditta deserved to have her life acknowledged. However, she had blown apart his whole existence. Could he put aside his complicated feelings to do the right thing?

Alex felt Danyal place his hand on his thigh again as Danyal said, "That's a huge decision, Mr. Brynmor. Please give Alex time to process his grief, and we will get back to you with his wishes presently."

Thomas nodded and stated if there were no further questions or issues, the board meeting was concluded until tomorrow's daily briefing. He thanked Alex and Danyal for their time and explained each department would schedule a one-on-one appointment with Alex this week. He ended the discussion by asking Mr. Tucker to escort them to the penthouse for a brief tour.

Alex thanked Mr. Brynmor for his time, but said they had other appointments they needed to keep, and so would tour the penthouse another time.

Walking down the hall, Alex asked Galen about the diversity of the board and wondered if it was by design. Galen affirmed Alex's observation and explained Ms. Dea had a company policy committed to diversity and representation. Galen added that the limo was ready to go to the university, or wherever else they needed to go, and that he had a portfolio for the penthouse, if they'd like to see it.

Alex replied he'd review it on the drive to the office, and whispered to Danyal that he wished everyone would stop pushing the penthouse on him.

While sitting next to Danyal in the limo, Alex opened the portfolio and was immediately struck. It seemed he'd accidentally walked into an episode of *Lifestyles of the Rich and Famous*.

"Welcome to 'champagne wishes and caviar dreams,'" quoted Alex.

"Was that your best Robin Leach impersonation?" said Danyal, as he intensely surveyed the portfolio.

"I'm pleased you caught the reference," Alex replied. Honestly, he had to admit that the penthouse was a feast for the eyes. Six thousand square feet spread over two stories, boasting sweeping, unobstructed views of Boston and the harbor with twenty-foot floor-to-ceiling windows. The decor was minimalist with a clean color palette, herringbone parquet flooring, and a wood-effect feature wall. The furnishings were all from Italian luxury brand Fendi Casa. Alex wondered what on earth they do with five bedrooms and five full bathrooms, including walk-in steam showers and oversized jacuzzi tubs.

"Don't forget the state-of-the-art kitchen," said Danyal. "More room for you to burn dinner."

"Ha ha, asshole."

Alex continued reading. Up the geometric staircase on the second floor, there was a pool and a four-hundred-square-foot observatory terrace with a garden. The theater/media center was awe-inspiring too, with first-run films available, so there would be no need to leave the penthouse. There was a personal chef on staff, plus valet, and service staff twenty-four hours a day.

Alex was enthralled, and had never seen such opulence and luxury. He never even considered where Ditta lived in all the years of knowing her, given how secretive she could be. This upgrade was more than a simple rags-to-riches story. He was starting to feel like Jed Clampett from *The Beverly Hillbillies*. A fish out of water seemed like an understatement; he'd yet to see the cement pond. He was struck there was more valuable art in the living room than in most museums: Van Gogh, Dalí, Matisse, Degas, Monet, Picasso, original Da Vinci paintings, not to mention classical sculptures.

"Who even keeps up with the art collection?" asked Alex.

"Director of antiquities, Dr. Caron," said Galen, sitting quietly across the limo, looking at the daily schedule on his iPad.

"Dr. Caron? Wynn Caron?" asked Alex.

"Yah. Ya know him?" said Galen.

Danyal sat up and abruptly closed the portfolio so hard he almost knocked it out of Alex's hands. Alex hesitated before responding, deciding how best to tactfully answer the question without causing a scene.

"Yes. Dr. Caron was my university professor, and I once considered him a mentor."

"Least ya'll have one mate on yur side."

"I'm not too sure that would be the case. We ended things on less-than-ideal terms."

Fuck, not Wynn.

Alex knew he'd soon have to face the biggest regret of his life.

Chapter Nine

Alex

February 21st, almost two years to the day since Cairo. The day when Alex and Wynn's lives changed forever.

The memories of when shit hit the fan in Egypt still haunted Alex, and he continued to have nightmares about the events. Cairo was the event that triggered Alex's panic attacks. He deeply regretted what happened, but was too ashamed to admit it and face Wynn. However, Alex needed to know about Wynn's connection to PGC, despite his regret and shame. He'd never have the courage to face him otherwise. Alex hoped meeting in a neutral location over a drink would help defuse the situation.

Cathedral Station had always been his favorite gay bar in Boston to drink and play billiards. Alex always thought he could have any guy in the bar he wanted––the ignorance of youth. Those days stopped when he met Danyal. Adding to his frustration, Alex could taste the beer, but alcohol no longer affected him since his transcendence. Against his will, he'd become one of the hipster gays who drank alcohol-free beer for the taste. Among the many "gifts" Ditta had bestowed upon him, this one seemed particularly cruel.

Seeing Galen sitting in the corner in his rugby jersey and jeans, sipping his beer, amused Alex. Seeing the swarm of muscle-bear hunters circling Galen offered thrilling entertainment, and a much-needed distraction. Perhaps Alex shouldn't have chosen Bear Night to expose Galen to his first gay bar.

Alex's amusement was interrupted by the man standing uncomfortably close to him at the bar. He could feel the man's hot breath on his neck. Alex turned to greet his guest.

"Thank you for joining me, Wynn. I didn't know whether you would. Would you like a drink? Guinness, if memory serves."

"No, I've no intention of staying long enough," said Wynn sharply.

"Suit yourself. Well, I have several questions—starting with your involvement with Palingenesis."

"Same old Alex, always right to the chase. No foreplay. Remember that black and white stray pup you found on the streets of Cairo? What did you name him?"

"Horus. How does that relate to my question, Wynn?"

Wynn said he was astonished Alex recalled the pup's name. He was all skin and bone. Horus was the runt even his mother didn't want—barely a few breaths from death. But Alex heard his screams from the garbage can along the streets where Horus was cowering. Wynn said Alex swooped in to save him, wrapped him in his Michael Kors jacket, and revived him.

"You nourished him, loved him, and protected him," Wynn said. "Watching you play with that puppy and care for him for the month we were there was perhaps the most human emotion I ever observed in you. Then what? You packed your Gucci bags and left Horus at the hotel. You didn't try to find him a shelter; you never tried to go through the official process to bring him back to the States, or find someone to care for him. He was a heartbroken puppy the cruel world had abandoned for a second time, and you left him alone at the hotel with nothing, not even food or water. Have you ever wondered what happened to that poor, forsaken puppy? Does it keep you up at night?"

"I remember it all vividly, Wynn. I don't need a recap," said Alex, noting that time obviously hadn't dissipated Wynn's anger.

"You see, the difference between us, Alex, is I cared enough to know what happened to Horus. The hotel threw him out as soon as they found him. He kept whining and howling about your betrayal. He was mistreated by the staff until, one day, he returned to the garbage can where he'd come from. He'd experienced love, happiness, and pleasure, but everything was taken from him by the person he loved most, and needed most to protect him."

"Look, Wynn, I know you're angry at me, and we didn't end on good terms..."

"Memories are funny things, Alex. You make it sound like there was a choice in how things ended. When the hotel security found us in bed together, you ran and never stopped, fleeing in fear of what a homophobic country would do to two gay men caught in the act." To add insult to injury, the contraband Klonopin Alex brought into the country was included in Wynn's arrest. "Did you try to contact the U.S. consulate when I was in custody? Did you try to get me an attorney to provide legal assistance? Did you even care about the violence I endured in an Egyptian prison as a faggot and American drug dealer? The months we spent together were nothing more than another notch on the bedpost for Alex Lieth. A story to tell your friends, if you had any, about the time you seduced your former professor and mentor."

"Wynn, I tried and did my best," said Alex. "I contacted Ditta, and she promised to help you. What more could I do? I was a twenty-three-year-old kid on the run from the homophobic police in a foreign country. I snuck out of the country in a crate, fearing every moment for days that I would be discovered. I still have nightmares and panic attacks about what happened."

"Well, bless your fucking heart. Always painting yourself as the victim," said Wynn.

Alex could feel his blood pressure rising as his face flushed, his heart began to race, and his breathing became shallower. The building, stabbing pain in his temples couldn't be ignored.

"It all goes back to your same character flaw," said Wynn. "You abandon and destroy everything around you that loves you, and discard them like trash. Horus and I were collateral damage in Hurricane Alex. Look at your life. The pattern is well-established. How is Shae? The thing about best friends is most people care about them and value them. When was the last time you reached out to him? Ignoring his texts doesn't count. I'll wait so you can think. Never mind, I'll save you time and energy. Nothing, since you met Danyal, is the answer. You had a new plaything or new puppy to spoil. Nothing else matters until you get bored, and you'll get bored with him. I pity anyone in your wake. That's what happens in natural disasters. Real, lasting damage occurs after the event ends, and brutal reality becomes the norm."

How dare Wynn fucking comment on my relationship and think he's the goddamn expert on my life.

Anger flashed in Alex's eyes, and he stood up abruptly. As he did so, every glass on the bar exploded, and the mirrors behind the bar smashed. All the patrons and bar staff fell to the floor covering their heads for safety. Only Alex and Wynn remained standing.

"There's the immature and emotionally volatile Alex I know. Are you brave enough to hit me, or is emotional damage your preferred weapon?" said Wynn.

"Step the fuck off, Wynn, and answer my question," said Alex.

Wynn went on to tell him that PGC recruited him to be the expert on all things Alex. He observed Alex every day at Yale. Wynn added Ditta thought he might be the lover to ignite the passion Alex needed to advance his progress. He said the only reward he received for being in Alex's bed was imprisonment and pain.

"I was ruined and shattered like Horus. PGC was the only reason I escaped from Egypt and prison after three months. So, I'll do my job as director of antiquities, but this conversation is over. I was a fool to believe you might actually offer an apology. Deity or not, you're damaged and need help. But I don't know if Dr. Sonja can perform miracles," said Wynn before turning and marching towards the door, stepping out of the threshold into the driving snow.

"Stop!" Alex yelled, following Wynn out onto the sidewalk. Alex approached him, remained silent, and looked shamefully into Wynn's eyes.

"Alex, did you just try using your god mojo on me? I have a rude awakening for you. All PGC employees receive vaccinations against the effects of their abilities. You can thank Ditta for this safeguard to ensure we gave her honest feedback without manipulation or undue influence. What's it like to have no power over us, even as a god? And for the record, it's probably karma for you to feel scared and isolated. I hope the feeling burns through you. You're not a coward; you're a fucking monster."

With that, Wynn walked off in the snow with a smile on his face.

Alex struggled to process what had just transpired. He turned back to return to the bar, but was met by Galen standing before him in the falling snow.

"Professor Lieth, ya right?" said Galen.

"Did you hear our conversation, Mr. Tucker?"

"Yah. Whole pub did."

"Were you aware?"

"Ware of what, sir?" said Galen.

"Did you know I can't influence the board and PGC employees because of the inoculations?"

"Yeah, Ms. Dea insisted on it to keep the board objective. Wanted people around her to call her on bad ideas."

"Are you immunized?"

Galen nodded.

Alex was alarmed by this revelation. It seemed like, at every turn, everyone around him had an agenda. "How can I be sure you're telling me the truth?"

"Ya can ask if I'm being truthful," said Galen.

"What's your agenda, Mr. Tucker?"

"That's not fair, sir. Can show you."

"How?" said Alex.

"Lend me yur hand," said Galen.

"Why?"

"Lend it to me, sir. Don't worry, I can't injure ya."

Alex hesitantly stretched his right hand out to Galen, who took the shaking hand and placed it on his chest.

"Ya can't see mah energy or spark. Ya can feel it through touch if I let ya."

"If you let me?" said Alex.

"Enough chitchat. Focus on feeling the energy," said Galen.

Alex sensed the warmth and tenderness of Galen's skin in the drifting snow.

"Ask mate, can ya trust me?"

"I didn't need to ask you, Galen; I sense it. You're not lying to me."

"Can we go back inside? It's nippy."

"Thank you, Galen."

"Eh, for what?"

"For...this. How did you know touch would work? Does the board know?"

"Yu're welcome, and dunno if the board knows. Ms. Dea shared that secret with me on her last night. Said there would come a day ya'd use that nugget. Carpe diem. Anyway, maybe we should blow this joint before all the bears attack me."

Alex laughed. "Yes, maybe it was too much for your first time in a gay bar."

"Not even. Many gay rugby teams in Australia loved to take us All Blacks to gay bars. They'd buy us a stubbie and see how pissed we'd get."

"You're full of surprises, Mr. Tucker. Would you be willing to try a new restaurant around the corner? I'm starving and have this new corporate credit card to break in. If you're uncomfortable, this is a business dinner. You could keep me safe from potential cutlery accidents while I get takeout for Danyal."

"Not sure that's a line to cross with mah boss."

"Maybe our relationship is unique," said Alex.

"Reckon there's a compromise. Sit at the same table, but I'll pay with mah scratch."

"That'll do. Let's get your coat. I think you're freezing."

"I'll skull my stubbie and grab my jacket. The warm limo awaits," said Galen.

Alex watched Galen laugh as he stepped out of the limo.

"Ya got me. Expected a fancy French restaurant. Not a Mexican/Asian fusion food truck," said Galen.

Alex chuckled. *So Galen didn't know everything about me from social media.* He had heard this place did a killer Thai peanut chicken burrito. Danyal and Alex had tried to eat here a few times, but the lines were far too long. Luckily, the snow tonight had driven the lines away. He'd been living as a student for so long and, most recently, on a new professor's salary, that treats like dining in fancy establishments were few and far between.

"If you live paycheck to paycheck, you learn quantity is more important than quality," said Alex.

"Gotcha. Know what it's like to be flat broke growing up in a wop-wops village. Didn't know how strapped we were until I grew up," said Galen.

"Now that we have this delicious food, should we wait to eat at the apartment or savor the moment here?" said Alex after returning to the warmth of the limo. He was teasing because Galen had already unpacked his burrito and taken several large bites.

"Apologies, sir. Bad habit from the military. Had a limited amount of time in the mess and the field. Ya ate fast for safety reasons."

"What other lasting effects do you have from the military?" said Alex.

"Used to go jugging, but military ran me ragged."

"Danyal likes to jog, and he dragged me along when he could get me out of bed on weekends. I probably wouldn't run if I weren't chased these days."

"Getting a swole on has many benefits. Improves sleep. Works as a natural happy pill and helps anxiety."

"I guess. First, we'll need the weather to get warmer."

"Will get out mah running gear, sir."

"Do you enjoy listening to music while running?" asked Alex.

"Like all types of music, but EDM is mah jam. Keeps the energy pumping."

"I love EDM," said Alex. "Who are your favorite DJs?"

"Alesso, Tiesto, and Utah Saints."

"Wow, Utah Saints are old school. They were popular way before either one of us was born," said Alex.

"Classics jams are the best. Annie Lennox's 'Little Bird' is mah all-time favorite remix. Reckon it reminds me of my twin sister, Amara. She's mah 'little bird.' Current favorite songs? Tie between 'Drugs from Amsterdam' and 'Lionheart,'" said Galen.

"Damn, Mau P and Joel Corry," said Alex.

"Ya got any current favorites?" asked Galen.

"The Sam Smith 'Unholy' remix. But Danyal hates it and leaves the room when I play it. It's his kryptonite. Who's your musical kryptonite?" asked Alex.

"Skrillex. Grating noise."

"Agreed, Skrillex makes my ears bleed and should be banned for public safety. How were the clubs in New Zealand and Australia?"

"Top discos were gay bars. Better music and stronger drinks," said Galen.

"You surprise me, Mr. Tucker. We may have found some common ground. I used to love going to clubs to dance all night. Being on the dance floor is tribal, even primal. I miss the feeling. Maybe that's one of the homework activities I could do for Hoko."

"Haven't visited a club in the United States. Mah job keeps me busy. Will sit in the corner drinking club soda to ensure yu're safe if ya go, though."

Alex said it might happen sooner than Galen thought. He explained he was the faculty chair for the LGBTQI+ student union at the university, and that they were holding a fundraiser next month at one of the local dance clubs for homeless queer youth. It was a noble cause and an opportunity to blow off steam. Galen smiled and stated he was up for the challenge.

"You aren't what I expected, Mr. Tucker. I find you 'curiouser and curiouser,'" said Alex.

"Lewis Carroll," said Galen.

"An EDM aficionado and a literary enthusiast."

"*Alice in Wonderland* was mah sister's favorite book. Made our parents read it every night. Book started to fall apart, but Amara knew the story backward."

Galen smiled, and he noticed Galen's dimples for the first time.

"Can I request a favor, Mr. Tucker?"

"Could I stop ya, sir?" said Galen.

Alex laughed. "Probably not. Can you stop calling me 'sir'? I feel like I'm your drill sergeant or your master. Not master in the context of slavery, but..."

"What ya getting at, sir?"

"Never mind. This conversation has turned awkward," Alex said as his face turned beet red. There was no way he was finishing his thought about being Galen's bondage master.

"Agreed, *sir*. Will consider it. What would ya prefer?"

"Alex, mate, or professor––any would be suitable. 'Sir' makes me feel ancient."

"Danyal going to be OK with me calling ya Alex?" said Galen.

"You let me handle Danyal. May I ask you another favor, Mr. Tucker? May I call you Galen?"

"Yu're the boss. Must respond to reasonable demands. Ask ya a question before calling it an evening?"

"Sure. I think that's only fair," said Alex.

"Does yur body feel different now?" asked Galen.

"Good question. I know alcohol and Klonopin doesn't affect me anymore, and I'm a little bitter about it," said Alex.

"Agreed, mate. Reckon that must suck."

"Thank you for the company this evening, Galen. That's enough for one night. I have a course in the morning and have appointments at PGC in the afternoon."

"Ask ya another question, mate? For the road?"

"You may, Galen."

"Was that ya with the exploding glass and smashed mirrors?"

Alex sighed. "I assume so. It appears my temper got the best of me. I hope no one was hurt."

"Did ya attempt to use yur abilities on Dr. Caron?" asked Galen.

Alex hesitated. "You noticed. Regretfully, yes, I did."

"What did ya try to do?"

"I was trying to help reduce his suffering. I know how we ended things in Cairo was horrible, but he'd no right to speak the way he did about Danyal."

"Sounds a little sus," said Galen, crossing his arms and leaning back in his seat.

"Yes. I was trying to take Wynn's emotions down a few notches." Alex knew he wasn't being honest.

Galen raised one eyebrow as he looked at Alex. "Ya sure about that, mate?"

Alex looked away before turning back to answer. "OK, maybe I was angry and wanted him to shut the fuck up."

"If he was unprotected, might ya have hurt him?" asked Galen.

Alex sat in silence without responding. Galen was right, but Alex was embarrassed by his true motivation.

"I don't know, Galen. In retrospect, it was probably a risky move on my part. I got remarkably close to losing control of my anger, and I still don't know the damage my abilities can cause."

"Sounds honest, mate. Will have to report it, since Dr. Caron will probably make a report."

"I understand, and thanks for your honesty. I don't want to seem like a dangerous loose cannon."

"Least ya can admit it, mate. Will report ya regret it," said Galen.

"I guess that's a small victory. Can I request we head home now?"

"Am knackered too, mate. Time to hit the hay. Will let the driver know."

"I must ask for a final favor, Galen––please don't tell Danyal I met with Wynn. Danyal is a wonderful man, but extraordinarily jealous."

Galen nodded before agreeing to keep Alex's secret. He added that security would be stationed outside Alex's apartment until the security suite across the hall is ready. Alex asked what happened to Ms. Dundee in 3B, since she was the building's "grandmother" and had lived in her apartment for thirty years. Galen replied that Ms. Dundee was right as rain and being financially cared for the rest of her days by PGC, who moved her to a larger flat down the hallway. He added that until Alex lived in the penthouse, a security suite across the hall was the best way to protect him.

"So, how has your second day on the job been?" asked Alex.

Galen said, "All good, mate. Haven't given ya a reason to smite me yet."

Alex chuckled as he appreciated Galen's humor and honesty. He sat silently on the drive home, reluctantly admitting how much his interaction with Wynn had shaken him. It couldn't have gone worse. OK, he didn't take a swing at Wynn or implode him like the glassware.

The worst-case scenario would be Danyal finding out about his meeting Wynn, and Alex keeping it a secret. He was grateful Galen didn't push him further about what had happened in Egypt. Alex was keenly aware he needed to stop acting like a madman, as he could only imagine what Galen honestly thought about him.

Chapter Ten

Alex

As Alex turned from looking out of the windows in Dr. Sonja's office, his attention settled on the confidential digital file on her computer screen with his name. What harm could there be in looking through her notes? Alex stepped closer to the computer screen and quickly satisfied his curiosity, before turning to look back out of the window.

"I'm sorry to keep you waiting, Alex. My apologies," said Dr. Sonja as she walked into the office.

Alex wondered how many psychotherapists had a view of Boston Harbor from their office.

"This office is much better than the bland space we've been meeting in for the past two years."

"Yes, it is indeed. Please have a seat, and let's get down to business," she said.

Alex sat in the chair directly opposite Dr. Sonja. His blood was boiling as he sat with his arms crossed, staring past Dr. Sonja in her chair.

Dr. Sonja sat down after picking up a notepad. "You have every reason to feel hurt and confused," she said.

"Thank you for giving me permission for my feelings," he said scornfully. Alex wondered if she could relate to having her therapist lie to her for the last two years while secretly working for a company owned by a goddess who was keeping tabs on her.

The smile on Dr. Sonja's face evaporated. "I understand your anger, Alex. I assure you our prior work was confidential."

"You expect me to take you at your word?" said Alex as he turned in his seat and made uncomfortably intense eye contact with Dr. Sonja.

"I'm bound by the law, Alex. I'd only release information if you were a danger to yourself or others, or if a judge requested the records. I have your consent forms in your file if you want to review them."

"That's bullshit, Dr. Sonja, and you know it," he replied.

"I take my reputation seriously, so please don't make unfounded accusations," she replied, meeting his gaze while refusing to look away.

"It all boils down to trust, Dr. Sonja," said Alex. He trusted her with his coming out experience, shared his experience of being forced into conversion therapy at boarding school, his severe anxiety after Cairo, and his concerns about Danyal's controlling, jealous behavior. It took him months to trust her. "Little did I know you were deceiving me from the start. So, you think I can easily overlook the fact you were assigned to monitor me?"

"I like to think we did good work, Alex, and we can reframe our continued work as an extension of the foundation we've already built in therapy."

"That's naïve, Dr. Sonja, especially after I know what you truly think about me."

"I'm confused, Alex. What're you alluding to?"

Alex glanced toward her computer and nodded.

Dr. Sonja removed her glasses and placed them on her lap. "You read your file. We agreed you'd ask before reviewing any records."

"They're *my* records, and you keep repeating that all I have to do is ask. Maybe you should have locked your computer if you didn't want me to see it."

"You potentially violated several confidentiality laws, and could have viewed other patients' files," said Dr. Sonja, slightly raising her voice.

"I didn't look at other files, Dr. Sonja. How does it feel to take me at my word?" said Alex, glaring at her.

Dr. Sonja sighed deeply and placed her hands in her lap before saying, "Something you read disturbed you. Let's process your feelings."

"'Although Alex has excelled professionally, he lacks maturity, is quick to respond with anger while blaming others for his shortcomings, and his anxieties make him emotionally unfit to assume any responsibility within the company.'"

Dr. Sonja paused before responding, "I stand by that assessment, Alex. Your current struggles with anxiety are serious. Medication no longer works for you. I am concerned your stress levels will overwhelm you, with severe consequences for you and the world."

"You misled me that I was doing well in treatment."

"I didn't mislead you, Alex. You have made significant progress."

Alex's blood pressure continued to rise as he felt his face flush. The pain in his forehead was new, but he knew it was a precursor to his losing control. The lights in the office began to flicker, and the glass panels in the windows started to shake. He paused and focused on his breathing for several moments. Dr. Sonja had effectively backed him into a corner. If he reacted angrily or defended himself, he'd only reinforce her beliefs.

"What would you like me to say, Alex?" said Dr. Sonja. "I'm only looking out for you."

Alex shook his head from side to side. She had a funny way of showing it. "I'll ask again: did you share this information with Ditta or the board?"

Dr. Sonja sat quietly, and Alex could see by her furrowed brow that she was formulating her response.

"I acted within the law. You signed a release form naming Ditta as your emergency contact at the start of treatment, stating I could share information with her in an emergency since she was paying for your therapy. I made the call that your mental stability before your ascension met this criterion, and on one occasion, I provided Ditta with the information you read in your file."

"When we started therapy, you promised to let me know before releasing any information. Did you let me know?"

Dr. Sonja sat in silence. Alex knew the answer was no.

He leaned forward on the couch and ran his fingers through his hair. He waited several moments before continuing. "Can you even say any positive things about me?" he said, not meeting her eyes.

"Yes, you know I can, Alex. You're passionate, intelligent, caring, thoughtful, savvy, and fiercely defend yourself. Most importantly, you love Danyal deeply."

It was too little, too late. "You've made it very clear I must attend sessions if I remain associated with PGC. I don't trust you and will only attend therapy under the condition I see another therapist."

With that, Alex stood and left the room in deafening silence.

Chapter Eleven

Alex

It had been two weeks since Alex had come to PGC, and he dreaded meeting with Dr. Bruno after their recent reintroduction. In the exam room, he sat in his underwear and a flimsy medical gown. Bruno was not the gentleman Alex remembered and owed a debt of gratitude to. He aimed to get through his medical assessment as soon as possible and get out of Dodge without starting an argument.

Dr. Donalds entered the room and introduced herself. "Good morning, Dr. Lieth. I'm Dr. Donalds, and I'm here to take your vitals."

"Good morning, doctor. A pleasure to make your acquaintance." Alex guessed she was around thirty, and this was probably her first or second job directly out of medical school. He could tell she was nervous as she hesitated in taking his blood pressure and temperature. Was this just her demeanor, or was it the fact she was touching a "god" that gave her pause? Alex decided he didn't care because she had kind eyes, and they made him feel comfortable.

"So, tell me, doctor, is the patient going to live?"

Dr. Donalds laughed. "You're as fit as a fiddle, darlin'," she said in a Southern twang.

"You have a charming accent and a gentle touch. The gentlemen of Boston better be prepared."

"The gents of this city will have to go without––but my wife will think that's a real knee-slapper."

"Excellent, another member of the rainbow community. We need more these days. Maybe we should do a recruitment drive and plan an enormous event for Pride month?"

"If the creek doesn't rise, Charlotte and I will be there with bells on!" said Dr. Donalds as she winked at Alex.

"Excuse me for interrupting your party planning, Dr. Donalds, but I need time alone with the patient," said Dr. Bruno curtly as he stepped into the exam room.

"Yes, Dr. Bruno. Pardon me for my manners today."

"Is that only limited to today?" said Dr. Bruno.

"No, sir. My apologies." With that, Dr. Donalds scampered out of the room like a frightened child.

What an asshole.

"We were just making small talk," said Alex.

"She doesn't get paid for small talk, Mr. Lieth."

Maybe she got paid for having a kind bedside manner.

"Good day, Mr. Bruno." Alex knew not referring to him by the proper title would get under Bruno's skin, and he enjoyed the free entertainment.

"You'll refer to me as Dr. Bruno."

"Well isn't that a coincidence, *Dr.* Bruno? You can call me Dr. Lieth."

"Oh yes. Doctorates in twentieth-century literature and anthropology. They'll be useful in saving the world."

They might not save the world, but at least Alex had learned manners in boarding school. He had been correct in his reassessment of

Dr. Bruno during the board meeting. There was barely enough room in the room for Dr. Bruno's ego. If Alex was going to get out of the examination without a significant argument, he knew he'd have to stop needling Bruno and take a more deferential tone. What in the world had so changed the kind man he used to look forward to seeing?

"You never know, good doctor––the world can be saved by many disciplines. I can see from your diplomas on the wall you achieved your medical degree from Ruprecht Karl's university in Heidelberg. I spent a year in a boarding school near there."

"I know, Dr. Lieth. I've been following your biological and medical assessments since before you were born. I know more about your health than you know about yourself."

"I see. So, you were on the science team responsible for my creation?"

"Yes. There were several hundred failed attempts before you. You were specimen number 1021."

Ditta indicated as much on his birthday. In a way, this saddened Alex. From what she told him, she took each setback hard. From the pictures on the wall, Alex deduced Bruno had worked with Ditta for decades––nearly fifty years, if Alex recalled correctly.

"Ditta was extraordinary," said Bruno. "I miss her both personally and professionally."

The momentary vulnerability from Dr. Bruno struck Alex. Maybe under the cold, pragmatic German exterior, he did have a heart. Could it be Ebenezer Scrooge was human after all? Alex was not surprised when Dr. Bruno quickly put his defenses back up and continued his monologue.

Bruno stated he had agreed with Ditta on many things over the years, but he didn't agree that Alex was ready to assume her place in the universe. He vehemently opposed handing over the reins of existence to an "infant" in terms of life experiences, and with no prior preparation. Alex conceded that he agreed with Bruno and was ill-prepared to be thrust into godhood. He didn't want the responsibility and felt at sea without a life preserver.

What concerned Bruno most was that while the board knew Ditta's powers and influence, Alex was an unknown anomaly or––to put it less kindly––a freak of nature. Alex had no qualms about being viewed as such. He understood what concerned Bruno was that neither he, nor Alex himself, fully understood the limits of his abilities. Alex felt Bruno looking at him like Dr. Frankenstein viewed his creation: with beauty and disgust. Bruno quickly corrected Alex that he regarded him with a mixture of fascination and caution.

Bruno went on to explain that the wild card in Alex's creation was ichor. Scientifically, the team worked blind and stumbled through the dark with the supernatural elements of his origins. Ditta had become paranoid over the millennia and kept the scientific team entirely in the dark about the influence or properties of ichor. She never let the team test the substance, and kept all samples tightly hidden. Bruno explained Ditta was concerned about the potential damage to humanity if ichor fell into the wrong hands. Bruno had no clue about ichor's origins, the substance's abilities, or the long-term consequences of exposure.

Alex now completely understood why Bruno viewed him with such trepidation, and thanked him for being honest. He agreed that he had no idea what he could do, and it deeply scared him.

"I'm told you've had two events of late," said Dr. Bruno.

Alex nodded yes. "Sunday after Ditta's passing, and two weeks ago at the university."

"Were there any triggers?"

"I'm not sure if they're triggers, but a severe headache was involved in each incident."

"And after the headache?" said Bruno.

"A buildup of energy in my body and a release of an intense wave of energy."

Dr. Bruno stepped back and tilted his head. "You omitted blowing up a tavern..."

"That was only some glasses and mirrors, nothing like the other events. There was no wave of energy. Besides, the décor needed updating."

Bruno didn't respond to Alex's attempt at humor.

"Intriguing," said Dr. Bruno, "the first time took down the power grid on the Eastern Seaboard and the second only half of Boston. I guess that's progress."

Alex smirked at Dr. Bruno's attempt at levity.

"Hoko will work with you on controlling your abilities, but it sounds like the last two events involved telepathy in hearing the thoughts of others, plus the telekinesis you demonstrated in the bar. The largest episode was probably an aftershock from your ascension."

Alex sat silently, trying to process Dr. Bruno's information.

Dr. Bruno placed his hand on Alex's shoulder; it startled him to see an act of compassion that reminded him of the man he once knew. He took the opportunity to give Dr. Bruno his long-overdue thanks.

"I don't know if you remember, good doctor, but the last time we saw each other at boarding school in Europe, you saved me from a terrible situation––and I never had the opportunity to thank you."

Dr. Bruno looked confused. "Your memory is much better than mine. What did I allegedly do?"

"After the Jesuit boarding school discovered I was gay, they forced me into daily conversion therapy for months. It only stopped after I told you about it on your last visit. It was one of the worst experiences in my life, and I sincerely thank you for your help in escaping the situation."

"What makes you think I helped in any way?" asked Bruno.

"Because the day after your visit for my annual physical, Ditta moved me to another boarding school in the States. I owe you, and I won't forget it," said Alex.

Dr. Bruno appeared stunned by Alex's statement, as he stepped back and furrowed his brow.

"I think it's best to leave the painful memories in the past. Let's focus on the present."

Alex nodded in agreement as Dr. Bruno quickly moved on to his next task––establishing some baseline measures of Alex's functioning. Dr. Bruno pulled a small black box from his lab coat pocket and quietly held it close to Alex's body. He slowly moved the device along every body part, before making notes. He explained after Alex had asked that the device was an EMF detector which identified the strength of electromagnetic fields. Bruno was only slightly concerned Alex was emitting an unusually high-level EMF field––it wasn't dangerous to Alex, or other humans, but posed a risk to electronics around him. Bruno stressed that Alex would need to have repeated monitoring upon every visit. He advised Alex to keep wearing his biometric watch so he could analyze the real-time data and revise Alex's baseline level of biological functioning as needed.

Bruno then asked Alex to hold out his right arm. He pulled a needle from his lab coat and removed the protective cap. Alex was hesitant, but complied. Bruno explained that Ditta could not have standard medical tests in her human form due to her impenetrable skin. In the next test, he prepared Alex to attempt to give him a shot of saline, to see if he had the same physical limits. Dr. Bruno held Alex's right arm as he tried administering the shot. He pushed harder and harder until the needle broke. Bruno pulled out a second needle and obtained the same results.

"Your skin may also be impervious to damage," said Bruno as he pulled a metal tray with several instruments sealed in hygienic plastic coverings to his side. He peeled the cover back to reveal a surgical scalpel.

"OK, Dr. Bruno, what do you intend to do with that?" asked Alex.

Bruno stated he would attempt to make a small mark on Alex's arm after swabbing it with alcohol, small enough to draw a few drops of blood.

"Hold up, Bruno. Needles are one thing, but incisions..."

"For god's sake, man up," said Bruno. He explained that throughout Alex's life, he was given increasing doses of ichor. Alex's last dose was the maximum available, so any injuries should be moot. Bruno offered for Alex to hold the instrument and make the nick if it would make him feel better. Alex shook his head and looked away from his arm.

Bruno opened an alcohol pad and carefully cleaned the area of Alex's forearm where he intended to mark his mark. He offered to either give Alex a countdown so that he could close his eyes, or use the surprise method. Alex said, "Just do it."

His dread was interrupted by the sound of metal clinking on the floor. Bruno placed his hand on Alex's shoulder once more and told him he could open his eyes, since the scalpel had broken. Bruno appeared satisfied that the experiment showed Alex's skin was functionally impenetrable.

"Color me confused," said Alex.

Bruno cautioned that invulnerability complicates things. If Alex were to sustain severe trauma causing internal injuries, there would be no way to treat him. Also, as a result, there was no way of determining whether his muscles, tissues, and bones could be damaged. Alex conceded that would be a problem and wondered if other diagnostic tests would be helpful. Bruno stated MRIs and CTs would not be safe with the EMP field Alex was emitting, and could damage the diagnostic equipment or else cause an explosion due to massive feedback. Even with his non-scientific doctorates, Alex grasped explosions would be a lousy outcome. Bruno cautioned him not to walk away with the perception that he could not be injured––exposure to massive levels of lethal radiation was probably the most significant risk to his safety.

"The only objective measure of your internal biological functions will be to gather saliva, urine, and fecal samples."

"OK, Dr. Bruno. This conversation just got awkward."

"Awkward or not, Dr. Lieth, I'll need saliva and urine samples before you leave today, and a fecal sample on your next visit."

"It's a date!"

"Is everything a joke to you?" said Bruno, shaking his head.

"I think I've earned a little humor with everything that's happened to me over the past two weeks. On a serious note, though, I do have a few questions. You mentioned genetics and cloning earlier. Were there other male test subjects?"

"No. You were the only male offspring."

"How did that happen?" asked Alex.

"Ditta, for decades, insisted only a female vessel could control and wield the Eros force. But after so many failed attempts, she became desperate. Most test subjects didn't survive through the gestational phase, and only a handful survived infancy."

"Not that I don't mind being special, but I'm not sure how I can be male if I'm a clone of Ditta. Where did the Y-chromosome come from?"

"The genetic material for your X-chromosome and Y-chromosome was extracted from a hair sample Ditta provided."

"So, I'm not an exact clone of Ditta?"

"Not exactly--you're slightly different, but still the same," said Bruno.

"Do you care to make an educated guess?" said Alex.

"I'm a scientist, I don't guess. Some things are just unknown."

"So, what in someone's DNA makes them a god?"

"That would be the 'god' gene. Only you and Ditta have it. Two of them, to be exact."

Alex raised one eyebrow. "Interesting. What does this god gene do?"

"Everything that makes you divine. Never seen it before, will probably never see it again," said Bruno.

"Speaking of miracles of science," said Alex, "it has come to my attention that an inoculation exists, making the board immune to Ditta's--or my--assumed abilities. Is this the case?"

Bruno took off his glasses and crossed his arms. "Yes, every board member and employee working at PGC receives inoculations. Ditta insisted on this provision to ensure the staff couldn't be manipulated by her or by outside cosmic forces seeking to harm her or the rest of the board. She'd become paranoid over the decades we worked together. But tell me, how did you come to learn about the inoculations?"

"I have my sources. Thank you for your time today, Dr. Bruno. I look forward to working with you."

Dr. Bruno nodded and left the room abruptly. After supplying saliva and urine samples, Alex left the medical wing and met Galen waiting in the lobby.

"Can I ask you a question, Galen?"

"Suppose, mate."

"How long have you known Dr. Bruno?"

"Since starting PGC. Don't know him personally. Been to weekly meetings where he's present. Why ya ask?"

"I don't like the way he treats people, and especially how he treats his staff."

"We have a sayin' in New Zealand that applies to him. He's 'spitting the dummy.'"

"What does that mean?"

"Always having a tantrum or hissy fit."

Alex laughed so hard he snorted.

"Ya right, mate?"

"Yes I am, Galen. I must admit your saying perfectly surmises how he acts towards others."

"Security staff avoid him at all costs. His security designation is 'the Muppet.'"

"Oh, now I'm dying to know the meaning of that."

"An incompetent idiot."

"Thank you for explaining. I was thinking more about Jim Henson. What's my security designation, if I dare ask?"

"Not sure I should say, mate."

"It's insulting to leave your boss hanging, Galen." Alex could see from the look on Galen's flushed cheeks that he was embarrassed.

"If ya must know, yur codename is 'the Unicorn.'"

Alex laughed. "A magical, mythical stallion. It could be worse, and I've certainly been called worse names. How does one get assigned a codename? Is there an office pool, or can the subject select their codename?"

Galen didn't respond.

"I take your silence as yes on the office pool."

"Yu're the boss, mate. Ya can pick any codename if ya like. Limo is prepared and ready to go."

"OK, let's go. The Unicorn has left the building!"

"Already regretting sharing that," Galen said, shaking his head in disapproval.

Chapter Twelve

Alex

*F**uck Dr. Sonja, fuck PGC, and fuck this Eros bullshit.*

Alex sat in his shoebox office, processing the events of the past couple of weeks. He knew he was missing an appointment at PGC with Hoko, but he was still feeling angry and defiant after his last session with Dr. Sonja. A gentle knocking on the door disrupted Alex's stewing. He ignored it. *Go away, leave me alone.* The person at the door persisted with three louder knocks. *Go the fuck away!* But the knocking continued.

"The door is open," Alex reluctantly said, realizing his visitor wouldn't desist.

"Good afternoon, Alex," said Hoko as he entered the office.

"Good afternoon, Hoko. Did we have a meeting today? I forgot. I must admit I left PGC yesterday rather distracted after my session with Dr. Sonja." Alex didn't care that he lied—he didn't owe Hoko or PGC anything. The quicker he left, the better.

"I apologize for the intrusion, but I was hoping to meet you on your turf to help you become more comfortable and begin learning more about your life. I can only imagine how intimidating and overwhelming the situation is for you."

"Truer words have probably never been spoken," said Alex.

"I hope you'll find our relationship will differ from the other board members. My job is to help you develop your skills and abilities to your maximum potential. We can achieve this by strengthening your connection with nature and accessing the energetic fields flowing through the universe."

"That's a radically different approach from Dr. Bruno and Dr. Sonja."

"My colleagues are well-intentioned, but they come on a little strong. After years of working with them, I've grown to respect what they bring to the board. However, it can be like bitter tea: you either develop a taste for it, or learn how to sweeten it to your liking."

"I'm not sure my relationship with Dr. Sonja can be repaired. I believe she deceived me and seems to think I'm a psychopath."

"So, her deductions bother you?" asked Hoko.

Alex said that in some ways, they stung him deeply. He'd put himself first in the past because no one would look out for him. The board acted like Ditta was some ever-present influence in his life, but Alex admitted that he never truly knew her at all. She may have paid for his education and essentials, but did he know the real Ditta? He said he'd only spent time with her on his birthdays. Now, he knew she was dosing him with ambrosia without consent, so she'd had an ulterior motive. When you do the math, he said, four hours a birthday over seventeen years, he'd only spent sixty-eight hours face-to-face with her——less than three days total, Alex admitted. Did he know her? How could she have dropped this bullshit into his lap without talking about it? He added you don't do that to someone you allegedly care about.

Hoko looked around the room before responding, "I see from the books on your shelves that you're a fan of Sir Arthur Conan Doyle."

"Good deduction; he's my favorite author."

"Do you remember what the BBC version of Sherlock Holmes said about being a psychopath?"

Alex chuckled as he responded, "I'm not a psychopath; I'm a high-functioning sociopath. Do your research!" Alex liked Hoko's sense of humor, so he gave him a few more minutes.

Hoko acknowledged Alex's feelings were valid. The changes in Alex's life were disconcerting and represented a seismic shift to his worldview. Hoko recognized that he didn't ask for, or want, any of this. Hoko said he wouldn't waste Alex's time, and added he could say Ditta was deeply conflicted regarding how she had kept Alex at a distance over the years. For all her strengths, she'd become jaded due to the losses she'd experienced. Initially, Hoko indicated, she was incredibly involved in the lives of the offspring that were the results of Dr. Bruno's project, raising them as her children. But, Hoko said, when they didn't survive, she'd go into a deep depression with each loss.

"She cared deeply, but was afraid to suffer another loss by getting too close to you. But I know she was immensely proud of you and your accomplishments."

Hearing Hoko's account of events hurt Alex's heart. He understood why Ditta kept her distance, but it also scared him because she'd warned the world would suffer if she became depressed or lost control of her emotions.

Hoko replied that Ditta's emotions took time to manage, and eventually patterns emerged which benefited humanity. He explained having a problematic day wouldn't have an immediate impact, so it's OK to feel one's emotions without fear of causing lasting damage to humanity.

Alex felt relieved and thanked Hoko for putting his mind at rest. Hoko was the first person in this ordeal who'd taken the time to validate Alex's experiences and honestly talk to him about Ditta, which gave him a better perspective on her life and struggles. Hoko added he was glad his words helped Alex, and he was willing to talk to him about her struggles as much as Alex would like. Hoko asked if Alex was bothered by other things Dr. Sonja may have said about him.

Alex admitted he had a hot temper with a short fuse. His first response in many situations was anger, with anxiety being a close second. He was working on better handling his emotions, but rubbing his nose in it was cruel. Who wanted to be defined by the worst possible moments in their life?

"Alex, you've done well for yourself in your career. From what I gathered on my walk across the campus, and interacting with students along the way, Dr. Lieth has a reputation for being challenging. Still, his students enjoy his lectures and lively approach to literature. In short, they respect you."

Alex thanked Hoko for his kind words. Hoko had earned a few more minutes.

"Are you familiar with the work of Matshona Dhliwayo? He's a Canadian philosopher, entrepreneur, and author."

"No, I'm not familiar with his work," said Alex.

"His words help me keep life in perspective, and I think they can help you.

When they judge you, yawn.

When they misunderstand you, smile.

When they underestimate you, laugh.

When they condemn you, ignore.

When they envy you, rejoice.

When they oppose you, prevail."

Alex paused for a moment before responding, "That's genuinely inspirational. People can only define me if I let them."

"An eloquent summation. So how does the lesson apply at this stressful juncture in your life?"

"I see what you did there," Alex said with a smile. "Maybe I should slow down my anger and not be so quick to judge others. I know who I am; I'll define myself!"

"I think you could also give yourself some compassion by forgiving your past mistakes. From where I sit, you're your biggest critic, not Dr. Sonja. You have an inner saboteur in your head that appears to be working overtime, which stokes the fire of your anxiety."

Alex thanked Hoko for sharing his wisdom and being so easy to talk to. It was not lost on him that Hoko and Galen were the only people who had consistently treated him with respect and compassion since his world turned upside down. Most of the board viewed him as a problem needing to be contained, or else a ticking time bomb.

Hoko laughed, saying Alex's words reminded him of a line from a movie he watched recently: "'It's none of my business what you think about me.'"

Alex laughed, saying those sounded like words to live by. He joked maybe Hoko should be the board psychotherapist.

Hoko said he must graciously decline the offer as he preferred to deal with the spirit, rather than the depths of the mind. He added he hoped they could develop a relationship that genuinely helped Alex, one in which Alex would lead the way. "Alex Lieth is the expert on your mind, body, and soul. I am merely your guide."

Hoko further explained he had a theory Alex would be able to surpass Ditta's abilities to connect with others and to read electromagnetic fields. In her physical form, Hoko said her abilities were diminished to some degree. He said it was like an incompatibility between software and hardware, where information got lost in translation. Hoko hypothesized Alex wouldn't have this problem because he started with a physical body, so would have a greater affinity to electromagnetic energy––one which opened up so many possibilities, since our brains work on electrical signals. Hoko said through quantum entanglement, Alex might be able to access individual human memories remotely and access the electromagnetic fields generated by the Earth, which had implications from climate change to being able to channel healing energy.

Alex smiled. It was refreshing to see someone excited about what he may be able to do. He admitted to Hoko to doing casual research, and had questions about Ditta's abilities. Hoko asked Alex what he had uncovered, while cautioning he couldn't trust everything he heard or read, owing to centuries-old misinformation on gods.

Alex smiled and shook his head. "No need to worry about ancient Fox News talking heads, got it. Let's go down the list," he said. "Immortality?"

Hoko confirmed Ditta was functionally immortal. Reportedly, several weapons from antiquity could harm her, but ultimately, she couldn't transition until Alex became the Eros force. Hoko noted he was excited about Alex's interest in exploring his abilities, but cautioned they would need to take it slow. Hoko offered Alex a deal––exploring one potential ability every session––which he readily accepted. Hoko said he'd like to explore the abilities Alex had already experienced: telepathy, telekinesis, and amokinesis.

"What's amokinesis?" Alex asked.

"Well, in simple terms, it's the ability to feel, manipulate, induce, or remove love from a human being."

On hearing this, Alex knew he'd experienced it at the tavern the last night he met with Ditta. Hoko said Alex that Alex could touch a person's life force or feel and see their "spark," as Ditta called it. From what Hoko had gathered, Alex showed a natural affinity for amokinesis. However, Hoko cautioned that there was one limit to the ability——Alex couldn't reduce the impact of true love.

"With true love, if you try to remove or reduce it, the love will revert eventually to its original form," Hoko said.

Alex stated Ditta had mentioned he displayed the ability to convert Danyal's spark to Eros. Hoko agreed and confirmed Ditta didn't have that ability, and was very impressed with Alex. He smiled and asked if Alex was up for doing some field research.

"I'm hesitant to even experiment with these abilities. What do you have in mind before I agree to anything?" said Alex, feeling his heart beat faster and his anxiety spiking.

"Let's stroll in nature around the campus since it's such a warm, sunny day for late February. We can get some vitamin D and test your amokinesis skills," said Hoko.

"I must admit, all this talk about supernatural abilities scares me shitless. What if I do something wrong and hurt someone? I only wielded these abilities when Ditta guided me through them. The only other times I tried to wield my influence was out of anger. In both situations, I was close to losing control."

"I honor and respect your concerns, Alex. I'd be more worried if you *didn't* have fears about developing your abilities. Overconfidence leads to mistakes and bad decisions that can have grave implications. Trust in our relationship is vital. I promise we will go slow and I won't push you to do anything you don't want. I'll let you decide how far we go today."

"Since you've taken the time to listen and respect my perspective, I'll try it, so long as you assure me we won't force people to act against their will."

"You have my word——we will merely observe from a distance," said Hoko.

Alex nodded in agreement. *Please don't let this be a mistake.*

Hoko and Alex strolled past the brick teaching buildings and the student union before settling on a bench in the central tree-lined courtyard of Starling University.

Alex was encouraged to focus on breathing. Hoko explained to Alex how to breathe and connect with nature, since Alex's abilities came from nature and the universe. He said Alex was one with everything, and connected to the cosmic source. Hoko said he wanted to teach Alex the skill of box breathing.

"Why is it called box breathing?" asked Alex.

"Well, it's made up of equal parts of inhaling, retaining your breath, exhaling, and finally holding your breath before starting the process again. We all live such fast-paced and driven lives these days that we often forget to breathe, even though it's an essential part of our existence. You can't survive if you don't breathe," said Hoko. "While inhaling, we are bringing the elements of the universe into our bodies. This supplies the oxygen needed to survive. Breathing not only helps bring in healing energy, but exhaling also helps purge impurities, expel negative energy, and helps your body find homeostasis. Let's give it a try."

Hoko encouraged Alex to take a deep breath for four seconds, and hold it for a count of four.

"Now exhale for four seconds...one...two...three...four, and then hold for four seconds...one...two...three...four. And that's box breathing. Navy SEALs use it to help them focus on training, lower their blood pressure, and to reduce both anxiety and insomnia. Eventually, we'll build up longer intervals between breaths. Does this feel OK, Alex? Do you have any questions before we proceed?"

Alex shook his head no. He felt slightly more relaxed after the brief exercise.

"Excellent," replied Hoko, who then instructed Alex to go through this cycle for three minutes. Hoko sat patiently and watched Alex breathe slowly, his chest rising and falling in rhythm.

"How do you feel?"

"Much more relaxed. I feel lighter, somehow."

"That's not odd at all," explained Hoko. "When stressed, our brains dump cortisol, the primary stress hormone, into our bloodstream. The only ways to remove it are relaxation and exercise." He said if Alex can learn to relax through breath work, he would reap the benefits, since it was physiologically impossible to be stressed and relaxed simultaneously. Alex laughed and asked Hoko where he was when he was studying for grad school tests.

Hoko explained the next step was to work on connecting with nature. He instructed Alex to keep his eyes closed and to focus on his box breathing. Hoko asked Alex to reach out with his mind and feel the energy around him in the air, grass, and trees. All of the elements and living organisms have an energy field, he said. Human eyes can't see the energy, but Alex could, said Hoko. He instructed Alex to feel the energy and let it flow around him, and then to let it flow through him. Hoko added that Alex could control the energy and bend it to his will.

"What does energy look like, and how does it feel?" asked Hoko.

Alex replied it looked like he was standing in a Van Gogh painting, with vivid colors swirling around him. He continued on, saying it felt like he was standing on a beach with a warm breeze on his face as it flowed through his body--every cell tingled and craved more. His body felt like a conduit for an endless flow of lightning.

Hoko directed Alex to control the energy without opening his eyes, telling him how many trees surrounded the courtyard. Alex kept slowly breathing. Ten, five on each side, he answered. Correct, said Hoko.

"What's happening to your right?" asked Hoko.

"There's a man playing fetch with his dog, a German Shepherd," replied Alex.

"And immediately behind you?" asked Hoko.

Alex described four women sitting at a table discussing sophomore chemistry, and how attracted they all were to the sexy teaching assistant. Their fantasies about him were so vivid, they almost made him blush. Hoko laughed and told Alex to be careful when reaching out to other minds, because one never knows what private or intimate thoughts would be revealed.

Hoko challenged Alex to focus on the couple across the courtyard, sitting on the steps to the dorms. "What are they feeling?" he asked.

Alex laughed; it was the two guys from the tavern he had nudged to share a kiss. They deeply yearned for each other and didn't want to care about who knew about their relationship. Alex admitted Ditta knew they were ready to take the next step. They only needed a push.

"Maybe it's true love," Alex said, smiling.

Hoko asked Alex about the woman walking on the sidewalk holding a briefcase.

"That's Professor Dobry. She's in a foul mood, which isn't unusual," replied Alex. "Actually, it's more than a bad mood; she's going through a divorce. The relationship is ending because her husband slept with one of her students. Ouch."

Alex stopped momentarily and noticed some weird energy centered under the third tree to the left. There's a void in the energy field, he said. Hoko nodded and explained that one of Alex's plainclothes security guards, Templeton, was sitting watching them. Alex marveled at the strength of the Eros vaccination––it must be powerful to disrupt the cosmic energy flow.

Hoko told Alex there was one last test to help gauge his current range.

"There's a coffee shop three blocks away on Esplanade Street. What energy can you feel in the café?"

Alex replied there was no way he could do that. Hoko asked if Alex was letting his inner saboteur tell him what he could and couldn't do.

"You're more likely to succeed if you think you can do something. Are you willing to try?"

Alex nodded. He would try and sit quietly, focusing on his breathing and the energy flow around him. Alex began to chuckle before observing Michelle, the barista, had a crush on his favorite rugby-playing security guard, Galen Tucker. Alex couldn't feel Galen, but he could guess he'd entered the café by the increase in her spark. In fact, the level of Eros energy in the room increased dramatically, so it seemed more than a few people were crushing on Galen.

"Oh, and one more thing––our coffee is ready."

"Did you read Michelle's thoughts?" asked Hoko.

Alex said he did more than read her thoughts; he could see briefly through her eyes. She even drew little hearts on the takeout cups. He paused. "Before we stop, Hoko, can you help me reach out to my friend Shae? I miss him and want to know he's OK."

"We can try, Alex, but I'm concerned you're pushing your limits. From what Dr. Bruno tells me, you get severe headaches related to your abilities."

"I'm willing to risk it," said Alex.

"Remote viewing, or remote contacting, works through quantum entanglement," explained Hoko.

"Is this Einstein's 'spooky action at a distance?" asked Alex.

"Yes," said Hoko, "two points in space and time that are different but connected. And we're going to use this connection to our advantage."

Hoko instructed Alex to go back to his breathing for a couple of moments, and when he was ready, to picture Shae in his mind and to reach out to him. Alex tried but replied he was not getting anything. Hoko cautioned Alex he was pressing too hard and to let the energy come naturally. Hoko suggested Alex think of his best memory of Shae, and hold that image in his mind.

Alex focused on his breathing before responding, "I see him walking down a row of brownstone houses carrying, I guess, groceries. He's turning to walk up the snow-covered steps."

"Excellent," said Hoko. "Look for clues that will give you hints about his location, such as a sign or address."

"The address by the door says 2756 Penderson Street. That's an upscale part of town. But I know that building. The only person I know who lives there is..."

"Who lives there, Alex?" said Hoko.

"Wynn lives there."

Shae and Wynn? When the hell did that happen? I must have got the address wrong.

"OK, Alex, open your eyes. How did that feel?" said Hoko.

"Exhilarated...my body feels like I've been skydiving. I've never experienced such a rush."

Hoko smiled and said it was more like directing and surfing on the natural energetic field. "But how do you feel emotionally?"

Alex noted the dial on his stress had turned down several notches. Hoko said that was music to his ears and that he could access this energy whenever needed; however, he must center himself first through his breathing. Hoko said he was amazed that Alex briefly viewed the world remotely. He added remote viewing was a highly advanced skill and was astonished by Alex's development in their brief session. Hoko said Alex was a natural at reading cosmic energy, and that his results hint at emerging telepathic abilities.

"I only used my abilities with your support. But you were right; I do feel a migraine starting," said Alex.

Hoko cautioned Alex to take it easy, adding that he suspected Alex's abilities would develop as his mind and body became more accustomed to the cosmic energy flowing through every fiber of his being. Hoko said he suspected Alex's mind might be suppressing his true abilities as a coping mechanism, similar to a state of shock after an accident, given that he'd undergone so much trauma recently. He added they would continue to work on ways to soothe Alex's mind and body. Hoko said Alex's homework was to do his box breathing daily for at least thirty minutes, and that he would email Alex some other relaxation activities, too.

"Thank you, Hoko. I feel a little hopeful for the first time since this ordeal began. I'll work on forgiving myself. Maybe even forgiving others...and that's a gigantic maybe," Alex said with a crooked grin.

"We will take this day by day, Alex. A journey down the universal path begins with one step. Today, we took the first step; tomorrow, we will take another step. Hopefully, in time, we can have you running at full sprint. Before I leave, I need your input to help me guide you in your growth. I mentioned several spiritual practices the other day when we first met at the board meeting; I'd like you to select one that resonates with you."

"No need to even think about it. I want to go dancing."

"What draws you to dance?"

"When I'm on the dance floor, I give into the music and energy, and the feeling is primal or, better yet, transcendent." Alex smiled. "Plus, I promised Galen I'd take him to see a dance club here in the States. Seeing him cut loose and have a little fun would be interesting. He's too uptight, in my opinion."

"You're developing a strong bond with Galen. I'm glad you're establishing a friendship with him. I wonder if your connection to Galen helped you remotely view today, rather than connecting with the mind of a random stranger. We can test that hypothesis in another session."

"Before we finish, Hoko, I owe you an apology," said Alex.

"For what, Alex?"

"I'm working on improving and changing my immature behavior. I lied to you earlier when I said I forgot about our meeting. I intentionally ditched it, and I'm sorry. It wasn't fair to you."

"No need to be sorry; I won't judge you for your decision when you are doing your best to survive an overwhelming situation. It worked out for me to come to you, and helped me understand your world better. So, rather than being upset, I want to thank you for allowing this to happen today. If there's ever a time you're not feeling it, please tell me, and we can take a step back. Got it?"

"Yes. I need to get back to grading papers, but I'm already looking forward to our next session."

Chapter Thirteen

Alex stepped out of the limo outside the row of brownstone homes on Penderson Street, and his body was frozen with fear. He had the driver park a block away so as not to draw attention and to give him the time on the walk to fortify his nerves, but he misjudged the level of his apprehension. Alex stood silently on the bottom step of 2756 Penderson, petrified and unable to move. He couldn't make peace with Shae unless he was brave enough to ring the doorbell.

Galen quietly held back, about twenty-five feet down the sidewalk.

Alex cautiously reached out, rang the doorbell, and was greeted by loud barking. Shae slowly opened the door, but before Alex knew it, he found himself lying on his back with a large dog standing over him, licking his face.

"Horus!" Alex cried. "It can't be!"

"Boris!" yelled Shae. "Get off him. No jumping!"

"But how? How is Horus here?" Alex could barely speak as the black and white dog kept licking his face intensely.

"Let's walk to the park around the corner to have some space to talk. I'll get my coat," said Shae.

"Some space to talk, or so I won't be here if Wynn comes home?"

"Don't push your luck, Alex. My gut tells me to send you packing," said Shae.

Alex sheepishly asked if he could walk Boris, and Shae reluctantly agreed after warning that Boris likes to pull on his leash and to be careful not to trip on the ice. Shae explained that they called him Boris as part of his fresh start in America. Alex nodded that he understood.

Alex and Shae sat on a park bench in awkward silence as Galen and Boris played fetch with a tennis ball.

"Who's your handsome shadow?" said Shae, finally breaking the silence.

"Oh, Galen. He's my bodyguard."

"I'd let that fine specimen of a man guard my body any day."

Alex was amused that, as usual, Shae was more focused on the eye candy than the tension between them, or the fact Alex now needed a bodyguard. Shae lived purely in the moment, and Alex desperately wanted that ability. His friendship with Shae kept him balanced and focused on being present throughout college.

"Same old Shae. I've missed your flirtatious personality. Galen's a great guy; the New Zealand accent doesn't hurt his attractiveness."

"You always did have international tastes."

"Stop it, Shae--it's not like that."

"How is it, Alex?" said Shae as he refused to turn to look at Alex. "I know you better than anyone, and I'll call you on your bullshit. You're attracted to that man."

"I didn't say I wasn't. I may be in a relationship, but I'm not dead."

What was there not to like about Galen? He's handsome—tall, with broad shoulders, powerful legs, and arms with tattoos on each forearm. Galen was ever hotter in his rugby uniform pictures. Despite having a neatly trimmed brown beard, his chiseled jawline framed his face with its deep brown eyes, his soft, wavy brown hair bouncing in the wind.

"Definitely a 'Squirrel.'"

Shae laughed for a fleeting moment, breaking the tension. "I almost forgot about squirrel."

"Squirrel" was their code to alert each other that an attractive guy in the area deserved their attention. Galen was, indeed, an impressive example of a "squirrel."

"Mind in the gutter as ever," said Alex.

"I learned from the best," said Shae as he briefly made eye contact for the first time. "If you don't want Galen, he can always be my future ex-husband."

"I've missed you, Shae. How long has it been since we hung out?" Alex regretted the question as soon as the words had come out of his mouth.

"Let me think––that would be from the moment you met Danyal."

Shae's response was honest and stoked Alex's feelings of shame. "Ouch, I deserved that one."

"You deserve that and a few more from where I'm sitting," said Shae as he turned toward Alex, tears forming in his eyes. "You hurt me. I thought we were close friends who valued and cherished each other. But when you met Danyal, you discarded me like yesterday's trash. I tried to reach out to you, but you were always busy or didn't have time. There was no room for anything in your world but Danyal. I depended on you; you were there for my physical recovery after being gay-bashed. I thought we were ride-or-die friends. Little did I know it was ride until the next hot guy came along," Shae said, tears now rolling down his face.

Alex paused before responding, holding back his own tears. "I'm sorry, Shae. There's no excuse for how I behaved. I love you like a brother, and I behaved horribly. I've been hearing a lot recently how much my choices have hurt others, and I deeply regret it."

"Wow, the proud Alex Lieth saying he's sorry is not something I ever thought I'd hear. But it's not enough to let you back into my life."

"I promise, Shae, I'll earn back your trust if you let me."

Shae looked at Alex. "Damn it, Alex, I'm not forgiving you so easy."

Alex sat in silence, fighting back his own tears before saying, "I'm so sorry, Shae. This was a mistake. I'm sorry to bother you. I won't do it again."

"You don't get to walk away from me again, Alex," said Shae, standing and walking towards Galen and Boris.

After gathering up the dog, Shae started to leave the park, but Boris broke free from his leash and ran back to Alex's bench. Alex continued to sob as he petted Boris. Shae came over and looked down at Alex.

"One last thing I need to get off my chest––come here, asshole, and give me a hug before I change my mind and kick your ass across this park."

Alex stood and embraced Shae for several moments, while Boris returned to play fetch with his new buddy. Alex could feel the spark in Shae's chest pulsing. Shae sat back on the bench with Alex, and asked if he planned to ask about Wynn. Alex shook his head no; he had no right and wasn't brave enough to broach the subject. He was surprised when Shae said that Wynn had returned from Egypt broken and damaged. It was like a part of him was still there in prison. Shae explained that Wynn didn't sleep well due to nightmares and being hyper-vigilant, meaning his mood was often unpredictable. Alex said it sounded like PTSD, and Shae agreed. Shae added Wynn had been seeing a psychiatrist who'd prescribed medication, but that he wouldn't take it––he was too proud. Shae shook his head and stated that the handsome, stubborn man would be the end of him. Alex placed his hand on Shae's back for emotional support.

Alex asked Shae if he loved Wynn, and Shae nodded yes. He already knew the answer before Shae replied, because he could see the spark in Shae's chest pulse as he talked about him. Shae stated Wynn cared about him too, but that it was difficult when the relationship was between Shae, Wynn, and Wynn's demons. Alex leaned over on the bench and kissed Shae on the cheek before offering an ear if Shae ever needed to talk. Shae thanked him for the offer, but Alex knew Shae would never use it.

"You haven't mentioned Danyal," said Shae as he laid his head on Alex's shoulder.

"Danyal is, well, still as jealous as ever. He's not talking about it, but I know he's struggling with Galen being around."

"I'm sorry, Alex. It sounds like the men in our lives are less than ideal."

Alex added that dealing with Ditta's company was also proving very taxing. Shae sat up and gave Alex a confused look, quirking an eyebrow. He explained that Ditta had passed and left him her company and penthouse. Shae laughed with his hand over his mouth and said if Alex was living the penthouse highlife, he would be hosting the next party. Alex shook his head and told Shae he had rejected the penthouse, causing Shae to shake his head back in disapproval.

"I have a question, one I hesitate to ask...," said Alex. "But how did Wynn bring Boris back to the States?"

"From what he says, he refused to come back without him. The company he worked for pulled several strings to make it happen. The poor pup was sickly, but we nursed him back to health, and he soon got adjusted. We love him," Shae said, looking over at the dog.

"You've nothing to worry about, Shae. I have no claim on Boris. He belongs to his dads...you and Wynn."

"How did you know what I was thinking?" said Shae.

"An educated guess," Alex lied after having read Shae's thoughts about how much they loved Boris. Following his session with Hoko, his telepathy skills had improved since he'd learned to quiet his mind by focusing on breathing.

Alex told Shae it would be great if he could see pictures of Boris on social media and, maybe in time, they could have playdates in the park if it didn't cause any issues with Wynn. Shae assured Alex he'd handle Wynn, but that he'd have to think seriously about unblocking Alex. It'd take more than one successful meeting in the park to take that next step.

Alex laughed and said Shae was incorrigible when Shae stated Boris had taken a liking to his "Chippendale shadow." Deep down, Alex loved Shae's flirtatious nature. He went on to say that, if Shae wanted to see a show, the university was having a fundraiser for LGBTQI+ homeless youth in two weeks at Icon Nightclub.

"You up for a night of dancing?" said Alex.

"Oh, you know that takes me back down memory lane. How will Danyal take you being out on the town with two handsome men?"

"Let me deal with Danyal."

"You're thinking about not telling him," said Shae, as he locked eyes with Alex.

Shae had pegged Alex's thoughts about the situation, and he knew lying to Danyal was unacceptable. He had to tell him. Alex quickly turned the conversation back to the offer he had made, and after hearing Galen had never been to a gay dance club in the States, Shae gladly accepted the invitation. He said it was his duty to protect and help culture a club virgin. Shae told Alex to text him the details and smiled as he walked again towards Galen and Boris, who had resumed their game of fetch. Alex smiled and waved at Shae and Boris as they left the park.

Galen walked over to the park bench and took a seat, catching his breath. Alex commented that it looked like Boris put Galen through a workout. Galen laughed and said Boris was an energetic lil pup. Alex replied that Boris always had been. Galen asked if Boris was the pup he found in Egypt, and Alex nodded yes. Someday, he would have to find a way to thank Wynn for giving him a home.

Galen said that he didn't want to overreach, but that he'd seen the look on Wynn's face at the bar, and it matched many soldiers in combat. He recommended a PTSD specialist a mate of his used after leaving the service. The therapist wasn't in Boston, but many therapists had been doing online therapy since COVID. Alex thanked Galen and agreed to pass the information on to Shae.

With a big smile, Alex asked Galen if he was ready. Galen hesitantly asked what he needed to be prepared for. Alex updated Galen on the plans to go dancing in two weeks with Shae for the homeless LGBTQI+ fundraiser. Galen was excited, but added he had nothing to wear. Alex chuckled and said not to worry; Shae was a fashion guru who would pick something out for him, but to watch out as he was a notorious flirt. Galen stated the warning was received and that he would try not to encourage Shae too much, as he stood to walk back toward the limo. Alex had no clue how to read Galen's comment about encouraging Shae.

As they reached the limo, Galen opened the door for Alex and told him that Ryo had found alternative transportation. They'd take it out on their maiden voyage to go dancing, so they could have a memorable night on the town.

Chapter Fourteen

Alex

Alex stood in the shower, bawling as the warm water washed over his face, diluting his tears. He'd never had such an intense argument with Danyal than the one they'd had over going out dancing with Shae for the homeless youth fundraiser. Danyal had known the fundraiser was approaching for the past month, but he went to a new level of nuclear when Alex refused to stay home and cancel his plans. Alex stayed defiant and was proud he stood up for himself and his friendship. He'd sacrificed the last year with Shae because of Danyal's insecurities, and would not stand for it anymore. Danyal had stormed out the door, slamming it in Alex's face, and Alex was glad Danyal would be working late tonight at the café doing yearly inventory. He wouldn't let the argument ruin his evening, and began preparing to start his night.

While getting dressed, Alex picked up his phone to check his messages, and saw he had a text from Galen to meet around the back of the apartment in five.

No peeking!

What had Alex gotten himself into? Fuck it! He had one goal tonight: enjoying himself and having fun. He waited for the prescribed time before walking down the stairs rather than the elevator, to arrive at the first-floor door closest to the back alley. Alex exited to see Galen standing beside a shiny new black SUV.

"Ya chariot has arrived, mate."

"What's this, Galen? I'm not a car person, so please excuse my ignorance."

Galen gladly explained this beaut was a 2024 Lamborghini Uros Performante.

"It has a twin-turbo V-8 engine with 657 horsepower, and can go zero to 60 in 3.1 seconds, topping out at 190 miles per hour."

Alex laughed as he had never seen Galen as excited as he was about the new SUV. He joked and asked Galen if he needed to give him and the Uros some time to get properly acquainted. Galen ignored Alex's attempt at humor and added the Uros purred like a lioness. Galen proudly proclaimed that he was Alex's driver from here on out, before clarifying the color was "Nero Noctis" rather than basic black. Alex laughed again, eliciting a scowl from Galen. Alex shook his head. He didn't want the flashy limo, so they got him a flashy luxury SUV. After he asked how much the Uros cost, Galen said the invoice in the glove compartment said $265,000 before the security modifications.

"Great, now the entire neighborhood will think I'm a drug dealer."

"Ya are a drug dealer, Alex," Galen said. "Just the drug ya deal is, love."

"Hilarious, Galen."

Galen was in a rare relaxed mood tonight. Not that Alex minded it; he could stand to loosen up a little and have fun. Alex held up a bag and pulled out a shirt Shae had picked for Galen to wear tonight, based on the color of Galen's eyes. With his right hand, Alex threw the shirt to Galen before saying he better get changed quickly, otherwise, they'd be late. He offered to protect the SUV while Galen changed.

Without a moment to waste, Galen began changing shirts right there in the alley. Alex started to turn around to give Galen privacy, but stopped when Galen began laughing and said he wasn't ashamed of his body. Galen threw his old shirt over at Alex, hitting him in the chest. Alex tried not to look up, but he couldn't resist. He noted that Galen's muscles and hairy chest were even more enticing than he'd imagined. Alex internally cursed Shae for contagious filthy minds. He demanded his eyes stop staring, but they refused to comply. He looked up and met Galen's eyes, as he asked if Shae had bought the right shirt since it was a bit tight. Alex chuckled, knowing it was the right shirt because, in Shae's eyes, the tighter the better. He smiled at Galen and admitted royal blue was definitely his color, and that he should wear it more. Galen snickered and asked if basic black was Alex's color, to which Alex replied his shirt was black, just like his heart. Alex then checked his watch and told Galen they needed to get the show on the road if they were going to meet Shae at midnight and make their grand entrance.

Alex and Galen walked to the entrance of Icon Nightclub, where they met Shae. Shae hugged Alex before introducing himself properly to Galen, since Alex had obviously forgotten his manners. Alex rolled his eyes before making formal introductions. He added that he expected everyone to play nice, and that there was only one rule tonight: have fun!

As they entered the club, their senses registered an onslaught of pounding rhythms and flashing lights. Shae immediately pulled Alex to the dance floor. Galen stepped to the side and watched as Alex and Shae let free their emotions and moved to the music. Before long, Shae got hot from the packed dance floor. He pulled off his shirt and encouraged Alex to do the same.

Shae leaned over, saying, "It's OK if we put on a show for our demanding public."

Alex reluctantly complied and continued to dance, not wanting to glance at Galen standing in the corner. *Why am I so self-conscious? Fuck the world; I'm here to have fun.*

Alex leaned over to Shae and yelled over the music that he needed to hit the bathroom. Shae nodded as he walked away. Upon returning to the edge of the dance floor, Alex quickly noticed Galen was not in his place in the corner. He scanned the bar intently. Did Galen leave? No, he's on the dance floor with Shae.

Alex watched Shae and Galen dance among the sweaty men on the dance floor. To Alex's surprise, Galen had both moves and rhythm. Alex was glad Galen was happily enjoying the moment for once. *Let's make this more interesting.* Alex closed his eyes and focused on his breathing. He reached out to the DJ's mind and placed a suggested playlist in his head, consisting of all of Galen's favorite songs that he'd shared with Alex. It was a small action that still caused a severe headache, but the pain was worth it to see Galen's face light up as 'Little Bird' began to play. Galen looked towards Alex and smiled, acknowledging what Alex had orchestrated. Galen danced and grew freer with each beat.

While his favorite songs continued to play, Galen leaned to say something to Shae and began to walk toward Alex.

"No fun, mate. When ya promise to go dancing, and ya stop dancing. DJ is lit," shouted Galen over the blaring music.

"I'm giving you some space to cut loose," said Alex.

"Plenty of room on the dance floor. If ya don't join us, will have to leave with the fancy new Uros."

"Fine, I'll join, but you better not report me to HR," responded Alex.

Alex and Galen returned to the dance floor as the DJ continued to play Galen's favorite songs. In the heat of the moment, Alex was freed of his worries and fears. He danced as Shae helped Galen pull off his shirt. Instinctively, Alex turned away, not wanting to embarrass Galen. A hand on his shoulder turned Alex around, and Galen gave him a disapproving look with one eyebrow raised. With his other hand, Galen made a circular motion, instructing Alex to turn around to dance with them. Alex awkwardly nodded, trying not to look at Galen's handsome face with the sweat rolling down his cheek and bouncing off his furry chest and abs. Galen's hand on his bare shoulder sent shockwaves through Alex's body.

Fuck it. It's only another body among the hundreds on this dance floor.

Alex gave into the moment, focusing on the life force and sexual energy dancing around him. He instinctively pulled the energy into his body until nearly every cell burst. He reached over to Galen and touched him gently on the forehead with his right index finger. From Galen's reaction, and the light reflecting in his eyes, he saw that Galen could now see the fantastic energies surrounding them. All three men danced, feeling the primal energy flowing through Alex. With each movement of his hands, arms, and body, Alex was the director, commanding the orchestra of energy around them.

When the bar announced it was closing at three a.m., Shae said his goodbyes by hugging Alex and Galen before waving as he made his way to the nearest metro station. Alex and Galen walked silently back to the parking lot to retrieve the new Uros.

"Gotta ask, mate——was ya pushin' the DJ in his set?"

"Why would you think that?" said Alex innocently.

"Cuz he played every song I like, including 'Little Bird.' Track's a lil old to be making a comeback."

Alex just smiled. He may have given the DJ a little nudge, but in his defense, the DJ played all of Shae's favorites, too.

"Cheers, anyway. Meant a lot, mate. The light show was bang-on."

"Yeah, they have good lighting in that place."

"Nah, not talking about that. Cosmic energy ya allowed me to see. Never seen anything so awesome. Can still see the energy around ya. Still glowing and bursting with energy."

"You're welcome. I'm learning to tune it out if needed," said Alex.

"Are ya blushing, mate?"

Alex knew he had been caught thinking about all the energy and sexual desire swirling on the dance floor. He hoped Danyal was in a better mood when he got home, because Alex had plenty of pent-up energy of his own he needed to release. Whether Galen knew it or not, he turned the head of every man looking in his direction, including Alex.

"You were the center of attention," said Alex.

Galen blushed and said, "Can't help being a 6'4 rugby god from New Zealand. There's no way to hide it. Ya learn to embrace it."

Alex laughed so hard he slipped on the ice. Reflexively reaching out, Galen caught Alex and pulled him up with their bodies moving closer than ever before. Alex could feel the intense heat of Galen's body, and he smelled so enticing.

"Excellent catch," said Alex, steadying himself and hastily stepping away from Galen's embrace.

"Cheers, all in a day's work. Let me take ya home," said Galen, his face flushing again.

Alex smiled and laughed to himself. *I see I'm not the only one embarrassing myself.* "I have one more favor: how do you open this car door? I'm afraid to break it."

"Ya pull the handle here..."

Before Galen could open the door, they were caught off guard by the jarring alarm emanating from their phones.

911 return to PGC immediately.

Chapter Fifteen

Alex

Alex paced back and forth as the private elevator at PGC made its way up the building. With each passing floor, his feelings of dread increased. *What the fuck was happening?*

Ryo had called the emergency security meeting, but had refused to share any information when Galen had called seeking further details. He felt like every time he entered PGC, something ominous would happen. Alex and Galen exited the elevator and walked down the hall to the conference room. As they arrived, they were met by Ryo and all the other board members sitting around the table.

"Thank you for coming in on short notice in the middle of the night," said Ryo.

"Call me paranoid, but my mind tends to run amok when I get called in for an emergency meeting. Can you put me out of my misery?" said Alex.

Ryo nodded and insisted all the information shared in the room wasn't to leave the building. "I've called this emergency briefing to discuss events that occurred today at 2:20 a.m. EST--events that involved Danyal Sarif."

Alex sat forward in his chair, immediately concerned. "You're scaring me, Ryo. Where's Danyal?"

Ryo explained that at 2:30 a.m., PGC received notification from Danyal's plainclothes security detail of a potential hostage event. The security detail had observed five men in military gear and assault weapons breaking into Excalibur Café. The security detail engaged and returned fire with the unknown assailants but was injured, preventing him from any pursuit. Before backup from Boston PD arrived, the assailants had fled with a hostage.

Upon entering the scene, the police found Danyal was the only employee missing, and several other employees were rushed for emergency care due to exposure to an unknown toxic gas. As of now, they didn't know Danyal's whereabouts. Ryo added that the only evidence they could recover from the scene was Danyal's phone. He placed it on the table as Alex's heart sank into his stomach. He closed his eyes as his breathing became fast and shallow. His head began to pound like a jackhammer. He couldn't focus as his vision blurred. His hands tingled as the room began to spin, before letting out a primal scream of "NO!" All the items on the conference table flew across the room and crashed against the wall, barely missing several board members' heads. Hoko moved quickly as he sat beside Alex and touched his shoulder.

"Alex, it's Hoko. Listen to my voice. Come back to the moment. You're safe in the boardroom. Focus on your breathing, breathing slowly in and out. Take deep breaths. You can do this. You have the power, and you're in full control."

Alex slowly brought his breathing under control.

"That's it," said Hoko, "I'm proud of you."

Galen placed his hand on Alex's other shoulder in support.

Alex opened his eyes and said in a weak, wavering voice, "How do we find Danyal?"

Ryo explained the PGC forensic staff would examine the café before Boston PD contaminated the scene. Then, they'd need to eliminate known terrorist groups in the area as suspects.

"Terrorists?" said Alex, as the fear in his heart made it feel like it would burst.

Ryo nodded and added Ms. Dea had powerful enemies that needed to be individually eliminated as suspects.

Alex's heart skipped several beats as he remembered Ditta's warning: "Beware of the Sons of Enyaluis."

"What did you say, sir?" asked Ryo.

"Ditta warned me the night she vanished. She said, 'Thanatos doesn't get his hands dirty. Beware the Sons of Enyaluis.'"

Ryo agreed it may be their only lead in the case, and he would have the counterterrorism group working on it immediately. He then insisted that Alex stay at the penthouse for safety.

Alex shook his head no. "I'll go back to my apartment in case Danyal returns home."

"Please, sir, that's a bad idea," pleaded Ryo.

"You can't stop me. I'm leaving."

Ryo stated he would assign additional security to Alex's apartment building. Alex nodded in agreement before asking to take Danyal's phone with him. Ryo slid the phone across the table to Alex. Despite offers of assistance from Hoko and Dr. Sonja, Alex asserted that he wanted to be alone, before asking Galen to get him as far away from fucking PGC as possible.

Galen nodded.

The ride down to the security entrance was as quiet as a graveyard. Alex looked as if the life had been sucked out of his body. His face was pale, and he slumped forward like an empty shell of a man. Galen's face showed obvious concern for Alex's well-being, but he didn't violate Alex's request for space.

Upon entering the backseat of the Uros, Alex was alone; he could no longer hold his emotions in check. He wept uncontrollably with his face in his hands, holding Danyal's phone for the remainder of the drive, before pulling himself together upon arriving home.

Exiting the elevator, he entered his apartment and slammed the door behind him. His world was on fire, and the flames threatened to consume him.

Chapter Sixteen

Galen

Although Galen was worried for Alex and his wellbeing, he needed an opportunity to enter Alex's apartment. Time was running out to achieve his mission. It had been forty hours since Alex entered his apartment, and since then he'd made no contact with the outside world. As long as Alex's biometric monitoring remained stable, Galen had been instructed not to enter the apartment by his supervisors, and Alex made it clear he wanted his space.

Galen was dead asleep when someone touched his shoulder. He instinctively grabbed the hand touching him and forced his unknown assailant into an armlock.

"Easy soldier, I'd like to keep my fucking arm," said Templeton. "There's an alarm on the Unicorn's biometric sensor."

Galen released Templeton's arm as he looked at the clock. *12:57 a.m.? How the hell was this my problem?* "What the hell, mate? Not mah concern in the middle of the night."

Templeton replied Galen was crazy if he thought he would be going into Dr. Lieth 's apartment. He said he hadn't met the Unicorn yet, and didn't want to barge into a god's abode unannounced in the middle of the night. Galen replied the Unicorn wouldn't bite unless provoked and asserted Templeton was just afraid to be in a gay bloke's apartment. Templeton stated Galen's accusation was absurd--it just didn't feel right since he was a stranger to Dr. Lieth.

"Ya want me to do yur dirty work," said Galen.

"No, well... maybe. You spend all day with him, so you know him. Please, I'll buy you Bruins tickets. You always said you wanted to check out a hockey game."

Galen considered Templeton's offer. This was Galen's first opportunity to enter the apartment. He didn't know if he'd get another chance, so had to take it without being too obvious.

"Shite, ya owe me tickets to two Bruins games *plus* a case of stubbies."

Templeton nodded, agreeing to the arrangement.

Before entering the hall, Galen checked the video monitors to ensure there were no threats. He crossed the threshold to Alex's apartment, taking his 9mm Ruger from its holster by the door. He knocked on the door firmly, with three consecutive knocks. Waiting impatiently, Alex didn't answer the door.

Shit, shoulda asked for two cases of stubbies.

Galen drew his Ruger to his line of sight with his right hand and turned the doorknob with his left. He carefully opened the door, looking to identify any threats. Having opened the door fully, he lowered his handgun after determining Alex was sitting on the floor in the darkness of his apartment, clutching Danyal's pillow to his chest. Only the light from the streetlamp dimly illuminated the room. Galen recognized the look of despair on Alex's face. Danyal had only been gone two days, but Galen could see Alex was drowning in grief.

Placing his Ruger on the dresser by the bathroom door, Galen spoke softly so as not to alarm Alex. "Sorry to bother ya so late, mate.

Needed to verify that ya are OK. Yu're not wearing yur watch. The biometric alarm triggered."

Alex didn't respond. Galen walked over to Alex and sat on the floor next to him, leaning up against the wall by the window. He'd seen such despair in his own life and recognized the paralyzing grip of grief. Galen knew grief was a primal emotion that destroyed even the strongest souls. The closer the relationship and the more intense the love, the stronger it became.

Galen sat quietly before softly saying, "Ya know, grief is like the ocean. Sometimes, the ocean is hectic and rough. Other times, the sea is calm. Ya can't hope to control a force like the ocean and grief. Grief will control ya, mate. The secret is to ride out the rougher seas to get to the calmer moments. There can be rogue waves that turn yur life upside down—part of the process. Ya learn to live with it and ride it out to the calmer moments."

"Who did you lose?" Alex whispered without raising his head.

"Mah twin sister Amara. Thought grief and anger were going to destroy me. Nearly did. Survived by grabbing a lifeline and riding out the rough waters. Ya live one second at a time, one hour at a time, or one day at a time. Ya do whatever ya need to find a purpose to survive. Ya have a warrior's fire in yur soul. Ya will survive."

"I don't feel like a warrior. I feel like I'm in hell. How did my life disintegrate so quickly? How did our happiness evaporate? When will the anguish end? Ditta warned me eternity would be a lonely existence."

"Ya don't recognize all the strength ya have," said Galen.

"You're in the minority opinion if you think I'm strong," Alex said through his tears. "In the past week, I've been called a coward, a monster, a cosmic mistake, and mentally unstable."

"They can all bugger off. Don't mind what people have to say. For what it's worth, I admire how ya refuse to let expectations define yurself. Wish I had that strength. Maybe life would have turned out different."

Galen didn't believe Alex was a coward and a monster. Yes, he fled from Wynn and Egypt, but any scared young gay bloke in his situation would have done the same—simple fight or flight. Alex chose flight and couldn't go back and change it.

"Wynn's dumping heaps of his anger onto ya. Ya can see the suffering in his eyes. Seen it on the battlefield. Shell shock, battle fatigue, or post-traumatic stress disorder...ya can't fight Wynn's demons for him. What happened to him was horrific, but none of his suffering happened by yur hand."

Galen could see Wynn wanted Alex to save him, because he loved Alex. No amount of anger and guilt would change the past. What could Alex have done to save Wynn? It'd taken PGC months to secure his freedom. Would suffering with Wynn in prison have changed anything? No.

"Ya can either learn from experience or keep making the same mistakes. Ya make the choice."

"I'm still a cosmic mistake," said Alex.

A cosmic mistake? The thought was hilarious to Galen. The universe had chosen Alex as the god of love, rebirth, and prosperity. He couldn't have a higher purpose than that. "Ya have been a god for a few weeks, mate; give yourself a break. Ya will adjust, and ya will learn the rules. When ya do, ya will be unstoppable. It's yur game; own it."

Was Alex mentally unstable? Galen had seen too many stressful and traumatic situations in his life. Alex was holding up better than most, given the circumstances. "Yur mental health is fine. Stop listening to those wankers. My military buddy Andrea has a crude way of putting it––unless they're feeding ya, fuckin' ya, or financing ya, they don't get an opinion on yur life."

Alex softly chuckled. He paused before saying, "It's my fault Danyal is missing," before crying into Danyal's pillow once more. "We argued the night he was kidnapped. The last thing I said to him was that I was tired of him controlling who I could be around and that I needed space to breathe. He was so angry when he left. What if those were the last words I ever said to him?"

"Danyal is missing because a terrorist group kidnapped him. Not yur fault. He loves ya. Every couple has issues." Galen deeply respected Alex for owning who he was and who he loved. "Hold onto the hope that ya get him back, Alex. Depend on Hoko to help ya access your god mojo. Ryo will help ya investigate the facts. Ya and Hoko can develop yur abilities to help find Danyal."

"There are times when I'm holding his pillow, I feel like I can sense Danyal near me. At other times, I see shadows or glimpses of energy of his image moving around the apartment, lying in bed beside me, or taking a shower. They're brief, but I see them like ghosts taunting me. Am I going crazy, Galen?"

"Yu're not going crazy, Alex. That's grief."

Alex instinctively laid his head onto Galen's bare shoulder. Galen recognized Alex's vulnerability and voluntarily allowed Alex access to his energy. The brief exchange of energy gave Alex the spark to escape his despair. Alex pulled his head back as if he'd been shocked by electricity.

"No worries, Alex. Ya can leave yur head on my shoulder if it helps. Yu're not going to hurt me. Can withdraw mah consent at any time. My gut said ya needed human touch."

Alex asked how Galen got so wise. Alex said in his life, basic touch and connection with men––especially outside of sexual situations––was taboo. Growing up with no parents and a distant provider in Ditta, he only had physical contact with male friends at boarding school when he was fighting his bullies or wrestling. He added he used to go to practice early to watch the older boys change, and that he wanted to be one of them. Alex relayed he used to stay late for more coaching to be close to another human body; not in a sexual way, but rather acknowledgment or validation he existed.

"Glad mah shoulder helped ya. Understand locker room behavior and touch in sports. Rugby allows ya to take out yur aggression physically. Be part of a team and build self-worth. Rugby players also engage in a lot of behavior that looks 'gay.' The naked rugby calendars were money-makers for the league. It's OK if they act gay in the locker room as long as they say, 'No, homo bro.'"

Alex laughed. "So, are you in a naked rugby calendar?" asked Alex.

"Plead the fifth. Conversation is getting uncomfortable. Shoulder is close to being revoked."

"You know you did walk into my apartment wearing basketball shorts, which are basically gay lingerie," Alex said, laughing. "I'm sorry; I'll stop teasing you. It's not appropriate."

Galen squirmed for a moment.

"Galen, could we sit here for a few more minutes? These have been the most peaceful moments I've had in weeks."

Galen nodded yes.

"Thanks again. You've been a lifesaver that walked me back from the edge of self-destruction."

"Doing mah job, Alex."

"And by the way," Alex said as he yawned, "don't think I didn't notice this was the first conversation you called me Alex."

"Mate, felt right in the moment. Will make sure it doesn't happen again. Won't cross that line."

"Nonsense," said Alex. "It's a requirement, not a request. Besides, if you keep my secrets, I keep yours--such as naked rugby calendars. Quid pro quo." Alex attempted a nefarious laugh.

"Made a deal with the devil..." said Galen, shaking his head.

"Not the devil, the Master of Eros," said Alex.

Alex closed his eyes and quickly fell asleep on Galen's shoulder. Galen waited a few minutes to ensure Alex was soundly asleep before picking him up and gently placing him on the bed, with Danyal's pillow supporting his head. Hopefully, Alex would have his first night of good sleep in weeks tonight. Galen quietly stood and cautiously walked over to the dresser to retrieve his weapon. After placing surgical gloves on his hands, he carefully rummaged through each drawer, not stopping until he found the box of birthday chocolates. He opened the box and removed the one piece of chocolate that remained. He carefully placed the chocolate in a small plastic bag he'd pulled from his shorts pocket.

After walking to the door, he pulled his private cell out of his pocket and sent a text: *Sample obtained*. Galen anxiously watched his phone for a response.

Deliver the sample tonight to 756 Highland Drive at once. Maintain communication silence until further instructions were the messages he received back.

Galen took an uneasy deep breath and quietly left Alex's apartment to return to the security suite, where Templeton asked if everything was OK. Galen stated the Unicorn had a mare but was better now. He told Templeton he owed him hockey tickets and two cases of stubbies. Templeton protested that his demands were highway robbery, but Galen insisted that if Templeton was unwilling to put skin in the game, he needed to stay on the sidelines. With that, Galen entered his room and closed the door behind him. He sat in the chair in the corner of his room, staring at the solitary piece of chocolate in the plastic bag he'd placed on the corner of his bed while he dressed. Walking back out to leave, he told Templeton he needed some air.

Galen sat in the Uros outside the all-night pawn shop at 756 Highland Drive, while he placed the chocolate in a white envelope. As he turned the engine off, his mind raced. Was he doing the right thing? Would Alex ever forgive him? Would he lose his job? Would they hold up their end of the bargain? It was the thought of betraying Alex that pained him the most. He hadn't felt as alive in years as he had in his brief time spent with him. He didn't take his betrayal lightly. Alex didn't need the chocolate. Galen had to act––otherwise, Amara would be doomed. He prayed Alex would never find out, and that Amara could be saved.

Galen took a deep breath and exited the warmth of the Uros. Walking into the pawnshop, the smell of cigarette smoke nearly knocked him over. The slightly built, balding older man at the counter turned toward Galen.

"Can I help you, young man?"

"Got a delivery, mate," said Galen as he laid the envelope on the counter.

The older man nodded and picked up the envelope. "Thank you for the delivery, son. It's a rather cold night for you to brave the weather. This must be important."

"It is," said Galen. "Let them know done mah part. Expect that they hold up their end of the bargain."

"No need to worry. The Sons of Enyaluis always pay what's owed. They'll be in touch."

Galen turned and quickly left the pawnshop. Upon entering the Uros, he repeatedly punched the steering wheel until he had bruised his knuckles. He was so focused on helping Amara that he never stopped to consider the motivations of those he'd aligned himself with. Until now, he didn't care. His stomach churned and his head pounded.

FUCK, FUCK, FUCK!

If Alex found out, he'd never forgive Galen for helping the terrorists who had kidnapped Danyal.

Chapter Seventeen

Galen

Galen vigorously scrubbed his body in the shower, trying to remove the guilt permeating from every pore of his body. The shower door clicked as it opened and closed behind him. He didn't turn but smiled as shower sex was his favorite. Chills spread over his body as his lover touched his shoulders and softly lathered the body wash down his back and buttocks.

"Easy," he said, "both have to go to work soon. Round three will have to wait."

As Galen turned around, he stepped back and banged his head on the showerhead.

"What's wrong?" said Alex, wearing nothing but a smile.

"Alex!" yelled Galen as he sat up rapidly in bed, his pillow and sheets drenched in sweat.

"Easy, big guy. You're having a nightmare," said Zoe as she took her hand and rubbed his back.

Galen took three gasping breaths before trying to speak. "Yu're right, a mare."

"You know," said Zoe as she rolled on her side, "most women would turn you away when you knock on their door at three a.m., especially after it took you six months to show up again on my doorstep. The sex was spectacular, but having you yell out a man's name while sleeping might be a deal-breaker."

"Told ya it was a mare. Alex is going through a lot of shite, which rolls downhill."

"Oh, you're on a first-name basis with the new love god. *That's* not a red flag," Zoe chuckled.

"Yu're a riot," said Galen, "don't quit yur day job." He knew he needed to get out of there and get ready for work. He would be showering at home with the bathroom door locked.

Zoe asked when Galen would bring Alex to the office so she could meet him. She said she'd heard the Unicorn had a hot college professor vibe.

"Sounds like a fantasy of yurs," said Galen, leaning forward to kiss Zoe. "Can roleplay that sometime."

"Don't make promises you're not prepared to keep, Galen," said Zoe.

"Gotta go and be ready for work. Cheers for last night. Needed the company."

"You know you can shower here," said Zoe. "I can always join you."

Galen's skin reddened as the vision of Alex in his dream flashed vividly in his mind. He could feel himself getting aroused, so he turned and quickly pulled on his Calvin Klein black boxer briefs.

"You're a man of mystery," said Zoe. "I hope to see you on my doorstep again. Try not to take so long next time. Have a good day on the love god express."

Galen finished dressing quickly and winked at Zoe lying in bed, as he closed the door behind him.

Sitting in the traffic, Galen couldn't stop playing and replaying the evening in his mind. Seeking out comfort in Zoe's bed hadn't been part of the plan. Office relationships always ended badly, but he needed comfort amongst the shitshow his life had become, and he had nowhere else to turn. Zoe helped dull the guilt for a few hours, but who was he not deceiving in his life? He was caught in a tangled web. With one wrong step, it was only a matter of time before his house of cards came tumbling down. He couldn't leave; he'd promised Ms. Dea to protect Alex with his life. But now Galen couldn't fight the thought that Alex probably needed protection from him.

Galen rushed up the stairs and was startled by Alex and Templeton coming down the other end of the hallway, coffees in hand.

"There's the man of the hour," said Templeton. "Someone's doing the walk of shame."

Galen could see Alex trying to stifle a chuckle, which further stoked Galen's anger. Templeton would pay for his public shaming, especially doing it in front of Alex.

"Out for some air," said Galen.

"Maybe six hours ago," said Templeton.

Galen shot Templeton a "shut the fuck up" look before Alex interjected, "OK, boys, we've all been there. How about some coffee? A flat white for the Kiwi?" said Alex.

"Cheers, mate," said Galen as he swiped the coffee out of Alex's hand. "Ready in fifteen. Today's agenda?"

"PGC, Boston PD, and ending the day at the university."

Galen nodded as he stepped into the security suite, with Templeton following behind. As soon as the door was closed, Galen turned to Templeton and released his fury.

"Ya got some fucking nerve, arsehole. Fronting me out in front of the boss."

"Chill, Galen. Just some lighthearted ribbing. You'd do the same. Maybe you were getting some air; normally people are in a better mood after they get laid."

"Ya was quick to get over yur fear of the Unicorn. Awful chummy with him. Ya fancy him now?"

"Screw you. You were right. He's a decent guy and an excellent listener. He wanted to follow the rules and not go and get coffee alone, so he asked me to go with. We mostly talked about Joy's due date. He was genuinely excited for us. Don't worry, we weren't discussing your lack of social skills."

Galen huffed as he sat his coffee on the counter and entered his bedroom, slamming the door behind him. He locked the door as a precaution to prevent uninvited visitors in the shower. Galen showered quickly, dressed, and skulled his coffee before entering the hall where Alex was waiting.

"Sorry for the wait, sir," said Galen.

"Oh, so I'm back to being 'sir'? Last night I was Alex."

Last night ya were many things, and ya were naked in my dreams this morning. Thank god he can't read mah thoughts.

"I also want to thank you for last night," said Alex.

Galen looked up, surprised. *Can he read mah thoughts? Does he know about the dream?*

"Doing mah job, mate," said Galen nervously.

Alex stated it was more than the job. Alex added he was at rock bottom, and Galen helped him tie a knot and hold on for dear life. He said he wouldn't forget it, and that he owed Galen.

If ya only knew Alex. Ya'd fucking hate me. Not yur savior, I'm yur Judas.

Galen watched Alex pull Danyal's iPhone out of his pocket and enter the passcode. They must really trust each other to share phone passcodes, Galen thought. He acknowledged he'd never trusted another living soul to that degree, except Amara.

From Alex's apparent dismay, Galen knew something was wrong and asked if Alex was having issues with his phone. Alex replied he tried to turn on Danyal's phone, but the notification he received was "Service unavailable. SIM card failure issue." Galen asked what he was trying to access. Alex explained he was trying to see Danyal's social accounts, messages, and anything that might give them a clue to what happened the night he went missing.

After a momentary pause, Galen suggested Alex access Danyal's accounts from his phone. Alex smiled and said that was an excellent idea, and that Galen had earned a gold star for the day. Galen continued observing. Alex pulled out his cell phone to check Instagram. Alex looked at his phone for several minutes.

"Ya right, mate?"

"No, Galen, everything isn't OK—no luck with Instagram or social media."

Galen impulsively responded, "If ya are having issues with yur phone, the technology team at PGC might be a good shot. Mah mate Zoe would be thrilled to help. Can make the introduction." Galen regretted the words as soon as they crossed his lips, and he prayed Alex would decline the offer.

Alex thanked Galen, adding he might take him up on the offer if they had time today.

Although Zoe would be thrilled to meet the Unicorn, Galen knew it would be a mistake, and was more concerned about Alex picking up on his vibe with Zoe.

Chapter Eighteen

"**A**ny update from Ryo on Danyal?" asked Hoko.

Alex shook his head, and said he planned to contact Boston PD today to see if they had any leads. Hoko asked Alex to please keep him updated, and to feel free to contact him anytime, day or night. Alex thanked Hoko for his support.

"So, how are you holding up?" said Hoko.

"I'll admit, I hit rock bottom the other night, but Galen helped me relax enough to get through it." Hearing his words out loud, Alex worried they could be misinterpreted as Galen helping him relax in another way, and was embarrassed. "I mean, Galen helped talk me back from the edge."

Hoko nodded and asked if Alex was doing his breathing exercises, to which he responded he did them several times a day, and that they were helping. Hoko said he was glad to hear it and recommended trying cinnamon tea for its relaxing properties. Hoko added he started every day with it.

Alex smiled and told Hoko he had the strangest thing happened last night. Most nights, he dreams about Danyal, but last night, he had a dream about his boarding school boyfriend, David. Alex had thought about him, of course, but never had any dreams about him. Dr. Sonja's walk down memory lane must have opened some old wounds in his last session. Alex said they had a rough ending. When they were outed after being found kissing, David's family pulled him out of the school, and Alex was forced into daily conversion therapy for months. Alex said it was a traumatic time. He often thought of David, but was scared to find him.

"What scares you?" said Hoko.

"His hyper-religious family pulled him out of school due to the scandal. I'm afraid…what if he hurt himself?"

Hoko replied he could understand Alex's reservation. He added that Ditta said if you try to connect with a person who may have passed, you may be able to connect with the person's essence. But if Alex was not ready to know, there's no need to push. Hoko encouraged Alex to talk to him about his dream.

Alex sat with tears starting to form in his eyes. He said in the dream, David was still handsome, but that his face had filled out. He was married with two kids, a boy and a girl. David and his family were in California. He was happy. Alex said he woke up crying happy tears. Hoko smiled and said that he didn't think it was merely a dream, before explaining that the mind and perception expand when asleep or unconscious. Alex said he didn't understand. Hoko said he had access to Alex's records and could tell him exactly what happened to David, if that was what he wanted. Alex hesitantly nodded yes.

Hoko opened Alex's file and smiled, before saying David lived in CA, was married to his husband, had two kids, and was happy. Hoko said he was amazed Alex had reached David in CA on the other side of the country through quantum entanglement and emotion. At this, Alex burst into tears. Hoko moved to Alex's side and put his hand on his shoulder.

Alex turned and hugged Hoko, saying he could only use his abilities when asleep or with Hoko without getting severe headaches or losing control. "You're my Obi-Wan Kenobi."

"I recall Obi-Wan said, 'These are your first steps.' We'll get there, Alex, where you can use your abilities pain-free. In our two sessions, you've made remarkable progress. So, I promised to discuss Ditta's potential abilities in each session. Dealer's choice, you pick."

Alex smiled and said super strength was rather passé as abilities go, so he'd go with something else. Hoko nodded, confirming Ditta had super strength and endurance.

"I guess one of the more fascinating abilities would be teleportation," said Alex.

"Well, Dr. Lieth, jump right into the deep end of the ocean," said Hoko.

"OK," Alex said with a smile, "now I'm intrigued."

Hoko said Ditta and all the gods of lore could teleport. He hypothesized it was like riding the Earth's electromagnetic fields from one place to another. Hoko added it was more like "world walking." Alex sat forward before saying that "world walking" sounded ominous. Hoko agreed and said Ditta shared it was more like stepping out of one dimension in time and space into another world, which allowed her to appear at any point she wanted on Earth.

"Did you ever see her do it?" said Alex.

Hoko said no, before adding Ditta told him she hadn't "world walked" in years due to advances in modern transportation, not to mention the fear of being discovered. As she adapted to modern society, she used her abilities less and less. Hoko cautioned Alex that Ditta did warn that teleportation was the hardest of her abilities to grasp.

"Understood, no teleporting," said Alex.

"Before you leave, can I ask a favor?" said Hoko.

"Anything. You've done so much for me and asked for nothing in return."

"Would you be willing to discuss your difficulties with Dr. Sonja?"

"That's a rather massive ask...but I trust you. After our last session, I don't know if we can ever have a trusting relationship after she deceived me for the past two years, as well as her harsh assessment of my progress."

"I understand, Alex. I can't pretend to know her thoughts, but I've known her for over twenty years, and she's shaken by how the session played out."

"Did she say so?"

"Yes, she did. She's regretful, personally and professionally. It's difficult for me to see two people I care about needlessly suffering. Are you open to finding a way forward?"

"Only if she apologizes," said Alex.

"It won't be an issue, Alex. You can pick the time and place where you are comfortable and in control."

"Would you be willing to sit with us as a referee?"

"Yes, it would be my pleasure," said Hoko.

"I'm trying to be in a forgiving mood. Can you call her into your office now before I lose my courage?" said Alex.

"I can try, Alex." Hoko picked up the phone and made a brief call. After about thirty seconds, he hung up the phone and looked up at Alex. "Are you sure you're ready for this? Didn't let me pressure you in any way."

Alex closed his eyes and took a deep breath. "She's at the door, Hoko; ask her to step inside."

Hoko stood and walked to the door, opening it for Dr. Sonja. She entered the room and sat in the chair next to Hoko across from Alex.

"Thank you for agreeing to meet with me, Alex. I couldn't blame you if you never wanted to be alone with me in a room again," said Dr. Sonja.

"I'm only doing this as a favor to Hoko. So, if you've something to say, say it so I can move on with my day," said Alex coldly.

Dr. Sonja said Alex didn't have to say anything because she needed to apologize. She added she had been practicing psychotherapy for nearly forty years and had never encountered such regret as she had about the disintegration of their relationship. She agreed Alex had been deceived. She admitted she was at fault for breaking a cardinal rule and not meeting him in treatment where he needed help, which biased her thinking by comparing him to Ditta and prior clients.

"You are a unique person, Alex Lieth, who deserved to be treated with caring and compassion to help you navigate the minefield that your life has become. It's my responsibility to fix the rupture in our alliance, if we are to have a healthy working relationship going forward."

"Thank you for the apology, Dr. Sonja. I've made mistakes too, and apologize for accessing your digital records without permission. I know humility can be a bitter pill to swallow."

"It's a new start, Alex. Please call me Diana. I hope you allow me to fix any damage I may have caused. My sole clinical purpose is to help you adjust to your circumstances and to help you find Danyal––if you accept my apology and my help."

"I accept your apology, Diana. I need to go, but I'll consider scheduling a session later this week." Alex stood to exit the room, "Good day to you both."

With that, Alex walked out into the waiting room and sat down next to Galen.

"Ya look weird, mate. Cat that ate the canary," said Galen.

"I think I accepted a truce with Dr. Sonja... Diana."

Galen furrowed his brow. "Knew the forecast was for freezing weather, but guess hell froze over."

Alex chuckled, "Hoko brokered the truce and she apologized."

"Humility is a good look, mate. Wear it more."

"Plus, I have a theory. I think Diana has a crush on Hoko."

"Come again?"

"It's just a hunch. She's different around him, and we tend to covet what we see. Working closely with someone can lead to strong feelings."

Galen rolled his eyes and resumed reading his magazine.

"Hilarious, Galen. Anything good in your magazine?"

"Nah, no rugby news."

"You miss rugby. Why did you quit playing?"

"Many reasons, none worth discussing."

"Message received; back off, Alex. I want to detour before leaving for Boston PD and the university. Can you have your friend Zoe look at Danyal's phone?"

"Yep, will make it happen. When?"

"Excellent. Let's do it now. I need the steps, and it's not every day I get to meet one of your friends," said Alex.

Chapter Nineteen

Galen

It had only been three hours since Galen had been in Zoe's bed. He prayed she wouldn't be in her office when he arrived with Alex. As they stepped out of the lift to the tenth floor, Galen still held out for lady luck to be on his side. Of course, his luck had always been shite.

"So, this is where the magic happens?" said Alex. "The Area 51 of PGC?"

"In a way, mate. PGC has an extensive research and development department."

"What are they working on? Is it super-secret spy technology?" asked Alex.

"Mah friend Zoe, one of the division leaders, plays her cards remarkably close to her chest. She arrived in Boston from the South Korean division at about the same time I started. Corporate espionage is a real concern. Her division engineered the tech for the PGC satellites, communication systems, and yur watch."

"Impressive. I'll take any help I can get at this point if it will help me find Danyal."

Galen approached the first lab to the left and gently knocked on the door.

"Knock, knock. Anybody home?" *Please don't be here.*

A petite young woman with shoulder-length black hair looked up from her workstation. Galen noticed a flash of excitement in her eyes when they entered the lab. He knew the look was meant for him, but the look on her face turned to surprise as she acknowledged Alex's presence.

"Hi Galen, long time no see. Welcome back to the technology division, where all the magic happens behind the curtain. Who do you have with you today?" she said with a wide, knowing smile.

"Zoe, this is Professor Alex Lieth."

Galen could see the amazed look on her face as she registered the Unicorn was in her office, in the flesh. He appreciated her wide-eyed amazement and excitement for even the minor things in life. Her free spirit was what had initially attracted him to Zoe.

"Good morning, Zoe. It's a pleasure to make your acquaintance," said Alex.

"Good morning, sir. What a wonderful surprise. Thanks for the heads up, Galen," she said as she flashed Galen a look of disdain before shaking Alex's hand.

Alex told Zoe he needed help with Danyal's iPhone, which had been recovered after his abduction. He said he charged it but got an error message when he tried to turn it on. Zoe smiled as Alex handed her the phone, and she said she could run a few diagnostics. She connected the phone to her computer and looked earnestly at the screen for several minutes. Sighing, she closed her laptop screen to focus all her attention on Alex and Galen.

"OK, I've good news and bad news. Which would you like to hear first?"

"Please, the good news," said Alex.

"Well, the good news is I can extract any pictures from the phone's memory, but it will take time and energy. I'll need to deconstruct and reconstruct the entire memory chip."

"OK, not the good news I was hoping for. What's the bad news?" Alex said.

Galen could see Alex stand up straight, bracing for the worst. Zoe said the bad news was that the internal processor appeared damaged. She added she expected to see damage from the recent EMP, but that wasn't the case. She said she hoped they had phone insurance. Zoe bragged that the PGC phones included shielding for EMPs, and had made it through the recent event unscathed. She said she was sorry she could not do more for Alex. Zoe then abruptly asked Alex if she could see his phone. Alex reached into his pants pocket and handed Zoe his personal cell phone. She promptly opened her laptop and conducted a series of diagnostic tests. Her furrowed brow said it all.

Galen recognized the confused look Zoe displayed. "Something isn't making sense," he observed.

"So where were these phones the day the lights went out in Boston?" said Zoe.

"They were both in the apartment," said Alex.

"Where exactly in your apartment, please? Be specific," replied Zoe.

"My phone was on my nightstand by my side of the bed, and Danyal's was across the room on the dresser."

"So, there's no special shielding by your side of the bed?"

"No, nothing but a wall."

Zoe took a deep breath and let out a long sigh. "We have a mystery, gentlemen. According to my diagnostic results, your phone only shows evidence of minor exposure to EMP. Not enough to disrupt its functionality. Why would that be the case if the prevailing theory from Dr. Bruno is that you were the source of the EMP pulse?"

"I met with Dr. Bruno recently, and he tells me I'm emitting a high EMF field, which could disrupt electronics," said Alex.

Galen watched Zoe's face light up like a firework. She jumped up from her chair and grabbed a grey instrument from her workstation across the room. "Is it OK if I take some readings, Dr. Lieth?"

Alex nodded yes, and Zoe began to measure the EMF field and radiation level around Alex. She said her readings confirmed Dr. Bruno's findings: Alex emitted constant high-level electromagnetic fields. She hypothesized Alex's biological EMF protected their phones from the larger EMP by producing a protective bubble or cocoon. Zoe said this finding was amazing, and asked Alex if he would be willing to do further tests so they could isolate Alex's specific EMF signature.

"Sure, you've piqued my curiosity. But will these tests help me find Danyal?" asked Alex, desperation in his voice.

"Unfortunately, no, but I do have a suggestion. Have you tried looking at Danyal's cloud backup? Depending on how he set up his phone, there may be a digital copy you can access."

"Thanks, Zoe. The thought never crossed my mind," said Alex.

"Do you also share the same wireless provider? You can access your account and potentially any text messages from his phone."

"Yes, we share an account––I'll check. Thank you so much, Zoe. I appreciate your help and won't forget it!"

"You're welcome, sir." Zoe blushed, "OK, Galen, you can bring this one around more often. He's a charmer, and literally electric."

"Will keep that in mind," said Galen. *Please, can we now leave the room? PLEASE!*

"You're also welcome to visit anytime you want, Galen. I can't have you being jealous. Now, are you coming for darts and beer on Friday night? You've missed a few weeks, and the team has suffered."

"Mah responsibilities have changed," Galen said, glancing sideways at Alex standing beside him, "Will see how mah new schedule works out. Things to do and lives to save."

"Keep missing our darts league, and *you* may need a bodyguard," Zoe said with a scowl.

"Gotcha. Professor Lieth, where's the next stop?" asked Galen.

"The Boston PD. Thank you again, Zoe," said Alex.

With that, Galen and Alex left the lab and entered the lift.

"She's a keeper. Intelligent, sexy, and personable," said Alex.

"Why would ya bring that up, sir?" Had he picked up something? Did he read her energy?

"She likes you," said Alex.

"Ya playing matchmaker? We're mates." *OK, mates with benefits.*

"I'm sorry, Galen. I can see I've touched a nerve, and I apologize if I've offended you."

"Ya just mind yur own damn business. It's mah job to keep ya safe. Our relationship needs boundaries," said Galen.

Galen and Alex stepped out of the lift after their tense interaction. The ride to the Boston PD precinct was in stone-cold silence.

Chapter Twenty

Alex

Alex knew dealing with the police as a member of the queer community was a double-edged sword. The police can either genuinely help you, or they could harass you, becoming an oppressive force in a vulnerable moment of need. Alex walked slowly up the five steps into the Boston District B-2 Police Station, his brooding shadow following.

"Afternoon," Alex said to the Officer whose name tag read Lieutenant B. Bledsoe. "My name is Alex Lieth, and I'd like to follow up on a missing person."

"What's the missing person's name and their relationship to you, Mr. Lieth?"

"His name is Danyal Sarif, and he's my boyfriend. Three days ago, he was abducted by armed men at Excalibur Café."

"I see. I'll need to gather some information." Officer Bledsoe shuffled his papers before turning his attention fully to Alex. "When did this alleged kidnapping happen again?"

"Three nights ago," said Alex.

"Did you and Mr. Sarif have a lover's quarrel that evening?"

"We had a minor disagreement, but our relationship is stable." Alex was annoyed by the question. What did it have to do with Danyal being kidnapped? Besides, he didn't consider arguing over going dancing a life-altering lover's quarrel.

"Did Mr. Sarif meet with any other friends or acquaintances that evening after work?"

"I don't know," said Alex.

"Did you happen to check, Grinder? Maybe he got a better offer. For that matter, did Mr. Sarif habitually frequent the bathhouses or sex clubs? As the saying goes, any hole in the storm is a goal."

Alex could feel the anger welling in his chest. To stifle his rage and to avoid being arrested for assault, he looked deep into the core of Lieutenant Bledsoe's soul before responding.

"I bet you find this amusing, Lieutenant Bledsoe. Another missing homosexual, what a loss for society! You have two options here. You can find me an officer who's not a living piece of shit to do the job for you, or you can shut the fuck up and do your job. Before you decide, I'd like you to consider the following information. How would your employer feel about your internet browsing and porn viewing habits? Questionably, legal teenage girls are a choice, considering you coach your daughter's softball team. If that's too much for your small mind to wrap around, maybe your lovely wife Denise would like to know when you allegedly have beers with the guys, you're soliciting sex workers down by the pier. Think it over carefully, Officer Bledsoe, because your decision may decide your career, marriage, and future." When Alex finished his sentence, all the papers on the precinct desks flew into the air.

The fear in Officer Bledsoe's eyes burned brighter than a supernova, and his arrogance melted faster than ice cream on a sweltering summer afternoon.

Galen introjected, "Cuse me, Officer. Most police charters have officers who serve as liaisons for underserved minority groups, such as the LGBTQI+ community. Boston Police Department's Commitment to Diversity, Equality, and Inclusion Initiative. Whom would that be?"

"Officer Lucia Gonzalez. Please have a seat, and I'll see if she's available," responded Officer Bledsoe in a quivering voice.

"Cheers," Galen said.

Lieutenant Bledsoe couldn't walk away fast enough as Alex stared daggers through him with each step.

"Ya think that was a little overkill, mate?"

Alex asked Galen what he meant. Was he supposed to take the abuse like a good faggot and bite his tongue? Alex stated Galen would never defend the officer if he experienced discrimination and homophobia. He angrily said his best friend Shae nearly lost his life after a group of drunk high school kids fractured his skull and broke both legs with a baseball bat for kissing his boyfriend on the subway. Alex added every LGBTQI+ person in this country has a target on their back, and they risk death at any moment. The next murder or mass shooting is around the next corner. Trans women of color are murdered every week in this country. No one gives a damn, said Alex. The government, politicians, and the church either fan the flames of hate or ignore their suffering. Today, there won't be target practice if he can help it.

Galen replied he was not defending the officer because his behavior was horrible. He added he wasn't minimizing the plight of Alex's community. "Ya looked like ya were about to lose control. Luckily, nothing exploded. Sometimes, you need the hammer. Other times, a more strategic approach is needed. Can ya leave the precinct without ruining any lives or fighting the way out of the building?"

"Oh, so don't hurt the bigots or rattle their cage? He deserves more than tongue-lashing for his disrespect. At this moment, I can think of many ways to make him and his kind suffer...."

Galen interrupted Alex before he could finish his speech. "May have missed the briefing where Eros was the source of wrath. From mah perspective, this feels hate-filled and Thanatos. Have ya considered part of mah job is keeping the public safe from ya losing control? And for the record, how do ya know?"

"How do I know what?"

"How do ya know I haven't experienced hate or discrimination? Ya are quick to make assumptions and judgments. No one community has the exclusive right to suffering and abuse."

A soft but firm voice broke the tension in the room. "Good afternoon. My name is Office Gonzalez, and I understand you have a loved one who is missing. Please follow me to my desk. I'll investigate and discuss options for proceeding. How should I address you, and which pronouns would you like me to use?"

"Alex and he/him/his are fine."

Alex walked towards the young officer after reading her aura and the spark in her chest to verify her compassion and caring. He was relieved he could trust her, yet saddened by all the suffering he could see in the memories she'd endured by her fellow officers for being the LGBTQI+ liaison.

Galen stepped forward to follow, but Alex turned to him and said, "You can stay here until I return. As you said, we're safe in a police precinct. I'll call you if I need to fight my way out."

Galen stopped and nodded. "Yes, sir. Will wait with the limo, ready if ya need to make a getaway. Hope ya find the help ya need to find Danyal."

Alex walked away, sulking like a chastised child with their hand caught in the cookie jar. He knew Galen hadn't tried to make him feel guilty when he'd been the victim of a homophobic verbal assault, but it stung that Galen had intervened in the counterassault on Officer

Bledsoe. On top of Galen's outburst over Zoe, this deeply upset Alex, and he was over Galen's foul mood today.

Forty-five minutes later, Alex emerged from the building and returned to the limo. Standing by the door, Galen opened it for Alex and closed it behind them. The awkward silence was deafening. Alex's face flushed as he stewed in his anger and avoided all eye contact.

"Ya still upset, mate. Ya only need the cartoon smoke billowing from yur ears to complete the picture."

Alex locked eyes with Galen before saying he wouldn't apologize for defending himself and Danyal against a homophobe, but maybe he needed to read the room or energy more before going scorched earth. Why did he not take the time to assess Officer Bledsoe's energy before engaging the enemy? The best way he could describe is it was a reflex. He hit Alex's nerve, and Alex kicked him back. "Years of abuse, condescension, and hate for being who you are and who you love take a toll. It leaves damage. Some scars last longer than others, Galen. It may be cliche, but I don't know my powers, which is starting to scare me. I've only had these abilities for a few weeks, but I've lived in a homophobic society for 25 years. I have a question: how did you know about the LGBTQI+ liaison?"

Galen took a deep breath before responding. "Did mah research, mate. Anticipated ya would be contacting the authorities for any updates on Danyal. Based on the history of neglect from police towards the LGBTQI+ community, looked for existing resources to help ya. Had mah own interactions with hostile police. In New Zealand, discrimination is rampant based on skin color, geography, and gender. My grandfather was Māori. Mah family faced discrimination our entire lives even though we were mainstream New Zealanders. Even one drop of Māori blood made us tainted. Mah twin sister especially suffered the most. Women of Māori descent are the lowest class of citizens. Know the pain of racism, discrimination, hate, and being hassled by the police for simply existing."

"I'm sorry," responded Alex. "I didn't know. Most of your records were sealed."

"Dark time in mah life, sir. Don't want to talk about the worst moments of mah life."

Alex could see Galen trying to stifle his emotions, but he couldn't hide the pain expressed by his eyes. Alex recognized Galen's struggles to share his vulnerabilities with others, and he knew Galen would not start sharing today.

"The only way to get through the fire is to get closer to it until the demons have no control over ya. Growth and healing come to the willing who risk being vulnerable. Ya need to learn a new way. Ya, willing? Part of mah job is to support ya in the field and keep ya safe."

"I think I'll be safe because of the gift of immortality."

"Ya sure of that? Yur abilities protect ya from physical harm, mate. Emotional harm can be even more painful. There are some fates worse than death. Why do you think they took Danyal? Where ya headed now?"

"Please take me back to the university; I've got papers to grade. I want some space when we arrive. We both appear to be in a foul mood today."

Galen said, "Been a momentous day, mate. Confronting my boss about being an Angus. Piss off a god in the process. Be asked to share the darkest moments of mah life. Can only go up from here."

"I don't need your sarcasm, Galen; maybe you should take your advice and look in the mirror at your anger issues," said Alex as he pulled out his phone, abruptly ending the conversation. Alex couldn't understand what had happened to the kind and caring Galen who had talked him off the edge last night. He didn't care for the asshole who had replaced Galen today.

Chapter Twenty-One

What the fuck was Galen's problem? Alex thought they were building a rapport, but today, Galen acted like a raging knuckle-dragging stranger. He replayed the day's events to identify any cause for Galen's repeated bouts of anger towards him. He ruled out lack of sleep, since there had been plenty of late nights for Galen, so exhaustion couldn't be the reason. Alex rehashed the events of the night before when Galen helped Alex pull himself up by his bootstraps and find the strength to hope. Galen didn't have to help Alex or offer physical comfort in his time of need. Did he cross a line in some way? Did Galen feel threatened? Could Alex's need for comfort have been perceived as sexual? It had to have been Galen who put him on the bed with Danyal's pillow. Why would he make such a caring gesture in one moment and direct his anger at Alex the next? What had changed? He put his pen down, leaned on his desk, and breathed deeply. He ran his fingers through his hair before leaning back in his chair against the wall. His life had become like the desk chair—shaky, unbalanced, and ready to topple over and crash at any moment.

Alex admitted his behavior in the police precinct was not his finest hour. He lost control of his anger and was lucky no one got hurt. Although he only grudgingly admitted it, he was unsure what would have happened if Galen hadn't been there to stop him. What if next time he actually hurt someone? This made Alex pause; it was one thing to think angry thoughts, but his emerging abilities could actually put them into practice. He needed to work more with Hoko and Diana to gain control of his abilities, or risk becoming too much of a threat to himself or others.

Why did Galen get so upset when Alex mentioned Zoe liked him? It was an innocent comment with no ill intent. It was merely an observation, since Alex couldn't read any energy coming off Galen or Zoe because of their vaccinations. He had trusted his eyes to conclude Zoe was attracted to Galen. Honestly, who wouldn't be? He does have the 6'4 rugby-god vibe working for him. Galen was a private man, and Alex didn't push earlier that morning when Templeton teased him about his walk of shame. Alex placed his hand over his mouth and chuckled as he put two and two together.

Had Zoe been Galen's late-night rendezvous?

It was only a theory, but it would certainly explain a lot. Alex had gotten too close to the truth, and Galen pushed back to cover his tracks. Alex didn't mind Galen was out having sex, but it only heightened his longing for Danyal, whose absence had left a Grand Canyon-sized hole in Alex's heart. All physical touch, comfort, and sexual energy had been stolen from him in one fell swoop. Galen's innocent physical contact with Alex had been his only skin-to-skin contact with a man other than Danyal in over a year. He remembered the warmth of Galen's skin, the pulsing core of energy in his chest, and the peace the moment had brought him. Galen had helped Alex recharge his spark.

OK, maybe Alex *was* jealous Galen was having sex when he was living in a dark hole deprived of love, sex, and desire. A brief flash of Galen and Zoe intertwined in an intimate embrace passed through Alex's mind. The quick image sent a pulse of electricity through his body. He missed Danyal, and his soul longed for intimacy, which fed his sexual desires.

Alex thought back to the night on the dance floor, where he channeled the primal and sexual energy in the club through his body. He focused on breathing and pulling the Eros energy from around him on campus. He brazenly embraced more energy than he had ever dared before. His body tingled with pleasure from head to toe as he slowly levitated off his chair. He had never known such euphoria, which was his for the taking. The overwhelming sensation began to scare Alex as he felt his desires and urges before glimpsing images of people in Boston having sex. He abruptly stopped and sat back at his desk, gasping for air as sweat poured off his brow onto the papers he was grading. Ditta had been right; he could tap into the Eros force if he dropped his inhibitions and let his nature flow free with the universe. Now, he needed a cosmic cold shower.

Alex gathered his papers and placed them in his briefcase as he steadied his nerves to face Galen. He walked over to the bookcase and pulled out a copy of *The Hound of the Baskervilles* that he would give to Galen as a peace offering so he could prepare for tomorrow's lecture. Sherlock Holmes had always made Alex feel better. He placed the book in his coat pocket and locked the office door behind him.

Walking down the sidewalk in the bitter cold towards the staff parking, Alex observed Galen sitting on a bench. He walked up to the bench and motioned to the space beside Galen with his hand. Galen nodded in agreement; Alex could sit. He smiled, pulled the book from his pocket, and gave it to Galen. Alex started to speak, but Galen shook his head. Alex could see the sorrow in Galen's eyes, but didn't want to push him. He took the risk of placing his hand on Galen's shoulder. Galen turned to Alex and nodded yes. The two men sat together in silence in the frigid air.

Galen eventually turned to Alex and nodded as he motioned with his right hand to the parking lot. Alex stood and followed Galen through the snow and ice on the sidewalk. Galen approached the driver's side door of the Uros, and Alex followed behind.

Just then, a blazing flash and intense wave of energy thrust Alex and Galen backward. Alex, disoriented and confused, pushed himself up from the ground. His vision was blurred, and smoke obscured the immediate area around him. He could not concentrate because of the ringing in his ears. The smell of burning fuel stung his nose.

"Galen! Galen! Galen, please speak to me! Someone help us; call 911!"

Chapter Twenty-Two

Alex

Alex burst through the emergency room doors as Galen's unconscious body was rolled into the triage room. His head still pounded from the explosion, and his ears rang like church bells on a Sunday morning. He could sense Galen's life force draining away. Alex could see only a single sliver of energy holding Galen to the mortal plane. Alex knew Galen was dying in front of him. He might have been a god, but he was helpless to stop it.

The EMT rattled off Galen's vitals to the waiting ER trauma staff. Without missing a beat, the doctor barked orders to the surrounding nurses. What caused the injuries? yelled the surgeon. Alex impulsively responded it was an explosion. The surgeon responded by asking who Alex was. He replied that Galen was his security officer and was with him when the explosion happened. The doctor told Alex to leave the emergency room so they could treat Galen. The nurse asked Alex if he knew of any next of kin or advanced care directives. Alex shook his head and feebly responded he would check with PGC.

"Is that your blood?" said the nurse.

Alex shook his head again. He looked down at his hands covered in Galen's blood, where he'd tried to apply pressure to his head wound. Galen's blood was a mixture of red hues, which had begun to crust and fall off Alex's hand onto the floor, like pieces of his life crumbling around him.

The surgeon demanded the nurse check Alex over and get him out of the ER immediately so they could do their work. The nurse guided Alex out the swinging doors and into the hall.

Sitting in the examining room in a paper gown, Alex's mind raced as he tried to piece together the events that had taken place. He played the scene over and over in his mind, like a broken loop. Guilt coursed through his veins like adrenaline. He knew he couldn't be hurt, and now Galen was lying in the ER fighting for his life. In the entire sequence of events, time slowed down for Alex as he focused on recalling the scene—the initial flash of flames in the explosion, Alex grabbing Galen by the shoulder, throwing his arms around him to put his body between Galen and the explosion. It all happened in an instant, and he acted purely on instinct.

The nurse disrupted Alex's concentration by informing him he'd been cleared of any injuries. Not even a scratch. He asked about Galen, but the nurse didn't have any news and promised to provide him with updates when she could. Who could he call? Who did he trust?

Alex's hands shook so violently, he could barely dial the phone. Alex called Hoko and said he needed his help. He said there had been an explosion, and Alex was unharmed, but Galen was at Mass General Hospital. He was severely injured, and the triage team was working to stabilize him. They needed to know his next-of-kin information and if he had an advanced care directive. He told Hoko that he didn't know where to get that information. Hoko said he'd get the information and forward it to Alex. He'd also have Ryo deploy additional security to the hospital, and would let the rest of the board know about the situation. He added Ryo would deploy a forensic team to the scene to prevent the Boston PD from contaminating evidence. Hoko said he'd be there as soon as possible and asked Alex if he needed anything. Alex said he needed a change of clothes since his were scorched and covered in Galen's blood.

"Galen is young, strong, and a fighter, Alex. He'll be OK."

Alex hung up the call and sat his phone on the examining room table as tears started streaming down his face, before his entire body began shaking and wouldn't stop. It felt like he was crying more than breathing these days. Although Alex couldn't reach Galen's energy or soul, he could support the doctors and medical staff providing his care energetically. He'd never been religious, but he closed his eyes to pray.

Alex held his face in his hands. It had been hours since he'd received any updates on Galen's condition.

His prayers were interrupted by a deep voice. "Mr. Lieth? I'm Dr. Anderson; we met in the ER. Galen is a fortunate man. He's out of emergency surgery for a subdural hematoma on his brain. We performed a decompressive craniectomy to remove a twenty-centimeter portion of the skull to reduce intracranial pressure and swelling."

"Is he going to make it?" Alex said, holding his breath as he asked.

Dr. Anderson said the next twenty-four hours would be crucial to determine the procedure's success. Galen was recovering and would be moved to an ICU room shortly. Dr. Anderson added there was no timetable for when he might regain consciousness, but he was hopeful because Galen was young and healthy, which would hopefully help his recovery.

Alex asked if he could see Galen, and Dr. Anderson said only for a few minutes––what Galen needed now was rest. He agreed to keep his visit brief and relayed the next-of-kin information he'd obtained. Galen only had a sister in New Zealand, but the records showed she was disabled. Dr. Anderson thanked Alex for the information, saying he would add it to Galen's records. Dr. Anderson touched Alex's shoulder before saying he could see how much Alex cared about Galen. Although it was against his better judgment, he'd allow Alex to stay with Galen in the ICU if he cleaned himself up. He instructed Alex the nurse would escort him to a place to shower and provide him with sanitized protective clothing to wear in the ICU to reduce the risk of infection.

Alex thanked Dr. Anderson, but was confused when Dr. Anderson thanked Alex for *his* support. Alex said Dr. Anderson must be mistaken, but he explained PGC was one of the biggest benefactors to the hospital, and they would do everything within their power to return Galen to health. Dr. Anderson turned and walked down the hall toward the nursing station. After giving his instructions to help prepare Alex for the ICU, he disappeared around the corner.

Alex quickly showered and dressed in hospital garments and protective gear. The ICU nurse led him into room 101, where the sight of Galen in the hospital bed was jarring. All the tubes, wires, monitors, and bandages around his head and face reinforced the severity of the situation. Alex sat quietly by the hospital bed, watching each breath and heartbeat on the monitors, hoping they'd not be Galen's last. Alex reached out and placed his hand on Galen's forearm. Alex didn't know if Galen could feel the small gesture, but he wanted him to know he was there. He could see the spark in Galen's chest slightly intensify with his touch.

Hoko was right. Alex could influence others when they were dreaming or unconscious. Still, he wouldn't abuse the situation and read Galen's soul or memories without his consent. Such a violation could destroy the trust and relationship they'd established. Alex focused on his breathing, drawing cosmic energy from nature, and focused with the singular intent on Galen and his struggle to survive. He watched as the energy flowed from his hand and encircled Galen's body, forming a protective bubble. He didn't know if this would help, but he had to try. If only Hoko were there to help him.

Alex didn't recall when during the night he fell asleep, but he couldn't outrun his exhaustion. The dawn light streamed through the window and dimly illuminated the room.

"Why?" said Galen in a weak voice.

"You're awake!" Alex said with a look of pure excitement as he raised his head from the side of Galen's hospital bed. "Don't try to talk. Let me get the nurse."

"Ya had no right. Should've let me go," Galen tearfully said as his heart rate and blood pressure monitors steadily climbed, setting off multiple alarms.

Alex didn't know what to say. Why was Galen so angry and upset that Alex had helped save his life?

"Save your strength, and I'll be right back with the nurse."

Alex returned to the room with the ICU charge nurse, who paged the neurosurgeon to do an assessment. Alex stepped out of the room and let the medical staff do their work, but only after checking their energy and spark to ensure they had good bedside manners.

After the medical staff left the room, Alex approached Dr. Anderson and asked if this was a good sign. Dr. Anderson said it was a great sign, and that in his many years of treating brain injury patients, it would usually take weeks to obtain Galen's level of responsiveness. He added it was truly a miracle that he hadn't observed before in his career. Walking out the door, Dr. Anderson said what Galen needed now was rest. Alex nodded and said he wouldn't overstay his welcome. Alex walked back to the ICU room and quietly watched Galen sleep.

Stepping out of the ICU unit after an hour, Alex was met outside by Hoko and Ryo, who immediately asked how Galen was doing. Alex filled them in on Galen's condition, to which Hoko and Ryo expressed relief. Ryo said they needed to update Alex on several events.

"Several events? I'm exhausted, Ryo, and I'm not sure I can take any more bad news," said Alex.

Ryo said, unfortunately, that was all he had to share. Ryo explained that several other events raised concerns about Alex's safety and security last night, in addition to the explosion. He stated he believed the explosion was not an accident, but rather a diversion.

"A diversion?" said Alex.

Ryo said at the same time of the explosion, the officer assigned to surveillance at Alex's apartment was assaulted and killed--or, more accurately, assassinated. Ryo said the assailants also burglarized Alex's apartment and were clearly looking for something specific, but he didn't know what.

Templeton? They had just gone out for coffee yesterday morning, and he was so excited that he and his wife were expecting in just six weeks. "Why would someone kill Templeton?" said Alex.

Ryo said they didn't know. The security suite was raided, all security footage from the incident was erased, while all security footage for the past several weeks was taken. This was a professional job. At the same time, Ryo said they had an electronic security breach at PGC. Alex was confused, asking how--given the military-grade security at PGC--that could have happened. Ryo said that's what they need to find out. The incursion was precise. The research and medical servers, plus Ms. Dea's personal files, were hacked. Ryo added they were working to figure out the extent of the breach. However, he said preliminary indications were that the thieves were looking for research on ichor.

Alex sat down in the chair in the hall. "Please tell me, that's all," he said in a broken voice.

Ryo shook his head no, before adding that at the same time as the hack and explosion, three masked assailants broke into Dr. Bruno's house and attempted to kidnap him. His wife, Greta, was in shock, and Dr. Sonja was with her now. Ryo said the details were limited, but evaluation of the scene showed Dr. Bruno resisted his kidnappers and was injured. Ryo explained the assailants were fought off by PGC security.

Alex closed his eyes and leaned his head against the wall. A car bombing, murder, attempted kidnapping, and corporate espionage all at once? What the fuck was happening? Whoever was attacking Alex and PGC was twenty steps ahead. He took a deep breath before asking why Ryo was at the hospital rather than at headquarters. Ryo replied that Alex's safety was their priority, and that Alex couldn't safely return to his apartment. He added the board had asked him to escort Alex to the penthouse since PGC had the full force of their resources to protect him there. Alex shook his head and said he didn't want to leave Galen at the hospital alone. Hoko pleaded with Alex to let them help him, and to go to the penthouse for his safety.

Alex noted the concern in Hoko's eyes before he begrudgingly nodded yes, but said the only way he'd go to the penthouse was if PGC protected Galen as if they were protecting him or Ditta. Ryo nodded in agreement, and Hoko said he'd stay with Galen until the security detail arrived. Ryo escorted Alex to an armored vehicle at the hospital's back entrance.

Alex's mind raced a million miles an hour as he tried to piece everything together. He'd found himself as the central character in an espionage novel. His previously simple life would have been canceled for being too boring if it were a reality show, but now his life had become a Tom Clancy thriller. His body filled with dread as he thought about what would happen next.

Stepping off the private elevator into the penthouse, Alex was a foreigner in a strange land. Standing at the floor-to-ceiling windows, admiring the Boston skyline, provided a momentary respite. Every worldview Alex had developed in his life was being challenged. Danyal, his rock, was missing, but the events of the past twelve hours had shifted his disappearance to the back of Alex's mind.

His thoughts drifted back to his conversation with Hoko. Alex vowed to protect the people he cared about, being a force for good. The events of the past twelve hours had convinced him he must do all he could to fight back against the darkness. But for tonight, the best thing Alex could do was rest.

He slowly walked to the main bedroom and fell forward, fully clothed, on the bed. Alex could no longer avoid his exhaustion by running on adrenaline.

Chapter Twenty-Three

Alex

It had been three weeks since Danyal was abducted, and two weeks after Galen nearly died, but PGC and Alex were no closer to learning any new information. He sat at the conference table in the boardroom, impatiently waiting for the meeting to begin. Alex hadn't left the PGC building in days and had taken an indefinite sabbatical from the university. He spent his days between training sessions with Hoko and therapy sessions with Diana, which he admitted were the only things maintaining his sanity. Although his days were busy, at night, when he was alone, he wrestled with his demons. Right now, the demons were winning.

The usual subjects were in attendance, but Zoe from the technology branch was also in attendance today. She looked nervous as she shuffled some papers on the table before her. Alex was surprised to see Dr. Bruno at the meeting after his recent assault. His head was bandaged from a laceration, and his right eye blackened. Alex didn't like the man Bruno had become, but he certainly didn't wish physical harm upon him. Still, in Alex's mind, something didn't feel right.

How could Bruno survive an assault when a trained security team member, Templeton, was murdered?

"Good morning," said Ryo. "Nothing said in this meeting today will leave this room. We have two issues that we need to discuss. The first issue is the forensic team has completed their evaluation of the truck involved in your hit-and-run accident, Alex."

Alex took a deep breath to calm himself. "I've never told anyone here at PGC about that accident, Ryo. How did you know about it?"

Ryo said a security detail had been following Alex for weeks before his ascension, and that they reported the incident to PGC. The truck was stolen, but DNA testing helped identify the driver's identity. Ryo stated the driver's name was Douglas Austin, an Irish national with links to organized terrorist groups. He added that word in the counterintelligence world was that Douglas had been recruited from within the former IRA, and had aligned himself with the Sons of Enyaluis.

Alex took a deep breath and leaned against the conference table.

"So, you're telling me the Sons of Enyaluis tried to kill me the day before my ascension?"

"Yes," said Ryo, "that's exactly what I am saying. We have asked for an APB for all U.S. authorities and with Interpol. He's likely already gone underground because the trail has gone cold."

"Fuck," said Alex. "Doesn't anyone ever share good news in this room?"

"I'm afraid that's not the worst news, Alex," said Ryo. "The forensic technology team has concluded its preliminary findings on the recent data breach, and has drawn several conclusions. First, the computer breach was because of a virus uploaded internally within the building. Specifically, the entry point was at your computer, Ms. Palmer."

"I've no idea how," said Zoe, her voice quivering. "We take every precaution in our department to maintain computer security."

Ryo said he believed her, but the data was undeniable––her workstation was the virus's entry point.

A sharp pain grew in Alex's chest as he picked up Danyal's phone, and Ryo said the virus was introduced three days after Danyal was abducted.

"Ryo," said Alex, "I think I know what may have happened. I asked Zoe to look at Danyal's phone. She examined it using her computer but couldn't pull any information from it."

Zoe clasped her hand over her mouth before responding. She said their computers had state-of-the-art virus and malware protection. She added that whoever coordinated the attack must know their security protections; otherwise, it would take her best staff weeks to hack into the system.

"This company has been safe for decades, and you bring it down by connecting an outside device to our system?" yelled Dr. Bruno. "Your incompetence has led to the injury of two staff including myself, not to mention Templeton's death. You both have blood on your hands and ought to be terminated immediately."

"Bruno," said Ryo, "please keep it together. This is unacceptable."

"How dare you. If she had a grave, Ditta would be turning in it," said Bruno.

"That's enough, Dr. Bruno," said Diana. "I know you're hurting, but please get it together. If you need to step out, I'll go with you, and we can have an emergency session."

"I'm not one of your headcases, Diana. I appreciate your help with my wife, but my head doesn't need shrinking."

Hoko broke the tension in the room by asking what information was taken. Ryo replied that, by following the digital trail of the virus, any records on ichor and ambrosia were targeted, as well as the personal data archives of Ms. Dea.

"This wasn't a random breach," said Alex, "they knew what they were looking for. The question is, did they get the data?"

Ryo said the best they could determine was that the data on ichor had been accessed, but there was no data to steal since Ms. Dea wouldn't allow any research on the substance.

Hoko asked if they had breached Ditta's files. Ryo said they had no idea since he didn't know these files were even on the PGC servers until the breach.

Alex leaned forward in his seat and asked, "If we didn't even know these files existed, how did they know they were on the servers? How did they even know what they were looking for?"

Ryo said that was an excellent question for which he didn't have an answer, but their attackers were likely hoping to find out where Ms. Dea may have obtained or stored ichor.

"What kind of damage could they do with this data or, heaven forbid, if they obtained ichor?" asked Alex.

"Your shallow mind may not grasp it, but the damage would be unimaginable if they could perfect or weaponize the substance," said Bruno.

"That's your one insult of the day, Dr. Bruno," snapped Alex. "Don't push your luck unless you want to see my temper."

The two men glared at each other like rams trying to show dominance. Ryo interrupted the staring contest and reminded everyone to maintain cooler heads. He added they were on the same team, and it was time to act like it. Ryo resumed the meeting by saying the best they could determine was that the attack on the security suite and ransacking of Alex's apartment had been related to obtaining samples of the ambrosia chocolate Ms. Dea had given Alex. He turned to Alex and asked if anything was missing.

"The last piece of chocolate was missing," said Alex, silencing the room. Alex repeated Bruno's warning internally that ichor in the hands of the wrong people could be catastrophic. However, he chose to withhold that he still had one piece of chocolate in his jacket at Starling University, because he had no clue who he could really trust at PGC.

Ryo said, unfortunately, they had no electronic surveillance of the event since it was all erased. He added they did gather footage from the university parking lot, which showed the moment of the bombing. However, no one approached the SUV the entire time it was parked.

"So, you're saying," said Alex, "the bomb must have been planted earlier in the day. PGC and the police station were the only places we went." Alex was frustrated there was no clear timeline of when the bomb was planted. Thank god no one else was injured.

Diana asked how Galen was doing, and Alex said he was doing remarkably well, physically at least. However, emotionally, he was depressed and withdrawn. He added Galen could be discharged as early as today. He knew he had stretched the truth because Galen, on his visits, was silent and refused to talk to Alex. Dr. Anderson had warned mood and personality changes could occur after a head injury.

Ryo said that was good news, and he'd make arrangements for Galen's aftercare. Alex thanked Ryo, but stated Galen would be recovering in the penthouse, where he could ensure Galen's safety and have him receive the best medical care.

"Is that a good idea?" asked Zoe. "It's a strange environment." She paused before continuing, "Galen is a proud man, and he's embarrassed. He feels like a failure for not detecting the threat and protecting Dr. Lieth. He's likely worried the recent events will cost him his job."

"You know a lot about Galen," said Alex. His suspicions had been confirmed. Zoe was the person Galen had been with before his recent walk of shame. The events seemed so long ago, and meaningless now.

"He's not talking much," said Zoe. "But he's starting to open up to me."

Alex felt a stabbing pain in his chest as Zoe spoke about Galen. Was it jealousy?

"If you were concerned about his safety," interrupted Bruno, "maybe Dr. Lieth shouldn't have been gallivanting around in public when we knew outside forces were attacking us."

Alex slammed his fist on the conference table. "Shut your fucking mouth, Bruno," he said as he raised a hand, resulting in the coffee cup in front of Dr. Bruno flying across the room and shattering against the wall.

"Alex," yelled Diana, "stop this at once!"

"I think Dr. Bruno owes me an apology."

"I owe you nothing. You're proving to be the downfall of this company. You're a blunt tool, and all you know is violence. Show us what we already know; Ditta made a catastrophic mistake in choosing a petulant child to replace her."

Alex stood from his chair as the conference room began to shake. His eyes filled with rage, and bolts of bright white cosmic energy began to burst from his eyes.

"Alex," Hoko said as he placed his hand gently on Alex's shoulder, "let it go. It's not worth it. Be the better man."

Alex slowly took his seat at the table as the room stopped shaking.

"If we can't respect each other," said Ryo, "we need to bring this meeting to an end."

"With all due respect," said Zoe, "I must present my findings. Dr. Lieth needs to know."

"I need to know what, Zoe?"

Ryo nodded for Zoe to continue.

Zoe said she'd been researching the EMP, which occurred when Dr. Lieth ascended. Based on the data, she'd discovered that the EMP signature that resulted in the failure of the power grid on the Eastern Seaboard didn't match the EMP field Dr. Lieth emitted. As a result, she stated the data indicated the EMP was a targeted emission, and that she believed it was intended to either weaken or eliminate Dr. Lieth when he gained his divine abilities.

"That's absurd!" said Bruno as he slammed his fist on the table. "You're saying someone set off a thermonuclear pulse in Boston?"

"Yes," said Zoe, "that's exactly what I'm saying." She explained she had consulted with a colleague in the military who specialized in EMP research, and he confirmed the findings. Dr. Lieth was responsible for the second pulse around eleven a.m., but not for the first pulse, which did most of the damage.

"So, you're asking us to believe the woman who allowed a breach of the corporation and broke company policy by taking data to an outside entity? I demand termination on the spot for your incompetence," yelled Bruno as he stood and shook his finger at Zoe.

"Shut your mouth, Bruno, and let her finish," demanded Alex, snapping his fingers. Bruno kept talking, but the words didn't come out of his mouth.

"Stop!" Diana begged. "Don't hurt him, Alex."

Alex asked Diana why she always assumed the worst of him. He said he hadn't injured Bruno in any way. Alex turned to Bruno and said, "You were warned, Bruno. Let her finish." Alex hadn't tested his theory, but his recent sessions with Hoko had him suspect the world around him went silent when he used his abilities.

Alex snapped his fingers again. "Please proceed, Zoe. You won't be interrupted. So, I wasn't the main source of the damage?"

Zoe said no, he wasn't the main reason––and for the record, she did obtain permission from Ryo before consulting outside of PGC. Alex thanked her for her research and said she'd given him the gift of peace of mind, but that her findings indicated the Sons of Enyaluis had attacked him on multiple occasions.

Ryo abruptly ended the meeting by saying he trusted Zoe's findings and that PGC would redouble their efforts to find Danyal and keep Alex safe. As the board members stood to leave, Ryo asked if he could speak with Bruno and Alex alone.

"There's no way I'll stay anywhere with this thug after he threatened and assaulted me. Is this what you're teaching him, Hoko, how to abuse others? Mark my words; he's a ticking time bomb," Dr. Bruno said as he left the boardroom, slamming the door behind him.

"I'll stay, Ryo, with Hoko and Diana present. My trust in PGC is wavering," said Alex.

Chapter Twenty-Four

Alex

"Is this going to be a lecture, Ryo? If so, I'm not in the mood for it," said Alex.

"We can discuss what happened in the meeting later, but first, I need to start with an apology," said Ryo.

"That would be a new experience in this conference room," said Alex.

Ryo said he understood Alex's experiences at PGC had been negative recently. He admitted he must take responsibility since he accepted the scientific opinion that Alex was the origin of the initial EMP blast, which crippled the city. He said he had spoken with Bruno and his team about the issue before the meeting, which might go some way to explain Bruno's foul mood. Ryo cautioned that Bruno was a very proud man and had difficulty admitting he was wrong, especially considering his team insisted they made a scientifically sound determination based on available data.

Alex laughed; he knew there was no apology coming from Bruno. He'd dealt with many condescending assholes in academia; any evidence they were imperfect was taken as a narcissistic injury. Ryo asked that the board allow Bruno to calm down, because he had been a valued team member.

"So, we have to tolerate him?" asked Alex.

"No, you two need to be separated for a while," said Ryo.

"I have an honest question: why does he hate me so much?" said Alex.

Ryo looked at Hoko and Diana. "We need to brief him."

"Brief me on what?" asked Alex.

Ryo shifted files in front of him and pulled out one with a green cover.

Diana said the core of Bruno's feelings likely had little to do with Alex, as she handed him the file Ryo had given her. Alex opened the file and looked at the picture of a young girl stapled to the first page. He recognized the girl and recalled seeing her in the photographs in Bruno's office. Looking down at the floor, Diana said that the girl's name was Nyssa, and she was Bruno's adopted daughter.

"Nyssa was another test subject in Bruno's research," said Hoko. "Bruno raised her as his child to provide her with a stable and loving environment."

Alex recalled Bruno told him none of the other test subjects lived into adolescence. In this picture, he'd guess she'd be about fourteen years old. "So, I had a sister, genetically speaking? She looks like Ditta. It's uncanny."

Hoko nodded yes and said she would have been Alex's "sister" biologically, since she was also a clone of Ditta.

"What happened to her?" Alex said, as the room went quiet.

Diana began to cry and eventually broke the silence. "She's dead, Alex."

Alex sat confused, trying to process the information being presented to him. "If she had lived to be a teenager, how did she die?"

"It was a dark time for Ditta...there came a time when she had to determine whether you or Nyssa would be the most viable replacement," Diana said, sobbing. Hoko stood beside her and placed his hand on her back for support.

Alex sat in silence, waiting for Diana to continue.

Through her sobs, Diana explained Nyssa had begun to display several concerning behaviors. She exhibited symptoms of depression and mania. In addition to her mood swings, Diana said Nyssa had begun to exhibit violent behavior toward herself and others, which forced Ditta to make a difficult decision based on Nyssa's mental instability. Ditta indicated she didn't have enough resources to continue the experiment with both Alex and Nyssa, because it was draining her life force.

Alex took a deep breath and braced for what he feared was the next revelation.

Diana met Alex's gaze with tears running down her face. "Ditta ordered Bruno to terminate the experiment and to focus all resources on your development."

Alex leaned forward, closed his eyes, and shook his head no. "Ditta ordered him to euthanize...kill his adopted daughter?"

"Yes," said Hoko. "Ditta didn't order her death, but she refused to provide Nyssa with any ichor."

Diana wiped her eyes before responding, "The board advocated vehemently for Ditta to change her mind, but she would not listen to our objections."

"So, you're telling me Aphrodite let a child die so I could survive?"

Ryo, Hoko, and Diana didn't respond.

"It's no wonder the man hates me," said Alex. "I'm a constant reminder of everything he's lost."

Diana nodded, adding she believed the more anger and potentially violent behavior Alex exhibited, the more it reinforced he might also be emotionally unstable like Nyssa. She said this was all re-traumatizing for Bruno. He may not have raised Alex, but was involved in his creation, so feels responsible for Alex's well-being.

Alex acknowledged all of the pieces were starting to come together now. He understood why Bruno looked at him with both fascination and fear. He agreed to stay away from Bruno under one condition: he asked that Dr. Donalds care for Galen upon his release. He didn't want Bruno's negativity anywhere near him.

Ryo nodded and said he'd work it out with the medical staff. Alex also made the group agree Zoe won't be terminated or disciplined in any way for trying to help him.

Ryo, Hoko, and Diana nodded in agreement.

"Now, let's get to the elephant in the room––who are the Sons of Enyaluis?" said Alex.

Ryo said the limited information they had came from international counterintelligence groups. Whomever they were dealing with, he said, they had considerable resources and demonstrated unparalleled sophistication in their execution and planning. Ryo admitted he'd never in his wildest dreams believed PGC could be so vulnerable. Alex said he understood, but that it felt personal. Danyal was missing with no ransom or specific demands. They attacked Alex both before, and at the moment of his ascension, manipulated him into introducing the virus to the PGC system, murdered Templeton, and almost killed Galen. More than ever, Alex knew Danyal was in danger.

"If I were Sherlock Holmes, I'd deduce our enemy had outsmarted us at every turn. Only they know the rules of this deadly game and dominate the playing field with deadly precision. Holmes would also say we may have a spy in our camp," said Alex.

Ryo looked toward Hoko and Diana before saying they were all in agreement. Ryo added they needed to take all actions possible to level the battlefield, or else this war would be over before they even made their first counterstrike.

"Alex," said Hoko, "how did you silence Bruno's voice?"

"I improvised on the spot. I imagined it and made it happen," said Alex.

"Your powers are growing, Alex. It would be best if you were careful with your emotions," said Diana. "When they spike, you act on instinct, which could lead to someone getting hurt or even killed."

Hoko sat beside Alex before saying they needed to ask Alex questions about the explosion that injured Galen.

"Could you break it down as best you can?" said Hoko. "What happened?"

Alex said he wasn't sure. He'd been playing it repeatedly in his mind, but it all happened so fast.

"We have something to show you," said Ryo. They'd obtained video from the traffic camera across the university parking lot. He said at the start of the video, they could see Alex and Galen walking down the sidewalk. Galen approached the Uros and then came the explosion. After the explosion, Alex and Galen were lying on the ground.

"What am I supposed to be looking for?" said Alex.

Hoko asked Ryo to slow down the video at fifty percent speed. Alex could see he started about fifteen feet behind Galen, and at the moment of the explosion, he was in front, shielding Galen from the blast. Alex told Hoko he was confused. That's exactly how Alex recalled it. Hoko asked Ryo to slow the video down to twenty-five percent. Hoko said he wouldn't believe this if he hadn't seen it, but based on the video evidence, there was no way Alex could have moved fast enough to shield Galen unless Alex teleported.

"Teleported?" said Alex.

"Yes, Alex, the video evidence shows you teleported," said Hoko.

Alex said they had discussed it as a possibility, but Hoko said it was an advanced ability and one probably beyond his grasp at this stage. Hoko agreed and said Alex acted on instinct; his fight-or-flight reflex kicked in. "Lucky for Galen that it did; you saved his life."

"Given everything happening with the breach, please keep this information between us," said Alex. "It's time to assume there's a traitor in PGC."

Chapter Twenty-Five

Galen

The walls closed in on Galen as he felt trapped in an ivory tower, sitting in his wheelchair in front of the fireplace in the penthouse. The glass of bourbon in hand and pain meds did nothing to dull the guilt and sorrow tormenting him. Why did Alex save him? For every sin Galen had committed, he should have let him pay for them with his life. Death was what he deserved for stealing from Alex and unwittingly working with the enemy. He might as well have abducted Danyal himself. If Danyal died, his blood would be on Galen's hands. Galen and blood were not strangers, as hurting others had been the driving force of his life. No matter where Galen ran, there was no escaping his past. People died, and he was responsible.

Galen was so deep in thought he didn't see Alex walking down the main hall of the penthouse towards him.

"Can't sleep, Galen?" Alex said softly. "And should you be drinking? The doctor said no mixing of your medication and alcohol after your surgery."

"Bugger off," said Galen, without turning to look at Alex.

"I see your mood hasn't improved," said Alex.

Galen took another drink of his bourbon. "Why did ya save me?"

"Usually, people are more grateful when you help save their life," said Alex.

"Didn't want it. Ya pulled me back to suffer."

"OK, Galen. I'm calling Diana. You need professional help," said Alex, pulling out his phone.

"Why am I here in this penthouse with ya doting over me? Not yur fuckin' responsibility."

"You're here because I want you safe while you recover."

"Ya don't know me. It's ya that needs to be kept safe from me."

"Is it the alcohol and medication creating this pity party or something else?"

Galen sat silently, staring at the fire, ignoring Alex's question.

"Galen, look at me," said Alex.

Galen didn't respond.

"Fine, if you don't talk, I'll do the talking," Alex said as he walked over to Galen and knelt between his wheelchair and the fire. "Dr. Anderson said there could be mood issues during your recovery. Let's start by stopping the drinking." Alex reached for the glass in Galen's hand.

"Don't touch me!" yelled Galen, throwing the glass past Alex's ear towards the fireplace. The glass shattered against the mantle and landed on the floor like falling stars.

"Galen, you're starting to scare me. I've never seen this side of you, and I don't like it."

"It's the real me!" exclaimed Galen as he grabbed Alex's shirt and pulled him toward him. Galen could smell Alex's cologne, which was always enticing. He didn't know if he wanted to hit Alex or kiss him. Maybe both.

"I know you're not going to hurt me, Galen," Alex said as he placed his hand on Galen's, grasping his shirt.

"All mah fault," said Galen, sobbing with tears running down his face. "I'm a killer!"

"Galen, you're not making sense."

"Killed a man with mah bare hands," Galen said, tears streaming down his face. "Son of a bitch brutally assaulted and raped mah sister, Amara." He stopped talking and continued to sob uncontrollably. "Found her beaten. Unconscious in the street. He left her in a coma, all because she refused him. Eight years later, and hasn't opened her eyes since."

Now Alex knew what he meant when Galen had said he'd lost his sister and grieved for her. "I'm so sorry. I didn't know anything other than she was in a care facility back home. I can't imagine what she went through."

"Took the light of mah life away. Made him pay. His family was rich, so the police did nothing to find justice. Found him and gave him the same mercy that he gave Amara. He died of severe head injuries. Keep playing it over and over in mah mind and mah dreams. Never stop until I watch the life drain from his eyes." Galen stopped talking, his face still in his hands.

Alex leaned forward, his forehead touching the crown of Galen's head.

"Avoided prison 'cause the All Blacks wanted to avoid scandal. Was mandated to serve in the military for seven years. The minimum sentence for manslaughter. Now I've killed again."

"Killed again?" said Alex, fear in his voice.

"Templeton," said Galen between sobs.

"Galen, I'm not following you. We know the Sons of Enyaluis killed Templeton."

"Was mah fault they were there," said Galen, sobbing even harder as he pushed Alex away from him. "Betrayed ya, Alex...did a horrible thing...ya should hate me."

"Nothing you've done, Galen, could make me hate you."

Galen blurted out, "Danyal's gone 'cause of me!"

"What did you say?" said Alex as he moved backward, tripped, and landed on the floor in the field of broken glass.

"Didn't mean to do it. Wanted to save Amara."

"Galen, you aren't making sense."

"Ya don't fuckin' get it! Stole the ichor and gave it to the Sons of Enyaluis."

Alex began to breathe rapidly, and the furniture in the room started to vibrate.

"Didn't do it intentionally. Tricked me into helping them."

"How?" said Alex between rapid breaths.

"Anonymously contacted me about obtaining the chocolate. Promised they could help Amara with her coma. Wuz my only hope. Thought it was just a piece of chocolate. Didn't know they were the enemy."

Alex tried to stand, but fell against the window. His silence deepened Galen's sorrow. Alex stood and exited to the terrace, going out into the biting cold. Alex had stirred feelings in Galen in the past few weeks that he hadn't dared experience in years. He'd given up his career and betrayed his friend for the pipe dream of saving his sister.

Galen stood from his chair and stumbled his way to the terrace door. He wanted all the pain to end. Stepping outside, he shuffled towards the balcony. Realizing what he was about to do, Alex tackled him to the cold stone floor covered in snow.

"What the fuck are you doing? Do you want to die?" yelled Alex.

"Let me end the pain," sobbed Galen.

Alex picked up Galen and brought him back inside to warmth and safety. Alex sat Galen in his wheelchair and knelt in front of him.

The two men stayed in silence, both weeping. Eventually, Alex broke it.

"I've two questions for you, Galen. When did you steal the chocolate?"

"Night I came to yur apartment."

"Are you the spy?"

Galen wiped his tears and shook his head no.

"How can I believe you?"

"Give me yur hand," said Galen. "Look into mah spark. Will show ya everything."

"You fooled me before; how can I trust what I see now?"

"Hadn't decided to betray ya yet. Wasn't lying."

Alex hesitated, but extended his shaking hand to Galen, who placed it over his heart.

Galen let everything flow as Alex touched his energy. Amara, his murderous rage, the military, ichor, and the Sons of Enyaluis––he shared it all.

Alex pulled back his hand with tears falling down his face.

"I believe you, Galen. They preyed on your love for your sister and manipulated you. I can't say I wouldn't have done the same thing to keep Danyal safe. I promise to do everything I can within PGC's resources to help Amara. It's only fair I return the favor, but I'm going to make you take your advice. We're going to ride out these waves until the sea is calm. To start with, we need to get you to bed so you can sleep off the booze. I'm not taking no for an answer," Alex said as he rolled Galen's wheelchair down the hallway to his bedroom. "I'll watch you tonight to keep you safe," he said, getting onto the bed across from Galen.

Galen felt something like peace for the first time in years and closed his eyes to sleep. Alex across from him on the bed was the last image in his mind as he drifted off.

Chapter Twenty-Six

Galen

Galen sat on the workout bench wondering, *how do ya thank someone for saving ya from jumping off a high rise? They don't make a thank ya card for this occasion.* Though the thought had crossed his mind over the years, and his reckless behavior in the military had been an apparent death wish, he was still surprised he came so close to ending it. Galen's attention was diverted as Alex walked up the staircase to the second-floor gym, where Galen was doing his physical therapy. Galen was surprised as Alex had been avoiding him for the past two days since the incident––he couldn't blame him for needing space.

"I'm glad to see you up and moving, Galen. Would you like some coffee?" said Alex.

"Nah, need to finish mah physical therapy. Doc finally released me to do more."

Galen couldn't take the tension anymore as Alex took a seat on the bench across from Galen without speaking.

"Don't know what came over me the other night. Lost mah head."

"I know, Galen. I had a front-row seat. A volatile mix of sorrow and alcohol."

"Betrayed ya. Must leave. Will resign immediately."

Alex paused before saying, "I needed some space to clear my head, Galen. You could leave, if that's what you want, or stay and help bring the enemy to justice."

"How could ya ever trust me again?"

"You did betray me, but you were honest about why. You did a bad thing, but you're not a bad guy. You were so remorseful you wanted to die. You didn't have to confess, and I've no room to judge. I've made mistakes with life-altering consequences––Wynn is a prime example. Plus, I've touched your life energy on multiple occasions. I know, at your core, you're a good person. Besides Hoko, you're the only person I've connected with since this ordeal began. With your help, I want to discover the true villain's identity. I can't do it without you; Sherlock needs his Watson."

"How?"

"We're going to root out any traitors in the company."

Galen leaned forward and laid his head on Alex's shoulder. "Will do anything to fix the damage I've caused."

"I know, Galen," Alex said as he wrapped his arms around him, holding Galen.

Galen basked in the warmth and compassion of Alex's embrace. He didn't want it to end.

"I do want you to get help, though," said Alex. "You must agree to see Diana for counseling."

Galen nodded his head. "Deal, mate."

"Not to be intrusive, but I can see the spark in your chest, and you're growing stronger."

"Yeah, the doc says can't have any shots until the noggin has healed."

"No worries. I promise I won't read your mind or energy."

"Look all ya want, mate," Galen said as he stopped doing his biceps curls. "No more secrets. Sherlock and Watson."

"I know, but I want to ensure you can be comfortable around me. So, I had this created while you were in the hospital." Alex reached into his pocket and pulled out a small item to hand to Galen. "Open your hand, please."

The request made Galen worried. He extended and opened his right hand, where Alex placed a silver and black ring.

"What's this? Bold to ask me to put a ring on it so soon."

"OK, Beyoncé, don't get too excited. Inoculations aren't the only way to block my abilities. I learned from Hoko that wearing an item treated with the 'magical substance' has the same effect. Hoko wears a treated medicine bag instead of taking the injections."

Galen held the ring between his thumb and forefinger to examine it. Black onyx with a silver fern--the symbol for the All Blacks.

"It's amazing what you can find on the internet. I didn't find you in any rugby calendars, but I did find numerous videos of the team when you were a member, and your pregame dance was nothing short of impressive," said Alex.

"Called a 'haka.' Ceremonial Māori war dance or challenge. Haka represents the team's pride, strength, and unity. Not that I'm ungrateful, but ya had a replica championship ring made?"

"Yes, they made it to the championship the year you left, so I thought you'd earned it. They wouldn't have made it to the championship without you."

"Cheers, Alex," Galen said as he flashed his boyish grin and placed the ring on his finger.

"I'd never seen you wear any jewelry, so I was clueless about whether you'd wear it."

"Ya did good. Let me know if it works. Try to read mah thoughts."

"You're thinking about what a wonderful guy I am."

Galen smiled and his face flushed; he was actually thinking that, if Alex were single and sitting closer to him, he'd have been tempted to kiss him. Galen's heart skipped; he'd shared his energy with Alex. Did Alex see the shower sex dream or his lewd thoughts?

"Wrong. Works because yu're way off base, mate." Galen sat quietly, looking at the ring. "Any new leads on Danyal?" he asked.

"No, the pawn shop you visited had already been cleared out. It was only a front. I did meet with the board a couple of days ago to review what we know to date."

"Eh?"

Alex shook his head. "Well, our work is cut out for us. I may have scared them."

"What did ya do now, mate?"

"I *may* have gotten upset at Bruno and caused a coffee cup to fly across the room and the conference tablet to vibrate uncontrollably."

"Sweet Jesus," laughed Galen, "can't leave ya alone for five minutes before ya threaten Bruno."

"He had it coming since he insulted Zoe and me. I *may* have also silenced him by taking away his voice."

"Come again? Hope ya have a video. Want to see his face."

"He was outraged because Zoe disproved his theory that I destroyed the electrical grid."

"Figures, ya can't do anything right," said Galen, shaking his head. "Can ya bring me the twenty-pound dumbbells?"

Galen watched as Alex reached out with his hand and, in one smooth motion, levitated the two dumbbells from the weight rack and floated them over to Galen at the weight bench. Galen laughed when Alex couldn't stick the landing, the dumbbells crashing at Galen's feet.

"Bombs away!" yelled Galen. "Showboating. Showing off your abilities like a peacock."

"I've been called worse, but I need practice. I haven't even mentioned the teleportation."

"Huh? Out for a few weeks, and yu're teleporting?"

"Afraid so; it appears I teleported at the moment of the explosion to shield you from the blast."

"Aye...Guess I should formally thank ya for saving mah arse twice."

"I'm keeping track, and might even offer a two-for-the-price-of-one special."

"Trying to be sincere, arsehole."

"I know; I feel bad I put you at risk in the first place."

"Ya didn't put me at any risk I wasn't willing to take. Been thinking..."

"Did it hurt?" said Alex.

Galen put the dumbbell down and flipped Alex off with his right hand. "What was the point of the explosion?" he said.

"Ryo thinks it was a diversionary tactic for the PGC breach."

"Only reason I came up with is..."

"You were the intended target because you'd delivered the ambrosia sample, and they were wrapping up loose ends," said Alex.

"Zactly, Sherlock. An explosion would never hurt ya, but could eliminate a loose end."

"It would also inflict emotional suffering on me if you were injured, since you and Hoko are my only allies. As I told the board, this feels personal."

"Agreed. Spot me for the bench press?"

"Sure, but only if you take it easy."

"Only a hundred pounds."

Galen couldn't avert his gaze from Alex, who intently watched him move the weight bar up and down.

"Be less awkward if ya weren't gawking at me," Galen said, finishing his last rep.

"Sorry, I was looking at your surgery scars. As soon as your hair grows out a little more, you won't even be able to tell you were injured."

"Doc Anderson did excellent work with an assist from ya. At least I won't be ugly."

"You're not ugly, but I think you know that, Mr. Humble New Zealand rugby god. It's my turn to bench press."

"How much weight do ya want?"

"Let's start with three hundred pounds."

"Yur funeral, Hercules."

Alex lay with his back on the weight bench, grasping the bar with each hand. He tried to lift the bar, making strained faces.

"OK, mate. No shame admitting defeat."

"I can do it--want to place a bet? The loser buys the other a burrito for lunch?"

"Will take yur burrito. It's a deal."

Alex took two deep breaths before gripping the bar again. Letting out a third breath, he lifted the bar and slowly counted each repetition out. "One, two, three, four, five, six, seven, eight, nine, ten," before gently returning the weights to their resting position on the arms of the weight bench.

"Cheater!" snapped Galen. "Took advantage of an injured bloke."

"For the record, I only suspected I could do it based on my sessions with Hoko."

"Bro, ya look weird doing bench presses with yur eyes closed."

Alex smiled. "When I worked out with Danyal, he'd say, 'Look at my eyes, not my crotch.' I didn't think either would be appropriate, so be grateful they were closed."

"TMI," Galen said, playfully punching Alex's shoulder.

"Ouch. That's workplace violence. Saved by the bell," Alex said, going to answer his ringing cell phone.

Galen instantly noted the look of concern on Alex's face.

"OK, I understand. We'll be there immediately," Alex said, as he ended the call. "Ryo wants us in the boardroom for an emergency meeting. The burrito you owe me will have to wait."

Alex and Galen stepped off the private elevator and walked down the hall toward the boardroom.

"Pardon our attire," said Alex, "we were working out."

"Please sit. Glad to see you up and about, Galen," said Ryo.

"Glad to be breathing," said Galen.

Ryo said at 11:30 a.m. today, they received an email request for a meeting at noon. He indicated the request was initially from one of their technology subcontractors, but further investigation revealed several anomalies.

"If we don't know who we'll be talking with today, is it wise to take such a call?" Alex asked.

Given the recent security breach that could have compromised the secure servers, Ryo shared Alex's concern. He added they had enacted every security protocol possible, but would find out in thirty seconds.

Galen could feel the dread building in his stomach, and he wanted to vomit. Something terrible was about to happen.

Chapter Twenty-Seven

Alex

Alex's fear was replaced by confusion when the video screen remained black, before it slowly illuminated to reveal Danyal sitting on a metal chair dressed in a white t-shirt and red basketball shorts, his feet and hands bound in front of him. Alex's entire body jolted like he'd touched a downed power line. Diana let out an audible gasp.

Danyal, in a shaky voice, began to talk. "My name is Danyal Sarif, and this message is for Alex Lieth and the Palingenesis Corporation. You'll deliver all samples of ichor to the coordinates provided in seven days. If you don't comply with this request, the Sons of Enyaluis will kill me and detonate a dirty bomb in an urban area in the United States. This isn't an idle threat; recent events prove the Sons of Enyaluis have the resources to enact this plan. If you seek help from the authorities or the military, the plan will be executed immediately, and the blood of millions of people will be on your hands." Danyal stopped speaking and looked directly into the camera, tears streaming down his face. "Please, Alex, give them what they want; I love you."

Danyal could barely say the last words before the screen faded to black once more.

The atmosphere in the boardroom was deathly silent. Galen reached over and placed his hand on Alex's shoulder, which startled him.

"Sorry, mate, my bad. Ya right?"

Alex stared at the video monitor as it shattered and crashed to the floor. The faces of everyone in the room, including Dr. Bruno, were pale. No one dared break the silence. As Alex's panic grew, the windows to the boardroom began to shake violently and crack. Galen strengthened his grasp on Alex's shoulder.

"Alex, focus on your breathing to help regulate your emotions," pleaded Hoko.

Alex slowed his breathing enough to respond as the shaking dissipated. "What the fuck just happened?"

"Let's stick to facts, Alex——we need to try and gather as much information as we can from the message," said Ryo.

"I'll give you a fact: these motherfuckers will pay!" yelled Alex as he slammed his fist on the table, breaking it into splinters.

"Alex," said Hoko, "focus again on your breath. We know Danyal is alive, and we need you here to figure this out."

"How?" asked Alex.

Hoko said they needed him to review the video as slowly and methodically as possible. Alex could see things they couldn't. Hoko asked if Alex saw anything unusual with his abilities.

Alex closed his eyes to concentrate on feeling the energy of the transmission. He nodded yes. Alex said he couldn't see the spark in the Danyal's chest or in the chests of the hostage-takers. "What does that mean?"

Bruno said it meant they were able to reach more of the PGC medical research than they'd anticipated, and they had synthesized an inoculation. Hoko said he suspected Bruno was right because it would prevent Alex from tracking them with his abilities.

"Know I'm late to the scrum," said Galen, "but did we find anything in the database about the Sons of Enyaluis?"

Ryo said the only information in the world criminal and terrorist database was that they're a low-level terrorist group with minor engagement in disruptive behavior across Europe, the Middle East, and Africa. He added they've never shown any organization on the level required for their attack on PGC. He wondered aloud how they went from the minor to major leagues so quickly, saying the video was planned down to the second to prevent them from tracking it to the source, as it appeared to be routed through several remote servers. He paused before asking, "Is Thanatos behind this?"

"Ditta did warn us shifting the balance of power may provoke the forces of darkness," said Diana.

"What makes ya think, Thanatos?" asked Galen.

Alex interjected, "Because, from Greek mythology, Enyaluis was the son of Aphrodite and Aries. He was the god of soldiers and warriors."

"What's their plans for the ichor? Why would Thanatos need it? Bloke's a god. May have access to it already," said Galen.

Bruno said ichor in the wrong hands would be devastating. It was immediately lethal to humans by all accounts and, if perfected, could create an immortal being or a god, so the damage could be unlimited.

"Imagine an army of immortal soldiers," Dr. Bruno added as he looked around the room, eventually focusing on Alex. "Alex, I know you'd do anything to save Danyal, but we can't let ichor fall into the hands of these terrorists. It's a good thing we have no samples."

"What if we did have a sample?" Alex asked.

"What're you saying?" responded Bruno.

Galen placed his hand on Alex's knee under the table before Alex could respond.

Alex paused until Galen removed his hand before responding. "I'm not saying I have any samples, but what if I could obtain one? Historically, ichor is the golden blood of the gods. Maybe I can locate a source."

"Heed my warning––that would be a terrible mistake. There would be no feasible way to obtain your blood, given your invulnerability," responded Bruno.

"So, you wouldn't do it for someone you loved?" asked Alex.

Bruno sat in silence.

"I figured as much. I need a moment," said Alex.

Ryo said he'd get the tech department working on the video. He doubted there would be any clues, but they would leave no stones unturned.

Alex stood to leave the room but was stopped by Diana, who extended her arms toward Alex for an embrace. Alex surprised himself by accepting it without resisting.

Hoko placed his hand on Alex's shoulder before saying Alex knew where to find him when he was ready, and that Hoko would start searching his resources for any mystical information to help ensure Danyal's safe return. Alex nodded in gratitude. Galen stood to leave the room after all the other occupants had left, but Alex stopped him by grasping his forearm.

"Please stay. I don't want to be alone," Alex said, as tears sprang forth from his eyes, and he wept uncontrollably.

Galen turned to Alex and placed his new protective ring on the table. He put his arms around Alex. "Not going anywhere, mate. Will hold ya as long as ya need me. Let it out."

Chapter Twenty-Eight

Alex

Galen and Alex worked together to slide open the warehouse door. Upon entering, they walked over to Hoko and Ryo, standing by a fire barrel.

"When you said you wanted to get out of the building, Hoko, I would never have guessed we'd be visiting the warehouse district. You do take us to the fanciest places."

"It's good to hear you still have your sense of humor, Alex, given the circumstances," said Hoko.

"It keeps me from falling apart," said Alex.

"Understood, Alex. Galen, make sure the doors are completely locked and secured."

"This all sounds very cloak and dagger," said Alex.

Ryo said they needed privacy because they must assume the enemy knows everything they know. Hoko smiled and said he and Ryo had a plan to discuss.

Alex could see Galen as he shivered intensely from the cold, and asked if he should be outside this long in the cold weather while in recovery.

"Fine, mate."

But Alex said he could see Galen was not OK and asked the group to step back from the fire barrel. He waved his hand over the flames, which caused them to leap higher and higher, before motioning with his hand for the heat to move in Galen's direction. Alex smiled, knowing heat was a form of energy he could easily control.

"Cheers, much betta."

"So, let's get back to this plan. Tell me everything," said Alex.

Ryo explained there was no way they could let any ichor samples fall into the hands of the Sons of Enyaluis. However, there was no way they could allow Danyal to be hurt, or risk the terrorists following through on their threat to release a dirty bomb on U.S. soil. He said the only way to ensure a positive outcome was to locate the terrorists first and launch a preemptive strike.

"Preemptive strike?" said Alex.

Ryo replied Galen had identified several mercenaries he worked with in the military who would serve as the strike team. He explained the team would be small, probably five or six members, since they weren't prepared to conduct a large-scale assault on American soil. He said they needed to use stealth and surprise to our advantage; they needed to get in and out with minimal bloodshed. Ryo added each team member had a specialized skill set, with Galen being their sniper, and Ryo serving as the explosives expert.

"What's my role?" asked Alex.

"Even with your remarkable abilities, Alex, I can't put you at risk," said Ryo.

"So, are you prepared to stop me? Think it over; I can remotely view, have super strength, and telekinesis."

"You're getting stronger," said Ryo, "but your control is erratic at best, and things get destroyed when you get upset. I will not risk having you fall in the hands of the enemy."

"If you need my help finding these sons of bitches, then you will have to let me participate," said Alex.

"Not gonna let this go, Ryo. The stubborn is strong with this one," said Galen.

"Thanks for the vote of confidence, Yoda," said Alex.

Hoko added that wherever Alex goes, he would go with him as his mentor to keep Alex focused and on task.

Ryo took a deep breath before saying he'd consider letting Alex monitor things from a distance, but what he needed from Alex right now was to help locate the terrorists. He said the IT staff identified the origin of the video was from within a nine-hour radius of Boston, because of the transition data rate. This was more information than they had to go on yesterday, and it placed the group firmly on the Eastern Seaboard.

"But how can I find them? They stole the vaccination, so I can't track their energy?" asked Alex.

Hoko said he had a theory that if they could narrow the parameters, Alex could focus on dead areas in the electromagnetic field. For example, he asked what Alex saw when he looked at the electromagnetic field around Ryo.

"The area is pitch black," said Alex.

Hoko smiled and asked Alex if he'd come across other areas of black fields in nature. Alex said no and added all organic and inorganic matter had some electromagnetic field that he could see. So, if the enemy grouped together, he could look for the area with the most significant absence of energy. Alex smiled and said it might work, and asked when they could test the theory. Hoko said they could start this afternoon when Alex and Galen had time to rest, recover, and eat a healthy meal. Galen and Alex nodded. Hoko said they'd reconvene at two p.m. in the penthouse.

"Please give me the keys, Galen. I don't like driving the Hummer, but you need more recovery time before driving," said Alex.

Galen walked over to Alex and offered the keys before dropping them by Alex's feet in the snow.

"Oops, mah bad."

"Real mature, asshole," said Alex.

Alex reached down to the ground and scooped up some snow, which he formed into a perfect sphere, before hurling it toward Galen and hitting him in the chest.

"With yur shite aim, surprised ya hit anything," Galen said as he hid behind the side of the Hummer.

Ryo and Hoko stepped out of the warehouse to close the door. "OK, boys," said Ryo, "save it for the enemy."

Galen and Alex looked at each other and nodded before throwing their snowballs at Hoko and Ryo, who casually stepped aside to save being hit. Alex and Galen jumped into the Hummer and quickly made their getaway.

Chapter Twenty-Nine

Alex

Alex and Galen turned toward the elevator, anxiously awaiting Hoko's arrival to start the remote viewing search for Danyal.

Hoko stepped out of the elevator, holding what appeared to be a sizeable rolled-up map. He unrolled the map on the kitchen island and said the map showed states within nine hours of Boston. Since they had the Atlantic Ocean to the east, he added, it helped limit their search to the mid-Atlantic region of New York, Pennsylvania, Maryland, and the northern parts of Vermont and Maine.

"Still heaps of ground to cover," said Galen.

"It is," said Hoko, "but I'm not worried about Alex's range since he connected with David in California."

"But I could only connect with David through the quantum entanglement of our emotional connection," said Alex.

"Correct," said Hoko. "I think the solution to our problem lies with ayahuasca."

Galen looked confused and said, "Gonna get him high? Substances don't work on him."

Hoko said ayahuasca worked differently because it was a psychedelic. He explained that the senses became enhanced, sharpened, or heightened with ayahuasca. Hoko said he'd facilitated vision quests for decades with ayahuasca, with Ditta even participating in some of his research. It affected her for thirty minutes, so he was hoping it would have the same effect on Alex.

"I trust you, Hoko. I'll do it if there's a chance it will help find Danyal. How do we do this?"

Hoko pulled a small thermos from his backpack and said he'd brought everything they needed. He indicated he'd warm the tea while Alex and Galen cleared the living room floor, where they could get comfortable to perform the ritual. Galen and Alex moved the furniture around while Hoko warmed the tea on the stove.

Hoko said he'd start with a cleansing prayer for the ceremony, and they'd drink the tea.

"What's mah role?" asked Galen.

Hoko said, "Given your recent brain injury, Galen, I don't think it would be safe for you to ingest ayahuasca."

"Supposed to just sit here and watch?" said Galen.

"Yes, Alex and I need you to be our anchor. If something goes wrong, I need you to pull us back into the moment."

Hoko instructed it would work best if they sat cross-legged on pillows, and asked Alex to join hands with him. Alex nodded and complied. Hoko asked if Alex was ready, before starting the ritual by singing a traditional song called "Icaros." He proceeded to shake leaf rattles and use tobacco smoke to anoint them, and protect the space for the ritual. Finally, Alex and Hoko drank the tea.

Alex felt lightheaded, as if he was floating. Otherwise, he didn't feel any effect.

"I don't feel anything." Then he opened his eyes and looked down to see his body below him as he hovered over the scene. *What the fuck?*

"It's OK, Alex," said Hoko, as his spirit floated out of his body to meet Alex's.

"What's happening, Hoko?"

"My best guess, Alex, is that between the ayahuasca and your abilities, we're having an out-of-body experience. Amazing, I've never encountered this vivid of an experience in the decades I've worked with ayahuasca."

"So, what do we do now?"

Hoko said he wanted Alex to focus on the electromagnetic energy and look for the dark areas in the energy field in the building. Hoko asked how many energetic voids Alex felt in the PGC building. Alex replied forty-two. Hoko asked him to focus on one of those voids and let the energy take them there. Alex closed his eyes and focused on an energy void on the tenth floor, and they were immediately transported to Bruno's lab, where Bruno stood tearfully looking at the pictures on his wall.

"OK, Alex. Now take us outside of the building."

With the simple thought, Alex and Hoko instantly floated high above the city among the clouds. Hoko directed Alex to focus on any void in the energetic field outside PGC, and specifically to look for clusters in the EMF field since the enemy would likely be grouped together. Alex closed his eyes and sent out a wave of energy like a ripple in a pond. He kept his eyes closed and focused on his breathing until the energy wave bounced back to him.

"Southwest," Alex replied, "there are fifteen voids in the energetic field grouped together."

"Concentrate, Alex, and take us to the clustered voids."

Alex opened his eyes to see the swirling, energetic fields around him and Hoko as they moved instantaneously. Alex looked around for signs of where they had arrived. Alex and Hoko descended to the ground, until they were standing in front of the York County Prison in Pennsylvania, which looked abandoned. He could sense that there were fifteen voids in the energy field on the first floor. As their spirits passed through the door of the building, Alex could see recent signs of activity in the building due to the crates and boxes stacked in the hallways.

"How do we find Danyal? Do we look in every room? When will the ayahuasca wear off?" asked Alex.

Hoko suggested that Alex focus on an item with a strong connection between him and Danyal, given them being in closer proximity.

"Danyal and I wear matching necklaces. He never takes it off."

"Focus on his necklace and take us there, Alex."

Alex opened his eyes to see Danyal sleeping on a dirty mattress on the floor of a locked cell. Alex's spirit moved quickly towards Danyal. He attempted to touch Danyal's face, but there was no response.

"I can't reach him, Hoko. He's right here in front of me, and I can't reach him," said Alex in desperation.

"Focus, Alex; if he's asleep, you may be able to reach him subconsciously."

Alex knelt by Danyal's body. *I love you, Danyal. We're coming to save you.*

As Alex sent his thoughts, Danyal rolled over and softly said, "Alex."

"He heard me, Hoko!"

"I think he did, Alex. We need to go. I've no idea how time works in this state..."

Chapter Thirty

Alex

Alex frantically yelled for Hoko and Galen to help him as he helplessly watched the scene unfolding on the living room floor. Fuck, he couldn't return to his body. Would he be stuck in his astral form without Hoko to guide him back?

"What happened, Galen?" asked Hoko, as he opened his eyes.

"Not sure," said Galen. "Alex's body violently went into a seizure and broke yur physical contact. Turned him to the recovery position on his side. Still not responding."

"How long were we gone?" asked Hoko.

"Two hours. Was afraid to break the connection."

"Two hours? Alex's abilities are certainly different from Ditta. We shouldn't have been gone so long."

Galen and Hoko reached to secure Alex's head and body as he started having another seizure.

"How's this happening, Hoko? He's invulnerable."

Hoko replied this was a spiritual crisis, and he had no idea how it would affect Alex. He told Galen they had found Danyal and suspected Alex didn't want to return to his body. Hoko said they must bring Alex back, or there could be permanent damage.

Galen knelt next to Alex's body and shook him by the shoulders. "Alex, ya have to come back! Please come back! Can't do this unless ya return. Ya can't abandon us!" yelled Galen with tears pricking his eyes, cradling Alex's head to his chest. With that, the seizures stopped.

"I knew you missed me," said Alex softly.

"Thank heavens," said Hoko.

"Not that I mind waking up in a man's muscular arms, Galen, but could you loosen your grasp so I can breathe?"

"Fuck ya, arsehole!" yelled Galen as he pushed Alex away. "Ya nearly died!" he exclaimed as he stood and stormed down the hallway, slamming his bedroom door behind him.

"I'm sorry to have worried you and Galen, but I couldn't find my way back into my body. I saw and heard everything happening floating above the room, but couldn't do anything to reenter my body."

"So, what changed?" asked Hoko.

"I don't know. When Galen was holding me, I was suddenly drawn back."

"Did you learn any other vital information?" asked Hoko.

"Yes, I did. The Sons of Enyaluis aren't bluffing. They have a bomb prepared to detonate in Harrisburg, PA. We have to act now!"

"I'll reach out to Ryo, and we need to formulate a plan."

"I'll go with you," said Alex.

"No, Alex. You need to rest. You've just been through several seizures. I'll ask Dr. Donalds to come to check on you."

"I'm fine."

"We'll see. Do you know who's not fine, Alex? Galen. He really panicked when you didn't immediately return. You two have been through some traumatic events together and have developed an intense bond. Don't underestimate his suffering; remember what it was like for you to see him lying unresponsive in a hospital bed."

Alex vividly remembered that helpless feeling and said he would talk to Galen as Hoko got up to walk toward the elevator. He took a deep breath before walking down the hall and gently knocking on Galen's bedroom door three times.

"Can we talk, Galen?"

"Bugger off!"

"Fine, I'll say what I have to say through the door...I'm sorry for being flippant about scaring you. I'm scared shitless, and I don't want to go through this ordeal without you. Sherlock needs to have Watson to succeed, so please forgive me. I'm doing my best in a horrible situation."

"Yu're still an arsehole," said Galen as he opened the door to look at Alex.

"Yes, I am, and it's not one of my endearing qualities."

"No, it's not," said Galen as he took his right hand and grabbed Alex by his shirt to pull him closer, looking directly into his eyes. "Scare me like that again, and ya don't have to worry about the enemy kicking yur arse. Will do it personally."

Alex placed his right hand on Galen's, grasping his shirt. "I'll do my best, Galen. But if you haven't noticed, I can be a little reckless. That's why I need you to keep me inside the guardrails."

"Don't get paid enough," said Galen as he gently pushed Alex back out of the doorway. "Sit yur arse down on the couch until the doc can check ya out. Ya need fluids. Once yu're hydrated, ya better tell me everything ya observed down to the last detail."

"Yes, sir. Dr. Donalds is on her way. I also need to thank you, Galen."

"Eh, for what?"

"I don't know if I would have found my way back into my body without you. You were the anchor pulling me back. Without you, I don't know what would have happened. Thank you for caring," said Alex as he leaned forward to hug Galen.

"Not much would happen," Galen whispered into Alex's ear, "only the world falling into chaos and destruction."

"Thanks for reminding me; no pressure," said Alex as he held Galen tighter.

Chapter Thirty-One

Alex

"**F**inish your meal, gentlemen, and start packing," said Ryo, stepping out of the elevator. "We're leaving in an hour. You must pack light and not bring any PGC electronics or credit cards that could leave an electronic trail. We're going off-grid. Meet Hoko at the exit to the private elevator at the back loading dock at six p.m. The cameras in the area will be off to allow us to slip out under the cover of night."

Alex and Galen hurried down the hall with their marching orders. Upon rounding the corner, Alex turned to Galen. "OK, I've never been off-grid. What the hell does it even mean? I've no idea what to pack," said Alex.

Galen said it meant they would rough it and avoid contact with other people. Pack light, primarily t-shirts, jeans, and a good winter jacket, and nothing flashy or that you don't want to ruin. Don't forget the toiletries, Galen cautioned; they had no idea what conditions they would be living in, and to pack for at least seven days.

"No Gucci boots?" said Alex.

Galen gave him a disapproving scowl.

"Tough crowd tonight. What was your longest period off-grid in the military?"

"Two separate year-long tours in the Afghan desert. Get yur arse in gear, Alex," Galen said as he entered his room.

Alex and Galen met Hoko and Ryo at the loading dock at PGC, where Ryo said they were early and told them to load their gear in the back of the Grand Wagoneer. He suggested they sleep if they could, since they had a six-hour drive ahead of them. Ryo turned from the driver's seat to look at Alex and Galen. He said from here on out; they were operating on military rules of engagement, which meant following his orders without hesitation and with no questions asked. Ryo smiled and said his first order was not to make him stop the Jeep, or they would regret it. Galen and Alex nodded in forced compliance. Although Alex recognized Ryo's attempt at humor, he knew Ryo was deadly serious.

Two hours into the drive, Alex leaned over and nudged Galen with his elbow. Galen opened his eyes and slowly turned his head to glare at Alex.

"Aye?"

Alex motioned for Galen to take off his ring. Galen raised an eyebrow and looked at Alex, questioning. Alex again gestured for Galen to take off his ring, and Galen reluctantly complied. Alex reached over with the ring finger on his right hand and tapped Galen on the forehead.

Galen, can you hear me?

"Aye, Alex?"

Alex raised one finger to his lips and shook his head no.

Please don't say it, Galen. Think it.

Galen nodded. *Are ya showboating telepathy now?*

Maybe I wanted to test a theory and have a private conversation.

Yur theory works. What conversation is so private that Hoko and Ryo can't hear it?

I'm scared, Galen. I can't get the image of Danyal lying on that dirty mattress, suffering, out of my head.

Show me, Alex. Show me the scene.

Alex closed his eyes and sent the mental image to Galen, whose face turned pale.

Sorry ya had to see that, mate. It's cruel. Keep an image of Danyal in yur mind of what it will feel like when he returns.

Alex briefly imagined him and Danyal lying in bed naked, embracing before this whole ordeal started.

Galen took his hand and covered his face.

Didn't mean to start thinking about it now, arsehole. Give a bloke a warning next time!

Alex quietly chuckled.

I think I established that my memory is pornographic.

Galen sharply punched Alex on the shoulder.

Try to sleep, Alex. Got four hours left.

Galen, one last thing.

Eh, Alex?

Stop talking so much about my ass and giving it orders. You're giving me a complex. I've worked hard on my glutes.

Galen rolled his eyes and sucked his teeth as he put the ring back on and turned away, resting his head upon the pillow he'd made with his jacket against the window.

A sharp poke to his ribs awakened Alex.

"Wake up, sleeping, beaut. Have arrived," said Galen.

Alex wiped the sleep from his eyes and looked at his watch. One a.m. was late for a meeting, but Alex was ready to make a plan to save Danyal.

"Where are we, Ryo?" asked Alex.

Ryo said they were at a construction site in Manchester, PA, retrofitting a high school outside town, far enough from York to not draw attention. He told Alex PGC had paid the construction company to stop work for the week so they could come and go as they needed. Ryo added it had plenty of space and amenities for their needs, and locals would think they were part of the construction crew. He told the group to grab their stuff and meet in the cafeteria in ten minutes for a sitrep with the rest of the strike team.

Alex and Galen walked into the cafeteria to see Hoko and Ryo greeting three other strike team members. The only woman in the bunch, dressed in camo pants and an army green t-shirt, ran over to Galen and jumped towards him, where he caught her in a warm embrace. Alex could see she was beautiful, with long dark hair pulled back into a ponytail, a lean, muscular body, and perfect cheekbones. By any beauty standards, she was striking, and Alex could see the spark in her chest pulse when she hugged Galen.

Before Alex could introduce himself, a bald man with a long brown beard walked toward Galen and put him in a bear hug. He was a couple inches shorter than Galen but as broad and muscular, with multicolored tattoos completely covering his bulging arms that now wrapped around Galen. The third man didn't approach but observed from a distance. He was slender but muscular, with dark black hair and thick five o'clock shadow, highlighting his dark eyes and handsome face.

"Listen up, soldiers, let's get this meeting going. You might as well start with a quick introduction and your specialties. I'll start. Yuzuru Ryo, Navy SEAL, breach specialist, and head of security at PGC. Let's go around the room to the right."

"Andrea Cane," said the tall, attractive woman standing next to Galen. "Canadian Special Forces, and hand-to-hand combat."

"Galen Tucker, New Zealand Special Forces, sniper, and tactical planning."

"Michael Christie," said the bald, bearded man standing on the other side of Galen, "Canadian Special Forces, sniper, and all-around badass."

Galen rolled his eyes. "Second-best sniper."

"Zoltan Ivonav, Russian Special Forces, and I'm the 'bomb whisperer.'"

"Hoko Mahomet, shaman, and I'll be helping with the logistical coordination of this operation."

"Alex Lieth, college professor, and I guess I'm your backup."

"You're going to make sure our papers are graded on time, Pretty Boy?" laughed Michael.

"Stop being an arse," said Galen, "ya haven't changed."

"Go ahead and tell them your abilities, Alex. We need to be honest and on the same page," said Ryo.

"My abilities are super strength, invulnerability, telekinesis, remote viewing, and energy manipulation. Oh, and limited teleportation...when it's working."

Michael let out a deep belly laugh. "I can see Pretty Boy left out stand-up comedian from his list. He's our mascot."

"Shut up, Michael," said Galen. "Can smite ya where ya stand. Don't mock him."

"It's OK, Galen. I can defend myself. Which ability would you like to see, Mr. Christie?"

"Dealer's choice, Pretty Boy."

Alex looked around the room at a four-person cafeteria table sitting to the right. With the motion of his hand, he telekinetically lifted the table off the floor and began slowly spinning it before it crashed to the floor after ten seconds. The pounding headache was well worth the look on Michael's face. He turned to see the other stunned faces in the room, but Hoko, Ryo, and especially Galen, all wore gigantic smiles.

"Enough show and tell," said Hoko as he placed his hand on Alex's shoulder, "you need to save your strength."

Alex nodded.

Ryo told the group to gather around as he unrolled blueprints onto the cafeteria table. He explained these were the blueprints for the abandoned York County Prison. Based on intel gathered by Alex and Hoko, he outlined there were fourteen hostiles from the terrorist group, the Sons of Enyaluis, and one hostage.

"Where's Danyal being held, Alex?" said Ryo.

"He's being held in a cell here, the third from the left on the first floor," said Alex.

Ryo marked the position on the plans before outlining what would happen––in order to reach Danyal and get out as fast as possible. The plan was to breach the southern wall closest to Danyal's cell. Ryo placed a second X on the map before telling the group they needed the element of surprise for this operation to be effective. He indicated it was best to breach the building at night while most of the group slept. Alex and Hoko would be at a safe distance in the cargo van, while Alex used his abilities to put a noise-dead zone around the building so the enemy couldn't hear, giving them an element of surprise.

"Who are these Sons of Enyaluis? I've never heard of them," inquired Zoltan.

Ryo replied that they were a rogue terrorist group that, until recently, hadn't made much impact. However, they'd now jumped to the major leagues and represented a high-level threat.

"What do they want?" asked Andrea.

Ryo said they wanted a powerful substance that couldn't fall into their hands. He went on to suggest that the substance was so dangerous, the potential impact it could have on the world didn't bear thinking about.

"Better yet," said Michael, "who's this hostage we're risking our lives for?"

"His name is Danyal Sarif," said Alex. "He's my boyfriend, and they're holding him hostage because they think I have access to the substance they're demanding."

"Since this is personal for Pretty Boy, should he be near this operation?" asked Michael.

Ryo said they wouldn't have any information about the situation without Alex. He admitted it was highly unusual, but Alex's abilities brought too much to the table to be ignored. Ryo turned to Galen and said that, given his recent injury, he wouldn't be going out in the field.

"Ryo, come on," Galen protested.

"The PGC staff hasn't medically cleared you," said Ryo.

"Where do I fit into this plan?" asked Zoltan.

Ryo said he needed Zoltan to be in Harrisburg, PA, to defuse a dirty bomb the Sons of Enyaluis planned to detonate. He cautioned that Alex had identified the location, and the loss of life could be catastrophic if the bomb exploded Ryo indicated projections for the fallout distribution based on wind pattern forecast models suggested the radioactive material could hit urban centers, including Harrisburg,

Washington, Baltimore and Philadelphia. He stated millions of lives could be at risk. Ryo said they needed to be smart and not rush or make mistakes. He outlined they would take shifts conducting surveillance for the next twenty-four hours, wrapping up the briefing by saying they would review the plans again tomorrow and, all being well, would launch the offensive at three a.m. on Tuesday morning--a little over twenty-five hours from now.

"Hit the sack," said Ryo, "you'll need all the rest you can get to operate at optimal capacity."

Fuck, this shit's getting real!

Alex didn't know if he could go back to sleep with all the adrenaline coursing through his veins.

Chapter Thirty-Two

Alex

Alex could hear a loud commotion down the hall, which had awakened him. He looked down at his watch. *Five a.m.? What the hell is going on?* He dressed quickly and walked down the hallway toward the other strike team members' rooms. Turning the corner, he was shocked at the sight of Galen standing over Hoko's body.

Alex yelled, "Step back! No one approach Hoko or touches him until I've determined the scene is safe!"

He quickly scanned the surroundings to assess the situation as Galen stood and stepped back from Hoko. Alex could see Hoko was unconscious, lying on his side. He concluded there was no danger in the immediate area, such as standing water or risk of electrical shock. He knelt by Hoko and rolled him onto his back, where he could see his breathing was shallow. Alex could sense Hoko's heartbeat was feeble. He pulled up Hoko's eyelids with his fingers to see his pinpoint pupils. The skin on his face was cold and turning a shade of pale blue. Alex knew what these signs meant; this was a drug overdose!

Alex calmly instructed Galen to get the medical kit and ensure it contained Narcan and an Automated External Defibrillator. He knew with a drug overdose, every minute was precious. Alex yelled instructions to Andrea to call 911 immediately. Galen ran to get the medical supplies and returned, kneeling by Alex.

Alex told Galen to stand back and that even brief contact with a substance like Fentanyl could be deadly. Galen took several steps back to give Alex room to work as the other team members arrived to see the commotion. Alex removed the Narcan nasal spray from the package and put his hand under Hoko's neck to raise it. He sprayed once in the right nostril and waited for a response, but nothing happened. Alex repeated the process in the other nostril.

Please, please respond, Hoko. Damn it, please, I need you.

Galen prepared the AED as Alex opened Hoko's shirt and placed the pads on Hoko's chest. Galen plugged the wire into the pads and turned the machine on by pushing the red button.

AED powering on, please place the pads on the chest...please step back...assessing heart rhythm...abnormal rhythm detected...shocked advised, declared the AED.

"Everyone, stand back!" Alex said, standing and stepping back. Galen pressed the red button.

Administering shock...shock administered...assessing heart rhythm...abnormal rhythm detected...shock advised.

Galen pressed the button again, and everyone stood back.

Shock administered...assessing heart rhythm...no heartbeat detected...immediately start CPR and rescue breathing.

Alex knelt over Hoko's chest and began making chest compressions. His muscles ached, but he couldn't stop; no one else could safely touch Hoko's body. *Damn it, Hoko! Keep fighting; I can't lose you!*

Galen pleaded with Alex to let him help, but Alex shook his head. He couldn't risk exposing Galen. Alex didn't stop even when he heard Galen yelling the ambulance had arrived.

"What do we have?" said the first of three EMTs arriving on the scene. Galen said it was a suspected opiate overdose. He relayed two rounds of Narcan were administered, and the AED administered two shocks before CPR was started. Galen also told them Alex had been performing CPR for around thirty minutes. The EMT asked how Alex wasn't exhausted and expressed concern about him not wearing gloves or using a face shield. Galen explained that everything had happened so fast. The lead EMT asked Galen to have Alex step back so they could reassess the situation.

But Alex didn't stop.

"Please, Alex, let the EMTs do their job," pleaded Galen.

Alex reluctantly stepped back from Hoko's body to let the EMTs do their work. He watched silently, running his hands through his hair. He had no time to panic since he'd jumped into action, but now he could feel the growing anxiety in his chest.

The third EMT asked if Alex was OK. Alex, visibly shaking, nodded. The EMT asked Alex to accompany him while they moved Hoko to the ambulance. Alex stared blankly into the distance as the EMT decontaminated his hands and face. The EMT commented Galen needed to watch Alex to monitor if he exhibited any additional symptoms of shock. Galen nodded and sat with Alex while the EMTs loaded Hoko in the ambulance.

As the ambulance with Hoko and Ryo prepared to pull away, the lead EMT asked Alex how he knew how to respond so quickly. Alex weakly replied he was a college professor and trained yearly in CPR and responding to opiate overdoses. As he closed the ambulance doors, the EMT said Alex was a lifesaver and told him he needed to shower immediately to prevent any potential cross-contamination.

Chapter Thirty-Three

Alex

How the fuck did this happen?

Alex stood in the communal shower room with hot water running over his head, face, and body. He played the scene back in his mind, using his abilities to touch Hoko's mind. The cinnamon tea...someone must have poisoned his tea. *Did it happen here or before we left PGC?* Alex's train of thought was disrupted by Galen, who knocked on the shower room door.

"OK to come in, mate?"

"Yes," he said as he turned off the shower and quickly wrapped his towel around his waist.

Galen stepped into the locker room, only wearing black boxer briefs with a toiletry bag in his hand and a towel draped over the other arm.

"Sorry if I interrupted yur moment of peace. Wanted to check on ya," Galen said as he sat across from Alex's bench. "Worried about ya...ya were starting to show symptoms of shock."

"I'm fine."

"Alex, it's me. Ya don't have to put up a strong front. Know ya was shaken. You can't hide the fear in yur eyes. Alex, look at me."

Alex raised his head to look at Galen, who had his towel draped over his shoulder. At any other time, the sight of Galen nearly naked would cause Alex to avert his gaze, but he was too exhausted in his current state to look away, so he sat there shaking his head from side to side.

"Know that look, mate. Ya know what happened. What did ya see?"

"I know you found him."

"Aye, and?"

Alex said he played Hoko's memories back. He'd gotten out of bed to start his morning routine, beginning with the cinnamon tea he loved. Alex looked up, making eye contact with Galen before saying the opiate was in the tea. Someone here, or at PGC, accessed Hoko's property and tried to kill him. Due to Hoko's condition, Alex couldn't take the memory back to the point he needed to see.

"Why would anyone harm Hoko? He's the gentlest soul I know..."

"'Cause they wanted to stop ya, Alex. Everyone at PGC knows ya are stronger, with Hoko guiding ya. Hurts ya and yur control of yur abilities without him."

"These motherfuckers will pay dearly for kidnapping Danyal and hurting Hoko."

"Can't let this change the plans. Still need to attack while we got the advantage of surprise," said Galen.

"Agreed. I'll check with Ryo for an update on Hoko's condition and let Diana know so she can be there for him."

"Can ya trust her?" asked Galen.

"Yes, she loves Hoko and would never hurt him."

"Secret office romance?"

"No...Well, Diana has never been brave enough to act on it, but maybe now she will. If Hoko makes it."

"*When* Hoko makes it," said Galen.

Alex nodded and said he was going to get dressed and call Ryo and Diana. He asked if Galen wanted to train because he needed to blow off some steam.

"I'm game. Ya been working out more lately? Yur muscles are swole."

Alex shook his head and blushed as Galen had made him feel awkward in the shower room. He stood, holding his towel around his waist as he walked toward the door. Alex heard the shower turn on behind him, and looked over briefly at the mirror over the sink to his right to see the reflection of Galen standing naked under the shower, washing his hair. *Goddamn it, Alex, why did you look? Fuck.* He'd never forget that image. Danyal was holding on for dear life, and here he was scoping out Galen in the showers. *Dirtbag.*

Alex looked away quickly and closed the locker room door as fast as he could, hoping Galen was unaware of his stolen glance.

Alex and Galen walked into the auditorium, where Andrea was cleaning her weapons, and Michael was at the other end of the gym, shirtless, playing basketball.

"Hell of a way to start the morning, amigos," said Andrea. "Any word on Hoko?"

"Ryo says he's in ICU in critical condition," said Alex.

"I'm sorry. I hope he pulls through. Only talked with him briefly, but he's a fascinating man," said Andrea.

"He's an exceptional person," said Alex. "I owe him a lot."

"What're you two looking so determined for?" asked Andrea.

"I need to practice my abilities to be strong for the fight ahead," said Alex.

"I'd love to see more of your abilities in action," said Andrea. "But first, do you remember how to clean a weapon, Galen, or do you need a remedial course?"

Galen laughed. "Always beat yur arse on weapon inspections."

"Do you know how to fire a weapon, Alex?" asked Andrea.

"No, I don't like guns."

"Pity," said Andrea. "Galen could teach you how to do a T-stance and the cute little ass wiggle he does."

"Watch it, Andrea," said Galen. "Anyway, don't play for yur team."

"I don't care which team he plays for, Galen. I can recognize a hot ass when I see one. Can you?"

Galen sneered at Andrea and said, "Ya missed a spot."

"You know I didn't," said Andrea, looking at the handgun barrel from several angles.

"Made ya look!" laughed Galen.

"How'd you gain these remarkable abilities, Alex?" asked Andrea.

Alex said he guessed he owed it all to his surrogate mother, Aphrodite, but the process of how was too convoluted to explain right now.

"The goddess of love? Can you make Galen love me again?" asked Andrea as she tried to give Galen a sultry look with her eyes.

Alex could see Galen was upset by her comment as his face turned red, and he kicked a piece of wood up against the wall. Alex replied, probably not, since he couldn't make people genuinely fall in love unless it was fated for them to do so. He added he could give Galen a mental push toward her bed, though.

Galen punched Alex hard on the shoulder. "Mah bed is fine as it is. Send her to Michael."

Michael, in response, started to flex his arms and make muscle-man poses, showing off his upper torso covered in brightly colored tattoos.

"Gross," exclaimed Andrea as she made fake retching movements. "I'd rather eat broken glass every meal for the rest of my life than touch that vile piece of meat."

Michael scowled at her response. "Ask anyone who's had a piece of this prime beef. They always come back for more. Right, Galen?"

Galen said, "Shut up, Michael. Don't pull me into yur shite."

"Put your money where your mouth is, or have you gone soft? Bring it on, a game of one-on-one basketball. High stakes!"

"Never turn down an opportunity to humiliate ya," said Galen as he ran across the basketball court, pulling off his t-shirt.

"Those two seem to be highly competitive," commented Alex.

"That's one word for it. They're always chirping at each other about something," said Andrea. "So, 'Love God,' do you have any hand-to-hand combat skills?"

"Only Greco-Roman wrestling," said Alex. "I won medals all four years in high school."

"I see some mats in the corner. Show me what you got."

Alex smiled as he helped Andrea pull out the mats and set them up. Andrea said they'd do two three-minute rounds, and she'd even teach Alex some rules about hand-to-hand combat. Alex and Andrea each went to their respective corners, as Galen and Michael stopped their basketball game to be spectators, walking closer to watch the wrestling match.

"Rule number one, Alex, size does not matter. Proper leverage and technique are more important," Andrea said before lunging toward Alex as he forcefully pushed her away with his forearm.

"Rule number one of wrestling, Andrea, never underestimate your opponent."

Alex moved towards Andrea as they locked arms to tussle. Andrea made her sudden movement while flipping Alex to the floor, where he landed on his back, and she straddled him.

"This feels nice," she said as she winked at Alex.

"This won't," said Alex as he shifted his weight, kicking Andrea to the side, where he surprised her with an armlock.

"Ouch! That hurts," yelled Andrea.

"Don't hurt her, Pretty Boy," warned Michael as he fired the basketball in his hands at the back of Alex's head.

Alex turned toward Michael, and with a wave of his hand, sent the basketball hurling back at Michael, hitting him in the face.

"You bastard, I'm going to wreck your pretty face!" Michael yelled, blood pouring from his nose and onto his tattooed chest.

Alex released his grip on Andrea as he turned to face the charging Michael and levitated him off the ground.

As Andrea completed a perfect leg sweep, Alex and Michael hit the ground in a thunderous crash. "Rule number two of engagement: don't turn your back on a threat. Now put your dicks back in your pants, boys. It's all fun and games until you make it about who's the biggest cock. The pissing contest is over. Save it for the fucking enemy. Galen, get the medical kit and clean Michael up in the washroom. Alex, you're not done. Get a mop and clean up this bloody mess you made."

Alex sulkily headed to the supply room while Galen took Michael to get first aid. Once Alex returned with a mop and bucket, he could see Andrea was still upset by her scowl.

"So, should I apologize to him?" said Alex.

"No, meathead needs plenty of time to cool off before he can use words. You'll have to keep it to short syllables," said Andrea.

Alex chuckled. "For the record, it was an accident. I'm still getting a handle on my abilities, and when I'm angry, I might lose control."

"I believe you, Alex. Hell, I don't see how a broken nose could make him any uglier, and he always starts a kerfuffle. It will sting a little more with it happening in front of Galen, because he was trying to show off."

"He's not ugly; he's hot if you're into inked, rough-around-edges bikers who might choke you out in the bedroom."

Andrea gagged. "Fuck you for putting *that* image in my head."

Alex laughed so hard he fell off his chair. "So, I take it you were all close once upon a time?"

"We were remarkably close. Combat does that to you."

"Galen doesn't talk much about his previous life."

"We all have reasons for entering the military, but his was barbaric."

"I understand. Galen told me about the events with Amara."

"Well, you two must be close if you know his secret. Galen is a very private man."

"I'm going to go get some lunch and try to meditate. Do you need anything?" asked Alex.

"No thanks––rest if you can. A midnight operation takes it out of you."

Chapter Thirty-Four

Galen

Galen sat alone in the dark, enjoying the campfire. So much had happened in his life of late, and he'd hardly had time to catch his breath since leaving the hospital. Maybe it was his brush with death, but he needed to get his priorities in order. Then there was Alex; he was never far from Galen's thoughts. Alex was focused and tenacious in his struggle to get Danyal back. Galen admired Alex's devotion and wished someone would feel that way about him. Galen dared not dream it could be Alex. OK, maybe in his dreams.

Galen was so deep in thought he didn't hear Andrea sneak up behind him.

"Gotcha!" she yelled, grabbing him around his neck.

"Real mature," said Galen as he jumped. "Ya know, sitting alone means stay away."

"Thought you needed the company. From the look on your face, the demons were winning the battle."

"Ya can stay if ya sit in silence," he said.

Andrea nodded and sat next to Galen, leaning her head on his shoulder and wrapping his blanket around her.

After a few moments of silence, she said, "Are we going to talk about you and Love God, Galen?"

"That's not silence."

"It needs to be said."

"Nothin' to say," said Galen.

Andrea locked eyes with him. "You can't lie to me, Galen. I see the way you look at him. You get a spark in your eye when he's around. You used to look at me that way once."

"Making me regret it. Leave the past dead and buried."

"We had fun until we didn't. You ran away; it's your way of coping. Maybe you've found someone that will make you want to stay."

"Didn't run far enough if yu're still beside me."

"You know, Michael and Alex were strutting around like rams in the heat for you."

"All in yur head," said Galen.

"No, it's not. You shared your past with Alex. How many people know about your life?"

"Ya and Michael."

"You've fucked both of us. Is..."

"Don't let those words come out yur mouth. Might throw ya in the fire."

"No, you won't. You don't want to talk about Alex. If things go bad tomorrow, you might get a chance..."

Galen shoved Andrea off the side of the bench with his arm. "That's a terrible thing to say. Why would ya even think that?"

"Jesus Murphy," said Andrea as she picked herself up off the ground. "I'm joking. You're unlucky in love, and I'd like to see you happy."

"I'm happy."

"No, you're not. How stable are Alex and Danyal?"

"Solid."

"Even solid stone can break, Galen. Life is about taking risks. You color too much inside the lines. Live a little." Andrea looked up at the gymnasium, where Alex walked toward the campfire.

"Speaking of Cupid...," said Andrea.

Galen smiled. "Not Cupid, the Unicorn."

"Great, a horny stallion. I'll leave you with your unicorn," said Andrea as she kissed Galen on his forehead. "Anyone want some pizza?" she said as she started to walk away. "If I have to lie in my cold bed alone, I can at least ensure I have a full stomach."

"I'm chocka," said Galen as she walked away.

"No, thanks," replied Alex, "I'm watching my carbs." Once Andrea was out of earshot, Alex said, "She's a badass, Galen. Where have you been hiding her? She scares me a little. I don't want to be on her shit list."

Galen laughed, "Don't let her hear ya. Would only feed her ego."

"She cares about you...and from where I'm sitting, she'd like to care for you again."

"Ya using yur god mojo, mate?"

"No, I'm respecting her privacy. I'm using my eyes for this deduction."

"Yu're talking about ancient history. Don't dredge it up."

"Understood. Speaking of ego, how's Michael's nose?"

"He'll live," said Galen.

"Should I offer to try to heal it?"

Galen shook his head no. "He's too proud. Let him wear his badge of honor. He's not a bad bloke once ya get to know him."

"I'll take your word for that. I've dealt with plenty of guys like him at the gym. Give me one decent quality Michael has, and I'll drop the subject."

Galen took a deep breath. *Should I say it? What if it changes things? Already fucked things up too much. Take a risk for once. Tell him.*

"He's...he's...he's a passionate kisser." Galen sat back from the fire and tilted his head to gauge Alex's reaction better.

Alex's eyes grew wide. "Did you just come out to me, Galen? Are you bisexual?"

"Don't like labels, mate. Sayin, in the past, was involved with Andrea and Michael in the military."

"OK, I have to ask," said Alex, "were you involved with them simultaneously or at separate times?"

Galen rolled his eyes and shook his head. "At different times, ya pervert."

"How did it end?"

"Both helped fill an emotional void at a dark time in mah life. Andrea doesn't like to share her playthings. Michael can get intense. When mah sentence in the military ended, left and didn't look back."

"So, this is the first time since you've seen them since?"

"Aye."

"Are you OK? You've seen me with my ex. We can't even be in the same ZIP code."

"Won't lie. Opening heaps of old wounds."

"So why would you reach out to them for this operation?"

"Cause we needed a team we could trust. When the shite hits the fan, they're the people ya want beside ya in combat."

Galen raised his head to look at Alex directly seated across the fire. Galen wondered what Alex was thinking. Would things be the same between them?

"Not everyone is ya, Alex. Proud and don't give a fuck about what the world thinks. Ya live yur truth. Deeply admire that bout ya. What ya have with Danyal is a gift. Ya will do anything to protect it."

Leaning forward, Alex asked, "Is it OK if I move closer, Galen, to better support you?"

Galen nodded yes and offered a part of his blanket to put around Alex's shoulders as he sat on the wooden bench. He leaned over and placed his head on Alex's shoulder. The two men sat in silence, taking in the moment. Galen appreciated the company and could feel the heat from Alex's body despite the roaring flames.

"Everyone's path is different, Galen. Would you be willing to share your path with me?"

Galen said he'd always known he was different from an early age. When he played chase or kissing games in primary school, he wanted to chase both the boys and the gals. He knew to keep his feelings inside, because his father was a rural minister. Galen added he had a long and painful relationship with religion. He said he had girlfriends in high school, but didn't have sex with a bloke until he was on the national rugby team. They both were so deep in the closet, and so scared. Relationship ended upon his being forced into the military. Galen indicated he never got to say goodbye to Bernard, and heard he left the team a couple of years later, and was now married to a woman and had two kids.

"The military's pretty homophobic. Suppressed that side and eventually got involved with Andrea. But couldn't suppress mah attraction to blokes, so got involved with Michael. Cared for them both, but needed a fresh start and so came to the States to work at PGC."

"This puts our whole conversation about discrimination and homophobia after going to the police station in a completely different light. Have you dated anyone in the States?"

"Hooked up with Zoe. She wants more, but try to avoid office romances."

Alex nodded. "So now I understand why you got so mad when I commented on Zoe liking you."

"Zoe's a great gal. Fishing off the company pier never works out."

"So, how was it when we went to the club?"

"Like a pig in shit, finally letting loose. Shae is a great bloke. Envy yur friendship. Haven't made any gay mates in mah life."

"Hello, there's one sitting beside you!"

"Present company excluded."

"Shae would be delighted to be your friend. He calls you his future ex-husband."

"Tell him ya already put a ring on it," Galen said, waving his hand around.

Alex smiled and said that would kill Shae. Alex thanked Galen for trusting him enough to share his story with him and said he felt honored and would not share his sexuality with anyone. It was Galen's story, and he was in control of it. Alex added he had been the university's staff advisor at the LGBTQI+ group for a couple of years and always advised the students to refrain from saying or doing anything they were uncomfortable with. He said he'd always support Galen, but he did have one last question.

"Are you more attracted to the gender or the person?"

"Fall more for the person. The plumbing doesn't matter."

Alex giggled and said he'd never heard it put that way, and that he was stealing the line. He added that a couple of students in his group identified the same way; the new terminology was "pansexual."

"Sounds like something outta *Peter Pan*. Students are lucky to have ya."

Alex smiled. "I have to say this for my conscience; I hope I haven't said or done anything, which made you feel uncomfortable."

"Fun to watch ya squirm when ya embarrass yurself."

"I do stick my foot in my mouth a lot. I think it may be another divine gift bestowed on me." Alex took a deep breath and looked Galen directly in the eyes. "Is it OK if I hug you? I feel you need one."

Galen nodded yes, tears glistening in his eyes. Alex and Galen hugged as the fire raged beside them.

Alex whispered gently to Galen, "You're a beautiful soul, Galen Tucker, inside and out. Any person would be blessed to love you. If they give you any shit, send them my way, and I'll turn them into a toad." He gave Galen a gentle kiss on the forehead.

Galen sat, wiping the tears from his eyes. "What's with this asking consent for a hug and already treating me differently?"

"I'm just trying to respect your boundaries in a highly emotional moment."

"Like when ya stole a glance in the shower?"

"I'm deeply sorry, Galen. That was not my intention. I was shocked by the reflection."

"So yu're sayin' I'm ugly. Cheers, mate."

"Never!"

"No worries, Alex. Not afraid for people to see my body. Guess I learned it from rugby."

"I guess it's part of the 6'4 rugby god persona," said Alex.

Galen laughed. "Caught a glimpse of ya first. Yu're not as fast on the draw as ya think. When ya put yur towel around yur waist in the shower, ya flashed yur arse. It was a full moon last night."

"You cheeky bastard."

"Nope. They were yur cheeks, and Andrea is right."

"Right about what?"

"Do recognize a nice arse when I see it."

"OK, Galen. I'm walking away to get another slice of pizza, and I'm dialing HR as I do so," said Alex, rolling his eyes.

"Don't have any cell phones, Alex."

"Screw you, Galen. I'll write a memo on the pizza box. Enjoy your fire."

"Will be in shortly. Don't let Andrea eat all the pizza. And don't spell mah name wrong in yur memo to HR."

Chapter Thirty-Five

Alex noticed the look in the eyes of the team members, a look he'd never seen before, and the seriousness of the faces scared him. He recognized the look of anxiety and the color of fear he detected in the aura of the strike team as they dressed in their gear to prepare to launch their assault on the enemy stronghold.

"Ya right, Alex?" asked Galen.

"I'm quietly praying we can save Danyal and that the entire team makes it back safe."

"They're trained soldiers, Alex. Trust 'em."

Galen was helping Alex put on his gear when Michael came over and pushed Galen aside.

"Go help Andrea with her gear, Galen. Pretty Boy and I need to have a chat."

Alex nodded toward Galen, who reluctantly stepped away.

"Michael, I'm sorry about your nose."

Michael didn't speak as he fixed Alex's tactical vest.

"Got one question, Pretty Boy," said Michael. "Is Galen safe and happy?"

Alex smiled and looked Michael directly in the eyes before responding, "He's working on making a new start and being happy, Michael. I've faith he's on his way."

Michael stood, meeting Alex's gaze. "He's a grown man, but all this god shit is pretty batshit crazy. I can't believe it myself. You better keep him safe, Pretty Boy, or I'll do my best to mess up your square jawline." Michael turned to step away, but Alex grabbed him by the shoulder.

"Come here, you brute," said Alex, raising his hand to Michael's nose. "I don't know my own strength. Let me see what I can do to fix this," he said, placing his hand over Michael's broken nose to heal it with cosmic energy.

"Make me a movie star, Pretty Boy."

"I can only do so much--you're more suited to adult films."

"You flirting with me, Pretty Boy? I would break you while you beg for more."

Alex chuckled, knowing his inappropriate sense of humor was coming out because he was scared. "That's the most handsome you can be today, but I think it's an improvement. At least the swelling is gone."

Michael laughed. "Stay away from the action, Pretty Boy. Grade some papers while we bring your man back."

Alex nodded and smiled. Just then, he noticed Galen had been watching his interaction with Michael with intense interest. Was Galen jealous? Alex had never seen the look on Galen's face as he tried to decipher it.

"Ya ready for this, mate?" said Galen, stepping back to help Alex finish with his gear.

"As ready as I can be," said Alex. "I'll sit on the sidelines and wait."

"Looked like ya and Michael had a civil conversation."

"I took Andrea's advice and used words with short syllables," said Alex, grinning. "Mostly, I apologized for his nose, and he let me heal it a little to reduce the swelling. Really, the conversation centered on you."

"Huh?"

"The strapping ogre wanted to know if you were safe and happy."

"How'd ya respond?"

"I told him you were making a life in the States and thought you were on the path to happiness. He made me promise to protect you, which was odd since it's your job to protect me," said Alex.

"Michael's a kidder. Can't trust anything he says. Lies like a rug," said Galen before he was interrupted by Ryo speaking to the group.

"Listen up, everyone. I have an update on Hoko. He's still in the ICU but stabilizing. Now it's time to put on your game faces and prepare to leave in twenty. To have another soldier on the battlefield, Galen, I'm putting you on the strike team. Alex, you'll be in the surveillance van, parked about half a mile from the scene. Under no circumstances should you get near the engagement, even if things go south. We can't risk you falling into the hands of the enemy—not only would it jeopardize your safety, but destabilize the balance of peace on the planet."

The plan was still the same: they would breach the door at the south side of the building, deploying flashbangs and smoke bombs to disorient the enemy and extract Danyal Sarif.

"Lethal force is authorized, and you'll all be wearing gas masks besides your gear. Wheels up in fifteen!" he yelled.

The group all loaded into the cargo van, with Ryo driving. Michael serenaded the group with his versions of pop songs with filthy lyrics added to cut the tension in the air. Andrea put in her earbuds to drown out his singing.

Alex leaned over to Galen and whispered, "Do you trust me, Galen?"

"Ya know I do, Alex. What do ya want? Ya only ask that question when ya've a wild idea."

"Take off your ring." Galen complied and removed his ring. "I'm going to monitor the situation from here in the van, but I have a favor to ask."

"Spit it out, mate."

"Let me remotely view the situation through your eyes."

"Ya want to ride shotgun in my head?" Galen paused before responding, "I'll do it, mate, but ya have to avoid mah thoughts."

"I promise, scout's honor. It'll be a two-way connection. If you need to reach me, think of my name."

Galen nodded as Ryo said they had arrived and would approach from the tree line after Alex was in position.

"Locked and loaded!" yelled Michael as he jumped out of the van.

Alex put his hand on Galen's shoulder and leaned in close. "Stay safe, Galen, and bring Danyal back to me."

Galen said, "Promise."

Alex drove the van to the spot predetermined by the GPS and turned the van to face the old county jail. His heart raced in his chest as he watched Galen and the team methodically approach the building from the south. Their speed and precision were incredible, as he watched Ryo set the explosives on the outer door. Alex, as instructed by Ryo, had used his abilities to deaden the sound in the immediate area to cover their surprise attack further.

Each team member entered the building in a barrage of flashbangs and smoke bombs, which hindered Galen's vision through his gas mask. The team approached the cell where Danyal was held, and Alex could see him lying helplessly on the mattress as the team set a charge to open the old, barred door to the cell.

Shit, there are motion detectors, Alex!

Alex opened his eyes abruptly as the scene went black in his mind.

What the fuck happened? Galen! Galen, do you hear me? Fuck, what do I do? Think, Alex. Alex reached out to Andrea and Michael with his mind. *Fuck, I can't reach anyone. They must be unconscious. What would Hoko do?*

With shaking hands, Alex started the van and floored the gas, speeding toward the jail. He stopped about three hundred yards away as he exited the van and crept close to the ground as he approached the building. Alex sent out an energy wave with his mind to count the voids in the energetic field. Alex detected sixteen gaps in the energy. Fourteen combatants, plus Danyal and Ryo. Alex jumped as he viewed an image from Galen's eyes of their captors kicking Ryo in the stomach.

I need to know what's happening.

With a thought, Alex released the sound barrier.

"Where the fuck is Alex Lieth and the ichor samples?" demanded the hooded terrorist, pointing an AR-15 at Galen's head.

"Protected back at PGC. Where ya will never reach him," yelled Galen.

The soldier responded by hitting Galen in the chest with the butt of his rifle. Galen slumped over in pain from the blow.

"You're dead, motherfucker!" yelled Michael.

"So brave when you have a M16 to your head, asshole. Maybe if I kill one of your partners, you'll talk. I'll start with the lady. It's such a waste; she's pretty. Maybe we can save her for last," said the lead combatant.

Using Galen's senses as his guide, Alex snuck up to the outside wall where the terrorists interrogated the team.

Galen! I need you to hear me. On the count of three, the entire team needs to get flat on the floor.

Hear ya, Alex.

Alex stepped away from the outside wall, positioning his hands in front of him.

One...two...three...

"On the floor now!" yelled Galen.

At that exact moment, Alex released a massive wave of energy, blowing a hole in the outside wall and directing all the bricks and debris toward the Sons of Enyaluis. Alex stepped through the gaping hole in the wall and smoke where his team was on the ground, shielding their heads.

"Galen, get everyone out of here. I'm going after Danyal."

"Alex, wait! There still may be others armed..."

Alex turned and moved away down the corridor towards Danyal's cell before Galen could finish his sentence.

"Fuck, everyone out!" Galen yelled as he took the M16 from an unconscious terrorist lying on the floor.

Alex approached Danyal's cell, stepping over the carnage of bodies littering the floor. "Danyal!" he yelled as he shook the locked cell door. He grabbed the iron door with both hands, ripped it off its hinges, and threw it at a combatant trying to pull himself to his feet. Alex didn't care when the man yelled in agony as the door crushed his body and pinned him on the floor. Alex moved across the cell to Danyal, who was lying motionless on the mattress.

"Danyal!" yelled Alex as he shook his body.

Alex, get the fuck out of the building now!

Alex hurried to heed Galen's telepathic warning as he picked up Danyal's body and carried him down the hall to the exit point in the wall, where he could see Galen waving him to safety. With each step, Alex moved closer to safety and Danyal's freedom—only three more steps...

But then, Alex looked away as a bright flash of light and wave of heat engulfed them.

Chapter Thirty-Six

Galen

Galen and the team were thrown backward from the shockwave of the first blast. They watched helplessly as the initial blast set off a series of coordinated explosions around the foundation of the prison, sending the three-story brick building crashing down like a house of cards. The entire mound of rubble burst into blue flames, which spread uncontrolled.

"Alex!" Galen yelled.

Michael grabbed Galen by the shoulders and pulled him back as he tried to rush into the burning rubble.

"Galen," pleaded Ryo, "those blue flames aren't normal. They burn up to three thousand degrees. There's no way we can safely approach the building."

"Not leaving them!" screamed Galen as he broke free from Michael's grasp and ran toward the collapsed building, now entirely engulfed in blue flames. He made it only a few feet before Andrea and Michael tackled him.

"We can't let you risk your life, Galen," begged Andrea. "If he's truly invulnerable, he'll make it."

Galen, through his tears, cried, "Let me go! Goddamn it! Let me go!"

"Excessively high radiation readings are coming from the rubble," Ryo said. "We need to get away now before it's too late and the authorities arrive. There are too many questions we don't want to answer. Get into the van now, soldier!"

Galen continued to struggle against Andrea and Michael, as Ryo nodded and motioned with his hand toward the van. Andrea and Michael complied by dragging Galen across the field. Upon arriving at the van, they threw Galen in the back and slammed the door behind them. Galen sobbed so hard he couldn't catch his breath, while Ryo got behind the wheel and floored it.

"Breathe," Andrea instructed, "breathe; you're hyperventilating."

"Fuck ya! Fuck ya all. Could have saved them!"

Ryo demanded, "Galen, get it together, or you'll be restrained."

Galen picked up a helmet and slammed it against the van wall, bouncing past Michael's ear.

"Galen, I don't want to hurt you, buddy, but if you don't calm your ass down, I'll knock you out. You need to bring your anger and heart rate down before someone gets hurt or you stroke out," begged Michael.

"Heart rate..." said Galen, putting the pieces together. "Ryo, ya have the only phone. Ya can check Alex's biometrics from his watch!"

Ryo unlocked his phone while driving and tossed it back to Andrea. She looked intently at the phone before responding that the app had stopped recording all biometric data from Alex ten minutes ago.

"Fuck! Fuck! Fuck! Fuck!" yelled Galen as he punched the van wall with his fist repeatedly until Michael grabbed his arm and stopped him.

"Galen, get your head back on and move forward. We've got to move forward like we always do," said Michael.

Galen took a deep breath and abruptly stopped yelling. With his eyes closed, he thought, *Alex! Alex, where are ya? Follow mah thoughts! Please follow mah thoughts!*

Andrea dropped to the floor of the van, kneeling beside Galen, and grabbed his face between her hands. "Has he stroked out?"

"No," growled Galen, "reaching out to Alex with mah thoughts. Telepathically linked at the time of the attack. Can't concentrate. Shut the fuck up. Can usually feel him when we're connected."

The team sat in silence for several moments.

Andrea eventually broke the silence. "Do you feel him, Galen?"

Galen silently shook his head as the tears streamed down his face. Michael held Galen securely to prevent him from causing any more harm to himself as the van sped down the dark country road.

Ryo said they had to get back to the school and regroup before they moved out, leaving no trace of their presence.

Galen sprang up from the floor and yelled, "Stop the van, Ryo!"

"I can't, Galen."

"Stop the fucking van now!" yelled Galen.

Ryo slammed on the brakes, throwing the passengers forward, crashing against each other and into the front seats.

"What the fuck, Ryo? We survive the attack to be killed by your driving?" yelled Michael.

"Get the medical supplies and get out of the van, now!" said Ryo.

"Are you hurt, Ryo?" asked Andrea.

"Get out now!" demanded Ryo again.

As Andrea grabbed the medical kit, Galen and Michael jumped out of the van. Rounding the van until they could see the road in front of them, they all froze in disbelief at Alex standing in the middle of the road, holding Danyal's motionless body. Alex dropped to his knees but held on tight to Danyal.

"Help, I'm not sure what's wrong with Danyal. I can't tell if he's breathing," said Alex in a weak voice.

Michael jumped into action, taking Danyal from Alex's arms, and took him to the back of the van with Andrea to medically assess the situation. Alex fell forward, but Galen caught Alex's body before he hit the road.

"Got ya, Alex."

Alex smiled at Galen as he rolled his cheek against Galen's chest before losing consciousness. Galen picked up Alex and carried him to the back of the van, where Michael helped him load Alex to safety and Ryo got them moving once more.

"What's the situation?" barked Ryo.

"Danyal is severely dehydrated, so I started an IV. His heartbeat is weak, and he looks in bad shape," Andrea replied.

"Alex?" questioned Ryo.

"Not sure," said Galen. "His clothes are scorched. Don't see any obvious injuries. Heartbeat is strong. May have passed out from the exertion required to escape."

"We're almost at the school. Andrea, I want you to shed your gear and change your shirt, then take the Jeep and get Danyal to the hospital. The address is in the GPS. Your cover story is he's a friend you were checking on and found unconscious."

"Alex?" asked Galen.

"We can't risk taking Alex to the hospital. There's no way they could give him an IV or traditional care. I'll call PGC and have Dr. Bruno come in the helicopter; he can be here in a couple hours."

"No!" demanded Galen. "Not Bruno. Alex would prefer Donalds."

Ryo nodded. "Fine, fine, Dr. Donalds will be here within a couple of hours. Galen, I want you to stay with Alex and let me know immediately if there are any changes."

"What about me?" asked Michael.

Ryo said he needed Michael to pack up the camp while Ryo started on damage control. He'd begin by anonymously warning local authorities they were entering a potential contamination situation due to the rumored activity of terrorists in the local area. He pulled into the high school parking lot, and the crew unloaded Alex and Danyal. Galen watched Andrea speed away in the SUV with Danyal as he carried Alex into the building, Ryo holding the door open.

Galen carried Alex down the hall to his room and laid him gently on the bed. Galen looked down at Alex as tears returned to his eyes. Galen couldn't fight his fatigue and adrenaline crash anymore as he reclined on the bed beside Alex, watching his chest rise and fall.

"I've got ya, Alex. I'll protect ya," was Galen's last thought before he closed his eyes and drifted off. *Anyone who wanted to hurt Alex would have to go through me.*

Chapter Thirty-Seven

Alex

Alex opened his eyes, and he blinked several times trying to make out the outline of a man lying next to him. *Danyal!* Alex leaned forward out of joy and passionately kissed the man facing him, who recoiled as the object of his affection pushed him away.

Alex blinked again, and was mortified that the man lying at the edge of the bed he'd kissed was...Galen.

Galen, wide-eyed and breathing heavily, fell off the side of the bed as he backed away from Alex.

"What the hell?"

Alex sat up, trying to piece everything together, but his head was ringing like the church bells on Sunday morning, and his double vision made moving difficult.

"Galen, I'm so sorry. I woke up and thought you were Danyal. Please forgive me. I didn't mean to offend or scare you," said Alex, placing his right hand on his forehead as he continued to assess the situation.

"Never pull a fuckin' stunt like that again," said Galen.

"Which part, the unwanted kiss or nearly getting myself killed?"

"Both," said Galen as he jumped up from the floor and slapped Alex's shoulder with his wounded hand.

Alex still couldn't see clearly, but he felt Galen physically wince.

"What's wrong with your hand, Galen? I can't see much, but it sounds bad."

"Picked a fight with a wall, and the wall won."

"I'm sure there's a story there, and I'll try to heal your hand if I can, but I feel like a speeding cement truck hit me."

"Take it easy, Alex. Ya've been through a traumatic experience."

"Not to be ungrateful, but where's Danyal? The last thing I remember is Michael taking him from my arms."

"Safe at the local hospital. Couldn't risk ya going there. Andrea took him. Will take ya to him as soon as ya have regained yur bearings."

"I'm fine; we need to go now," said Alex as he tried to stand up from the bed and fell shoulder-first into the wall. Galen pulled him back up and positioned Alex on the edge of the bed.

"Yu're not fine, Alex." Galen looked at his watch. "Ya've been unconscious for over three hours."

"Three hours?"

"Do ya even remember what happened?"

"I remember a bright flash of light and the building collapsing. It was like time was moving in slow motion. I thought the explosion killed us," said Alex, tears in his eyes. "The next moment, we were lying in a field freezing. I could hear the explosions and see the blue flames in the distance. My instinctive need to escape activated my teleportation abilities, like when you were injured. But this time, I was disoriented and couldn't concentrate."

"How'd ya find us?"

"Over the severe pain and noise in my head, I heard your voice calling me. So, I closed my eyes and followed your voice. The next thing I remember, I was standing in the road in front of the van."

"Thought we'd lost ya and Danyal. Lost it and went a little ape shit crazy," said Galen as he handed Alex a bottle of water.

"Was that when you picked a fight with a wall?"

"Wall, Andrea, and Michael."

"Wow…I'm sorry I scared you. I had to do something after seeing the team captured."

"Was a major risk ya took, but will give ya points for the dramatic entry. Exploding the wall inward to take out the terrorists was a boss move. Ya made a quick and decisive action, which presented little risk of injury to yurself or the team. But going down range by yurself was stupid."

"I guess watching anime with Danyal gave me the idea. All I could think about was saving Danyal while going down the cellblock. Ripping the cell door off with my bare hands was also pretty badass––you should have seen it."

Galen shook his head. "Show off."

"My vision is getting better, Galen. I want to try to stand."

Galen helped Alex stand and take a few steps toward the door, but Alex stumbled and fell to one knee. "Easy, Alex; before we can go to the hospital, ya need to change yur scorched clothes and walk under yur own steam. Can't have the hospital trying to admit ya."

Alex nodded. "There are fresh clothes in the bag. I'll need your help changing."

"Will help since ya asked nicely." Galen picked up the duffle bag and pulled out a t-shirt and jeans. He knelt to remove Alex's boots. "Can do the shirt or try the pants first."

"Go with the shirt; my legs are still wobbly."

Galen pulled off Alex's shirt. "Hold out yur right leg and work on the pants," Galen said. He began laughing as Alex sat on the bed in his underwear. "Did ya go into combat wearing hot pink boxer briefs with unicorns on?" said Galen, shaking his head from side to side, laughing uncontrollably.

"Too much?" said Alex as he smiled. "Does it not go with my unicorn persona?"

"Plead the fifth, mate."

"Let's try the shirt first." Alex raised his arms to help Galen slide down the shirt over his head and torso. "Now for the pants." Alex held out his right leg, and Galen slid on the jeans and completed the process on the other leg.

"OK, Alex. Put my arms around you from the front. Want ya to stand if ya can and pull up yur pants while ya are vertical."

Alex nodded and followed Galen's commands perfectly. "This is unique; I've never had a man dress me first thing in the morning. Usually, they undress me."

"Ya must be feeling better since yur inappropriate sense of humor is back. What's the word of the day?"

"Boundaries," said Alex.

Galen helped Alex stand by his side and put his arm around his shoulders. "Will move toward the cafeteria; Dr. Donalds is on her way," said Galen.

"Why Donalds?"

"Wasn't letting Bruno near ya."

Alex smiled. "My hero."

"Don't ya forget it."

Alex and Galen turned the corner into the cafeteria, where they were met by Ryo and Dr. Donalds coming into the room through the back door. Dr. Donalds rushed over to Alex and helped sit him at a table.

"Dear lord, Alex. Looks like you picked a fight with a train, and the train won. Thank you, Galen. Let me do my work," said Dr. Donalds, who opened her medical bag and asked Alex various questions. Galen stepped away to give them privacy, but Alex listened to the conversation between Galen and Ryo.

"How's he doing?" said Ryo.

"He's in shock and probably has a concussion. Any updates from the hospital?"

"No, nothing from Andrea on Danyal's condition. On a positive note, Diana is with Hoko in the ICU. He's on the mend."

"Some good news, finally," said Alex as Dr. Donalds crossed her arms and told him to sit still as he continued to listen in.

"Hesitate to ask," said Galen, "but did Zoltan have any better luck?"

"Yes," said Ryo. "The bomb was real, and Zoltan's team disarmed it. It's now in the custody of the feds. He's already cleared out and headed to his next assignment."

"Nice to get a win. One less crisis for now," said Alex.

Dr. Donalds set down her stethoscope next to Alex. She said the best she could tell, Alex had no lasting physical damage. She said she knew she was preaching to the choir, but Alex was emitting higher than normal radiation levels than his baseline readings.

Galen looked at Ryo. "Tell her."

"Tell her what?" said Alex.

Ryo paused before saying after the explosion and collapse of the building, the wreckage burst into blue flame and was giving off dangerously high radiation readings. The readings were so high, they couldn't risk a rescue.

Dr. Donalds pulled out her Geiger counter and took measurements from Galen and Ryo. She said Galen's level was higher due to his close exposure to Alex, while Ryo's levels were acceptable. She added they could count their blessings, given the situation Ryo described.

"So, what's the verdict, doc?" asked Alex. "Can I go to the hospital to be with Danyal?"

Dr. Donalds said, "Hold your horses, Alex. I'll be going with you to give my expert opinion on Danyal's condition after consulting with his attending physician. Galen, I'll need you with me. There's no way I'll be able to lug this ox around if he collapses again." Dr. Donalds winked at Alex.

Galen nodded. "Got a vehicle, Ryo?"

"Michael retrieved the SUV from the hospital before he took off with the van." Ryo tossed the keys to Galen. "Drive safe and keep me updated while I tie up the loose ends."

Galen helped Alex into the front passenger seat while Dr. Donalds climbed into the back. Pulling out of the school parking lot, Alex rolled down his window and extended his arm into the breeze.

"What're ya doing, Alex?" Alex ignored Galen's question. Galen took off his ring.

What're ya doing, Alex?

Ouch, Galen, inside voice, please.

If ya answered my question, I wouldn't have to yell in yur head.

I heard you the first time; I'm recharging with cosmic and electromagnetic energy. I've a theory it will help me focus and heal.

Make sure ya don't hurt yurself.

Could you give me your right hand, Galen? Let's see if it works.

Glen stretched his damaged right hand toward Alex, where Alex gently collapsed his hand over Galen's bloodied knuckles.

Could you try it now?

Galen pulled back; his hand had now healed. Only the dried blood showed his former injury.

Cheers, mate. Ya need to save yur energy for yurself and Danyal.

Alex didn't respond, so Galen returned to the GPS, providing directions to the hospital. Upon pulling into the hospital parking lot, Galen parked near the emergency room entrance.

Alex sat paralyzed in the passenger seat.

"Ya right, Alex?" asked Galen.

Alex shook his head no. Galen could see Alex's respiration rapidly increasing.

"Doc, may need yur help."

Alex raised his hand to stop Dr. Donalds from approaching the door.

"Talk to me, Alex. Know yu're scared.

"Terrified," said Alex between gasps of breath. "Danyal's been gone for weeks, and I'm fucking terrified to walk through those doors to see him." His shoulders slumped forward as the tears came streaming down his face.

Galen raised his hand to wave Dr. Donalds off, giving them space. "Let it out. We'll walk in that door together and face whatever awaits ya. Won't let ya do this alone. Focus on yur box breathing and center like Hoko says."

Alex breathed slowly for several minutes, in and out, until he nodded his head and opened the door to step out of the vehicle. Dr. Donalds led the way through the entrance to the nurse's desk.

"Good morning, my name is Alex Lieth, and I'm here to see my boyfriend, Danyal Sarif. He was brought in earlier for emergency attention."

Nurse Johnson checked her computer screen before looking up. "Yes, Danyal is here, but I can only allow family to see him."

"This is Dr. Donalds, and she's Danyal's physician."

"Thank you for the introduction, Alex. I want to meet with his attending physician as soon as possible to consult about his case, ma'am."

Nurse Johnson nodded. "And this fine young man behind you? Is he family?"

"Yes," said Alex, turning to smile at Galen. "This is Galen, and he's family--wherever I go, he goes."

"Please wait while I get you visitation badges so you can be with Danyal in a jiffy."

"Thank you, Nurse Johnson, you're a lifesaver."

Keep it together, Alex; you've got this. Keep it together for Danyal.

Chapter Thirty-Eight

Alex stood at the door of hospital room 303 as severe dread gripped his body and paralyzed him. On the other side of the door was either the promise of a joyful reunion with Danyal, or a profound loss that would change his world forever. As his thoughts shifted between these two alternatives, the cycle stopped when Galen placed his hand on Alex's shoulder.

"Ya right, Alex?"

Alex shook his head no, unable to speak. He stepped back as the room began to spin, disrupting his balance.

"Easy, mate," said Galen, "let's keep ya vertical. Focus on yur breathing like ya did in the parking lot. Won't enter the room until yu're ready. Will open the door for ya if ya need it."

Alex took some long, deep breaths and slowly exhaled. He completed this cycle several times before nodding at Galen.

"Open the door," he said in a broken voice.

Galen turned the doorknob and opened the door so Alex could cross the threshold.

He stepped toward the single hospital bed in the middle of the room, a white curtain obscuring his view of the person in the bed. The constant beeping of monitors was the only sound to be heard in the room, which smelled of harsh cleaning chemicals. Alex steadied himself against Galen and reached out his shaking hand to pull back the curtain. Tears filled his eyes at seeing Danyal lying motionless in the hospital bed. Danyal's smooth olive skin looked pale, and his handsome face was sunken. Danyal's breathing was shallow but consistent. Tears began rolling down Alex's face. Alex leaned over to kiss Danyal on the forehead. He cupped his head and held his face against Danyal's cheek.

Galen pulled a chair from the corner of the room and slid it behind Alex. He sat back in the chair and clasped Danyal's right hand.

"I hardly recognize him, Galen. Why does everyone I care about wind up in a hospital bed because of me?"

"Ya didn't put me, Hoko, or Danyal in a hospital bed. Because of ya, each of us survived."

Alex didn't feel that way as he leaned forward and placed his hand on Danyal's heart, assessing the spark in his chest.

"His spark is weak, and that scares me. I'm sending energy through his body; I can't find anything physically wrong with him."

"Can ya reach his mind like with mah coma?"

Alex closed his eyes and breathed slowly, concentrating on reaching out to Danyal's mind. Alex opened his eyes and shook his head no. "His mind isn't available to me. I can't feel him."

"Can ya heal him as ya did me?"

Alex shook his head no again. He said he didn't know where to start. He had known Galen had suffered a head injury, so knew where to focus his energy. He had no clue what was wrong with Danyal, so the best thing he could do was to try and boost his spark. Alex closed his eyes again and channeled all the cosmic energy he could control into Danyal. He wished Hoko were here; he'd know what to do since Alex's abilities were much stronger when Hoko guided him.

"Talk to him, Alex. Would talk to Amara every day."

Alex picked up Danyal's hand and squeezed it. He said Danyal had napped long enough. It was time to wake up so he could hug him and tell him how much he'd missed him.

"I'm lost without you; you are my anchor," Alex said.

There had been so many changes in his life he needed to tell Danyal about, and Alex was doing his best to keep it together. In some ways, Alex found a strength inside he never believed existed. He'd made some wonderful friends, fascinating people who challenged him to be better.

"I know you had issues with Galen, but he has a heart of gold. I think you'll like him if you give him a chance."

Alex paused as his tears increased, and said he thought he'd started to mature a little into the man Danyal knew he could be, and that he couldn't wait to show Danyal how much he'd grown. He smiled and said he also had some fancy new tricks that'd blow Danyal's mind.

All he wanted was to hold Danyal and hear his voice. Alex would even be happy to hear one of Danyal's rants about his favorite anime series. It didn't matter what they did, as long as they were together. Alex was never going to let Danyal go again. He sat quietly, gently stroking Danyal's arm while wiping away his tears. Galen handed him a Kleenex and touched Alex's back for support.

The moment was interrupted by a gentle knocking on the door. Alex turned to see Dr. Donalds standing in the doorway.

"Is it a good time to enter, gents? I can come back if you need more time alone with Danyal."

Alex said, "Come in, doc, and please bring me some good news."

Dr. Donalds approached the bedside and placed her hand on Alex's shoulder. She said from what she could tell from Danyal's records, the local physicians had comprehensively assessed the situation. She added that, other than severe dehydration, they'd ruled out head trauma, and his preliminary blood work didn't indicate any concerning findings.

"So why has he not regained consciousness?" asked Alex.

Dr. Donalds said that was the million-dollar question they were trying to answer. She explained six types of comas had specific underlying origins. So far, they'd eliminated all six conditions that could account for his coma.

"Is that good news?" asked Alex.

She nodded. Dr. Donalds said his vitals were getting stronger, and Danyal was young and strong as an ox, so she had her fingers crossed.

Alex said he'd tried scanning Danyal's body and couldn't find any injury, and couldn't reach his mind as Alex did when Galen was injured. She replied they had resources at PGC that standard hospitals wouldn't even begin to understand, so they would use their state-of-the-art facility to assess Danyal further. Dr. Donalds added, medically speaking, moving Danyal back to PGC for assessment and treatment was their best option, and that she promised she wouldn't rest until they'd considered every alternative. She winked at Alex and said she would fight for Danyal as if he were her kin.

Alex stood and hugged Dr. Donalds. "Thank you. How soon can we move him?"

She said if Danyal's vitals continued to improve, they could move him that evening. She'd work out all the details for the medevac. In the meantime, she wanted Alex to stay put and try to rest.

"How's Hoko?" asked Galen.

Dr. Donalds said he was still in the ICU but stable. He hadn't regained consciousness, so it would take time to figure out what long-term consequences Hoko might experience, and that he had a long road to recovery ahead of him.

"Will be praying for him," said Galen.

"We could all use a little prayer these days, Galen," Dr. Donalds smiled as she sat Danyal's chart on the bed.

"One last question," said Alex, "would it help if I tried to heal Hoko?"

"Heavens no," she said, "Hoko can fight this battle." She wagged her finger at Alex and chastised him that he was only a couple hours removed from being unconscious after a traumatic event, and reminded him he'd had multiple seizures in the last week. It would be in everyone's best interest that he leave the supernatural healing alone.

"Will watch him, doc. Keeping him in line is a full-time job," said Galen.

Alex turned and smiled at Galen. "You can try."

Chapter Thirty-Nine

Alex

Alex looked through the window of the ICU room door, and the sight of Hoko lying helpless in the bed nearly broke his heart. The crippling guilt in Alex's mind almost kept him from seeing Hoko before leaving with the medevac taking Danyal back to Boston. But Alex couldn't just go; he owed so much to Hoko and needed him to know the depths of his feelings. Since Hoko was not wearing his medicine band, Alex could see Hoko's spark was faint, but he knew Hoko was a fighter. Plus, Hoko had Diana sitting next to him, holding his hand. Although Alex and Diana had had a tumultuous relationship of late, Alex knew she'd fight for Hoko.

Diana noticed Alex standing by the door. She smiled and waved him into the room. She stood to hug him, which made Alex burst into tears.

"It's OK, Alex. Let it out."

"I'm sorry," he said, "it's my fault he's in this bed."

"You're right, Alex. It's your fault he's in this bed..."

"What? You're not supposed to agree with me. Kick me when I'm down."

"You didn't let me finish," she said as she stroked the hair on the back of Alex's head. "He's in this bed because you saved his life. Not with supernatural abilities; you saved him with your knowledge and decisive action. If you weren't there, we would have lost him. I don't have words to convey my gratitude."

Alex stepped back from her embrace. "Because the enemy targeted me, he was in harm's way."

Diana shook her head. "Alex, he was in this battle for decades. Hoko knew the risks of working at PGC and with Ditta. We all accepted it could place a target on our backs. So, this isn't your fault."

"Dr. Donalds said I could put myself and Hoko at risk if I tried to heal him."

"Let's listen to her. You've been through severe trauma; allow yourself time to heal. Hoko will heal on his own. The only instance you could heal was with Galen, and you did it by instinct. The most pressing question now is, how's Danyal?"

"He's unconscious, and the medical staff can't determine why."

"I'm so sorry, Alex. What's the next step?"

"Dr. Donalds is arranging the medevac. We will be leaving within the hour. Galen is with Danyal now, protecting him."

"How's Galen doing? Ryo told me he broke down when you were missing and feared dead."

"He's putting up a good front, but I can see he's exhausted physically and emotionally."

"Proceed with caution, Alex. Be careful with the emotions of those around you. Even with the best of intentions, people can get hurt."

Alex was confused by Diana's statement. What was she talking about? Never mind, he didn't have the time for more therapy. Alex leaned over to Hoko and touched his forehead to Hoko's. He stood and turned to Diana with tears and a huge smile. "Give me your hand, Diana."

Diana looked at Alex, confused, but she complied. Alex picked up Hoko's hand. "Close your eyes and think of Hoko…Now say something."

"Please, Hoko, come back to me."

Diana opened her eyes, surprised as she heard Hoko's voice, "I'm on my way."

She immediately burst into tears. "Was that real, Alex?"

Alex smiled and nodded. "When I made physical contact with Hoko, his mind reached out to me and asked me to give you the message. I allowed him to do it himself. Now I can return to Boston with Danyal, knowing Hoko is safe."

Diana hugged Alex so tight he winced.

"Easy there, you've got a grip like a grizzly bear."

Diana laughed. "You amaze me more and more every day, Alex Lieth. Ditta made the right choice when she picked you."

"OK, let's not over-inflate my ego. We've only recently brought it down to a size that will fit through your office door. Stay here and protect Hoko. I'll keep you updated on Danyal."

"Safe travels, Alex. Godspeed."

Alex and Galen walked with the medical staff as they rolled Danyal out of the hospital toward the helipad. Alex scanned the area with his mind to find any threats waiting to ambush them, but didn't see any voids in the energetic field within the immediate area. Alex nodded to Galen to proceed.

Galen said he'd take it from here, and motioned with his hand that it was safe to approach the helicopter before the PGC staff moved Danyal across the parking lot.

After Danyal had been loaded on board, Alex sat next to Galen and motioned to Galen to remove his ring. Galen complied.

We won't be able to hear each other over the helicopter noise, Galen.

Ya screen the medical and PGC staff on board, Alex?

Alex nodded. Because the staff hadn't been inoculated, he could see they didn't carry any negative energy or register any malice.

Ryo intentionally brought them in from outside the Boston head-quarters. They didn't have any knowledge of the security breach or information leaks. Also, I visited Hoko, and he's doing his best to recover. We touched our minds, and he had a message for Diana.

Excellent news!

He also had a message for me, Galen.

Don't leave us hanging, mate.

He said to end this, I must find the traitor before they can do more damage. From here on out, my goal is to help Danyal recover and to root out the traitors from within the company. We have a mystery, Dr. Watson, that needs solving.

Ya know, Mr. Holmes, ya don't even have to ask. Going down the list, starting with the board, Hoko, Diana, and Ryo can be eliminated.

Can we automatically eliminate Ryo, Galen? How well do you know him?

He was devastated when we thought we'd lost ya when the operation went to shite. No commander wants to lose a soldier. Can't see him being that good of an actor. Believe he'll also give ya consent to scan him if yu're willing to share that secret.

Alex nodded in agreement. *What about Thomas Brynmor? He knows Ditta's personal and corporate legal secrets.*

Thomas was deeply devoted to Ditta. Why would he betray her? Money isn't a good enough reason. He could easily embezzle money from PGC business dealings instead. Why would he turn to terrorism?

Galen was right. Those pieces didn't fit together. The same logic applied to the CFO, Kylie Peters. She didn't stand to benefit from Alex being eliminated or forging an alliance with terrorists.

I don't want to anger you, Galen, but should we consider Zoe?

Need to consider all options, Alex. Everyone's a suspect. Zoe could be a perfect spy hiding in plain sight. She has the knowledge and skills to hack computer and surveillance systems. She was close to me before ya arrived. Would place her in a position to attempt to obtain access through me. The perfect cover to deflect blame for the data breach. Could have quickly introduced the virus into the system using Danyal's phone. She's from outside the core group. The rest worked together for decades. Zoe could have prior existing ties with her international background. Would be foolish to drop her as a suspect.

There's one thing giving me pause, Galen. She has feelings for you. What would she stand to gain from the bombing that nearly killed you?

Could be reasons for that, Alex. May not have had a choice. May not have known about it. Mah injuries may have been unintended. Her feelings may have been accidental. Sometimes, spies develop feelings for their marks before they eliminate them. Situation gives me an awful feeling, Alex, in the pit of mah stomach. Give me yur impression of Dr. Donalds.

Alex looked across the helicopter at Dr. Donalds, who stared intensely at her tablet.

From the beginning, I sensed a good vibe from her, but then I could be more inclined to trust her since she's part of the rainbow community. Well, I must trust her because I'm letting her treat Danyal. She's only recently out of medical school, so I'm struggling to see how she'd be involved with terrorists unless...

Aye, what, Alex?

Unless someone she loved, like her wife, was threatened--perhaps she's being forced to comply? That's a terrible thought, but our enemy manipulated you, using your love for Amara as leverage. Then again, you must trust her since you demanded she come care for me.

She was the lesser of the two evils. It was either her or Bruno. No way was I letting that guy near ya.

Dr. Bruno, let's unpack this one. He's not the kind-hearted man I knew who saved me from a horrible situation at boarding school. Life may have turned him into an asshole, but it doesn't make him a spy in league with terrorists.

Don't leave any stone unturned, mate. How did life change him?

This all came out after your injury, but another test subject survived the experiments. Her name was Nyssa, and Bruno raised her as his child. He has pictures of her in his office. She is a carbon copy of Ditta. However, Nyssa became emotionally unstable and a danger to herself and others, and Ditta determined I was the more viable option to replace her. She ordered Bruno to euthanize Nyssa and distribute all resources to me.

Yu're only telling me this now, mate?

At the time, I was a little distracted worrying about someone I care about dying from a severe head injury, so please cut me some slack.

Galen scowled but continued, *Ditta making him watch his daughter slowly die is undoubtedly a reason to hate her. Could explain his animosity toward ya. Could be a motive to want revenge on PGC.*

I know the loss of Nyssa still bothers him. I accidentally observed him in his office crying, holding her picture when Hoko and I were remote viewing. His grief genuinely struck me. I admit my part in the conflict with Bruno. I threatened him and took away his voice. Reviewing all the evidence, Bruno did warn me not to try to save Danyal or to surrender any ichor samples.

Can't discount him as a suspect based on one moment of decency. Ya tend to be stubborn. Would tell ya to do the opposite to trick ya. Playin' mind games. Gives him cover to claim he warned ya against any rash actions. But why now? Had plenty of opportunities to take revenge on Ditta over the years.

It's the same answer for all the suspects, Galen; I'm an unknown player on the board they want to remove. They want to strike while I'm distracted and weak.

Galen nodded. *But the world goes to shite if yu're eliminated. How does that help Bruno? How does ichor fit into the picture?*

I've been mulling that problem; maybe he intends to attempt to clone his daughter. If he had any of her DNA, he could potentially only need the ichor and time to clone Nyssa. Hear me out; Bruno created me from genetic material harvested from a hair sample and infused with ichor.

Galen tilted his head to think. *That's a long-term gambit. Bruno is the oldest board member at sixty-eight. Does he have twenty-five years to watch his plan come to fruition? Yu're Nyssa's brother. Wouldn't killing ya be murdering the only part of Nyssa still left in the world?*

I don't think he views me with any affection. In his mind, I'm potentially the reason he lost Nyssa.

How do the Sons of Enyaluis become involved with this theory? Are they the muscle to do the dirty work? What do they get out of this?

I'm not sure. Maybe they've designs on the ichor and are playing him. The theory still has holes, such as who is financially backing the terrorists. Bruno may be brilliant, but he does not have the computer knowledge to coordinate the data breach.

Bothers me, mate. Bruno survived a kidnapping attempt by terrorists. Templeton was a trained Special Forces soldier. Bruno is an older dude and overweight. Only weapon he knows how to use is sarcasm.

Agreed. So, how do we eliminate Zoe, Donalds, and Bruno from our suspect list? I have a plan, Galen. I want to switch out the injections with a placebo and assess each suspect by screening them with my abilities, placing them in circumstances where they'll play their true hand.

Need to think this through and figure out the details once we arrive at PGC. Yur main priority is keeping Danyal safe. Will start drafting the specifics of our sting operation. Rest while ya can, mate. Going to need ya at full strength, moving forward.

Chapter Forty

Galen debated waking Alex, who had fallen asleep on the helicopter with his upper body leaning toward Danyal lying on the medical gurney. He gently shook Alex by the shoulder and said it was time to wake up.

Alex sat up, wiping the sleep from his eyes. "How long was I asleep?"

"Two hours. You needed it. Ya get Danyal settled when we land. Have a few things that need to be done. Time to start eliminating suspects from our list."

Alex nodded and said he was demanding Danyal be treated in the penthouse, where they could tightly control access with only one way in and out.

Galen smiled. Alex had clearly started to think more strategically. He watched as Alex helped roll Danyal down the hall to the penthouse elevator. He was glad the weather was better than predicted, making landing and unloading Danyal safe and easy.

Galen sought out Ryo, who was sitting at his desk. "Got a sec, boss?" he asked.

Ryo said he was running behind preparing for a meeting, but that he did. "Alex and the medical team are back safely?"

"Getting Danyal's medical care set up in the penthouse. Will get right to my request. Need access to the computer files and employee records for Zoe Palmer, Dr. Bruno, and Dr. Donalds."

"I won't give you access to those records just because you want them."

"Bullshite, Ryo."

Galen had been reviewing the contracts each employee had to sign. They stipulated all computer and phone records within the building were subject to electronic monitoring. PGC contracts said that under duress, employee records would be released without consent if their safety was at risk or they were under suspicion of a crime. Could Ryo really argue their current situation didn't meet these criteria?

"Damnit, Galen, as head of security, it's *my* job to investigate. You need to step off and remember your place. You're a grunt who needs to stay in his lane."

"Let me help ya."

"You mean you or your partner-in-crime? You two are getting too close; it's clouding your judgment."

Ryo and Ms. Dea assigned him to protect Alex, and now Ryo judged him for it. That was rich. He'd protected Alex by putting his life on the line.

"Some people could judge ya for yur security failings, Ryo."

Ryo took a deep breath, stood up from his desk, and stepped closer to Galen until they stood nose to nose. "Choose your words carefully, Galen, because they will have consequences. You have no authority here, and don't delude yourself; you're replaceable. You're a mere cog in the machine."

"Not yur enemy, Ryo. We're on the same side. Let me help ya find our spy before other people are hurt. Ya can even claim mah actions were unknown to ya. Plausible deniability."

Galen could tell by Ryo's scowl he was mulling over options.

"Galen, I have a meeting I'm going to be late for. It's funny how our computers don't lock themselves for ten minutes. It's an annoying fact, but one I've come to live with. Someday, I must change the policy." Ryo passed Galen in his doorway. "Disregard or challenge my authority again, and you'll find yourself on the street where not even the Unicorn can save you. Don't be here when I get back, or else I'll stick a boot up your ass, and you'll need even more surgery."

Galen sat at Ryo's computer, quickly searching all the personnel files he needed. Looking through the files, he downloaded the home addresses, information on significant relationships, and the financial disclosure records PGC required. Phone records were kept separately, so he'd need to get them from communications. Galen locked Ryo's computer and carefully wiped the keyboard to remove any fingerprints that could associate him with a data breach. He closed the door to Ryo's office behind him and headed to the elevator to the communications floor.

Upon leaving the elevator and walking down the hall, he gently knocked on the last door on the left.

"Knock, knock," said Galen. "Good afternoon, Monica. How ya doing?"

"Galen!" exclaimed the tall, athletically built African-American woman, who enthusiastically jumped up to hug Galen. She said she was glad to see him and was delighted he was recovering so well from his accident. She smiled and said they missed him at the darts league.

Galen said he missed playing, but his world had become a mix between a telly soap opera and a Tom Clancy thriller.

"I'm so sorry," said Monica. "The darts league truly misses Templeton. That skinny little guy could talk trash, but he sure was endearing. We're taking turns checking in on his wife, since she's due any day with the twins."

"That's why I'm here, Monica. Tracking down leads to help bring the people who hurt Templeton to justice. Need access to PGC phone records."

"Galen, I could lose my job for giving you access. I'm afraid I can't help you."

"Might be against policy, and could get ya into trouble, I know. However, ya could also help end this black cloud over this company."

"I know it sounds easy enough to just print the records, Galen, but will you pay my rent and put food on my table when I get fired for helping you?"

"Yu're skilled, and ya can do this without anyone finding out."

"Sneaky––now you appeal to my ego, you little shit."

"Do it for Templeton."

"That's not fair, Galen. You're playing dirty."

"Will play any way that helps find the people responsible for his death."

Monica massaged her temples. "So, if I help you, I get to live with the fear of getting fired and even prosecuted. If I don't help you, I live with the guilt I could have helped identify Templeton's killers. Fuck you, Galen. You've no right to put me in this situation." After a long pause, Monica said, "I'm only doing this for Templeton and his family. What do you need?"

"Need the communication records for Dr. Donalds, Dr. Bruno, and Zoe Palmer."

"Zoe? I guess that shouldn't surprise me."

"Aye, what makes ya say that?"

"She's been different the past three weeks. More withdrawn and, honestly, quite unfriendly. I've tried to be a friend and offer a sympathetic ear, but she just shuts me down."

"Interesting. How long would it take to get the records?"

Monica said she couldn't get him recordings, but she could give him names and numbers related to calls from the PGC offices and cell phones. She added it would take a moment before she turned to her computer and worked feverishly until she looked up at Galen to ask if he wanted a digital or hard copy. Galen replied hard copy, because it was harder to trace. Monica printed the records and placed them in a black folder before handing them to Galen. She paused before releasing the file.

"Promise me, Galen, you'll get the bastards that killed Templeton."

"Promise to do my best. Might even have a little divine help as backup."

"Oh, Dr. Lieth. I've only seen him in passing. Then again, if I was in charge of casting the role of a god, he'd be more than adequate."

Galen laughed. Monica said maybe Galen could bring Alex along for darts and beer sometime. Galen smiled and said he'd extend the offer, but she needed to know Alex was a bit of a hustler who liked to use his divine abilities to cheat. Galen had learned that the hard way.

Monica smiled, shook her head, and said it was amusing they had to sign a nondisclosure agreement——no one would believe their stories anyway. Galen smiled and said he'd tell her all about Alex's exploits someday. He was badass for a mild-mannered professor, but would feed his ego too much if he heard Galen say it.

"Oh, so you're on a first-name basis with him."

Galen gave Monica an exaggerated frown. Monica, in response, rolled her eyes and sucked her teeth.

"Cheers, Monica. Owe ya a favor and several stubbies," said Galen as he turned to leave her office. He tightly held the folder with the phone records as he entered the elevator.

On to the next step of the plan!

Galen pulled out his phone to text Alex. *Going to be out in the field on recognizance. May be MIA for a few days.*

He received a reply before Galen could place his phone back in his pocket.

Galen, we're in this together. Dr. Donalds is drawing blood and running tests on Danyal. I'll work on her to determine if we can eliminate her from our suspect list. Please be safe; I'll hunt you down if you get hurt.

Real subtle, mate.

Chapter Forty-One

Alex

It was Alex's responsibility to determine if Dr. Donalds was an enemy or an ally. He wouldn't let anyone else hurt Danyal. Alex watched Dr. Donalds and her assistant draw vials of Danyal's blood for testing.

Alex asked what tests they would be running that the hospital couldn't complete. Dr. Donalds replied that PGC had more sensitive equipment, and some new tests could identify damage down to the molecular DNA level. Alex asked how long the results would take, and she said they'd process them in-house, so turnaround time is significantly reduced––at most, twenty-four hours. She added they would run a confirmation test to verify the results before she asked Nurse Ringwood to take the vials to the lab for analysis immediately. Nurse Ringwood nodded and quickly went down the hall to the penthouse elevator.

"Thank you, doctor. I appreciate everything you've done for me and Danyal."

"Don't thank me yet, Dr. Lieth. I can't promise I can find anything medically to help Danyal."

"Please, call me Alex. You're standing in my bedroom," said Alex with a disarming smile.

"Don't tell my wife. She'd not believe you, anyway. May I ask a question, Alex?"

"Yes, you may."

"Why am I treating Danyal in the penthouse rather than the medical wing?"

Can I trust her?

"Because I'm unsure how safe the company has become, and I don't know who to trust."

Dr. Donalds turned towards Alex and placed her hand on his shoulder. "I don't blame you, darlin'. I'm scared, too. Murders, kidnappings, and terrorist groups weren't what I signed up for. I'll do all I can to help Danyal, but I question your decision to treat him here. I'm not sure you're thinking straight. I can't predict what medical equipment he'll need, and moving him to the medical wing in a crisis will cost valuable moments that we may not have to spare. I think your decision is reckless. You're not seeing the forest for the trees."

"Thanks for making me feel worse, Dr. Donalds."

"That was not my intention, darlin'. As Danyal's physician, I need to let you know any issues I see which could affect his recovery." Dr. Donalds took a deep breath. "I sense you don't want to hear this, but I believe it's also a mistake not letting Dr. Bruno assist in Danyal's treatment."

Alex could feel his blood pressure rising as he closed his eyes and tilted his head. "Please, Dr. Donalds, enlighten me."

"If it were my Charlotte in this bed, I'd allow anyone with the knowledge and skills to help her recover to assist in her treatment. If I had my druthers, I'd eat my pride for her treatment."

"So, I should make a deal with the devil?"

"I wouldn't call him that, but you get what you get with Bruno. Is he too big for his britches and a condescending asshole? Yes. Is he the best boss in the world? No. He thinks the sun comes up to hear him crow. But to his credit, he knows more about cutting-edge treatment than any physician I've met. I've learned more from him in two years under his supervision, than in a decade in the private sector. We're not friends, but if he could save my beloved, a deal with the devil sounds like a small price to pay."

"May I ask you a question, Dr. Donalds?" asked Alex.

"Of course, darlin'. We're in your penthouse bedroom, so it's only fair you call me Veronica."

"OK, Veronica, do you completely trust Bruno?"

"That's a complex question; I trust him with science. He won't stop until he solves a problem. Do I trust him as a person? Will this answer leave this room?"

"No––I promise, any secrets shared in the bedroom stay in the bedroom."

Veronica chuckled. "He's probably the most miserable son of a bitch I've ever met. However, I'd gladly let him save Charlotte if he could." Veronica giggled again, "I should quit talking ugly, but if he were a superhero, his superpowers would be biting sarcasm and hissy fits."

"Sounds more like a supervillain."

"Your words, not mine."

"There was a time when he was kind and jovial," said Alex.

Veronica tilted her head to the side. "Two questions. Are we talking about a different universe, and what have you been smoking, child?"

Alex said that seeing Bruno used to be the highlight of his school year. He brought Alex's favorite Scooby-Doo Band-Aids and cherry lollipops for his yearly checkups. Alex thought Bruno cared for him, unlike many of the staff at the boarding school.

Veronica said she couldn't believe her ears. Alex said it was shocking, but it happened.

"So, can you give me your scientific opinion if I ask you a work-related question?"

"Of course," she said.

"What do you know about the inoculations?"

Veronica took a deep breath. "I'm afraid that's a company secret."

"You know I technically own the company."

"I'm unsure if answering your question would violate my NDA."

"I understand, and don't want to jeopardize your position. What if I asked you a hypothetical question?"

"Hypothetical questions are entertaining. Let's try it on for size," responded Veronica.

"So, if I wanted to replicate these injections, would I need chemical or organic materials?"

"That's an interesting question. I'd *speculate* you'd need organic materials. Stem cells would be the perfect thing if you were recreating similar research."

"Interesting––so genetic editing would take longer to make changes. What if I wanted to make an alternative for staff who didn't want to take injections?" asked Alex.

"In those situations, theoretically, you could treat an object the person wears to have a similar, but weaker, effect."

"So, how long would these new inoculations last?"

"Only a week or two at the most––the science says our bodies would reject the inoculations similar to how our immune systems fight off bacteria or a virus."

"So, how long would it take for the inoculation to leave the system if you ran out of injections?"

"Hmmm. That would depend on how long the person was taking the injections. It would be about a week for someone new to the process, and much longer if the subject had been on the injections for many years."

Damn, that wasn't what I wanted to hear.

"If a scientist wanted to get around the injections, could it be done?"

"Medically, no. There's no way around it."

"What if there was a supernatural workaround?"

Veronica moved her right hand over her mouth. "What're you telling me, Alex? Do *you* know a way around the injections?"

"*Hypothetically*, if I did know a supernatural workaround, would you be willing to test it?"

Veronica sat on the side of the bed before wringing her hands. "The scientist in me would like to test your theory, but I'd need to know if there could be any side effects."

"Not that I'm aware of. I want to see if I can share my energy with you and sense your energy, despite your inoculation."

"Will you have access to all my thoughts?"

"I promise I'll only stick to the questions asked."

Veronica nodded. "How does this work? I'm intrigued."

"I need to place my hand on your heart to feel your spark, and I can ask you questions to check their validity."

"So, you're a human lie detector."

"I guess you could see it that way. You're under no obligation to do this if you're not up to it."

"Let's do it––the scientist in me wants to know if this is real, or if you're selling me snake oil."

"I'll need to place my hand over your heart." Alex rubbed his hands together to warm his palms before placing his right hand over Veronica's heart. "OK, there's one more step; you need to give me consent. Do you give me consent to touch your energy?"

"Yes, I give consent."

"I'll start with small questions. Why did you join PGC?"

"Many reasons: paying off my student loans, wanting to live in Boston, and making enough money to support my wife. As newly-weds, money didn't come easy or grow on trees. My wife, Charlotte, is completing her social work Ph.D. at Starling University."

"You're being sincere. Good for Charlotte! I didn't know she attended Starling; I've probably passed her in the halls."

"Maybe I shouldn't tell you this, but she did look in the door during one of your lectures to see who the new owner of the university was."

"I'm not offended by that––I hope it was on a good hair day," Alex said with a smile.

Dr. Donalds grinned. "She thought you were a real looker. It's hard not being able to talk with your spouse about your work. Not that she'd believe any of this anyway. It's like living a dual life."

Alex nodded. "That's also true. I'm sensing there was another reason for joining PGC, a deeply personal reason involving Charlotte."

"Yes...Charlotte has stage two neuroendocrine cancer. The treatments are working for now, but I want to find a cure," said Veronica with tears in her eyes.

"I can feel how tenacious you've been in caring for her. No wonder you endure Bruno."

"He's my best chance for a cure," said Veronica.

"I'll ask a few questions and please answer them to the best of your ability. Do you hold any grudges against PGC?"

"No."

"Do you know who provided information about PGC to outside forces?"

"No."

"Do you have any connections with the Sons of Enyaluis?"

"Hell no. Those bastards need to pay for all the damage they've caused."

"Do you know anyone in the company with connections with the Sons of Enyaluis?"

"No."

"Everything you've told me, Veronica, was the truth. You have a gorgeous soul, and Charlotte is a real beauty," said Alex as he removed his hand from Veronica's chest. "I didn't know how long the energy I shared with you would last, but I expect it to wear off quickly."

"Believe me, she knows it," said Veronica. "She's a real peach. How'd you discover the injections weren't ironclad?"

"I know you can keep a secret, Veronica. Ditta passed this information on to me through Galen. I'm not sure she ever used it, but she made sure I knew about it." Alex paused before saying, "I would love to meet Charlotte someday. Maybe at the company Pride celebration?"

"That would be wonderful. She's always looking for a reason to get gussied up. I need to go, Alex; I want to supervise the tests on Danyal's blood. I hope I didn't come on too strong about asking you to consider Bruno's help."

"I've touched your soul, Veronica. I know you were being sincere."

"Please, try to rest, Alex. I promise to do everything within the company's resources to help Danyal."

"Thank you. I appreciate your dedication and support."

After Veronica had left the penthouse, Alex pulled out his phone to text Galen: *Drop Dr. Donalds from the suspect list. Text me back. She's one of the good guys, but I've bad news. The plan to switch the injections is a bust. The longer the person has been on the injections, the longer it will take to leave their system. It would take months to get the injections out of Bruno's system. It could also take weeks to get the injections out of Zoe's system, and we don't have time to waste.*

Alex placed his phone on the nightstand and straightened the blankets around Danyal before gently climbing into bed to lie beside his boyfriend. Alex closed his eyes but opened them again to take one last look and make sure he was next to Danyal before kissing him softly on the forehead. He was finally lying beside his boyfriend in bed once more.

Please don't let this be the last time.

Chapter Forty-Two

Alex looked at his reflection in the mirror; he looked like shit. The bags under his eyes were so enormous he'd have to pay a baggage fee to ride the elevator. He opened the bedroom door, smiled at Nurse Ringwood, and said good morning. She smiled and said she needed to check on Danyal and take some readings for Dr. Donalds. Alex said he'd leave her to her work before he walked down the hall toward the kitchen. He could smell bacon cooking––that meant Galen was making breakfast.

"Smells delicious. What's a guy have to do around here to get a home-cooked breakfast?" Alex stopped as he turned the corner to see Zoe sitting on a stool by the kitchen island. Alex could feel the anger boiling in his chest. "What the hell, Galen! Do you invite all our suspects for breakfast?"

"Alex, it's not what ya think. Yur face is red. We're all mates here."

"So, we're friends with the enemy now?" said Alex.

Galen turned to Alex and slid a file across the kitchen island. "I'd let ya sleep more if I knew this was the mood ya were packing."

"You didn't answer my question; why is she here? She could be a threat, and you brought her into the penthouse without consulting me," Alex said, as his breathing increased and his heart pounded faster.

Galen stepped between Alex and Zoe. "Alex, yu're starting to scare me. Don't know if Zoe can see it, but ya've streams of purple energy leaking from yur eyes. Focus on yur breathing because yu're close to losing control." Galen stood in front of Alex and placed his hand on Alex's chest. "Read the file, Alex."

"I'm not reading any fucking file; you need to get her out of her immediately."

Galen turned slightly toward Zoe. "Mind briefing Alex on the situation?"

Zoe nodded. "Dr. Lieth, I can assure you I mean you and Danyal no harm."

"I warn you now, don't let Danyal's name cross your lips again."

"Alex!" yelled Galen as he slammed his fist on the counter. "Please trust me and let her talk. Ya know I'd never put ya or Danyal at risk. Please continue, Zoe."

Zoe said Alex had every reason not to trust her, but she was not his enemy. She said his instincts were good to suspect she was withholding information. Zoe looked over at Galen, who nodded. She said there was no easy way to say it, so she'd tell him bluntly. She'd been working undercover at PGC at the request of Yuzuru Ryo. She said she worked for Interpol, and her presence was requested because unknown agents had stolen PGC intellectual properties and technologies, which had made their way to numerous international groups, including the Sons of Enyaluis.

Alex's face grew pale as Galen moved over to stand by his side, while sliding a plate of eggs and bacon on the counter in front of Alex.

"Interpol?" asked Alex.

"Yah. Interpol," said Galen.

"How do we know this isn't a lie?"

Galen tapped the file on the counter next to Alex's food. "It's all in the file, and Ryo will back her up." He added he butted heads yesterday with Ryo over employee files; initially, he thought Ryo was being an ass, but it turned out he was worried about blowing Zoe's cover.

Alex slowly opened the file. "So, how did you figure this out, Galen?"

"Did surveillance at her condo yesterday. Had enough evidence to confront her last night."

Alex raised one eyebrow. "So you confronted a suspect on your own last night?"

"Ya confronted a suspect on yur own yesterday. Let it go."

"May I proceed, Dr. Lieth?" asked Zoe.

Alex said yes without looking up.

Zoe explained that over the past two years, PGC technology systems and medical advancements were being sold on the international black market. Only someone deep inside the company could've done it. Her sole focus was to find the source of the leaks and stop them.

"How's that going?" said Alex sarcastically.

"Poorly, sir, and it gets worse. Mistakes were made."

Alex looked up with a hard stare. "What mistakes?"

"It's OK, Zoe. Go ahead," said Galen.

"We foolishly allowed the virus that resulted in the data breach into the system."

Alex took a deep breath as the cabinets and all the items on the counter began to shake. Galen's firm grasp on his shoulder brought him back into the moment.

"Alex, play nice," said Galen, as the shaking ebbed away.

"What do you mean you allowed?" said Alex.

"When you brought the phone to be analyzed, we suspected it had a trojan horse virus but had no clue what consequences it would cause."

Alex said with a clenched jaw, "So Galen almost getting killed and Templeton getting executed, are only 'consequences' to you?"

"You don't think I fucking know that?" said Zoe, with tears in her eyes. "You know I care for Galen, and Templeton was my friend. I know his wife. For god's sake, my mistake cost his unborn children their father."

"You also let me take the blame for introducing the virus."

"I know, and I'm sorry. But I did fight for you, Dr. Lieth; please recall I debunked the theory that you destroyed the city's electrical grid."

"So, inflicting emotional damage on me is OK?"

"I deeply regret it, but I also identified the enemy was trying to kill you."

"Like they could."

"The bottom line is, I deeply regret any pain I've caused you."

Alex, Galen, and Zoe sat in awkward silence.

"Can ya find in yur heart for some forgiveness, Alex?" Galen said.

"Forgiveness has to be earned, Galen."

"Not long ago, I betrayed ya. Ya forgave me."

"That's because I'd touched your soul and knew you weren't on the side of darkness."

"Light and darkness. Don't think it's that easy, Alex. Life has a lot of grays," said Galen.

"The only thing I want to know from Ms. Palmer, if that even is her name, is who's behind the leaks?"

"The evidence we've gathered is confusing. Sometimes it seems as if someone in research and development is involved, while at other times the data points to the medical staff."

"You can remove Veronica Donalds from the list; she's not a suspect."

"OK," said Zoe.

"Is Bruno a suspect?" asked Galen.

"At times, yes, and at other times no. The technology often stolen is his advancements, but he doesn't have the computer skills to pull this off. He's a scientist, but can barely reboot his computer when needed."

"Was his inoculation formula stolen in the breach?" said Galen.

"That's both true and untrue. The data was stolen, but kept on a computer system not connected to the mainframe."

Alex raised his head and looked at Zoe directly. "So you're saying someone internally stole the formula, and we have no idea when it occurred?"

"Yes, I'm afraid so," said Zoe.

Alex sat, running his fingers through his hair. "Galen, I'd like a moment alone with Zoe."

"Alex, I trust ya, but yu're in a rare mood this morning."

"She'll be safe, Galen."

"It's OK, Galen. I'll be fine," said Zoe.

"Will be out on the balcony. Both of ya behave."

Alex waited for Galen to leave before directing his attention to Zoe.

"So, I guess you want to read my energy to determine if I'm lying to you, Dr. Lieth?"

Alex said no; he wanted to apologize for letting his temper get the best of him. He admitted he could get a little paranoid when people were coming for him, and seemingly there was danger around every corner. Alex asked why she took so long to come forward with this information, given that it directly affected his and Galen's safety.

"Guilt," said Zoe softly. "I was dealing with the guilt of losing Templeton and Galen's injury."

"Don't leave out your feelings for Galen. He told me you briefly hooked up, and I know your feelings go deeper than friendship."

"You can see that?"

"I don't need special abilities to see you have feelings for him."

"That puts us in the same boat," said Zoe.

"Excuse me?"

"You might not admit it, but your relationship with Galen is more than employer and employee. Are you upset with me because you think I'm a traitor, or is it because he might have spent last night in my bed?"

"We're just friends, Ms. Palmer."

"So it's Zoe when you want something from me, but Ms. Palmer when you're brooding because I know him in a way you don't. At first, you were friends, but I heard every word and emotion when he thought you were dead."

"How could you know what happened and his feelings about it?"

"Ryo had me monitor all your communications equipment to get to the bottom of the assault, and I heard everything. Plus, I'm not blind. Galen dropped everything shortly after he met you and was devastated when he thought you were lost. Being his boss doesn't inspire such avid devotion."

"You're a clever woman, Ms. Palmer, but you are way off base here. Yes, Galen is more than an employee; he is now a dedicated friend whom I trust with my life. But the man I love is lying in a coma about a hundred feet down the hall. Don't diminish our fucking relationship."

"Which relationship? You have two of them. I'm a trained agent, Dr. Lieth. Learning how to read people can be the difference between life and death. Someone will get hurt, and I fear it will be Galen."

"Galen's physical and emotional safety is my priority, and I don't have to explain it to anyone. So where does that leave us, *Zoe*?" asked Alex coldly.

"It leaves us on the same side with no secrets," said Zoe. "Ryo and I will share our information with you and Galen going forward."

"Can you get Galen to witness this agreement?"

Zoe stepped over to the balcony window and tapped it three times to get Galen's attention. Galen stepped inside and walked back into the kitchen.

"We've called a truce, Galen, and have agreed to share information. I've one stipulation––I want Bruno under twenty-four-hour surveillance and all his calls monitored," said Alex.

"He has an agent on him, and I'll ensure additional agents are assigned. Galen, can you handle the phone monitoring?" said Zoe.

"One step ahead of ya. Reviewed all his company internal phone and cell phone records."

"And?" said Alex.

"It's confusing. Doesn't call on the company cell phone except in the building."

"That's alarming," said Zoe. "I'll see if I can get a warrant to monitor calls from his house. It may take a while to get a judge to sign off on it."

"Thank you, Ms. Palmer. Galen, can you show Ms. Palmer out?"

Galen nodded and escorted Zoe to the elevator door, which closed behind her.

Galen turned to walk back into the kitchen as Alex began to eat his breakfast. "Tasty; you're a good cook, Galen. Thank you for breakfast."

"That's all ya've got to say after nearly going scorched earth again? Thought ya were going to hurt her."

Alex turned to look at Galen. "I'm sorry. Emotions are riding high these days. I was half asleep and startled she was in the penthouse. I thought we agreed to keep it a safe haven?"

"We did, but ya needed to hear it ASAP."

"Go get some rest, Galen. You look exhausted. Did you get any sleep last night?"

"What did ya and Zoe talk about when I was outside?"

"We exchanged our favorite recipes."

"Alex, cut the shite. Ya get this little twitch over yur left eye when yu're being dishonest."

"Fine, we talked about you. Zoe feels guilty for putting you in harm's way and wants me to keep you from getting hurt physically or emotionally."

"Did ya think I might have a say in that conversation? Ya know what? Screw it, going to bed. Enjoy yur breakfast. Don't fuckin' expect it again."

Chapter Forty-Three

Every time Alex was in the boardroom, he felt his life crashing and burning around him. Sitting in the room gave him goosebumps, and his stomach churned like a blender destroying his intestines. Alex looked at Galen, who appeared on the surface to share his concerns.

"Ya right, Alex? Today is the day we finally catch a break," said Galen.

"We deserve one," said Alex.

Dr. Donalds and Dr. Bruno entered the room and disrupted Alex's response as they sat on opposite sides of the table.

"Good morning, Alex and Galen," said Dr. Donalds. "I'm glad you could be here on such short notice."

Alex could tell she was nervous with Bruno in the room––he would not make the mistake of addressing her as Veronica, which would surely draw Bruno's ire.

"Good morning, Dr. Donalds. Please tell me you have some good news for us?" Alex could see Dr. Donalds take a brief sigh of relief before continuing.

"I'm here to present the facts," she said.

"Why is Bruno here?" said Galen.

"I asked him to be here to help explain our findings," said Dr. Donalds.

At those words, the churning in Alex's stomach worsened. "As long as he's useful, I'll allow him to stay," said Alex.

"So, as we discussed," explained Dr. Donalds, "PGC has cutting-edge equipment, which can produce findings far beyond the limits of mainstream medical technology."

"OK," said Alex.

"We ran Danyal's blood work several times with no significant findings."

"Please tell me that's promising."

"We now know a little more," said Dr. Donalds. "Danyal's symptom presentation is unusual. So, I took a risk––I asked Dr. Bruno to look at the findings, which led to identifying the potential origin of Danyal's condition. If it's OK with you, I'll let Dr. Bruno explain the findings."

Alex nodded.

"I know you don't want me here, Alex. Still, I have the expertise to help Mr. Sarif...Danyal." Dr. Bruno nodded to Dr. Donalds before saying their findings uncovered an unexpected and highly unusual result. The blood tests showed the presence of radioactive isotopes.

"Is that a result of Danyal being close to me?" asked Alex.

Bruno shook his head and said the radioactive isotopes in Danyal's blood were in a degraded state. He explained that all radioactive isotopes emit radiation and result in cellular disintegration. The barely detectable levels in Danyal's blood couldn't have resulted from an exposure weeks ago. That length of exposure would have been lethal, said Bruno.

Alex leaned forward in his seat. "What are you saying?"

"I'm saying, Alex, I believe Danyal was exposed to a degraded dose of ichor while he was in captivity, resulting in a case of ichor poisoning," said Bruno.

"So let me get this straight——you're saying the Sons of Enyaluis intentionally poisoned him?"

"Potentially," said Dr. Donalds, "or they could have been experimenting on him."

Alex's heart raced faster, and he turned away from the table.

"Alex," said Galen, "ya need a moment?"

Alex shook his head before saying he was trying to wrap his head around the fact that Danyal may have been experimented on by those bastards. "Why would they do this?"

"Dr. Bruno has a theory," said Dr. Donalds.

Alex could see the look of concern on Dr. Bruno's face.

"What are you not telling me?" asked Alex.

Dr. Bruno cleared his throat. "I wouldn't have believed this myself, Alex. I ran the tests several times."

"Spit it out, Bruno," said Alex.

Bruno hesitated before saying, "Danyal has a dormant 'god' gene."

Alex fell silent, trying to process the information.

"What did you say?" said Alex.

Dr. Bruno repeated himself. Galen moved over and placed his hand on Alex's shoulder. The room sat in silence.

"What does that even mean?" said Alex.

"It means somewhere in his family line, he has a god as an ancestor," said Bruno. "Probably in the past two hundred years."

Alex put his hand over his mouth. "Ditta?"

Bruno shook his head. "I did the comparison myself several times. His god genes come from different sources."

Alex took a deep sigh of relief. However, a daunting question then hit him. "Then which god is it?"

"We don't know," said Dr. Donalds. "There used to be many gods, according to what Ms. Dea told Bruno. What do you know about Danyal's history?"

"Not much," said Alex. "He was born in Turkey and adopted shortly after birth."

Alex dared not say what he feared deep inside his heart. But he mustered the courage to say the words out loud. "Is it Thanatos? Ditta told me the night she disappeared, Danyal's core was surrounded by darkness. I was too afraid to look for myself."

Dr. Bruno shuffled his papers and looked down. Alex's fear grew with each passing second until his vision blurred, and his hands tingled. He knew these signs; a panic attack was coming. He stood and turned to look out the window while focusing on his breath work for several moments.

Without turning around, he said, "There is no way to know, is there?"

"No," said Dr. Bruno. "If Ditta is to be believed, Thanatos is the only other remaining god."

Alex turned and looked directly at Bruno. "So, what does a dormant gene mean?"

Bruno shook his head. "We don't know, Alex. We're in uncharted territory."

Galen leaned forward and asked, "Were they trying to activate the god gene?"

"Good question, Mr. Tucker. We don't know," said Bruno. "The ichor was degraded, so whatever their plans, it didn't work. His god gene likely kept him alive."

Alex turned to face the group with his face red and eyes glistening. "He has one god gene. What would have happened to him if the ichor sample had not been degraded?"

Bruno shook his head again and shrugged his shoulders. "It's an untested theory with one god gene. He could have ascended to some level, or it could have killed him."

"So, he could become a demigod or die?" said Alex.

Bruno nodded.

"Makes no sense," said Galen. "How did the Sons know about the god gene?"

Dr. Donalds shook her head. "Somehow, they must have had a DNA sample."

Alex ran his fingers through his hair before responding, "I gave him a DNA kit for Christmas for fun, to see if he had any relatives in the DNA databases."

"That could explain how they learned about his DNA," said Dr. Donalds, "but that suggests they are much more insidious and organized than we'd thought."

"Where do we go from here?" said Alex. "Can it be treated? Would dialysis or a blood transfusion help?"

"The isotopes, unfortunately, are in his brain tissue and organs," said Dr. Bruno.

Alex shook his head slowly, trying to hold back tears. "So what's the prognosis? Can anything be done?"

Dr. Donalds paused before responding and swallowed softly. "Without a way to purge the isotopes from Danyal's system, his condition will continue to worsen and become fatal."

Alex couldn't speak. Galen placed his hand on Alex's shoulder once more.

"In a perfect world, if you could do anything, doctors, what would you do to save him?" asked Alex.

Dr. Donalds said it was more Dr. Bruno's area, but if they had a sample of ichor, they might be able to retro-engineer a compound capable of purging the ichor from Danyal's system.

"An antidote?" said Galen.

"It's not that simple, but yes," said Dr. Bruno.

"How would this impact Danyal's god DNA?" asked Alex.

"No way of knowing," said Bruno.

Alex returned to face the table again. "If we had a viable sample, would this be an option?"

Both Dr. Bruno and Dr. Donalds nodded. "The problem is," said Dr. Bruno, "Ditta never shared the source of ichor. The other concern is how pure ichor would affect his god DNA. There are too many unknown variables to predict what would happen."

"So, how long does he have?" asked Alex, holding his breath.

The room fell silent at Alex's question. With tears in her eyes, Dr. Donalds responded, "At his current rate of disintegration, no more than a week."

Alex fell back in his chair as he held his hands to his face. No one dared break the silence. Alex, in a wavering voice, thanked the doctors for their help. Looking up, he asked Dr. Donalds if she could accompany him to the penthouse to discuss the plan for keeping Danyal comfortable. Dr. Donalds nodded. Alex walked to the other end of the conference table and extended his hand to Bruno, who reluctantly shook it.

"Thank you, Dr. Bruno. I appreciate your help." Alex could see Bruno was speechless as he finally nodded in reply.

The doors to the elevator were barely closed before Veronica turned to hug Alex.

"I'm so sorry; I wish I'd better news, darlin'. I'm not giving up on Danyal," said Veronica.

"I believe you," said Alex. "Let's not talk until the penthouse."

"Walls might have ears," said Galen.

Alex could tell by Dr. Donalds' face she was confused, but followed his request. After stepping out of the elevator, Alex and Veronica watched Galen walk down the hallway to close the door to the bedroom where Nurse Ringwood was sitting with Danyal. Galen closed the door and returned to the living room.

"Clear, Alex," said Galen. "Do yur thing."

Alex closed his eyes and opened them.

"Do what?" asked Veronica.

Alex said he'd turned off the sound in the area by manipulating the sound waves. No one outside of the room would hear their conversation.

"Why are we here, Alex?" she asked. "I know you don't want to discuss end-of-life care for Danyal. There's no way in hell you're giving up."

"You're very astute, Veronica; I'm here to ask for your help."

"Ask away, darlin'; I'll do anything I can."

"First, I need your assurance you won't discuss this conversation with anyone else, especially Bruno."

Veronica nodded. "I swear. But you're starting to scare me with all the cloak and dagger requirements."

"Not our intention," said Galen as he handed Alex a small metal box. Alex opened it and showed Veronica the contents.

"Is that what I think it is, Alex?" said Veronica.

"Yes, this is the only piece of ichor chocolate remaining that Ditta gave me on my birthday. Please tell me if you can do something with it."

"If I can isolate the ichor, and it's not too degraded, I might find a way to purge the isotopes from Danyal's system."

"Can you do the work here in the penthouse?" asked Alex.

"Unfortunately, no. The equipment I need is in the lab."

"We will have to increase the security in yur lab to keep the sample safe," said Galen.

"I understand," said Veronica, "but it will draw unwanted attention if you want to keep my work a secret. Bruno knows everything that is happening in his labs."

"What if I could get you a lab outside the building, with Ryo's permission?" said Alex.

"That could work, but I'd need special equipment requiring time to procure."

"Would Mass General have it?" asked Alex.

"Yes, I have a girlfriend who works there. But how would you make that happen?"

"Dr. Anderson, the head of surgery, is a fan of PGC and would help if further donations for the hospital would be forthcoming."

"How would I explain my absence to Bruno?" asked Veronica.

"Does he know about Charlotte and her treatments?"

Veronica nodded yes.

"What treatments?" asked Galen.

"My wife Charlotte is being treated for breast cancer."

"So sorry, mate," said Galen.

"I have a crazy idea. Would Charlotte be willing to help us with our ruse?"

"I think I see where you're going," said Veronica. "A 'setback' would require her to seek treatment, and I'd need to take a brief absence to be with her."

"I'm desperate, Veronica––I'll do anything to make this happen. Please help us."

Veronica smiled and said Charlotte was adventurous so it wouldn't take much to rope her into their plan. "But how will we get the sample to Mass General?" she asked.

"Leave it to me," said Galen. "Shouldn't raise any eyebrows for me to go for mah post-operative follow-up."

"Can we make this happen tonight?" asked Alex.

Veronica nodded.

"Galen will go speak with Ryo, and I'll reach out to Dr. Anderson," said Alex.

Alex thanked Veronica for helping as he hugged her before she stepped toward the elevator. Galen went to follow, but Alex stopped him by placing his hand on Galen's chest.

"Ya right, Alex?"

"I'm not sure. I have this growing tingling in my chest, and it's getting harder to breathe."

"It's OK. Sounds like hope. Been so long since ya experienced it. Feels strange, I bet. Hold onto that feeling."

Chapter Forty-Four

Alex

Alex sat by the bed where Danyal lay, holding his hand tightly as he watched the heart rate and breathing monitors drop with each moment. It had been five days, and still no update from Veronica. Lost in thought, Alex didn't hear Galen enter the bedroom behind him with a tray, bringing Alex breakfast.

"Alex," said Galen.

Alex jumped, startled by Galen's approach. "Shit, Galen. Give a guy some warning before you sneak up on him in his bedroom."

Galen said he thought all the noise in the kitchen would warn Alex he was coming down the hall. He begged Alex to eat since he hadn't left Danyal's side for five days.

"I'm not hungry; besides, I thought you'd never cook me breakfast again."

"Didn't cook, so keeping my promise. Got ya pancakes and the butter pecan syrup ya like."

Galen and Alex jumped as Alex's cell phone vibrated on the nightstand. Galen leaned forward to read the caller ID. "Alex, it's Veronica. Answer it!"

Alex took a deep breath as he picked up the phone and placed it on speaker.

"Hello," he said in a quivering voice.

"Alex, I have a serum Danyal must receive at once. I'll give you all the details when I arrive; this is probably our only chance," said Veronica.

"Should we come to ya?" asked Galen.

"No," said Veronica, "it would waste too much precious time moving Danyal. I'm fixin' to head to you in two minutes as soon as the security detail clears a path."

"Please, hurry." Alex hung up the phone and turned to Galen. "You heard that? I'm not hallucinating?"

"Yu're not hallucinating!" yelled Galen. "Finally gettin' a fuckin' break!" Alex hugged Galen and began to sob.

"Let it out," said Galen. "Not like I'm wearing a new shirt that can't be dry-cleaned."

"Screw you," said Alex as he cried and laughed simultaneously. "Now I'm wiping my snot on your shirt."

"If it helps," said Galen, "but sending ya the bill."

Alex stood up and looked at Galen. "Have I thanked you for everything you've done to help me get to this point? I wouldn't be getting Danyal back without you."

"Easy there, mate. Let's not jinx anything."

"I forgot, you're superstitious," said Alex.

"Cautious, not superstitious. Luck keeps biting us in the arse. Best not to tempt her. Mass General isn't far away. Saturday morning traffic should be light. What do we need to do to prepare?" asked Galen.

"We should call Ryo so they're ready to assist."

Alex and Galen both turned, surprised, as they heard the elevator arrive on the penthouse floor.

"That was too fast," said Galen. "Going to go check who arrived. Ya need to stay here in the bedroom."

"Galen, we're going down the hall together."

Galen nodded. Walking down the hall and turning the corner, the sight of Ryo standing by the elevator gave Alex a sense of relief.

"That was fast, Ryo. Were you on the elevator when Galen texted?"

Ryo turned toward Alex, and the disturbed look on his face stopped Alex in his tracks.

"The situation at Mass General has changed," said Ryo.

"Spit it out, Ryo," said Galen. "Don't keep us in the dark."

Ryo shot Galen an angry look as he said, "As of ten minutes ago, Mass General had a potential biohazard exposure and was placed on total lockdown."

Alex turned to punch the wall and put his right fist through the bricks. "Where's Veronica?"

Ryo said he wasn't sure. All communication in and out of the building was in the hands of federal authorities.

Alex frantically pulled out his phone and tried to call Veronica. "Fuck, no cell service available. We've got to get there, Ryo."

"No," said Ryo, "I can't risk you entering an unknown situation that could be a trap, especially not with the authorities and news cameras watching. PGC is now on lockdown until this is over."

Alex said Ryo couldn't stop him from leaving. "Danyal is dying and won't make it much longer. I'll take down every wall in the building or jump off the balcony if needed."

Ryo placed his right hand on his hip near his service weapon.

"That's how you want to play this, Ryo?" asked Alex.

"No, but I'll use the force necessary to stop you. This could be another trap, and I can't risk you being injured or captured."

"So ya think ya can just enter the home of a god and pull a gun?" said Galen.

"I don't have to stop the god; I only need to stop you, Galen. He won't risk your safety or go anywhere if you are injured."

"Ryo," said Alex calmly, "please remove your hand from your weapon."

"No."

"Answer this question for me…is this stunt worth losing your job or family for?"

"Are you threatening my family, Alex? You sound increasingly like a loose cannon. Perhaps Bruno is right."

"I wonder if they would understand losing you for making such a bad decision. I won't ask again--remove your hand from your weapon."

"No."

Alex snapped his fingers, and Ryo flew up against the brick wall, surrounded by an aura of pink energy that held him about three feet off the ground.

"Alex, don't hurt him!" yelled Galen.

"What happens now is solely up to him," said Alex as he stepped closer to speak to Ryo. "I may not be able to control or affect you directly with my abilities, but I can cause plenty of damage using the environment around you. Right now, I'm slowing your breathing and blood flow to your brain by constricting the bulletproof vest around your chest. Either you can get it under control, or I won't stop until you lose consciousness. Yes, or no."

Ryo nodded his head yes.

"I'll release you, but don't you dare threaten me or Galen again," said Alex as he released Ryo, who landed on his feet before falling forward to his stomach.

"He's stalling," said Galen.

"I know," said Alex. "Do you still have the gas masks and weapons from the field mission?"

"Yah. What're ya planning, Alex?"

"Get the masks from our gear, and I'll show you."

Galen rushed down the hall and returned with three gas masks and two pistols.

Alex turned to Ryo, still kneeling on the floor, trying to catch his breath.

"I'll give you a choice, Ryo. You can stay and keep Danyal safe or come with us."

"You'd trust me with Danyal after I threatened Galen?"

"Yes," said Alex. "It was a misguided attempt to protect me and the company. I don't need to read your soul. You're a good soldier who wants all of us to make it out of this alive."

"Shit," said Ryo. "Go before I change my mind."

"What's the play?" said Galen.

"Put on your gas mask and put your arms around me."

"What?"

"Put your arms around me and hold on tight. We're teleporting."

Alex could see the fear in Galen's eyes through the gas mask. "Here we go."

"Alex!"

Alex opened his eyes as he and Galen crashed on a cold, hard linoleum floor.

"Made it!" yelled Galen.

"You doubted me?" said Alex.

"Yah, ya don't have control over teleportation."

"If I let my fight-or-flight reflex kick in during life-or-death situations, I can harness the ability."

"How will we find Veronica?" asked Galen.

"She's down the hall to the left; I can feel her."

"Ya can feel her?" asked Galen.

"I shared some of my energy when we were in the penthouse earlier in the week. It serves as a beacon. We need to move."

Alex rushed down the hall with Galen behind him until they stopped at two secured large doors. Alex drew back his fist to hit the doors, but stopped when he heard Veronica cry out.

"Alex! Don't open the doors; I'm OK," yelled Veronica as she looked at Alex through the window of the safety doors.

"How do I get you and the serum out?" asked Alex.

Veronica said she was in a hermetically sealed negative pressure room that didn't circulate any air from outside, which kept her safe from the biohazard contagion in the air.

"Is Charlotte OK?"

Veronica nodded yes, saying she left early this morning and made it home. "Alex, you need to find Bruno."

"We'll deal with Bruno when this is over," said Alex through his gas mask.

"No," said Veronica as she shook her head, "you need to *stop* Bruno. He came to the lab and wanted to see my research. When I refused, several men with assault rifles threatened us. I'm so sorry, Alex. He ran off with the antidote."

"How long ago did this happen?" asked Galen.

"About eight minutes ago. Bruno and the armed men headed down the hall toward the back of the hospital. One more thing––Zoe was in the building and went after them."

"Galen," demanded Alex, "take my hand. We're going after Bruno."

"How?" asked Galen.

"I put the same energy on him recently when we shook hands. I can feel him now. He's moving fast. We need to go."

Alex opened his eyes and shielded them from the sun as he and Galen materialized on the hospital roof. Alex looked instinctively at the Mass General helicopter about a hundred yards away from the roof of the building. Alex reached up with his hands as if pulling a rope to drag the helicopter back.

"Alex!" yelled Galen, "ya have to stop."

"Bruno is on the helicopter, Galen. If he gets away, we may not find him again."

"Stop!" yelled Galen again as he grabbed Alex's arm. "The helicopter is struggling against ya. If it crashes, the serum is gone. There will be massive damage and civilian casualties in the streets below. Please stop. Find another way."

Alex released his telekinetic grip on the helicopter as a hail of bullets from the aircraft flew past him and Galen. Alex watched through his tears as Bruno and his only hope to save Danyal sped away from the city skyline and toward the harbor, before disappearing over the horizon.

"I won't give up," yelled Alex. He closed his eyes and disappeared.

Alex reappeared on the roof within seconds, holding Bruno by his jacket. He walked Bruno to the edge of the building and dangled him over the side. "If you want to fucking live, Bruno, you'll hand over the antidote."

"I can't," yelled Bruno, "you fool, what've you done? It's still on the helicopter."

Alex held Bruno further out over the side of the building. "You've condemned Danyal to death. I hope you see his face as you hit the ground."

"Stop!" yelled Bruno. "I know where SOE are headed, and I'll tell you, but only if you help me."

"You miserable piece of shit. Why would I help you?"

"Because you won't only condemn me to death––you'll kill your sister too. Nyssa is alive but must receive a full dose of ichor to survive."

"Alex, please," yelled Galen, "bring Bruno back from the edge!"

"He poisoned Danyal and Hoko, nearly killed you, and tried to kill me––why does he deserve mercy?"

"He doesn't. Would move heaven and earth to save my sister. Don't stoop to his level. Yu're not a murderer."

Alex paused before turning and throwing Bruno back onto the roof, where he skidded across the surface. Alex dropped to his knees and let out a primal scream which shook the building.

Galen turned and knelt to comfort Alex, but stopped as he registered the horrific scene behind them. He ran and picked up the lifeless body lying in a pool of blood in front of the entrance to the roof. "Zoe!" yelled Galen. "Please open yur eyes, please! Alex, help!"

Alex stood and ran to Galen, holding Zoe's body.

"She's not responding, Alex. Has a gunshot wound to the chest. Please! Please heal her!"

Alex closed his eyes to concentrate and touched Zoe's heart. He focused on directing life energy into her body, as he had when Galen was injured. Alex opened his eyes and shook his head. "I'm so sorry, Galen. She's gone."

Galen held Zoe's body close to his chest as he wailed uncontrollably, while Alex held Galen tighter than he ever had before.

Chapter Forty-Five

Alex

Alex sat at the table in the boardroom, replaying the siege at the hospital in his head. Galen and Ryo sat at the end of the table, listening to the television news report.

"A terrorist group named the Sons of Enyaluis," said the commentator, "has taken responsibility for releasing an airborne biotoxin at Mass General, which resulted in thirty patients and staff members being exposed. Currently, there are no medical updates available."

"Turn it off," said Alex. "I'll tell you how it ends; we lose!"

"Alex," said Ryo, "we need to know if there are any updates."

"Turn it off now!" yelled Alex as he slammed his fist on the conference table, resulting in the table splintering.

Ryo turned off the TV.

"Where's Bruno now?" asked Galen.

"He's in the medical wing under armed surveillance. Alex shook him up good when he threw Bruno across the hospital roof," said Ryo.

"Giving him to the authorities?" asked Galen.

"Eventually. That depends on the quality of information he provides," said Ryo.

"Wuz information provided by Bruno about the SOE accurate?" asked Galen.

Ryo said there was an old warehouse in Albany, New York, used as a home base for SOE. However, the building was now vacant.

"The helicopter?" asked Galen.

"Found in upstate Massachusetts––they ditched it for road vehicles as soon as possible," added Ryo.

"Can ya track them, Alex, as ya did before? Looking for voids in the electromagnetic field?" asked Galen.

"No," said Alex. "The bastards have learned from that experience, and were now scattered in different directions like cockroaches. I have no idea where to look or who to search for to find the serum. It's over; Danyal only has hours to live, and I have to be here with him."

Galen motioned for Ryo to leave the conference room. Galen walked over and sat in the chair next to Alex.

"Alex, know what yu're feeling. Please don't give up."

"You know what I'm feeling? Is a man you love near death? If I recall correctly, you ran away from all your relationships."

"Damn it, not fair. Ya don't have the exclusive right to suffer. Amara has been unconscious in a hospital for eight years, and now Zoe's dead."

Alex stood, and Galen followed suit.

"Do ya need an emotional or physical punching bag, Alex? Suggest ya try someone else, because I'll fight back," Galen said as he puffed out his chest and stepped forward until he came up against Alex's chest. "Come on, mate. Too afraid to get yur hands dirty as usual."

"Galen, I'm warning you, don't do that again."

Galen stepped forward and shoved Alex once more.

Alex reached out and wrapped both arms around Galen, pulling him tightly to his chest.

"Let me go!" yelled Galen.

"No. Please stop fighting. I'm sorry, you've been with me from the beginning. I've no right to take my anger out on you. You've suffered more than any person should."

Galen placed his head on Alex's shoulder as he began to sob.

"Sorry, too. Wanted to punch someone to make them hurt like I do inside."

Their embrace was interrupted by a knocking at the conference room door. Alex looked up to see Wynn standing on the other side of the glass door.

"What the fuck? I don't have the energy to deal with him today," said Alex.

"I got him," said Galen, wiping away his tears as Alex released his bear hug. "Ya go be with Danyal."

Galen stepped outside the room but quickly stepped back in before Alex left. "Alex, Wynn says he has information to discuss with ya that can't wait. Think he's serious."

Alex sighed and sat back down at the undamaged end of the table. He nodded to Galen to send him in.

"Ya want me to stay?" asked Galen.

Alex shook his head.

"Will be back in a sec," said Galen.

"I don't have the energy to fight, Wynn," said Alex. "I want to be with Danyal in his final moments."

"I'm not here to fight, Alex," said Wynn, sitting a file on the table. "But I'd like to start by saying I deeply regret what I said to you at our last meeting. I was insensitive about you and Danyal, and that was inexcusable. No one should have to suffer the way Danyal has suffered. I don't know how you're holding it together; I'd be devastated if Shae suffered this way."

"Thank you for the apology, Wynn. I owe you a long overdue apology, too. I'm sorry I panicked and left you alone in Egypt. There's not a day that I'm not ashamed of how I acted, and I can't fathom the suffering you endured because of my actions."

"It's not all your fault, Alex. I'm in therapy, and I understand I blamed you for a situation you couldn't control. Both of us in a prison cell wouldn't have changed the outcome. What hurt the most is I loved you, and that circumstances forced you to abandon me."

"I recognized your feelings were deeper than mine, and I panicked. You deserved better," said Alex.

"We can't change the past, Alex. I'm trying to move forward with Shae, but it's a daily battle. I wish the pain could magically go away."

Alex nodded and looked at his hands, holding them before his body. "I don't know how my abilities might work on psychological trauma, but are you willing to try?"

"Are you serious, Alex? Please, take the edge off so I can sleep without nightmares. It may be the help I need to be the man Shae needs me to be."

Alex said, "I need to place my hand on your heart, and I need your consent to touch your core energy."

Wynn nodded.

Alex lifted his hand, but was surprised when Wynn wrapped his arms around Alex to hug him. "This will work, too," said Alex as he returned Wynn's embrace. "You might feel some tingling." Alex drew the cosmic energy around them to form a pulsing orange, blue, and pink cocoon. Alex stepped back from Wynn's embrace to look at his spark.

"The good news is your spark is brighter. However, you'll still have to do the heavy lifting in therapy, but hopefully you'll now have a better chance of succeeding," said Alex.

"Boris, Shae, and I thank you, Alex," said Wynn as he leaned in and gently kissed Alex on the cheek.

Alex smiled as he wiped a tear from Wynn's cheek. "Consider it a thank you for saving Boris."

Wynn turned and picked up the file he had placed on the table. He said the information he was about to convey was top secret.

"Many years ago, Ditta developed contingency plans to help her recover if she was physically injured."

"Injured?" said Alex. "I thought she was invulnerable."

"Nearly," said Wynn. "Over the years, she was involved in several battles with the other gods, especially Thanatos. Several ancient weapons could injure her, and by her account, Thanatos nearly succeeded in killing her once."

Alex asked how she survived. Wynn said she could survive by healing herself via two methods. The first was to gather the Earth's healing energies at natural power sources or vortexes on the planet, such as Mount Shasta, Giza, Sedona, Göbeklitepe, and Tiwanaku. He added this method was the most powerful and immediate way she could heal herself.

"And what about the second?" asked Alex.

"This method is more frightening, and only to be used as a last resort," said Wynn.

"Go on," said Alex hesitantly.

"She could temporarily extend or supplement her life force by draining the life force from a mortal."

Alex sat in silence before responding, "So, are you telling me she's the basis for the vampire myths?"

"I'm not sure, Alex," said Wynn, "but she could drain the life from humans to ensure her survival."

"Why are you telling me this now? I don't need healing," said Alex.

"I can't predict it would help, but if you wielded pure healing Earth energy, could it give you a chance to heal or improve Danyal's survival chances? It's at least worth considering."

Alex sat up in his chair. "So the only other option is to try to heal Danyal by supplementing his life force, by killing another human?"

Wynn nodded.

"That's not happening," responded Alex. "Who else knows about these protocols?"

"Only three people: me, Hoko, and Bruno."

"The more I learn about Ditta," said Alex, "the more I understand how cunning and calculated she was."

The two were interrupted by Galen knocking on the boardroom door.

"Sorry to interrupt, but ya need to see this," said Galen.

Galen placed an elongated box about a foot long and six inches wide on the table. He opened it to reveal the dagger Ditta had given him for safekeeping.

"So, you bring me a dagger, Galen? Can I use it on Bruno?" asked Alex.

"Ms. Dea gave me this dagger on the night ya ascended. Swore me to only give it to ya when all hope appeared lost. Now feels like the right time," said Galen.

"May I inspect it?" asked Wynn. He looked over the knife carefully and said he'd only ever encountered one other dagger like this in the Egyptian Museum in Cairo. The tomb of Pharaoh Tutankhamun had a similar dagger. He said the dagger was unique because it originated from a meteorite that fell to Earth and was composed of cosmic materials. If he had to date it, he told Alex he'd bet his career this dagger predated Tutankhamun's.

"So how does this help me, Wynn?" asked Alex.

Wynn leaned the dagger forward. "There's an inscription I can't make out." As Wynn turned the blade, the weight shifted and fell out of Wynn's hands toward the floor.

Alex instinctively reached out to catch the dagger, but abruptly jerked his hand back before the blade bounced on the wood floor.

"Ouch," said Alex.

"Ya, right?" asked Galen.

"Yeah, I think it nicked me."

"How's that possible?" asked Galen as he handed Alex the cloth used to wrap the blade. "Alex," said Galen, "ya need to look at yur hand."

Alex looked down. "Shit, my blood's golden. That's new."

"Galen," said Wynn, "quickly hand Alex the empty water glass on the counter."

"You want to drink my blood, Wynn?" responded Alex.

"No, you handsome idiot––did you not learn anything in my lectures? What does gold blood mean in mythology?"

Alex thought momentarily, and his eyes widened.

"Gold blood means ichor. The pure blood of a god." Alex, with his other hand, carefully tried to catch the dripping blood in the glass. "It appears to have stopped bleeding," said Alex. "The cut has healed."

He lifted the glass, holding the drops of pure ichor to eye level, and turned the glass to inspect it from every angle before smiling. "Someone get Veronica here now––we've got work to do if we're going to save Danyal," said Alex.

Galen jumped up to dial Veronica's number on his cell as Wynn picked up the dagger to inspect it again after Alex had ensured it was safe.

"Careful," said Alex, "don't get any ichor on you. It can kill you."

Wynn nodded. "I think I can read the inscription now."

"What does it say?" asked Alex.

"It says rebirth. This is the knife of Eros."

"May I ask you a favor, Wynn?" asked Alex.

Wynn nodded.

"If you were to pick an Earth power vortex to try to heal Danyal, which would you choose?"

Wynn stroked his beard with his right hand as he considered the question. He said Giza was obviously out of the question, while Sedona and Mount Shasta were too public. That would leave the most ancient sites of Göbeklitepe and Tiwanaku. Göbeklitepe was the oldest known temple on the planet, but the province in Turkey was so war-torn it wouldn't be safe, and they'd have difficulty moving freely. Known for its monoliths and the Gate of the Sun, he said he'd choose Tiwanaku and the Lake Titicaca area in Western Bolivia. Wynn said all these sites were too far away, however, given Danyal's condition, as he handed Alex another file.

"Boston is located on one of the most powerful vortexes in the northern hemisphere. It's why Ditta picked it for the company headquarters. This file contains the exact coordinates of the energy vortex needed to tap into pure Earth energy. It's very close," said Wynn.

"How close?" said Alex.

"It's only twelve miles away under the Old North Church, the oldest church in Boston."

"The same church that was the location for the signal sent for Paul Revere's midnight ride, one if by land and two if by sea?" said Alex.

Wynn nodded and said many churches were built on top of pagan or spiritual sites of native cultures. He cautioned there was one problem: Ditta sealed the vortex decades ago to limit the flow of energy, because it was amplifying negative human emotions that led to more conflicts, and the open vortex served as a beacon, drawing Thanatos to Boston.

"So, how do I reopen the vortex, and what would be the consequences?"

"Unfortunately, Ditta took that information with her. All I know from her records is that it can be accessed in the catacombs beneath the church."

"Would you be willing to help us with this quest, Wynn?" asked Alex.

"Yes, it's the least I can do for the gift you gave me today. I'll meet with Ryo and get the ball rolling." Wynn left the room as Galen finished his call with Veronica.

"She's on her way," said Galen. "Ya looked pretty chummy with Wynn."

"It was long overdue. You afraid of graveyards or crypts, Galen?"

"No," said Galen, "why?"

"We're going to be headed to the catacombs beneath the Old North Church to open an energy vortex."

"Would follow ya anywhere. Promise me one thing, mate."

"What, Galen?"

"Promise me we'll never fight again."

"I promise," said Alex, "our faces are too pretty for fighting, so we must settle our differences with video games or wrestling."

"Remember how well ya wrestle. Michael's nose is still healing," Galen said as he rolled his eyes and pushed Alex down the hall towards the penthouse elevator.

Chapter Forty-Six

Alex

"Alex, darlin', I can't do what you're asking. It's impossible to recreate the antidote serum in twenty-four hours. I'm not a miracle worker," exclaimed Veronica.

"Please, Veronica," begged Alex. "This may be the key to saving Danyal's life. You did it before; why can't you do it now?"

Veronica said that the situation had changed. It took her five days to research a sample of degraded ichor before. The ichor he wanted her to use now was pure; there was no way she could predict how the purity of the sample would impact the research. She said Alex needed to understand that they couldn't rush science. She explained she couldn't do it in a month of Sundays, and it would be unethical to give a serum to Danyal that hadn't been properly researched. "It could kill him at once. There's no fixin' that mistake."

"You told me five days ago the best estimate was he had about a week to live. How am I supposed to live with myself knowing we didn't try every option at our disposal?"

Veronica said she understood, but there just wasn't enough time.

"What if I could get you help?" asked Alex.

"Who could you bring in that wouldn't get in my way? You bet-ter not be planning what I think you have in mind, Alex." Veronica paused and took a deep breath.

"You know he could help. He's the most experienced in this field. No one on the planet is more qualified. Those were your words."

"You don't understand, Alex; He's a monster. Less than twen-ty-four hours ago, Bruno had his cronies hold an assault rifle to my head."

"I'm sorry, Veronica; I know this is traumatic, but I wouldn't ask if there was any other option."

"An assault rifle, Alex, held to my head. I thought I was going to die and never see Charlotte again."

"Remember our conversation in the penthouse five days ago?"

"Don't go there, darlin'. Don't play that card with me."

"You told me if it were Charlotte in the hospital bed, you'd allow anyone with the knowledge and skills to help her assist in her treat-ment."

"Fuck you, Alex. That's not fair. That was before he tried to kill me and make Charlotte a widow. I think you also called him a 'devil.' I'm willing to admit I'm wrong; he is *the* devil."

"I recall you added that if he could save Charlotte, a deal with the devil sounded like a small price to save her life. We're wasting precious time, Veronica. I'm leaving for Wynn's earth vortex in a day. I need the serum as a backup."

"What're you proposing?" asked Veronica hesitantly.

Alex said he didn't want to traumatize her, but they needed Bruno's help. He said he didn't want Bruno's hands on the pure ichor sample, so he offered a compromise. He suggested she and Bruno work in different labs at PGC remotely. She would run the show, and he'd be out if he didn't follow her lead. They would only communicate via video conferencing and work on the computer server in real time. Alex said Bruno might be the devil, but he wouldn't get anywhere near her and would have armed guards on him. Alex asked if this arrangement would work for her.

Veronica closed her eyes and didn't respond to Alex for several moments.

"Yes, I'll try. But you'll owe me, darlin'," she said.

"Anything, thank you!" yelled Alex as he hugged Veronica.

"Don't count your chickens before they hatch, Alex. You've got to convince the devil to take part."

"Oh, he'll participate. I have the ichor that can save his daughter. I've all the leverage I need."

"Don't get overconfident, now. When playing poker with the devil, he always has a card up his sleeve. Cheating is all he knows; you won't know what card it is until it's too late."

"I won't forget your warning," said Alex as he ran down the hall to meet with Bruno.

Alex turned the corner and entered the medical wing, not knowing what to expect when he came face to face with Bruno. He looked through the door and almost didn't recognize the man before him. Gone was the bombastic figure who took every opportunity to bloviate about his intelligence, and in his place was a feeble-looking old man shackled to a hospital bed. He looked more like a dying man than a criminal mastermind. Despite the bruises and scrapes on Bruno's head and face, he'd get no fucking sympathy from Alex. He was directly responsible for the suffering of the people Alex loved. He opened the door and stepped into the room.

"I don't have any time to fuck around with you, Bruno. I'm going to offer you a deal. Take or leave it, but this is the only chance to save your hide and Nyssa."

Bruno sat up in bed and said he didn't expect to see Alex unless he had come to finish the job he started on the roof.

"Fuck off, Bruno. You don't get to play the victim. You're the architect of all the pain and suffering in my life. I suggest you let me do the talking before I decide to smite you."

"What do you want, Alex?" responded Bruno.

"I want your help with developing a serum to save Danyal."

"The plan has no chance of succeeding. You're missing the main ingredient––you have no ichor."

Alex took great satisfaction in holding up a small vial of his gold blood to show Bruno his treasure.

"Is the sample real? How did you obtain it?"

"None of your fucking business. All you need to know is Dr. Donalds has verified its pure ichor."

"I'll ask you again, Alex. What do you want?"

"I want your help. If you help Dr. Donalds develop a serum to treat Danyal, I'll ensure you're treated fairly by the authorities."

"As if I care about my situation..."

"Let me finish, Bruno. If you help Danyal, I'll do everything I can to help Nyssa survive––even if it means giving her a full dose of ichor."

Bruno took off his glasses with his unshackled hand, and Alex could see tears forming in his eyes. "Why would you help her? You have no reason to."

"Maybe I'm not a heartless bastard like you. I have no biological family, but I'm willing to help save my sister. What Ditta ordered you to do was ruthless. Help me fix her mistake."

"Don't you want to know why I took such extreme measures to replace you and risked so many lives in the process?"

"I don't think knowing your reasoning will help me, and we're wasting time."

"Everything I did was to save her. Since Danyal didn't consume any ichor the night you ascended, the degraded ichor was given to Danyal to force you to find another source of ichor. I want you to know I warned his captors this would end badly."

Alex breathed deeply. "Why didn't you fucking ask?"

"Ditta made the rules. She kept insisting there could only be one source of Eros."

"In case you hadn't noticed, I'm not Ditta. I make the rules now. Will you help?"

"Yes, I'll help if you promise to treat Nyssa with ichor."

"You may want to know all the details before you agree. You'll be working in your lab and remote conferencing with Dr. Donalds. You'll never touch the ichor."

"I agree," said Bruno.

"You've twenty-four hours to produce the serum."

"Twenty-four hours? You might as well ask for a biblical miracle. Who decided the timetable?"

"I did. Dr. Donalds was totally against it. The deadline is needed so I can try another possibility with Danyal."

Bruno laughed and said, "The resurrection protocols. Wynn must have stepped up to the plate. I warn you; you might get more than you bargained for with an Earth energy vortex. There are two kinds: one vortex takes in Earth's energy and filters it, and the other, which you are trying to wield, expels the Earth's energy and is easily polluted by the surroundings. I wonder if your body can handle the energy you are attempting to harness."

"What're you talking about, Bruno?"

Bruno shook his head. "Now I have a secret for you. You currently are only running at a fraction of the power Ditta possessed. I initially didn't think it worked, but now I can see it did."

"What're you blabbering about?" snapped Alex.

"The targeted EMP detonated at the moment of your ascension. It has hampered your development more than you know. You could be signing your death warrant if you try to wield pure Earth energy."

"I'll take the risk," said Alex.

"Yes, you're a risk-taker. Between you, me, and the walls, I respect that about you, Alex."

"Don't flatter me."

"Get me out of here and into the lab, Alex. Several lives hang in the balance, and I'll do my part to help. If you come back alive, I'll give you the details regarding Nyssa's location––that is, if the Sons of Enyaluis don't find her first."

"I can find her if needed," said Alex.

"Can you?" said Bruno. "I'll share another secret with you: gods can't track or control other gods. It's a defense mechanism to keep them safe."

Alex stepped toward the hospital bed as he leaned closer to speak to Bruno.

"If that's true, your inoculations must be based on Nyssa's biology."

"Smart man," said Bruno. "The inoculations were developed from her stem cells."

Alex stepped back. "This revelation changes nothing, Bruno. Don't try anything or double-cross me. I'll find new ways to make you suffer."

Bruno nodded. "Get me out of this gown and into a lab coat. I've work to do."

Chapter Forty-Seven

Galen stood at the loading dock of PGC with a nervous look on his face as he hung up his phone.

"Need to talk, mate. That wuz Veronica; she can't come. Charlotte needs emergency medical care."

"What?" asked Alex.

Galen said the doctors had run some tests at Mass Gen and identified her treatments weren't working as well as they'd believed. She was going into surgery tonight.

"Fuck, fuck, fuck, fuck, fuck!" said Alex.

"Take a breath, mate. Medical staff will be here shortly with the serum," said Galen. He knew that Alex understood Bruno was the only other option. "Ya right with this? If not, I can find another doc."

Alex shook his head.

"Alone in a truck with the man who tried to kill us and yur ex, Wynn. What could go wrong?" said Galen.

Alex smirked and responded by pointing behind Galen, who turned in time to sidestep an attempted kiss from Andrea. She scowled at Alex for warning Galen and punched Alex gently on the shoulder. As Galen was distracted, Michael snuck up behind him and placed him in a bear hug, which Galen quickly slipped out of and smacked Michael on the back of the head.

"Ya do this, Alex?" said Galen.

Alex smiled and shook his head as Ryo walked up the loading ramp with Bruno in handcuffs. Ryo responded he made the decision since they were bringing a known terrorist along.

Bruno said they had nothing to worry about from him, because he planned to keep his end of the bargain he had made with Alex. He cautioned Michael not to break the equipment he was loading; Alex might drop Michael off the side of a building.

"Still bitter?" asked Galen. He hoped Bruno remembered who had stopped Alex. Galen leaned close to Bruno and said, "If ya do anything except breathe in this truck, I will personally make sure it runs ya over for the simple pleasure of it."

Bruno nodded as he quickly sat, and Ryo handcuffed him to the wall.

Ryo told the group they were sending out three identical trucks to different locations across the city. If the Sons of Enyaluis tried to follow them, they would make it as difficult as possible. Ryo added that a severe nor'easter was raging outside, so it would be a bumpy ride.

"Yu're wrong, mate. It's the attempted murderer, yur ex, and mah exes in the back of a truck. Sounds like the start of a bad joke."

"I don't know, Galen," said Alex. "If you take the terrorist out of the situation, it's only our exes. Throw in some alcohol, and I bet things could get freaky."

Galen shook his head and rolled his eyes at Alex's sense of humor. He wondered how he could make inappropriate jokes at a time like this, but he knew the answer was that it kept him from crying.

"Take your seat; let's get this party bus on the road," said Alex.

Galen watched from across the truck as Alex sat by Danyal's hospital bed, holding his hand and stoking his hair as the truck left the loading dock at PGC. Galen knew these moments from his struggles after Amara's assault. He recognized all the stages of grief at once. Although he avoided organized religion for years, he quietly prayed for Alex and Danyal. They deserved a chance to be happy. Alex would be devastated if he lost Danyal. *Please let this work.*

Galen took off his seat belt and climbed into the truck's cab. "Didn't know ya could drive a big rig, Ryo," said Galen.

"There's a lot you don't know about me, Galen," said Ryo. "My father was a long-haul truck driver in Japan."

"Now that we're alone, wanna know yur problem."

"It's all in your head, Galen," said Ryo.

"Bullshite, ya've been riding me from the beginning. Let's not forget ya were willing to shoot me to stop Alex from leaving. Yur actions say otherwise."

"I don't like your attitude, and you have no respect for the chain of command. You think you're running something. I didn't want you to be assigned to Alex. Other seasoned security staff were better qualified."

"How's that my fault?" said Galen.

"It's not. Ms. Dea chose you personally."

"Eh, why?"

"You'd have to ask her, but I think she wanted to dangle a distraction in front of Alex."

"Come again?"

"Alex has a type. He likes tall, dark, and handsome international men. You fit the bill perfectly. Ditta didn't do anything without a reason."

Galen didn't respond as he processed the situation. Ryo had some fucking nerve to speak to him that way, but could he be right? Was he merely a distraction to Alex?

"I can tell by your silence that I hit a nerve. So, what happens to your intense bond with Alex when you become a third wheel? Are all three of you staying in the penthouse? Is it going to be a throuple?"

"Ya don't know anything, Ryo. Alex is exhausted and running on fumes. Ya better not add to his stress with yur conspiracy theories."

"The lady doth protest too much," said Ryo.

"That the only literary reference ya know, Ryo? Shut the fuck up and drive."

Galen stood to return to the back of the truck, but was bounced around like a rag-doll by the increasingly violent winds hitting them from all directions.

Ryo told Galen to sit back down, that the violent storm outside was worsening and everyone needed to stay buckled in for safety. Galen could see Ryo was concerned as he looked at the storm radar on the phone mounted on the dash. He saw that the storm was several hundred miles wide and had knocked out power across Boston, based on the dead streetlights. Many of the streets were blocked by downed trees. Ryo asked if Galen could get this information to Alex without moving. Galen nodded as he took off his ring.

Alex, we have a problem. Storm is getting worse. Downed trees blocking the route.

No! We can't waste time, Galen.

Galen could hear Alex in the back of the truck instructing Andrea and Michael to keep Danyal safe.

Don't come up here, Alex!

But Galen was too late with his warning, as Alex was already climbing into the cab of the truck. Ryo demanded Alex sit down, and

Galen chuckled when Alex blatantly ignored the demand. An argument ensued, with Alex asserting that they couldn't turn back because Danyal's vitals were dropping to where he might not survive if they diverted. Ryo yelled that Alex would get them killed.

"Give me a chance to get us there safely," said Alex.

Ryo shook his head as he stopped the truck just in time to miss hitting a downed tree in the road. Alex begged and said that storms were nothing more than energy that he could wield, since he felt stronger as they approached the vortex. Galen watched Alex put his hands on the cab ceiling and close his eyes. He watched Alex breathe in and out slowly. Galen was amazed, and his heart raced as Alex placed a protective electromagnetic barrier around the truck. Galen advised Ryo to slowly drive the truck due east while Alex cleared the roadways. Galen watched in disbelief as the clouds and severe rain in front of the truck began to separate, as a bright yellow energy barrier formed around the truck. Any trees blocking the road quickly moved out of the way like repelling magnets.

Prove this arsehole wrong, Alex!

Careful, Galen, we're still connected. I need to concentrate. Wearing your ring to protect you from stray energy is probably safer.

Galen smiled and complied.

After twenty minutes of intense silence, Ryo indicated they were about five blocks from the church. Ryo said he'd never been able to observe Ditta in action and wondered if every day with Alex was like this.

Galen shook his head. "Alex is getting stronger with each feat and becoming more magnificent."

Galen laughed again when Alex called Ryo out for being rude by talking about him while he was still in the room. Galen asked if Alex was right, and Alex nodded, adding that it had been easier than expected to use the energy from the storm to clear their path. Ryo accused Alex of bragging, but Galen knew Alex deserved all the credit and more. Ryo thanked Alex for the assistance and advised him to hydrate and rest since they were about five minutes from the church.

Galen turned to help Alex return to the back of the truck.

"Galen," said Ryo.

Galen turned to look at him. "Ya've said enough."

"My words to you were harsh. Whatever happens, you have a place with PGC if you want it."

Galen turned away without responding. He knew his priorities were more aligned with Alex than with protecting PGC any day.

Chapter Forty-Eight

Alex's head was pounding so hard he almost lost consciousness from the pain as they arrived at the vortex coordinates at the Old North Church. His heart raced faster and faster. The sweat poured off his brow as if he were in a sauna. Had he overtaxed himself with the storm? No, this was something different. He feared his headache would surpass the pain he experienced after his ascension. Each mile closer to the energy vortex brought him closer to achieving salvation for Danyal, but Alex was worried. Could his body deal with channeling this much energy?

"Alex, Alex," said Wynn as he slid beside Alex. "Are you OK? You don't look well."

"I'm fine," said Alex.

"Bullshit," said Bruno, sitting across the truck and looking at Alex over Danyal's body on the gurney. "You're starting to feel the vortex. Here, the energy is projected out from the Earth. Your body is like a water hose trying to funnel Niagara Falls."

"I know, Bruno. I feel the energy growing stronger the closer we get."

"Is he running a fever, Wynn?" asked Bruno.

Wynn placed his palm on Alex's forehead. "Damn, you're burning up, Alex."

"My health isn't the issue. Since we have arrived, Wynn, I'll defer to your expertise."

"You know we're in uncharted territory. Plus, arriving in the dead of the night during a city-wide blackout is hardly ideal," said Wynn.

"I tend to do my best work when I wing it," said Alex.

"You keep believing that, Alex. Follow the energy, but I suspect the energy will find you," said Wynn.

Stepping out of the truck, Alex stumbled and nearly fell in the rain.

"Easy," said Wynn. "Let me help you."

Alex nodded as Galen, Andrea, and Michael approached.

"Cupid, you've lost the color in your cheeks," said Andrea.

"You say the kindest things, Andrea," said Alex.

"What's the plan?" asked Galen, looking toward Ryo for an answer.

Ryo said, "The security detail needs to form a perimeter around the church. We don't want any surprises."

"Priest knows we are coming?" asked Galen.

Ryo nodded yes. He said a healthy donation to the parish helped grease the wheels, and that they thought the group was filming a paranormal documentary in the catacombs.

As they stepped through the large wooden arched doors, Alex pointed his finger to a hallway on the left past the altar.

"The energy is pulling me there. I'm going to need Galen's help to keep steady."

"Gotcha, mate," said Galen as Wynn stepped aside.

"We need more light," yelled Wynn. "I can't see a thing. The flashlights are all dead."

Alex closed his eyes and raised his right hand as a bright beam of yellow light sprang forth from it.

"Fancy," said Wynn. "You're a regular Rudolph."

Alex smiled, even though it hurt to move his facial muscles.

"What are we doing next, mate?" asked Galen.

"I feel the energy coming from down the steps. It's calling to me."

"Calling to ya?" said Galen.

"I can't explain it, but the vortex wants me to approach, and it wants to be unleashed."

"Will get you there, Alex," said Galen as they walked down the spiral stone staircase into the church's basement.

Alex pointed to an old metal gate on the basement floor.

"We need to go there," said Alex weakly.

"Gate is locked," said Galen. "The map says the entrance to the catacombs is at the other end of the basement."

Alex shook his head. He reached down with his right hand and crushed the padlock securing the metal gate. He pulled it open and said he needed to do the rest on his own.

Alex took a shaky step away from Galen and moved to the railing of the stone stairs like a toddler taking his first steps. He fell to his knees twice, but pulled himself up and slowly descended into the darkness of the catacombs. Walking down the long tunnel lined with skulls and bones, he stopped at a brick wall with a mental plate identifying it as the "Tomb of the Strangers."

Kneeling, he touched the ground with his right hand, and the tunnel began to shake violently as debris started to fall from the ceiling. A large circular white portal opened in the ground. Alex stepped into the blazing light and was enveloped by it as he descended further into the portal until he disappeared and the ground closed above him.

Chapter Forty-Nine

Galen stood next to Wynn as they watched from a safe distance in awe and confusion as the light from the gateway dissipated and Alex disappeared into the ground.

"Alex!" yelled Galen in a panic. His scream echoed through the catacombs until the only sound was the wind rushing through the tunnels.

The ground beneath their feet began to vibrate slightly, and the wind began to whirl until it was as if a tornado was ready to touch down, forcing Galen and Wynn up against the wall of bones. The air crackled with electricity, causing loose debris and scattered bones on the floor to rise from the surface before crashing back down. A flicker of light sparked within the ground, which grew in intensity until a bright lavender oval portal of light appeared.

Alex levitated out of the portal, surrounded by swirling energies of yellow, red, white, and orange. He levitated until he had passed Galen and Wynn before ascending the stone stairs. He levitated out of the basement and from the large wooden front doors of the chapel.

Alex was now fifty feet above the group of onlookers at the truck where Danyal's hospital bed had been placed on the ground. Galen watched Alex release a massive golden flare of light, illuminating the sky as if it were midday and causing the raging storm around them to stop. Galen stepped back as Alex slowly descended until he was standing next to Danyal on the gurney. Andrea and Michael stepped back cautiously away from Alex, who emanated enough light to illuminate the entire area.

Galen watched as Alex reached out with his arms and lifted Danyal from his bed. He closed his eyes and enveloped Danyal in a pink protective cocoon of cosmic vortex energy. Alex gently laid Danyal back on the gurney.

Galen helped Bruno carefully approach with an electronic monitor in his hand.

Bruno told Alex he must step back because his energy interfered with the equipment. Alex quietly levitated about ten feet off the ground from Danyal.

Bruno looked up at Alex and shook his head.

"It didn't work. You must stop. Whatever you did caused a spike in Danyal's radioactive isotope levels. Any further exposure will kill him."

"You're lying, Bruno," yelled Alex, telekinetically lifting Bruno two feet off the ground by his neck.

"Stop!" yelled Galen, looking at Bruno's equipment monitor.

Alex dropped Bruno on the muddy ground and descended to Danyal's side.

"We have to try again," said Alex.

"No," said Galen. "Bruno's not lying. Would kill him."

"Then the only option is the serum," said Alex.

Galen nodded and turned to Bruno, whom Michael had helped to his feet. Bruno opened the protective medical case and pulled out the preloaded syringe of bright blue glowing liquid.

Galen asked Bruno if it was supposed to glow, and Bruno shook his head. Galen removed the cap and turned to hand the syringe to Alex, whose hands shook uncontrollably. Galen steadied Alex's hand with his hand and placed the syringe in Alex's open palm.

"I'm scared," said Alex. "This could be the end of everything."

Galen raised his left hand to cup Alex's face.

"Yu're fuckin' Alex Lieth! Ya've got this."

Alex turned Danyal's right arm over and gently inserted the needle into his forearm. After a deep breath, he kissed Danyal gently on the forehead and pushed the plunger down.

Chapter Fifty

Alex

The harsh fluorescent lights stung Alex's eyes as he tried to open them. He looked around the room, not recognizing his surroundings. Despite his throbbing headache, he could determine he was in a hospital room. Where was he, and––more important-ly––where was Danyal? Alex looked down at the man sleeping peace-fully, leaning over the side of his hospital bed. He gently placed his hand on the back of Galen's head to wake him.

Galen turned his head with marks from the blanket on his face from where he had been sleeping.

"Yu're awake! Let me get Veronica."

"No," said Alex. "First, tell me where I am and what has happened to Danyal."

"Relax, Danyal is here unharmed. Let me get Veronica."

"No," said Alex. "Where am I?"

Galen took a deep breath before responding, "Promise yu're not going to overreact."

"Galen, you need to tell me now."

Galen sat back down by the side of the bed and said Alex was in one of the medical treatment rooms at PGC.

"How long have I been out?" said Alex.

"You've been unconscious for seventy-two hours."

"Seventy-two hours? That's three days!"

Galen said Bruno warned him about channeling pure vortex energy. "Ya overheated and needed time to cool down. Ya survived the ordeal, but yur body needed time to recover. Ya missed a bumpy ride back because we had to wait for the storm to clear, since no one could part the storm for us."

"Danyal?"

"Let me text Veronica to give you an update," said Galen as he pulled out his phone.

"Alex!" said Veronica as she entered the door on the other side of the room from Alex's hospital bed. She leaned in to kiss Alex on the top of his head. "Welcome back."

"Please, how is Danyal?"

"All in good time," said Veronica. "We need to address your situation first. You came here with the worst case of exhaustion I've ever seen, and we couldn't give you IV fluids until Galen had an idea to remedy the situation."

Alex looked down and wondered how he missed the IV in his right hand. The dagger must have been used for it.

"You are a resourceful bunch," said Alex. He reached his hand to his face. "Can I get this feeding tube out of my nose?"

"Of course, Alex. I want you to take it easy," said Veronica. "No extracurricular god activities, if you know what I mean."

"Understood. Please, just give me an update on Danyal."

Veronica smiled and said Danyal was at Mass General under Dr. Anderson's care and was being treated by the best coma specialists in the country. She added she was happy to report he had been showing steady improvement. The radioactive isotopes in his system were now undetectable, and he was displaying brain patterns indicating he might soon wake from his coma.

Alex dropped his head back on his pillow and took several deep breaths before responding through tears that he didn't know what to say; she'd given him the best news of his life. He said he wouldn't forget her efforts and would do whatever he could to repay her.

Galen placed his hand on Alex's shoulder and smiled.

Alex placed his hand on Galen's. "When can I see Danyal?"

"I see no reason why you can't see him today, as long as you didn't overexert yourself," said Veronica.

Alex nodded, and Veronica said she'd have a nurse to assist Alex getting dressed.

"I gotcha," said Galen. "Think I'm qualified to dress him, drive him to the hospital, and push a wheelchair."

Veronica gently removed the feeding tube. She left the room as Galen pulled the wheelchair to the bed. Galen helped Alex stand, and Alex placed his arms around Galen. They stood in silence, embracing.

"Yu're going to have to let go so ya can get changed," said Galen.

"I know," said Alex. "I just can't believe that, after all that's happened, the ordeal is nearly over. I truly wouldn't have made it here without you, Galen. I hope you know how much your friendship means to me."

"Feel the same, mate. Ya've changed mah life in so many ways. Mostly for the better," said Galen as he chuckled. "Where do we go from here?"

"I see a bright future for us, a lifelong friendship. But for now, help me dress and take me to Danyal."

Alex's heart raced the entire drive to Mass General. As Galen opened the door to Danyal's hospital room, Alex couldn't hold back his emotions.

"He looks so much better," said Alex through tears. "His color is returning, and he's starting to look like my Danyal again. Although I'm not sure about the beard. I think it hides his handsome face."

"Don't know," said Galen. "Clean up the beard, maybe; it could suit him."

Alex smiled. "Agree to disagree; I'll have to see how it feels when I kiss him."

Galen rolled Alex up to the side of the bed. "I can see his spark," said Alex. "It's much stronger than before."

"Good thing?" said Galen.

Alex said it meant he was healing as he picked up Danyal's hand and kissed it. "I'm going to nurse him back to health, and we're going to get our lives back on track. Everyone gets a happy ending."

"Not everyone," said Galen. "Zoe's memorial service is today."

"I'm so sorry, Galen," said Alex, "that was insensitive of me. I'm so sorry for your loss. It pains me I couldn't save her."

"I know, Alex."

"Are you going to the service?"

"Not sure," said Galen.

"I know it won't be easy, but you have to. I can hold down the fort here. Do what you need to do for you, and for Zoe. Don't leave any regrets."

"Andrea and Michael said they'd go with me. Andrea says she'll wear a dress. Gorilla says he'll wear a suit," said Galen.

"Oh my," said Alex with a laugh. "Sneak some pictures if you can. I struggle with imagining either of them wearing anything other than camo."

Galen said it had been a while, but they cleaned up well. He added he needed to head back and clean up. "Will need to discuss future arrangements for when Danyal moves into the penthouse so ya can have space."

"That's a conversation and a bridge we will cross much later. Be with your friends, and please share my condolences with Zoe's family."

Galen nodded and kissed Alex on the top of his head. "Ya deserve a happy ending, Alex Lieth," he said before leaving the hospital room.

Chapter Fifty-One

Alex sat by Danyal's bed, praying. Danyal's hand he held began to twitch. Alex looked up, scanning for any sign of consciousness, but didn't see any. He turned his head down again until he was startled by the sound of a voice.

"Water, please," Danyal said feebly.

Alex jumped up, grabbed a cup of water, and slowly held it to Danyal to sip through a straw.

"Slowly," said Alex, "drink it slowly."

"Thank you," said Danyal.

Alex could no longer restrain his joy as he grabbed Danyal, pulling him forward and kissing him on the forehead. "Stay still," Alex said, "I'll get the doctors."

Alex ran out of the room and returned with Dr. Anderson and Veronica in tow.

Dr. Anderson approached the bed cautiously. He introduced himself and said he needed to ask Danyal a few questions. He added it was OK if Danyal needed some time to gather his thoughts. Dr. Anderson indicated that Danyal had been through an ordeal and was in Mass General Hospital undergoing medical care. "May I look in your eyes?"

Danyal nodded yes.

Dr. Anderson said Danyal would see a bright light as he looked into each eye. "Excellent. Can you follow my finger?" Dr. Anderson asked as he moved his finger from side to side and up and down. Danyal tracked his finger perfectly.

Dr. Anderson asked if it was OK to ask a few questions.

Danyal nodded yes again.

"What's your name?"

"Danyal Sarif."

"Good. What's your birthday?"

"June 23rd," said Danyal softly.

"How old are you?"

"Twenty-four."

"Do you remember the events that brought you to the hospital?"

Danyal shook his head no.

Dr. Anderson said that's OK and not unusual.

"Do you recognize the handsome man standing next to me?" Dr. Anderson said as he looked toward Alex.

Danyal paused and looked at Alex. Danyal nodded yes. "His name is Alex. We met recently, and he asked me out on a date."

Alex's heart sank at those words. He knelt by Danyal's bed, grasping his hand. "Danyal, it's me, Alex—your boyfriend. We've been together for a year. I missed you so much."

Danyal abruptly pulled his hand from Alex's grasp. "Don't touch me," said Danyal, as he looked at Alex with a furrowed brow.

Dr. Anderson motioned for Alex to step back from the bed. "It's OK, Alex. Confusion after a coma is normal. Let me continue my assessment."

Veronica stepped up to Alex and grabbed him by the hand. "Step back, Alex. Let him do his work."

Alex stepped back, his heart racing and head pounding like a bass drum. He panicked at the scene unfolding in front of him.

"Where do you work, Danyal?"

"I work at Excalibur Café."

"What year is it?"

"2022."

"Which month?"

"February."

"Where are you from?"

Danyal paused. "Istanbul, Turkey."

"Are you currently involved in any relationships?

"No," said Danyal. "I've been single since I immigrated from Turkey to the U.S. in 2019."

"What's your sexual orientation, Danyal?"

"I'm gay."

"Where do you live?"

"I've been staying with friends and a friend of the family since I immigrated."

"Is there anyone you'd like us to call?"

"My adopted parents are in Turkey," said Danyal, with tears in his eyes. "They need to know I'm OK."

Alex fell to his knees, trying to process Danyal's responses.

Veronica pulled him up by the arm. "Alex, you can't cause a scene here," she whispered. "If you scare Danyal, he may not let you back in the room. You're not married, so medically and legally, you've no right to be here," she said, ushering Alex out of the room.

As soon as the door closed, Alex began to pace in the hallway, holding back tears before he turned and punched a hole in the drywall. Veronica approached him cautiously and held him as he began to sob.

Dr. Anderson stepped out of Danyal's room to address Alex and Veronica.

"What is going on, Dr. Anderson?" asked Alex, wiping away his tears.

Dr. Anderson said he knew it was difficult, but Alex needed to keep his emotions under control around Danyal, who was in a fragile state.

"Why doesn't he remember our relationship?"

Dr. Anderson said there could be many reasons, including ICU psychosis or ICU delirium, which are side effects of prolonged comas. Dr. Anderson also cautiously understood experimental treatments were used, so they didn't know what the side effects would be.

"So, this is my fault?" said Alex.

Dr. Anderson said it was no one's fault; Danyal's mind was trying to make sense of events. Danyal was oriented in all spheres, but to early 2022. He added retrograde amnesia might also be involved.

"So, what do we do?" asked Alex.

Dr. Anderson said they needed to be patient and keep assessing Danyal's mental status to see if there were changes. He added that Danyal's recovery would be a marathon, not a sprint. The best they could do at this time was to give Danyal some space to relax. Dr. Anderson ended by asking who they could call to support Alex.

"Galen," said Veronica.

"Galen is at Zoe's funeral today," said Alex. "Please give him space to grieve."

"I'll call Dr. Sonja," said Veronica.

"She's in York with Hoko," said Alex, "she won't be able to get here."

"You've been out of commission a while, Alex," said Veronica, "Hoko's now at Mass General, and Dr. Sonja is probably in the building. I'll get her for you and won't leave you until she arrives."

Chapter Fifty-Two

Galen

Galen sat in the back row of the small chapel at Zoe's funeral, as the smoke from the candles and incense burned his eyes. Tears rolled down his cheeks and stained the hymnal in his hands. His accidental desecration of the Old Rugged Cross on page 150 was another sin the Almighty would surely punish him for. Intense guilt in his heart ached for the many things he could never apologize to Zoe for. She would not know how sorry he was for leading her on in their brief relationship. She had supported him in his time of need, but he knew they only used each other for physical comfort. They would never have worked as a couple, because he knew he was damaged goods who would only bring pain and sorrow to those unfortunate enough to care about him.

Zoe never said it to him, but Galen knew from her intense interaction with Alex during their investigation that Zoe was aware of Galen's growing attraction to Alex. Life would have been easier if he could have loved Zoe, but she deserved so much better than being a consolation prize. Galen knew she was a highly trained operative, but he blamed himself for being unable to save her. The best he could do to honor her memory was to say goodbye and ensure she was remembered.

Galen hugged his friends silently as he stayed in the church, as the mourners passed by, and the service ended. He looked intently at his phone for any messages from Alex. Galen could not help but smile through his tears, reading a text from Veronica that said Danyal had awakened from his coma. He was glad Alex would get his happy ending.

Deep in his heart, after reading Veronica's texts about Danyal's memory loss, Galen wanted to return to the hospital to be by Alex's side. Alex needed him to be his friend and protector, but he knew all he could bring Alex was conflict and pain. He could no longer hide the fact he wanted to be the one living in Alex's heart. Galen couldn't bear being close to Alex daily, and not being free to act on his desires. They had connected mentally and spiritually, so he had no hopes of hiding his feelings. Alex had made him feel alive for the first time since before his military service. He now knew he wanted to live and needed to live for himself.

Although Alex had ignited the fire in his heart, Galen was under no illusion that he could compete with Danyal for Alex's affection. He knew Alex cared for him, but Alex was honorable and would do the right thing. It was the Unicorn's nature. He loved Alex's dedication. Maybe Ryo was right; he was nothing more than a distraction for Alex. Galen knew he was just the help who overstepped the mark and dared to think a god could love him.

It was a lose-lose situation. If he stayed, he would be tortured by his unrequited desires. If he left, he would walk away from the most profound feelings he had ever known.

On his phone, he hastily emailed his resignation to Ryo and booked a plane ticket to London, where he would seek shelter with Andrea. He slowly walked down the chapel steps with his duffel bag and hailed a cab to the airport.

Galen had finally found a reason to stop running, but it was best for everyone involved if he made a clean break and walked away.

Chapter Fifty-Three

Alex

Alex sat on the couch in the penthouse, staring blankly out the window.

"Alex," said Diana, "did you hear my question? How are you holding up?"

He said he was barely holding on to his sanity. It had been two weeks since Danyal emerged from his coma, and he'd shown no improvement. Dr. Anderson and the neurologists said there was no brain damage, but Danyal remembered nothing after February 2022. Alex said Danyal barely knew him, and had no memories of their relationship.

Diana asked if Danyal had agreed to spend time with Alex to see if it triggered any memories. Alex replied he spent a little time with Danyal daily, but he had been asked not to overwhelm Danyal with pictures and videos while he was still adjusting. Diana said she was sorry and acknowledged that it must be excruciating, but that hope remained. She said the love they shared didn't disappear. Maybe it was time to be Danyal's friend and go on a first date once more to recreate the magic.

Alex said he only wanted to hug and hold Danyal until he remembered him. Ditta told him their love was real, but he wondered what she may have done to meddle in their relationship. "Did he ever really love me? His energy is starting to look different. Eros energy is still there, but so is the darkness."

Diana said, "Of course your love was real; Ditta was amazed by the strength of your bond."

Alex said, through tears, "She also said the relationship shouldn't have lasted. Maybe we were on borrowed time."

"Alex, no one could blame you for being depressed. Are you eating?"

"Sparingly."

"Sleeping?"

"Even less."

Diana said, "This is grief talking. You can't hope to control it; it will control you."

Alex replied someone he cared about once told him something similar not too long ago. Now he had to grieve that loss too. Alex looked up to meet Diana's gaze. "Why did Galen leave?"

She said she could speculate, but only Galen knew the definite answer. "What was your last conversation with Galen?"

Alex said Galen brought up living arrangements after Danyal recovered. Galen kissed him on the head and told him he deserved a happy ending. Alex said he was so focused on Danyal that he didn't recognize Galen was saying goodbye. He thought Galen's heightened emotions were due to Zoe's funeral. "I should've stopped him."

Diana said, "We can't change the past, Alex."

"I guess he chose an exciting life with Andrea and Michael rather than staying to protect me."

"Andrea and Michael?" said Diana.

Alex nodded, saying they'd gone to Zoe's funeral with Galen. Diana replied she attended most of Zoe's memorial before coming to the hospital, and Galen was alone.

"Why'd he lie about it?"

Diana speculated maybe Galen didn't want Alex to think he'd be alone. She added all she knew was Galen resigned by email immediately after the service.

"So, he's out here alone grieving, too. Did our friendship mean nothing?"

"I think it meant a lot, Alex. More than you're willing to admit."

"You made a similar statement back in York, Diana. Speak plainly."

"Galen cared for you, Alex, cared for you deeply. What may have started as a trauma bond could have developed into more for Galen."

"I think you're reading too much into our connection, Diana."

"Alex, your chemistry with Galen was electric."

"Zoe and Ryo made a similar statement."

"And Hoko made the same observation. Ditta did pick him specifically to be your protector." Alex shook his head, but Diana continued, "Take it from someone who watched from the sidelines for years, not sharing my feelings and watching the person I cared about daily...It was unbearable."

Alex asked if she spoke with Galen at the funeral. She said they only hugged at the end, but Galen had a sorrowful look in his eyes. It was more than grief; she said she recognized the longing look on his face.

"Say it, Diana. It's my fault he left. I knew he was developing feelings for me. I connected with his energy so often, there was no way to avoid them. But I pushed his and my feelings aside. Was I supposed to look in the mirror and admit I had feelings for Galen, too? It nearly ate me up inside. Danyal was dying, and my thoughts were split between him and Galen."

Diana said she understood and asked if he had tried to reach Galen.

"Repeatedly. No answers to my calls or texts."

"Can you sense him with your abilities?"

Alex said no--Galen was either wearing his ring or had had an injection before he left. "With everything we went through, I thought our friendship meant more. I'd never imagined he'd abandon me when I needed him the most. No one gets a happy ending, except maybe Bruno."

Diana paused and took a deep breath before asking if Alex would honor his promise to help Nyssa.

"Yes, I gave my word. The serum saved Danyal's life, so it may help Nyssa."

"Please think this through, Alex. There are many factors to consider outside of your control."

Alex said Nyssa was also a victim, and he felt her pain. He wouldn't change his mind, but would have to find her first. The Sons of Enyaluis took her, and he vowed he'd save her and give those motherfuckers some payback.

"So, where do you go from here, Alex?"

"I don't know, Diana; I need some space to think."

Diana nodded and placed her hand on Alex's shoulder as she stood to leave the penthouse. She said Alex had people who loved him and were on his side when he needed them.

Alex appreciated the sentiment, but the words rang hollow as he sat in the barren wasteland that had become his life.

Chapter Fifty-Four

Galen

"Enough, Galen," said Andrea. "I've let you wallow in your self-pity for two weeks. It's time you get off my couch, shower because you reek, and take control of your fucking life."

The bright sunlight streaming through the window burned Galen's eyes as Andrea opened the curtains and blinds to let in the blazing midday sun.

Galen covered his head with his pillow, but Andrea quickly snatched it out of his hands.

"Fuckin' leave me alone," he said as he threw his other pillow at her.

"No," she said, "you're about to make one of the biggest mistakes of your miserable life, and now I'm kicking some sense into your ass."

Galen covered his head with the blanket until Andrea yanked it away.

Andrea asked why he was on her couch, hungover and depressed, instead of being in Boston. She commented Alex had been blowing up their phones, so he knew the situation with Danyal. Alex needed him, and here he was lying on her couch in his underwear, stinking of whiskey.

"Fuck off, Andrea. Ya don't know anything," said Galen.

"You've been whining for two weeks about your feelings for Alex. He's ignited a passion in you I've never seen before. Can you live with that regret?"

Galen sat up on the couch with his hand on his forehead.

"What would Amara think?" said Andrea.

"Don't go fuckin' go there!" yelled Galen as angry veins popped on his forehead and neck.

Andrea waited patiently for Galen to calm down before sitting on the couch beside him. She placed her hand on his bare back and started making gentle circles.

"Was a low blow," he said without looking up.

Andrea sat silently before speaking. "You didn't answer the question," she said softly. "What would Amara say?"

Galen was silent for several moments before responding. "She'd slap me on the back of my head and tell me to stop being daft. Probably quote something from *Alice in Wonderland.*"

Andrea smiled and asked which quote.

"Oh, "tis love, 'tis love, that makes the world go round!'" he said as tears rolled down his cheeks.

Andrea said she thought Amara was wise. "You have two choices, Galen. You can either find somewhere else to take your pity party, or you choose to take back control of your life."

"Can't compete with Danyal," he said.

"Then don't compete," replied Andrea. "Put the ball in the Unicorn's court. He might be a god, but he cares about you and needs you with him."

"I can still feel his pain, even with my ring on," said Galen.

Andera asked what was the source of his pain.

"Danyal."

"That's all that hurts him?" she asked.

"And grieving that I left. Feels abandoned."

Andrea said, "You don't feel that deeply for an employee, Galen. Hell, you don't care that deeply as a casual friend. You obviously meant more to Alex than that. Half his thoughts and pain were focused on you in the darkest moment of his life. You share a profound connection. Be honest with me; what's your biggest fear?"

"Being rejected," said Galen.

Andrea replied, "But so what if he does? You'll survive. Alex would still be your friend. And, if I recall correctly, Galen promised a goddess he would protect Alex with his life. That sounds like a divine purpose to me."

"What if Ryo is right? Was only a distraction."

Andrea gently slapped Galen on the back of his skull and asked why he was giving Ryo space in his head. What the fuck did Ryo know? She said if the goddess of love, a freaking universal force of nature, put Galen and Alex on the same path, who cared about her reasoning.

"The rest of the world isn't so lucky; you won't get any sympathy from me after this heavenly matchmaking," she said with a smile. "If Alex was here right now, what would you do?"

"I'd hold him till his pain goes away," said Galen.

"That's it? I bet you'd want to kiss him," said Andrea, teasing Galen as she kissed him gently on the cheek.

"Alex kissed me once by accident after the raid."

Andrea rolled her eyes. She said she didn't believe the bullshit it was an accident and asked how Galen responded.

"Pushed him away."

"Well, that was no fun. Close your eyes, Galen, and think about that kiss. Can you still feel it?"

Galen closed his eyes before responding, "With every fiber of my being." He twirled the ring Alex gave him on his finger. Should he run, or should he go back? Could he live with himself if he walked away from his feelings and obligations? Fuck it, take a leap of faith. He took a deep breath and picked up his phone from the coffee table. He scrolled for several minutes, reading through Alex's texts before opening the British Airways app.

"Will ya do me a favor?" said Galen.

"Anything, within reason," said Andrea with a knowing smile.

"Can ya give me a ride to Heathrow tonight?"

Andrea laid her head on his shoulder and said of course.

"Going to Boston," said Galen. "Have some promises to keep. Will blame ya if mah heart gets trampled."

"Oh, Galen. If Alex breaks your heart, he'll have to answer to me––and he knows I can kick his ass again."

Galen laughed as he hugged Andrea.

"I'd pay good scratch to see that rematch," he said.

She pushed him away and told him to get in the shower. "You smell like a distillery."

"Thanks, Andrea."

"For what, Galen?"

"For kicking mah arse when I need it."

"Don't think it comes for free, Galen; the Unicorn owes me a vacation with a hot man. My services don't come for free."

Galen laughed before heading off to shower and pack.

Chapter Fifty-Five

Alex

Alex sat slumped on the couch with his face in his hands, trying to sort through the carnage that had become his life. His tears seeped through his fingers and soaked the wood floor. How had everything gone to shit in such a brief period of time? He was fully ascended and one of the most powerful beings on the planet, but he was more alone and depressed than ever. Danyal was physically back, but he was not the same Danyal. It was all Alex's fault; would Danyal ever be the same again?

Galen was gone, and Alex wanted desperately to talk to him. He had risked letting someone else into his life, but he had been abandoned. A part of his soul was missing. A wave of sorrow washed over him, and his chest ached. With each beat, his heart came closer to bursting with anguish.

Alex was so deep in his misery that he didn't even look up as the bell on the elevator chimed. He didn't want any visitors.

"I'm tired of talking, Diana," he exclaimed without looking up.

Alex's statement was met with silence. He took a deep breath. Why the fuck could he not be left alone?

"Alex," said the deep, husky voice.

Alex looked up to see Galen standing about fifteen feet away, wearing a brown leather bomber jacket, a black rugby shirt, and jeans. Seeing Galen was a beacon in the darkness. Alex stood frozen as his heart pounded faster. He wanted to run over and embrace him tight, but was concerned about giving Galen mixed messages. He was also afraid of his guilt for wanting the embrace of another man, with Danyal still in the hospital. Whichever choice he made, he betrayed someone and didn't want to cause any more suffering. Alex's fears kept him paralyzed, helplessly staring across the room at Galen.

Finally, mustering the courage to speak, Alex said, "I thought I'd never see you again."

"Made it to London, but even with all the distance, could still feel ya. Andrea kicked my arse and dared me to acknowledge mah feelings. Decided to stop running and follow mah heart," said Galen.

Galen stepped closer to Alex, and with each step, he could feel the warmth and compassion radiating from him. Alex extended his hand to stop Galen at arm's length. Galen met Alex's gaze and smiled his disarming smile. Alex could see Galen's dimples through his neatly trimmed beard, and his heart melted. He was physically shaking as Galen took Alex's hand and placed it on Galen's chest. As they had done on several occasions, Galen let Alex touch his soul.

This time, though, the feeling was different: a high voltage energy ran through his body, followed by a euphoria he had never experienced. Galen extended his arms and wrapped them around Alex. He finally felt safe as he relented and placed his arms around Galen in a reciprocal embrace. Galen's thoughts and feelings were clear to Alex. Galen had found his reason to stop running, and wanted to kiss Alex with every fiber of his being.

Despite desperately wanting to kiss him back, Alex denied himself the pleasure and was instead ashamed of the intensity of his desires.

How could he want Galen so much when his love for Danyal had not changed? Alex wouldn't cross the line.

Galen started to speak with tears running down his handsome face, but Alex shook his head and touched his forehead to Galen's. In mere moments, he had gone from depression to elation. Alex was afraid to think of where he would go from here, but was unwilling to leave this moment with Galen, who had the potential to turn his world upside down.

The peacefulness of the moment was disrupted by Alex's cell phone vibrating in his pocket. Alex said he needed to take the call because it was Dr. Anderson. Galen stepped aside to let Alex answer it. The look on Galen's face grew concerned as the tone in Alex's voice immediately turned serious before he hung up the phone.

Alex said the hospital had called a crisis negotiation team to speak with Danyal. He'd barricaded himself in his room and was threatening the staff. Alex told Galen he needed to go.

"Everything is fucked up, but I don't want you to leave again; please...please stay," said Alex.

"Going with ya," said Galen. "Where you go, I go."

"You don't owe anything to PGC or Danyal, Galen."

"Mah allegiance is to ya, Alex. No one else."

Alex nodded, placing his arms around Galen as they teleported to the Mass General.

Chapter Fifty-Six

Alex

Alex opened his eyes as they materialized in the staff bathroom down the hall from Danyal's hospital room. He and Galen entered the hall, where all the chaos was occurring. Several security guards and Dr. Anderson stood outside the room, attempting to talk to Danyal. Alex pulled Dr. Anderson aside.

"What the hell is happening?" he asked.

Dr. Anderson said Danyal's memories started flooding back; he remembered everything. Alex breathed a sigh of relief--but then asked why Danyal had barricaded himself in his room. Dr. Anderson explained that Danyal started acting aggressively after his memories returned. Danyal had pushed a nurse, causing her to fall and injure her arm. Psychiatric staff had tried to intervene, but Danyal said he'd only talk to Alex.

Alex nodded and motioned with his arm for everyone to clear out and give him space. He approached the door and saw Danyal through the window, cowering in the corner of the room. Danyal was drenched with sweat. His eyes bulged from their sockets, and he was clasping his hands over his ears. Alex knocked gently on the door, but Danyal didn't hear him. He knocked louder, which got Danyal's attention.

"Alex, my love, where have you been?" said Danyal as he ran to the door.

"I'm here, Danyal. Please open the door."

Danyal frantically shook his head. "I can't. I've got to protect you. You need to get away!"

Alex investigated Danyal's core energy with his mind and saw the energy pulsing like a strobe light. He'd never seen such erratic and uncontrolled energy. Alex told Danyal he was coming in and to step away from the door. Danyal ran and hid behind his overturned hospital bed. Alex pushed the door, breaking the chair obstructing it. He stepped into the room carefully and looked around for any hidden threats. Alex knelt down, sat on the floor a few feet away from Danyal, and extended his arms, offering Danyal a hug. Danyal was agitated, and continued rocking back and forth.

"Make it stop!" yelled Danyal, before violently banging his head against the wall.

Alex grabbed Danyal by the shoulders, preventing him from hurting himself further.

"Please stop," begged Alex as he held Danyal tight in his arms.

"Why did you do this?" said Danyal through his sobs.

Alex held Danyal tighter and kissed him on the forehead. "It's OK, Danyal. I'll protect you."

"No, you can't! Get away! I'll hurt you!"

Alex knew Danyal couldn't hurt him, and he tried to reach Danyal's core with his abilities to help regulate his energy. But Danyal stood and pushed Alex backward onto the floor.

"You caused this with your serum!"

Alex stepped back, nearly falling over the overturned bed as the realization hit him. *Danyal's hallucinations might be real. How else could he have known the measures we took to save him?*

"Danyal, I need you to take a deep breath."

"NO!" yelled Danyal as he thrust out his fist and hit Alex in the chest with enough force to hurl him across the room, where he crashed against the wall, smashing the drywall. Danyal moved fast and stood over Alex, tears pouring down his face as his fists pulsed with dark, chaotic energy that flared like coal-black flames.

"I love you, Alex. He won't stop unless I hurt you!" said Danyal as he raised his fist to punch Alex again.

Alex slipped and fell as he tried to stand. He couldn't bring himself to respond, lest he risk hurting Danyal. He tried to dodge the assault, but Danyal landed a solid blow to the right side of Alex's skull that drove his head into the floor, fracturing the concrete and sending a cloud of debris into the air. Alex, dazed, could only instinctively raise his arm in a feeble attempt to block Danyal's next punch, but the attack never landed. He opened his eyes to see a tall figure standing behind Danyal, holding him in a chokehold until Danyal stopped moving. As the security guards and Dr. Anderson tended to Danyal, Alex could see Galen had saved him from Danyal's attack.

"Ya right, mate?" asked Galen as he knelt beside Alex. "Yur scalp is bleeding."

Alex, still dazed by Danyal's assault, raised his hand to his head and stared at the gold blood on his fingers. How could Danyal have injured him? Alex moved back abruptly to prevent Galen from encountering the ichor. Galen reached down, picked up a towel off the floor, and handed it to Alex to apply pressure to his injury.

Leaning on Galen to steady himself, Alex stepped out into the hall after ensuring he had safely cleaned up the blood on his scalp. Dr. Anderson was standing beside Danyal, who was now lying on a gurney, having been given a sedative injection. Dr. Anderson turned to

Alex and said something was seriously amiss, but that Danyal would be moved to the psych ward for further observation and tests.

Alex didn't respond to Dr. Anderson as he clung to Galen with a blank look on his pale white face, as he vacantly stared off into the distance. His vision was blurring, and his breathing was rapidly increasing. As he attempted to take a step on his own, he fainted and fell forward as Galen caught Alex's limp body before he hit the floor.

Dr. Anderson knelt by Alex and shook him by his shoulders before directing Galen to get Alex to a triage room so he could assess him for shock and a head injury.

"No," said Alex in a weak voice as he turned his head toward Galen.

Dr. Anderson insisted, but Alex ignored him.

"Get me back to PGC," said Alex as Galen picked him up from the floor and hastily carried him down the hall toward the elevator. Alex lost consciousness as the elevator door closed.

Alex lay in the hospital bed at PGC, while Diana and Galen nervously waited as Veronica carefully sutured the gash on the crown of Alex's head. He watched a live stream of Danyal's hospital room on his phone. His legs and arms were strapped to the hospital bed. Danyal looked so peaceful. Alex couldn't believe he could have exhibited such unprovoked rage.

"Give it to me straight, Veronica––how bad is it?" said Alex as he put down his phone.

Veronica sucked her teeth and shook her head from side to side. "You are lucky, Alex. After Danyal's assault, your body is not healing." She agreed with Dr. Anderson's assessment that Alex had a severe concussion. Since medical imaging was out of the question due to Alex's electromagnetic field, there was no way to determine the extent of it. Alex knew that he was fortunate that Galen had intervened, but struggled to understand how Danyal had injured him.

Alex's thoughts were interrupted by Ryo entering the room with Bruno in handcuffs.

As she stepped back from Bruno, Diana asked why he was there. Alex could see the fear in her eyes.

"I asked him to be here," said Alex. He knew Bruno was the expert on his physiology.

Galen stepped to Alex's bedside to stand guard over him. Alex nodded to Veronica to proceed as she displayed Danyal's most recent MRI results on the monitor for the group to view. Bruno stepped closer for a better view.

"Fascinating," he said, as he told the group the auditory areas and frontal cortex of Danyal's brain were functioning at superhuman levels. He added this type of activity didn't cause psychotic behavior before pulling up an additional scan on the monitor. Alex could tell Bruno was holding something back, based on his hesitation and avoiding eye contact.

"We're all thinking it, Bruno––fucking say it," said Alex.

Bruno cleared his throat before expressing that the serum had activated Danyal's dormant god gene. There was no way to know the impact on Danyal's mind, behavior, or the abilities he may exhibit. Bruno said it was the only viable reason he could injure Alex. Only gods or demigods could harm a god in battle, Bruno added.

Alex's heart jumped into his throat at Bruno's assessment. He couldn't stop thinking that he had also placed Galen in mortal danger by exposing him to his blood when Galen came to his rescue. He closed his eyes and turned his head away so the group couldn't see the fear on his face.

Alex said, "Danyal's core energy was going ballistic, like a battle being waged for his soul. He wielded dark chaos energy when he had me on the ropes. I sensed great rage when I touched Danyal's soul."

Alex knew Bruno was right. It was how Danyal injured him and why he wasn't healing like normal. Danyal knew things he shouldn't, such as the measures Alex had taken to save him. They had intentionally avoided sharing that information with Danyal. Someone commanded Danyal to hurt him. Alex stopped and took a deep breath. He knew what it all meant.

"Thanatos was guiding Danyal."

Diana audibly gasped before clasping her hand over her mouth.

After a prolonged silence, Galen asked, "is he as strong as ya?"

Alex weakly said he didn't know and was thankful that the sedatives seemed to be working.

Bruno stated that they had underestimated the Sons of Enyaluis. He hypothesized they were intentionally trying to activate Danyal's dormant god gene, but the ichor they had was degraded. He further speculated the Sons of Enyaluis wanted a god or demigod under their control. Nyssa was their primary option, but Danyal was their backup plan.

Ryo interjected that Bruno may be right. His Interpol contacts had been hearing whispers in terrorist channels that all the major insurgent groups feared the Sons of Enyaluis. They had likely gone rogue and broken away from Thanatos' agenda. Word was they were trying to create a super soldier, and either Danyal or Nyssa would be a tremendous asset. Ryo paused briefly before saying he had something that Alex needed to see. He pulled out his phone and cast a video to the large monitor in the room.

From the surroundings in the video, Alex recognized the façade of Excalibur Café. "What are we looking at, Ryo?" he asked.

          RICHARD E. WILLIAMS

Ryo said that the video had been recovered from the cell phone of Douglas Austin, who Interpol apprehended in Ireland as he tried to sneak back into the country.

Alex watched impatiently as the video shifted to viewing Danyal through the café's front window. "So what," said Alex, "they were casing Danyal at work?"

Ryo raised his hand for Alex to stop talking. Alex watched as Danyal greeted a group of three men sitting at a table. He sat and entered into an intense discussion. When the conversation ended, Danyal hugged a tall man with dark hair and a goatee, wearing a white shirt and khakis. The stranger kissed Danyal on both cheeks before Danyal took off his apron and left the café with the group of men.

Alex grew impatient and didn't understand what Ryo was getting at.

"What's your point, Ryo?"

Ryo turned to Bruno and said, "Do you recognize the man Danyal hugged and left with, Bruno?"

Bruno hesitantly nodded yes.

"Who is he?" said Ryo.

Bruno didn't answer.

Ryo said in a louder voice, "Who is he?"

Bruno looked up, visibly shaking. "He's the leader of the Sons of Enyaluis."

Alex's head began to pound like a jackhammer as he processed this revelation before yelling, "You're fucking lying!"

Bruno, still shaking, shook his head.

"What are ya trying to prove, Ryo?" asked Galen.

Ryo calmly replied to look at the time stamp on the video.

Alex gathered his composure to focus again on the video; the date was the day before Danyal was abducted.

"This proves nothing," said Alex. "So what if Danyal left with these men? They are master manipulators."

The room remained quiet until Ryo said the video proved Danyal had been in contact with the Sons of Enyaluis before his abduction. "We don't know Danyal's relationship with the terrorists, but it can't be denied that Danyal is a threat to your safety, Alex."

"He was manipulated," said Alex as he locked eyes with Ryo.

"It doesn't matter if Danyal met them; he severely injured you today. He's a threat and should be treated as such," said Ryo.

Alex closed his eyes and took several deep breaths before asking the group to give him some space. Veronica, Diana, Ryo, and Bruno promptly left the room. Galen stood by Alex's bedside and touched his shoulder. Alex placed his left hand on Galen's hand.

"Ya need me to stay, mate?"

Alex shook his head. Galen couldn't know how much strength his presence gave Alex and how grateful he was that Galen had stopped Danyal's assault. Even though he wanted Galen to hold him, having Galen's arms around him at that moment felt wrong and fueled Alex's guilt over his attraction to him.

"Promise me you won't leave," said Alex.

"Promise. Will stay to protect mah unicorn," said Galen, winking at Alex before he turned to leave the room.

Alex burst into tears as soon as the door closed, and his mind began to race. What the fuck was happening? Was Danyal connected with the Sons of Enyaluis? Was everything in their relationship built on a lie?

Alex promised himself Thanatos and the Sons of Enyaluis were going to pay: his retribution would be swift and merciless.

About the author

Richard E. Williams is a cisgender gay male and licensed clinical psychologist in North Carolina and California. With a Doctorate of Clinical Psychology (Psy.D.) and 28 years of experience in correctional psychology, he's dedicated his professional life to helping others overcome their mental health and substance abuse challenges. Despite his clinical career, writing has always been his true passion. He began as a writing major in college before switching to psychology and has been crafting stories for over 25 years.

His first novel, Eros Rising (Olympus Ascending Book One), is an MM urban fantasy romance/adventure that reflects his deep commitment to positively representing LGBTQI+ characters. He aims to create engrossing stories that keep readers engaged and invested while inspiring them to live confidently as their authentic selves. He hopes his readers see themselves in his characters, and through their journeys, find the courage to overcome their own obstacles.

As a lifelong fan of science fiction and fantasy, including graphic novels (especially X-Men) and Japanese anime/manga, these influences often permeate his writing. Outside of his literary pursuits, Richard is an avid sports fan, cheering for the Atlanta Braves, West Virginia University basketball/football, and the Sacramento Kings.

He's also an amateur bowler and a, proud member of the longest-running LGBTQI+ bowling league in Northern California.

Professionally, he's passionate about training new clinicians and helping them achieve their goals and dreams. Personally, his experience of growing up gay in a rural area has fueled his dedication to representing sexual minorities positively and authentically in his work. Richard believes in the power of storytelling to not only entertain but also to inspire and empower.

Richard's ideal readers seek to see themselves portrayed in positive, inspiring ways, who root for the underdog, and who are looking for an escape from reality while finding motivation in his characters' journeys. In both his clinical work and his writing, he's most often complimented for his dedication and the relatable, fully developed characters he creates.

For more about Richard's work and upcoming projects, visit his website at www.richardwilliamswriter.com. Let's connect through stories that celebrate authenticity, resilience, and the extraordinary within the everyday.

https://www.facebook.com/profile.php?id=100092648392354&mi
bextid=LQQJ4d

https://www.instagram.com/richard_williams_writer?igsh=OGQ5
ZDc2ODk2ZA%3D%3D&utm_source=qr

https://x.com/williamswr83157